# THE ULTIMATE PLAYBOY

BY
MAYA BLAKE

D1741111

MILLS
&BOON

Published in Great Britain 2014
by Mills & Boon, an imprint of Harlequin (UK) Limited,
Eton House, 18-24 Paradise Road, Richmond, Surrey, TW9 1SR

© 2014 Maya Blake

ISBN: 978 0 263 24669 8

Harlequin (UK) Limited's policy is to use papers that are natural,
renewable and recyclable products and made from wood grown in
sustainable forests. The logging and manufacturing processes conform
to the legal environmental regulations of the country of origin.

Printed and bound in Spain
by Blackprint CPI, Barcelona

**'Don't sell yourself short, sweetheart. I'd place you more as a deliciously forbidden dessert than as an appetiser. But one I intend to devour nonetheless.'**

'Look, Mr…?'

Narciso raised a brow. 'You're at a masked event, shrouded in secrecy, embroiled in intrigue and mystery, and you want to know my *name*?' he asked cynically.

How could she have forgotten? 'Why do I get the feeling that all this bores you rigid?'

His eyes gleamed. 'How very intuitive of you. You're right, it does. Or it did until I saw you.'

Ruby's heart gave a little kick. One she determinedly ignored. 'You were fully engaged when you played your game. And *that* had nothing to do with me.'

Again that reminder hardened his eyes. 'Ah, but I lost thirty million dollars so I could make what's happening between us happen sooner.'

'There's nothing happening—'

'If you believe *that* then you really are naïve.'

**Maya Blake** fell in love with the world of the alpha male and the strong, aspirational heroine when she borrowed her sister's Mills & Boon® at the age of thirteen. Shortly thereafter the dream to plot a happy ending for her own characters was born. Writing for Harlequin® is a dream come true. Maya lives in South East England with her husband and two kids. Reading is an absolute passion, but when she isn't lost in a book she likes to swim, cycle, travel and Tweet!

You can get in touch with her
via e-mail, at mayablake@ymail.com,
or on Twitter: www.twitter.com/mayablake

**Recent titles by the same author:**

WHAT THE GREEK CAN'T RESIST
WHAT THE GREEK'S MONEY CAN'T BUY
  *(The Untamable Greeks)*
HIS ULTIMATE PRIZE
MARRIAGE MADE OF SECRETS

**Did you know these are also available as eBooks?
Visit www.millsandboon.co.uk**

To David and Peter.
Life would be so much duller without you two!

# CHAPTER ONE

*New York*

NARCISO VALENTINO STARED at the box that had been delivered to him. It was large, made with the finest expensive leather, trimmed with velvet rope, with a horseshoe-shaped clasp made of solid twenty-four-carat gold.

Normally, the sight of it brought anticipation and pleasure.

But the ennui that had invited itself for a long-term stay in his life since he'd turned thirty last month leached excitement from him as the stock market leaked money after a juicy disaster.

Lucia had accused him of turning into a boring old man right before her diva exit out of his life two weeks ago.

He allowed himself a little grin of relief. He'd celebrated her departure with a boys' weekend ski trip to Aspen where he'd treated himself to a little palate cleanser in the form of a very enthusiastic Norwegian ski instructor.

But much too quickly, the jaded hollowness had returned.

Rising from his desk, he strode to the window of his seventieth-floor Wall Street office and stared at the New York skyline. Satisfaction eased through him at the thought that he owned a huge chunk of this city.

Money was sexy. Money was power. And The Warlock of Wall Street—as the newspapers had taken to calling him—never denied himself the pull of power and sex.

The opportunity to experience two of his favourite things lay within the package on his desk.

Yet it'd remained unopened for the last hour…

Shrugging off the lethargy, he returned briskly to his desk and flipped the clasp.

The half mask staring up at him from a bed of black satin was exquisite. Pure silver edged with black onyx and Swarovski crystals, its intricate design and flawless detail announced the care and attention that had gone into creating it. Narciso appreciated care and attention. It was what had made him a millionaire by eighteen and a multibillionaire by twenty-five.

His vast wealth was also what had gained him admission into *Q Virtus,* the world's most exclusive gentlemen's club, whose quarterly caucus invitation was the reason for the mask. Two four-inch-long diamond-tipped pins held the mask in place. Pulling them out, he flipped it over to examine the soft, velvet underside, which held the security microchip, his moniker—The Warlock—and the venue, *Q Virtus,* Macau. He ran his thumb over the smooth surface, hoping to summon a little enthusiasm. Failing miserably, he set the mask down and glanced at the second item in the box.

The List.

Zeus, the anonymous head of *Q Virtus,* always provided club members with a discreet list of business interests who would be attending the caucuses. Narciso had chosen not to attend the last two because he'd already dealt with those lists' major players.

His gaze skimmed the heavily embossed paper and his breath caught. Excitement of a different, dangerous kind sizzled through him as the fourth name jumped out at him.

Giacomo Valentino—*Daddy dearest.*

He perused the other names to see if anyone else on the list would make his attendance worthwhile.

His lips twisted. Who the hell was he kidding?

One name and one name only had become *the* deciding factor. There were one or two business interests worth cultivating during the two-day event, but Giacomo was who he intended to interact with.

Although perhaps *interact* was the wrong word.

Setting the list down, he fired up his computer. Entering the security codes, he pulled up the file he kept on his father.

The report his private investigator updated on a regular basis showed that the old man had rallied a little from the blow Narciso had dealt him three months ago.

Rallied but not fully recovered. Within minutes, Narciso was fully up to speed on his father's latest business dealings.

He didn't fool himself into thinking it gave him any sort of upper hand. He knew his father kept a similar file on him. But the game wouldn't have been this interesting if advantages had been one-sided. Nevertheless Narciso gained a lot of satisfaction from knowing he'd won three of their last four skirmishes.

He was contemplating the latest approach to his annihilation campaign when his phone buzzed.

Allowing the distraction, he thumbed the interactive surface and read the message from Nicandro Carvalho, the closest thing he had to a best friend.

Still caught in premature midlife-crisis mode, or are you ready to shake off that clinging BOM image?

*Boring old man.* A corner of his mouth lifted as his gaze slid to the list and his father's name. Suddenly energised, he whipped back a response.

BOM has left the building. Care to get your ass whopped at poker?

Nicandro's response—Dream on but bring it on—made him laugh for the first time in weeks.

Powering down his laptop, he slammed it shut. His gaze once again fell on the mask. Picking it up, he stashed it in his safe and shrugged into his suit jacket.

Zeus would receive his RSVP in the morning, once he'd devised exactly how he was going to take his father down once and for all.

The internet was a scary place. But it was an invaluable tool if you wanted to hunt down a slippery son of a bitch.

Ruby Trevelli sat cross-legged on her sofa and stared at the blinking cursor awaiting her command. That she was reduced to online trawling for a solution to her problem spiked equal measures of irritation and frustration through her.

She'd made it a point to avoid anything to do with social media. The one time she'd foolishly typed her name into a search engine, the sheer volume of false information she'd discovered had scared her into never trying again.

Of course, she'd also found enough about her parents to have scarred her for life if she hadn't already been scarred.

Tonight, she had no choice. Because despite thousands of pages featuring Narciso Media Corporation, every effort to speak to someone who could help her had been met with a solid stone wall. She'd already wasted a solid hour discovering that a thirty-year-old billionaire named Narciso Valentino owned NMC.

She snorted under her breath. Who on earth named their child *Narciso* anyway? That was like inviting bullies and snarkmongers to feast on the poor child. On the flip side, his unique name had eased her search.

Sucking in a breath, she typed in her next request: *Narciso's New York hangouts.* There were over two million entries. Awesome.

Either there were millions of men out there named Narciso or the man she sought was indecently popular.

Offering up a Hail Mary, she clicked the first link. And nearly gagged at the graphic burlesque images that popped up.

*Hell no!*

She closed it and sat back, fighting the rising nausea.

Desperate was fast becoming her middle name but Ruby

refused to accept that the answers to her woeful financial predicament would be found in a skin den.

Biting her inside lip, she exhaled and typed again: *Where's Narciso Valentino tonight?*

Her breath caught as the search engine fired back a quick response. The first linked the domain of a popular tabloid newspaper—one she'd become rudely acquainted with when she'd received her first laptop at ten, logged on and seen her parents splashed over the home page. In the fourteen years since then, she'd avoided the tabloid, just as she avoided her parents nowadays.

Ignoring the ache in her chest, she clicked on the next link that connected to a location app.

For several seconds, she couldn't believe how easily she'd found him. She read the extensive list of celebrities who'd announced their whereabouts freely, including one attending a movie premiere right now in Times Square.

Grabbing the remote, she flipped the TV channel to the entertainment news station, and, sure enough, the movie star was flashing a million-dollar smile at his adoring fans.

She glanced back at the location next to Narciso Valentino's name.

Riga—a Cuban-Mexican nightclub in the Flatiron District in Manhattan.

Glancing at the clock above the TV, she made a quick calculation. If she hurried, she could be there in under an hour. Her heart hammered as she contemplated what she was about to do.

She despised confrontation almost as much as her parents thrived on it. But after weeks of trying to find a solution, she'd reached the end of her tether.

She'd won the NMC reality TV show and scraped together every last cent to come up with her half of the hundred-thousand-dollar capital needed to get her restaurant—Dolce Italia—up and running.

Any help she could've expected from Simon Whittaker, her

ex-business partner and owner of twenty-five per cent of Dolce Italia, was now a thing of the past.

She clenched her fist as she recalled their last confrontation.

Finding out that the man she'd developed feelings for was married with a baby on the way had been shock enough. Simon trying to talk her into sleeping with him despite his marital status had killed any emotion she'd ever had for him.

He'd sneered at her wounded reaction to his intended infidelity. But having witnessed it up close with gut-wrenching frequency in her parents' marriage, she was well versed in its consequences.

Cutting Simon out of her life once she'd seen his true colours had been a painful but necessary decision.

Of course, without his business acumen she'd had to take full financial responsibility of Dolce Italia. Hence her search for Narciso Valentino. She needed him to stand by his company's promise. A contract was a contract....

A gleaming black limo was pulling up as she rounded the corner of the block that housed the nightclub. The journey had taken an extra half-hour because of a late-running train. Wincing at the pinch of her high heels on the uneven pavestones, she hurried towards Riga's red-bricked façade.

She was navigating her way around puddles left by the recent April shower, when deep male laughter snagged her attention.

A burly bouncer held open the velvet rope cordon as two men, both over six feet tall, exited the VIP entrance in the company of two strikingly beautiful women. The first man was arresting enough to warrant a second look but it was the other man who commanded Ruby's interest.

Jet-black hair had been styled to slant over the right side of his forehead in a silky wave that flowed back to curl over his collar.

Her steps faltered as the power of his presence slammed into her, and knocked air out of her lungs. His aura sent a challenge to the world, dared it to do its worst.

Dazed, she documented his profile—winged eyebrow, beautifully sculpted cheekbone, a straight patrician nose and a curved mouth that promised decadent pleasure—or what she imagined decadent pleasure looked like. But his mouth promised it and, well, this guy looked as if he could deliver on whatever sensual promises he made.

'Hey, miss. You coming in any time this century?'

The bouncer's voice distracted her, but not for long enough to completely pull her attention away. When she looked back, the man was turning away but it wasn't before Ruby caught another quick glimpse of his breathtaking profile.

Her gaze dropped lower. His dark grey shirt worn under a clearly bespoke jacket was open at the collar, allowing a glimpse of a bronzed throat and mouth-watering upper chest.

Ruby inhaled sharply and pulled her coat tighter around her as if that could stem the heat rushing like a breached dam through her.

The drop-dead gorgeous blonde smiled his way. His hand dropped from her waist to her bottom, drifted over one cheek to cup it in a bold squeeze before he helped her into the car. The first man shouted a query, and the group turned away from Ruby. Just like that, the strangely intimate and disturbing link was broken.

Her insides sagged and she realised how tight a grip she'd held on herself.

Even after the limo swung into traffic, Ruby couldn't move, nor could she stem the tingling suspicion that she'd arrived too late.

The bouncer cleared his throat conspicuously. She turned. 'Can you tell me who that second guy was who just got into that limo?' she asked.

He raised one *are-you-serious?* eyebrow.

Ruby shook her still-dazed head and smiled at the bouncer. 'Of course you can't tell me. Bouncer-billionaire confidentiality, right?'

His slow grin gentled his intimidating stature. 'Got it in one. Now, you coming in or you just jaywalking?'

'I'm coming in.' Although the strong suspicion that she'd missed Narciso Valentino grew by the second.

'Great. Here you go.' The bouncer placed a Mayan-mask-shaped stamp on her wrist, glanced up at her, then added another stamp. 'Show it at the bar. It'll get you your first drink on the house.' He winked.

She smiled in relief as she entered the smoky interior. If her guess had been wrong and she hadn't just missed Narciso Valentino, she could nurse an expensive drink while searching him out.

She'd worked in clubs like these all through college and knew how expensive even the cheapest drinks were. Which was why she clutched an almost warm virgin Tiffany Blue an hour later as she accepted that Narciso Valentino *was* the man she'd seen outside.

Resigned to her fruitless journey, she downed the last of her drink and was looking for a place to set the glass down when the voices caught her attention.

'Are you sure?'

'Of course I am. Narciso will be there.'

Ruby froze, then glanced into one of the many roped-off VIP areas. Two women dripping in expensive jewellery and designer dresses that would cost her a full year's salary sat sipping champagne.

Unease at her shameless eavesdropping almost forced her away but desperation held her in place.

'How do you know? He didn't attend the last two events.' The blonde looked decidedly pouty at that outcome.

'I told you, I overheard the guy he was with this evening talking about it. They're both going this time. If I can get a job as a *Petit Q* hostess, this could be my chance,' her red-headed friend replied.

'What? To dress in a clown costume in the hope of catching his eye?'

'Stranger things have happened.'

'Well, hell will freeze over before I do that to hook a guy,' the blonde huffed.

Statuesque Redhead's lips pursed. 'Don't knock it till you try it. It pays extremely well. And if Narciso Valentino falls in my lap, well, let's just say I won't let that life-changing opportunity pass me by.'

'Okay, you have my attention. Give me the name of the website. And where the hell is Macau anyway?' the blonde asked.

'Umm…Europe, I think?'

Ruby barely suppressed a snort. Heart thumping, she took her phone from her tiny clutch and keyed in the website address.

An hour and a half later, she sent another Hail Mary and pressed send on the online forms she'd filled out on her return home.

It might come to nothing. She could fail whatever test or interview she had to pass to get this gig. Heck, after discovering that she was applying to hostess for *Q Virtus,* one of the world's most exclusive and secretive private clubs, she wondered if she didn't need her head examined. She could be wasting money and precious time chasing an elusive man. But she had to try. Each day she waited was another day her goal slipped from her fingers.

The alternative—bowing to the pressure from her mother to join the family business—was unthinkable. At best she would once again become the pawn her parents used to antagonise each other. At worst, they would try and drag her down into their celebrity-hungry lifestyle.

They'd made her childhood a living hell. And she only had to pass a billboard in New York City to see they were still making each other's lives just as miserable but taking pleasure in documenting the whole thing for the world to feast on.

*The Ricardo & Paloma Trevelli Show* was prime-time viewing. The fly-on-the-wall documentary had been running for as long as Ruby could remember.

When she was growing up, her daily routine had included

at least two sets of camera crews documenting her every move along with her parents'.

TV crews had become extended family members. For a very short time when it'd made her the most popular girl at school, she'd told herself she was okay with it.

Until her father's affairs began. His very public admission of infidelity when she was nine years old had made ratings soar. Her mother publicly admitting her heartbreak had made worldwide news. Almost overnight, the TV show had been syndicated worldwide and brought her parents even more notoriety.

The subsequent reunion and vow renewal had thrilled the world.

After her father's second admission of infidelity, millions of viewers had been given the opportunity to weigh in on the outcome of Ruby's life.

Strangers had accosted her on the street, alternatively pitying and shaming her for being a Trevelli.

Escaping to college at the opposite end of the country had been a blessing. But even then she hadn't been able to avoid her roots.

It'd quickly become apparent that she had no other talent than cooking.

The realisation that the Trevelli gene was truly stamped into her DNA was a deep fear she secretly harboured. It was the reason she'd cut Simon out of her life without a backward glance. It was also the reason she'd vowed never to let her parents influence her life.

Which was why she needed a ten-minute conversation with Narciso Valentino. A tingle of awareness shot through her as she replayed the scene outside Riga.

With a spiky foreboding, she recalled the dark, dangerously sensual waves vibrating off him; those bronzed, sure fingers drifting over the blonde's bottom, causing unwelcome heat to drag through Ruby's belly.

God, what was she doing lying in bed thinking of some stranger's hand on his girlfriend's ass?

She punched her pillow into shape and flipped off her bedside lamp. She couldn't control the future but she could control the choice between mooning over elegant hands that looked as if they could bring a woman great pleasure or getting a good night's sleep.

She was almost asleep when her phone pinged an incoming message.

Exhaling in frustration, she grabbed the phone.

The brightness in the dark room hurt her eyes, but, even half blinded, Ruby could see the words clearly. Her CV had impressed the powers that be.

She'd been granted an interview to become a *Petit Q*.

# CHAPTER TWO

*Macau, China, One Week Later*

THE RED FLOOR-LENGTH gown sat a little too snugly against Ruby's skin, and the off-the-shoulder design exposed more cleavage and general flesh than she was comfortable with. But after two gruelling interviews, one of which she'd almost blown by turning up late due to another delayed train, the last thing she could complain about was the expensive designer outfit that spelt her out as a *Petit Q*.

She was careful now to avoid it getting snagged on her heels as she walked across the marble floor of her hotel towards the meeting place, from where they'd be chauffeured to their final destination. In her small case were two carefully folded, equally expensive outfits the management had provided.

An examination had shown that they, too, like the dress she wore, would be tight…everywhere. It was clear that someone, somewhere in the management food chain had got her measurements very wrong.

She'd already attracted the attention of an aging rock star in the lift on the way to the ground floor of her Macau hotel. It didn't matter that he'd seemed half blind when he'd leered at her; attracting *any* attention at all made her stomach knot with acid anxiety.

She'd let her guard down with Simon, had believed his interest to be pure and genuine, only to discover he wanted nothing more than a bit on the side. The idea that he'd assumed because she was a Trevelli she would condone his indecent proposal, just as her mother continued to accept her father's, had shredded the self-esteem she'd fought so hard to attain when she'd removed herself from her parents' sphere.

She wasn't a coward, but the fear that she might never be able to judge another man's true character sent a cold shiver through her.

Pushing the thought away, she straightened her shoulders, but another troubling thought immediately took its place.

What if she'd made a huge mistake in coming here?

What if Narciso didn't show? What if he showed and she missed him again?

No, she had to find him. Especially in light of the phone call she'd received the morning after she'd signed on to be a *Petit Q*.

The voice had been calm but menacing. Simon had sold his twenty-five-per-cent share of her business to a third party. 'We will be in touch shortly about interest and payment terms,' the accented voice had warned.

'I won't be able to discuss any payment terms until the business is up and running,' she'd replied, her hands growing clammy as anxiety dredged her stomach.

'Then it is in your interest to make that happen sooner rather than later, Miss Trevelli.'

The line had gone dead before she could say anything more. For a moment, she'd believed she'd dreamt the whole thing, but she'd lived in New York long enough to know loan sharks were a real and credible threat. And Simon had sold his share in her business to one of them.

Panicked and angry with Simon, she'd been halfway across the Indian Ocean before she'd read her *Petit Q* guidelines and experienced a bolt of shock.

No doubt to protect its ultra-urban-legend status, the *Q Virtus* Macau caucus was to be a masked event at a secret location in Macau.

*Masked,* as in *incognito.* Where the chances of picking out Narciso Valentino would be hugely diminished.

The memory of broad shoulders and elegant fingers flashed across her mind. Yeah, sure, as if she were an expert in male shoulders enough to distinguish one from the other.

Her fingers clenched around her tiny red clutch. She'd come all this way. She refused to admit defeat.

The redhead from Riga turned towards her and Ruby fought not to grit her teeth as the other woman dismissed her instantly.

As the door to the Humvee limo slid shut behind them another jagged stab of warning pierced her. Every cell in her body screamed at her to abandon this line of pursuit and hightail it back home.

She could use the app to find out when Narciso returned to New York. She could confront him on home turf where she was more at ease, not here in this sultry, exotic part of the world where the very air held a touch of opulent magic.

But what if this was her last chance? A man who would fly thousands of miles for a highly secretive event could disappear just as easily given half a chance. She'd been lucky to be in the right place to find out where he'd be at this point in time.

Fate had handed her the opportunity. She wasn't going to blow it.

The limo hit a bump, bringing her back to reality.

Despite the glitzy lights and Vegas-style atmosphere, the tiny island of Macau held a charisma and steeped-in-history feel that had spilled over from mainland China. She held her breath as they crossed over the Lotus Bridge into Cotai, their final destination.

Bicycles raced alongside sports cars and nineteen-fifties buses in a spectacular blend of ancient and modern.

Less than ten minutes later, they rolled to a stop. Exiting, she looked around and her trepidation escalated. The underground car park was well lit enough to showcase top-of-the-line luxury sports cars and blinged-out four-by-fours next to stretch limos.

The net worth in the car park alone was enough to fund the annual gross domestic product of a small country.

The buzz of excitement in her group fractured her thoughts and she hurried forward into waiting lifts. Like her, the other nineteen hostesses were dressed in red gowns for the first evening, and the ten male hosts dressed in red jackets.

Six bodyguards accompanied them into the lifts and Ruby stemmed the urge to bolt as the doors started to close. Five seconds later it was too late.

The doors opened to gleaming parquet floors with red and gold welcoming carpet running through the middle of the vast, suspended foyer.

On the walls, exquisite tapestries of dragons flirting with maidens were embellished with multihued glass beads. Red and gold Chinese-silk cloth hung in swathes from the tapered ceiling to the floor, discreetly blacking out the outside world.

Two winged staircases led to the floor below where a sunken section in the middle had been divided into twelve gaming tables, each with its own private bar and seating area.

All around her, masked men in bespoke tuxedos mingled with exquisitely clad women dripping with stunning jewellery that complemented their breathtaking masks. Granted, the number of women was marginally less than men, but from the way they carried themselves Ruby suspected these women wielded more than enough power to hold their own against their male counterparts.

A tall, masked, jet-haired woman wearing a sophisticated-looking earpiece glided forward and introduced herself as Head Hostess. In succinct tones, she briefed them on their roles.

Ruby tried to calm her jangling nerves as she descended the stairs and headed for the bar of the fourth poker table.

*A bar she could handle.*

Nevertheless, she held her breath as the first group of men took their places at the table. They all wore masks in varying degrees of camouflage and design. As she mixed her first round of drinks and delivered it to the table, Ruby tried to glean if any of them resembled her quarry.

One by one, she dismissed them. Eventually, they drifted off and another group took their place.

A grey-haired man—the oldest in her group—immediately drew her attention. He carried himself with command and control, but he was too old to be Narciso Valentino and his frame was slightly stooped with age.

He snapped his fingers and threw out an order for a glass of Sicilian red. Ruby pursed her lips and admonished herself not to react to the rudeness. Five men took their places around the table, leaving only one other space to be filled.

Safely behind the bar after delivering their drinks order, she watched their bets grow larger and bolder.

Music pumped from discreet loud speakers, and through a set of double doors guests took to the dance floor. It wasn't deafening by any means but Ruby felt the pulse of the provocative music through the soles of her feet.

She swallowed down the mingled distaste and latent fear as she noticed things were beginning to get hot and heavy as guests began to loosen their inhibitions.

She could do this. Just because she was a Trevelli didn't mean she would lose sight of her goals. Decadence and excess were her parents' thing. They needn't be hers…

The lights overhead dimmed.

A door to one side of the lift labelled The Black Room swung open and two men stepped onto the gangway.

One wore a gold half-mask that covered him from forehead to nose. The aura of power that radiated from him raised the very temperature of the room.

But the moment Ruby's eyes encountered the second man, her belly clenched.

The head hostess drifted towards him but he raised a hand and waved her away. At the sight of those slim fingers, recognition slammed into her. She watched, dry-mouthed, as he sauntered down the steps and headed for her side of the room.

He stopped in front of her bar.

Silver eyes bore into hers, drilling down hard as if he wanted to know her every last secret. The smile slowly left his face as he continued to stare at her, one eyebrow gradually lifting in silent query.

His silver and black onyx mask was artistically and visually stunning. It revealed his forehead and the lower part of his face and against its brilliance his olive skin glowed in a way that made her want to touch that chiselled jaw.

Piercing eyes drifted over her in a lazy sweep, pausing for a long second at her breasts. Her breath hitched in her throat as her body reacted to his probing gaze.

Narciso Valentino. If she'd had two dollars to rub together she'd have bet on it.

Her mouth dried as she looked into his eyes and lost every last sensible thought in her head.

'Serve me, *cara mia*. I'm dying of thirst.' His voice was raw, unadulterated sin, oozing what Ruby could only conclude was sex appeal.

At least she thought so because the sound of it had transmitted a tingling to parts of her body she hadn't known could tingle just from hearing a man's voice. And why on earth had her hands grown so clammy?

When his brow arched higher at her inactivity, she scrambled to think straight. 'W-what would you like?'

His eyes moved down again, paused at her throat, where her pulse jumped like a frenzied rabbit.

'Surprise me.'

He turned abruptly and all signs of mirth leached from his face.

Across the small space between the bar and the poker table, he speared the silver-haired man with an unforgiving gaze.

The man stared back, the part of his face visible beneath his mask taut despite his whole body bristling with disdain.

Animosity arced through the air, snapping coils of dangerous electricity that made Ruby's pulse leap higher. Her gaze slid back to the younger man as if drawn by magnets. She told herself she was trying to decipher what sort of drink to make him but, encountering those broad shoulders again, her mind drifted into impure territory, as it had outside the nightclub in New York.

*Focus!*

The older man had requested a Sicilian red but instinctively she didn't think the man she'd concluded was Narciso would go for wine.

Casting her gaze over the bottles of spirits and liqueurs, she quickly measured the required shots, mixed a cocktail and placed it on a tray.

Willing her fingers not to shake, she approached the poker table and placed his drink at his elbow.

He dragged his gaze from the older man long enough to glance from the pale golden drink to her face. 'What is this?' he asked.

'It's a…*Macau Bombshell,*' she blurted out the name she'd come up with seconds ago.

One smooth brow spiked as he leaned back in his seat. 'Bombshell?' Once again, his gaze drifted over her, lingered at the place where her dress parted mid-thigh in a long slit. 'Would you place yourself in that category, too? Because you certainly have the potential.'

Right, so really he was one of those. A Playboy with a capital *P*.

A man who saw something he coveted and went for it, regardless of who got hurt. The clear image of his hand on another woman made her spine stiffen in negative reaction, even as a tiny part of her acknowledged her disappointment.

Irritated with herself, she pushed the feeling away.

Now she knew what sort of man she was dealing with, things would proceed much smoother.

'No, I wouldn't,' she said briskly. 'It's all about the drink.'

'I've never heard such a name.'

'It's my own creation.'

'Ah.' He sipped the champagne, falernum, lemon and pine-apple mix. Then he slowly tasted the cocktail without taking his eyes off her. 'I like it. Bring me one every half-hour on the button until I say otherwise.'

The implication that she could be here for hours caused her teeth to grind. She looked from the dealer to the other players at the table, wondered if she could ask to speak to Narciso privately now.

'Is there a problem?' he queried.

She cleared her throat. 'Well, yes. There are no clocks in this place and I don't have a watch, so...'

The silver-haired man swore under his breath and moved his shoulders in a blatantly aggressive move.

'Hold out your hand,' Narciso said.

Ruby's eyes widened. 'Excuse me?'

'Give me your hand,' he commanded.

She found herself obeying before she could think not to. He removed an extremely expensive and high-tech-looking watch from his wrist and placed it on her right wrist. The chain link was too large for her but it didn't mask the warmth from his skin and something jagged and electric sliced through her belly.

When his hand drifted along the inside of her wrist, she bit back a gasp, and snatched her hand back.

'Now you know when I'll next need you.'

'By all means, keep me waiting as you try out your tired pick-up lines,' the older man snapped with an accent she vaguely recognised.

Silver Eyes shifted his gaze to him. And although he continued to sip his cocktail, the air once again snapped with dark animosity.

'Ready for another lesson, old man?'

'If it involves teaching you to respect your betters, then I'm all for it.'

The resulting low laugh from the man next to her sent a shiver dancing over her skin. On decidedly wobbly legs, she retreated behind the bar and forced herself to regulate her breathing.

Whatever she'd experienced when those mesmerising eyes had locked into hers and those long fingers had stroked her was a false reaction. She refused to trust any emotion that could lead her astray.

*Focus!*

She glanced down at the watch. The timepiece was truly exquisite, a brand she'd heard of and knew was worth a fortune.

Unable to stop herself, she skated her fingers over it, her pulse thundering all over again when she remembered how he'd looked at her before slipping the watch on her wrist. She shifted as heat dragged through her and arrowed straight between her legs.

*No!*

She wasn't a slave to her emotions like her parents. And she wasn't the gullible fool Simon had accused her of being.

She had a goal and a purpose. One she intended to stick to.

Exactly half an hour later, she approached, willing her gaze not to trace those magnificent shoulders. Up close they were even broader, more imposing. When he shifted in his seat, they moved with a mesmerising fluidity that made her want to stop and gawp.

Keeping her gaze fixed on the red velvet table, she quickly deposited his drink on the designated coaster and picked up his almost-empty one. He flicked a glance at her.

*'Grazie.'*

The sound of her mother tongue on his lips flipped her stomach with unwanted excitement. She told herself it was because she was one step further to confirming his identity but Ruby suspected it was the sheer sexiness of his voice that was the bigger factor here.

*'Prego,'* she responded automatically before she could stop herself. She bit her lip and watched him follow the movement. A deeply predatory gleam entered his eyes.

'I want the next one in fifteen minutes.' His gaze returned

to his opponent, who looked a little paler since the last round of drinks. 'I have a feeling I'll be done by then. Unless you want to quit while you're behind?' he asked, sensual lips parted in a frightening imitation of a smile.

The older man let out a pithy response that Ruby didn't quite catch. Two players quickly folded their cards and left.

The two men eyeballed each other, pure hatred blazing as they psychologically circled one another.

Narciso laid down his cards in a slow, unhurried flourish. His opponent followed suit with a move that was eerily similar and made Ruby frown. The connection between the two men was unmistakable but she couldn't quite pin down why.

When the older man laughed, Ruby glanced down at his cards. She didn't know the rules of poker, but even she guessed his cards were significant.

She held her breath. Not with so much as a twitch did Narciso indicate he'd just lost millions of dollars.

'Give it up, old man.'

*'Mai!'* Never.

Ten minutes later, Narciso calmly laid down another set of cards that won him the next game. Hearing Giacomo's grunt of disbelief was extremely satisfactory. But it was the indrawn breath of surprise from the woman next to him that drew his attention.

He didn't let himself glance at her yet. She'd proven a seriously delicious distraction already. He had plans for her but those plans would have to wait a while longer.

For now, he revelled in Giacomo's defeat and watched a trickle of sweat drip down his temple.

They were barely an hour in and he'd already divested him of several million dollars. As usual, Giacomo had been lured in by the promise of trouncing his son, enabling Narciso to lay the bait he knew wouldn't be resisted.

The last game had won him a midsize radio station in Anaheim, California.

It would be a superb addition to his already sizeable news

and social media portfolio. Or he could shut it down and declare it a loss.

It didn't matter either way.

What mattered was that he had Giacomo's financial demise within his grasp. How very fitting that he should be in the perfect place to celebrate once he'd hammered the last nail into the coffin.

His gaze flickered to the stunning woman in red who regarded him with a touch of wariness and a whole lot of undisguised interest.

The silky cognac-coloured hair begged to be messed with, as did that sinful, pouting mouth she insisted on mauling every time he won a hand.

But her body, *Dio!* Her dress was a little too tight, sure, but even the fact that it made her assets a little too in your face didn't detract from the fact that she was a magnificent creature.

A magnificent creature he would possess tonight. She would be the cherry on his cake, one he would take the utmost pleasure in savouring before he devoured.

But first…

'Do you yield?' he asked silkily, already anticipating the response. In some ways they were so very similar. Which wasn't surprising considering they were father and son.

Although a father and son who detested the very ground each other walked on put an interesting twist on their *relationship*.

'Over my dead body.' Giacomo snapped his fingers at the dealer and threw his last five-million-dollar platinum chip in the middle of the table.

Beside him, his hostess's mouth dropped open. The sight of her pink tongue sent a spike of excitement through his groin.

*Sì*…he would celebrate well tonight. For a while there, he'd begun to suspect that beating Giacomo would be his only source of entertainment in Macau. Which was why he'd sought the old man out instead of leaving him to squirm a little longer. He'd wanted to be done and out of here as soon as possible.

The other deals he'd come to negotiate had taken the necessary leap forward and he'd believed there was nothing left.

But now…

His groin hardened as he watched her mouth slowly press shut and her eyes dart to his with the same anticipated excitement that flowed within him.

He let his interest show, let her see the promise of what was to come.

Heat flared up her delicate neck and flawless skin into a surprisingly innocent face that could've graced a priceless painting.

*Dio,* she was truly entrancing. And yet she was in a place like this, where the likelihood of being hit on, or more, was very real.

He gave a mental shrug. He'd stopped trying to reason why people took the actions they took well before he'd grown out of long socks.

Otherwise he'd have driven himself mad from trying to decipher why the father whose DNA flowed through his veins seemed to hate every single breath he took.

Or why Maria's betrayal still had the power to burn an acid path in his gut—

*No.*

That train had long left the station. Giving it thinking room was a waste of time and his time was extremely precious.

Keeping his eyes on his hostess, he downed his drink and held out his empty glass.

'I'm thirsty again, *amante.*'

With a nod, she sashayed away in her too-tight dress and returned minutes later with his drink.

When she started to move away, he snagged a hand around her waist. The touch of warm, silk-covered flesh beneath his fingers short-circuited his brain for a few moments. Then he realised she was trying to get away from him.

'Stay. You bring me luck when you're near.'

'Shame you need a woman to win,' Giacomo sneered.

Narciso ignored him and nodded to the dealer. He wanted this game to be over so he could pull this magical being tighter into his arms, feel her melt against him, his prize for emerging triumphant.

Giacomo threw his chip defiantly into the fray. Narciso's chest tightened with the anger that never quite went away. For as long as he remembered, his father had treated him like that chip—inconsequential, easily cast aside. Underneath all the anger and bitterness, a wound he'd thought healed cracked open.

Ignoring it, he calmly plucked his cards from the table.

'Let's up the stakes.'

Eyes that had once been similar to his own but had grown dimmer with age snapped at him. 'You think you have something I want?'

'I *know* I do. That tech company you lost to me last month? If I lose this hand, I'll return it to you, along with all of this.' He nodded to the pile of chips in front of him, easily totalling over thirty million dollars.

'And if I lose?' His voice held a false confidence Narciso almost smiled at. *Almost.*

'You hand over the other five-million chip I know is in your pocket and I'll let you keep your latest Silicon Valley start up.'

Giacomo sneered but Narciso could see him weighing up the odds. Thirty million against ten.

He waited, let the seductive scent of his hostess's perfume wash over him. Unable to resist, he slid his hand lower. The faintest sensation of a thong made his groin tighten. Again, she tried to move away. He pulled her back towards him and heard her breath catch.

'My offer expires in ten seconds,' he pressed.

Giacomo reached into his tuxedo pocket and tossed the second chip onto the table. Then he laid out cards in a flourish.

Four of a kind.

Narciso didn't need to glance down at his own cards to know *he'd* won.

And yet…the triumph he should've experienced was oddly missing. Instead, hollowness throbbed dully in his chest.

'Come on, then, you coward. It's your turn to answer this—do you yield?'

Narciso breathed in deep and fought the tight vice crushing his chest. Slowly, the hollowness receded and anger rushed into its place. 'Yes, I yield.'

His father's bark of victorious laughter drew attention from other tables but Narciso didn't care.

His hand was tightening over her waist, anticipation of a different sort firing his body. He was about to turn towards her when Giacomo reached for the cards Narciso had discarded.

A straight flush. A winning hand more powerful than his father's.

The evidence that he'd been toyed with registered in Giacomo's shocked eyes. *'Il diavolo!'* He lunged across the table, his whole body vibrating with fury.

Narciso stood, his eyes devoid of expression. *'Sì,* I am the devil *you* spawned. You'll do well to remember that next time we meet.'

# CHAPTER THREE

*I AM THE devil* you *spawned*.

Had he meant that literally?

Ruby glanced at the man who had her imprisoned against his side as he steered her towards…

'Where are you taking me?' she demanded in a rush as electrifying fingers pressed more firmly into her skin. Who knew silk was an excellent conductor of heat?

She burned from head to toe and he wasn't even touching her bare skin.

'First to the dance floor. And then…who knows?'

'But my duties…behind the bar—'

'Are over,' he stated imperiously.

Despite the alien emotions swirling through her, she frowned. 'Can you do that?'

'You'll find that I can pretty much do anything I want.'

'You deliberately lost thirty million dollars two minutes ago. I think doing what you want is pretty obvious. What I'm asking is, am I risking my job by deserting my post?'

He ushered her into the lift, took hold of her wrist and held the smartwatch against the panel. When it lit up, he pressed the key for the floor below. 'You're here to serve the members of this club. I require your services on the dance floor. There, does that ease your anxiety?' He asked the question with a thread of cynicism that made her glance closely at him.

The tic throbbing at his temple and tense shoulders indicated that he hadn't shrugged off his encounter at the poker table.

'Who was that man you were playing with?' she asked.

Silver eyes hardened a touch before they cleared and he smiled. Ruby forced herself not to gulp at the pulse-destroying transformation his smile achieved.

'No one important. But you—' he faced her fully as the lift stopped and the doors glided open '—are much more fascinating.'

One hand brushed her wrist and slid up her arm. The shiver when he'd first touched her returned a hundredfold, sending soul-deep tremors through her.

*What on earth was going on?* She'd believed herself in love with Simon, enough to come within a whisper of making a fool of herself, and yet he'd not triggered an iota of what she was feeling now.

*Chemistry.*

The word fired alarm bells so loud in her head she jerked backwards. Her back hit the lift wall and panic flared high as he stepped closer. Heat waves bounced off his hard-packed, unapologetically male body straight into hers.

'I'm not fascinating. Not in the least,' she said hurriedly.

He laughed, a deep, husky sound that sent warning tingling all over her body.

Was this how helpless prey felt within the clutches of a merciless predator? She was nobody's prey; nonetheless she couldn't deny this man's seriously overwhelming presence.

'You're refreshingly naïve, too.' His gaze probed, then his smile slowly faded. Although the hunger didn't. 'Unless *that's* the ploy?' he queried in the same silky tone he'd used at the poker table.

Ruby's breath caught as the unmistakable sense of danger washed over her again. 'There's no ploy. And I'm not naïve.'

His fingers had reached her shoulder. They skated along her collarbone, perilously close to the pulse jumping at her throat. The doors started to slide shut. His fingers stopped just shy of touching her pulse, then returned to grasp her wrist. With a tap on the smartwatch the doors parted again.

'Come and dance with me. You can tell me how un-naïve and un-fascinating you are.'

He led her to the middle of a dance floor much larger than the one upstairs. Over a dozen guests graced the large space, moving to the beat of the sultry blend of Far Eastern music and western jazz.

They could've danced apart. In fact Ruby was counting on the brief reprieve from close contact. But he had other ideas.

He caught her close, one arm around her waist and the other catching her hand and imprisoning it against his chest as he began to sway. The fluidity with which he moved, his innate sensuality, told her that this man knew a lot about sex and sexuality. Would know how to take a woman and leave her utterly replete but desperate for more.

'I'm waiting for you to enlighten me.'

For a second she couldn't get her brain to work. Sensations she'd never felt before crashed through her as his hard thighs brushed hers.

'About what?'

'About why you think you're not fascinating. Those impure thoughts running through your head we'll leave for later.'

She sucked in a shocked breath. 'How…? I wasn't…'

'You blush when you're flustered. As endearing as that is, you'd make a lousy poker player.'

'I don't gamble. And I don't know why I'm having this conversation with you.'

'We're performing the requisite mating dance before we… mate.'

She stopped dead. 'In your dreams! I'm not here to be your, or anyone's, appetiser.'

'Don't sell yourself short, sweetheart. I'd place you more as a deliciously forbidden dessert than an appetiser. But one I intend to devour nonetheless.'

She was on a dance floor thousands of miles away from home, immersed in a debate about which food course she was.

Surreal didn't even begin to cover the emotions coursing through her as she glanced up at him and encountered that blatantly masculine square jaw and those hypnotic eyes.

'Look, Mr…?'

He raised a brow. 'You're at a masked event, shrouded in secrecy, embroiled in intrigue and mystery, and you want to know my name?' he asked cynically.

Damn, how could she have forgotten? 'Why do I get the feeling that all this bores you rigid?'

His eyes gleamed. 'How very intuitive of you. You're right—it does. Or it did, until I saw you.'

Her heart gave a little kick. One she determinedly ignored. 'You were fully engaged when you played your game. And *that* had nothing to do with me.'

Again that reminder hardened his eyes. 'Ah, but I lost thirty million dollars so I could make what's happening between us happen sooner.'

'There's nothing happening—'

'If you believe *that* then you really are naïve.'

Another couple danced closer. The flash of red hair distracted Ruby enough to make her look. *Redhead* was in the arms of another man but her hungry eyes were fixed squarely on Narciso.

Irrational irritation jerked up Ruby's spine.

Pursing her lips, she tilted her chin at the redhead. 'Why don't you help yourself to her? She definitely wants you.'

He didn't bother to glance where Ruby indicated. He merely smiled and shrugged. 'Every woman wants me.'

'Wow, you're not the shy type at all, are you?' she snapped.

He leaned forward, and a swathe of luxurious black hair fell over his forehead to curl over the top of his mask. 'Are those the types that turn you on?' he whispered.

The image of shy, self-effacing…*duplicitous* Simon fleeted

across her mind. She stiffened. 'We're not discussing my tastes here.'

'I've clearly hit a nerve. But if you don't tell me what your tastes are, how will I know how to please you?' His mouth was a hair's breadth from her ear.

Ruby fought to breathe. Her chest was a mere inch from his but her lower body was plastered against his in a way that made his body's response blatant and unmistakable.

He was aroused. And he meant her to know it.

Her abdomen clenched so forcefully, she lost her footing and stumbled.

Strong hands righted her and began to pull her back into his arms but Ruby quickly stepped back.

'You can start by buying me a drink.'

He reluctantly dropped his hand from her waist. Expecting overwhelming relief, Ruby frowned when it didn't arrive.

A white-jacketed waiter hovered nearby. 'Champagne?'

She shook her head. 'No. Something else.'

Something that would take several minutes to make and give her time to get her perplexing emotions under control.

'State what you wish,' he said.

She almost blurted her reason for being in Macau there and then. But this wasn't the right time. She needed to get him alone, in a place where he couldn't blow her off as easily as his employees had these past weeks.

Casting her gaze around, she pointed to the far side of the room. 'There.'

'The ice-vodka lounge? Is this a delaying tactic?'

'Of course not. I really want a drink.'

He watched her for several seconds, then he nodded.

This time her relief was tangible. But the reprieve didn't last long. His arm slid possessively around her waist as he led her off the dance floor.

She was suppressing the rising tide of that damned *chemistry* when he leaned in close. 'You're only trying to delay the inevitable, *tesoro*.'

'I have no idea what you mean.'

His laughter drew gazes and turned heads. Ruby had a feeling everything this man did compelled attention. And not just of the female variety.

Powerful men stepped aside as he steered her towards the vodka lounge. A faux-fur coat appeared as if by magic and he draped it over her shoulders before they entered the sub-zero room. She headed for an empty slot at the bar, near an ice sculpture carved in the shape of a Chinese dragon.

The bartender glanced at her unmasked face with a frown.

'I'd like a *Big Apple Avalanche*, please. Heavy on the apple.' She needed a clear head if she intended to stay toe to toe with Narciso Valentino.

The bartender didn't move. 'I don't think you're allowed—'

'Is there a problem?' The hard rasp came from over her shoulder.

The bartender snapped to attention. 'Not at all, sir.' He grabbed the apple mixer and the canister of top-range vodka.

'I'll take it from here.' Narciso took the drinks from him and waved him away.

Despite the warmth of her coat, she shivered when he turned to her.

'Ready?'

*God,* this wasn't going well at all. Far from feeling under control, she felt her thoughts scatter to the wind every time he looked into her eyes.

'Yes,' she said as she inserted the specialised drinking spout into the ice outlet and brought her lips to it.

Her eyes met molten silver ones and fiery heat rushed into her belly. He slowly tipped the canister and icy vodka and apple pooled into her mouth.

Cold and heat simultaneously soothed and burned their way down her throat but the power of the decadent drink came nowhere close to the potent gleam in his eyes.

Before discovering Simon's duplicity, sex had been something she'd imagined in abstract terms; something she'd accepted would eventually happen between them, once the trust and affection she'd thought was growing between them was solid enough to lean on.

Sex just for the sake of it, or used as a weapon the way she'd watched her parents use it, had made being a virgin at twenty-four an easy choice.

But looking into Narciso's eyes, she slowly began to understand why sex was a big deal for some women. Why they dwelled on it with such single-minded ferocity.

Never had she wanted to drown in a man's eyes. Never had she wanted to kiss sensually masculine lips the way she wanted to kiss him right now. She wanted to feel those arms around her again, holding her prisoner the way they'd held her on the dance floor. She wanted to spear her fingers through his luxurious hair, scrape her nails over his scalp and find out if it brought him pleasure.

'Have another one,' he commanded huskily. He raised the sterling silver mixer, his gaze riveted on her mouth.

He wanted to kiss her badly. The same way she wanted to kiss him. Or would have if she didn't know from painful experience how treacherous and volatile sexual attraction could be.

'No, thanks. It's getting late. I need to go.'

One beautifully winged brow rose. 'You need to go.'

'Yes.'

'And where *exactly* do you intend to go?'

She frowned. 'Back to my hotel, of course.'

He slowly lowered his arm. 'I thought you understood your role here,' he murmured coolly.

Icy foreboding shivered down her spine. 'What's that supposed to mean?'

'It means, the moment the last guest arrived, the whole building went into lock down. You're stuck here with me until tomorrow at six.' He discarded the canister and stepped closer. 'And I have the perfect idea of how we can pass the time.'

* * *

Narciso watched a myriad expressions dart over her face.

Excitement. Anxiety. Suspicion.

Two of those three weren't what he expected from a woman when he announced they were effectively locked in together. Most women would be salivating at the thought and making themselves available before he changed his mind.

Not this one.

Even the hint of excitement was fading. Now she just looked downright frightened.

He frowned. 'I expected a more enthusiastic response.'

Her gaze went to the watch—his watch—then back to his face. Narciso decided not to think about why the sight of his large watch on her delicate wrist pleased him so much.

He would gift it to her. She could keep it on during sex. Once he'd dispelled that unacceptable look from her face.

'You just told me I can't leave. And you expect me to be excited?'

'You have some of the world's richest and most influential men gathered in one place. Everyone who attends these events has the same agenda—network hard and party harder, especially the *Petit Qs*. You, on the other hand, are acting as if you've received a prison sentence. Why?'

Her eyelids lowered and she grabbed the lapels of her coat.

Faint alarm bells rang at the back of his mind. Going against a habit of a lifetime, he forced himself to ignore it as she raised those delicate lids to lock gazes with him.

Her sapphire-blue eyes held a combination of boldness and shyness that hugely intrigued him. She wanted something but wasn't quite sure how to get it.

He had every intention of showing her how to get exactly what she wanted once he got her to his suite upstairs. He might even tempt her into using the velvet ropes that held back his emperor-size bed's drapes…

Desire slammed into him with a force he hadn't experienced

in years…if ever. The strength of it struck him dumb for a few seconds before he realised she was speaking.

'…knew about the club, of course, and that my hostessing gig was for two days. I didn't know I'd be staying here for the duration.'

'Ah, one small piece of advice. Always read the small print.'

Her delicious mouth pursed. He had the sudden, clamouring urge to find out if it tasted as succulent as it looked. Her narrowed-eyed glare stopped him. Barely.

'I always do. I can't say the same for other people though. Especially people who have the small print pointed out to them and still wilfully ignore it.'

The alarm bells grew louder. 'That's decidedly…pointed. Care to elaborate?'

She opened her mouth, then shut it again. 'I'm cold. Can we leave?'

'That's an excellent idea.' He walked her to the door of the ice bar and helped her out of her coat.

The sight of her hardened nipples—an effect of the sub-zero temperature—fried a few million brain cells. That clawing hunger gutted him further, making him fight to remember whether he was coming or going.

*Going.* Definitely. Up to his allocated suite with this woman who sparked a reaction within him that left him reeling, and wanting more. He hadn't wanted anything this badly for a long time. Not since his eleventh birthday…

He shut off his thoughts and walked her to the lift, absurdly pleased when she didn't protest. Perhaps she'd accepted the inevitable.

They were meant to be together. Here in this place where the events of earlier this evening with Giacomo had nearly soured his experience.

She would take away the bitterness for a while. Take away his unsettling hollowness when he'd held the old man's financial demise in his grasp but hadn't taken it.

All would be better in the morning.

For tonight, he intended to seek the most delicious oblivion.

'Should I bother to ask where you're taking me now?'

His smile felt tight and his body on edge. 'No. Don't bother. What you should ask is how many ways will I make you like what's coming next.' He activated the electronic panel. When the chrome panel slid back to reveal the row of buttons he selected the fiftieth floor for his penthouse suite.

'If you're planning to throw a few more millions away, then I'd rather not watch.' Again there was that censorious note in her voice that strummed his instincts.

From experience he knew women always had hidden agendas, be it the urge to make themselves indispensable in his life the moment he so much as smiled their way or to take advantage of his power and influence—as well as his body—for as long as possible.

But the woman in front of him was exhibiting none of those traits. And yet there was something… Narciso didn't like the mixed signals he was receiving from her.

'Have we met before?' he demanded abruptly, although he was sure he would have remembered. She had an unforgettable body, and that mouth… He was absolutely certain he would have remembered that mouth.

'Met? No, of course not. Besides, I don't know who you are, remember?'

'If you don't know who I am then how do you know we haven't met before?'

Her eyes shifted away from his. 'I…don't know. I just think a man like you…I'd have remembered…that's all.'

He smiled at her flustered response, deciding he definitely liked her flustered. 'I like that you think I'm unforgettable. I aim to make that thought a permanent reality for you.'

'Trust me, you already have,' she quipped.

Narciso got the distinct impression it wasn't a compliment.

He stepped forward. She stepped back. Her eyes widened when she realised she was trapped against the wall of the lift.

His pulse thundered when her gaze darted to his mouth and then back to his eyes.

'Somewhere along the line, I seem to have made a bad impression on you. Normally I wouldn't care but...' He stepped closer, until the warmth of her agitated exhalations rushed over his chin. Her scent hit his nostrils and he nearly moaned at the seductive allure of it.

'But...?' she demanded huskily.

'But I find myself wanting to alter that impression.'

'You want me to think you're a good guy?'

Laughing, he slid his hand around her trim waist. 'No. *Good* is taking things a touch too far, *amante*. I haven't been *good* since...' he blunted that knife of memory again '...for ever.'

Her darkened eyes dropped to his mouth again and Narciso barely stopped himself from groaning. But he couldn't stop his hands from tightening on her waist. In contrast to her lush hips, her waist was so tiny, his hands spanned it easily.

'Then what do you want from me?'

Before he could succinctly elaborate, the lift doors slid open. The double doors leading into his suite beckoned. Beyond that the bedroom where he intended to make her his.

He grasped her wrist and tugged her after him. Using the smartwatch to activate the smaller panel, he pressed his thumb against the infrared scanner and pushed the doors open. He didn't bother to shut it because the doors were automatic. Security was exemplary at all *Q Virtus* events, especially the private suites. He had the whole floor to himself and no one would disturb them unless he wanted them to.

And he had no desire for any interruptions—

He noticed she'd stopped dead and turned to find her staring at him.

'You've brought me to your suite,' she blurted.

The pulse pounding at her throat could've been excitement. Or more likely it was the trepidation he'd seen earlier.

'Very observant of you.'

'Know this now—I won't be indulging in anything…illicit with you.'

'Since we haven't established exactly what it is we'll be doing I think we're getting a little ahead of ourselves.'

'I wish you'd stop toying with me.'

His shoulders moved with the restlessness that vibrated through his whole being. He couldn't remember the last time he'd had to work this hard to get a woman to acknowledge her interest in him. 'Fine. Do you deny that there's something powerful and undeniable happening between us?'

'I don't want—'

'If you really don't want to be here, say the word and I'll let you leave.' That wasn't strictly true. First he'd use his infinite skills to convince her to stay. Arrogance didn't come into his awareness that he was attractive to most women, and, despite her mixed signals, this woman was as attracted to him as he was to her.

She might need a little more work than usual—and the thought wasn't unpleasing—but he was more than up to the task.

He watched her debate with herself for an endless minute. Then she turned towards the window.

Narciso forced himself to remain still, despite his every cell screeching at him to grab her. Picking up a control device, he pushed the button that allowed the glass windows to turn from opaque to transparent.

Macau City lay spread before them in a cascade of lights, glittering water and awe-inspiring ancient Portuguese, Chinese and modern architecture.

Since he'd started doing business here, his fascination with the city had grown along with his bank balance.

But right now his fascination with her was much more paramount.

'Tell me you'll stay.' His voice emerged rougher than normal.

The thought that he wanted her badly, alarm bells or no alarm bells, made him frown. He'd trained himself not to want anything he absolutely could not have. It was why he calculated his every decision with scalpel-like precision.

That way he avoided disappointment. Avoided…heartache…

She turned from the window, arms crossed at that tiny waist. Her response took a minute, two at a stretch, but they were the longest minutes of Narciso's life.

'I'll stay…for a little while.'

He swallowed and nodded. Suddenly, his fingers itched to remove the pins in her hair, to see its silky dark gold abundance cascade over her shoulders.

'Take your hair down,' he instructed. The time for playing was over.

Her eyes widened. 'Why?'

'Because I want to see it. And because you're staying.'

Her fingers touched the knot at the back of her head. Anticipation spiked through him only to be doused in disappointment when she lowered her hand.

'I prefer to keep it up.'

'If you're trying to keep me hyped up with interest, trust me, it's working.'

'I'm not, I mean… My hair is no big deal.'

'It is to me. I have a weakness for long hair.'

Her head tilted to one side, exposing a creamy neck he longed to explore. 'If I take my hair down, will you take your mask off?'

As much as he wanted to rip his mask off, something told him to delay the urge. 'No,' he replied. 'My house, my rules.'

'That's not fair, is it?'

'If life was fair you'd be naked and underneath me by now.'

A blush splashed up her exquisite throat and stung her cheeks. Molten lust rushed into his groin and spread through his body. Feeling restricted and seriously on edge, he shrugged off his tuxedo jacket and flung it over the long sofa. Next came the bow tie. He left that dangling to tackle the top buttons of his shirt and looked up to find her gaze riveted on him.

Good, he was not alone in this. Sexual desire pulsed from

her in drenching waves. Which made the reticence in her eyes all the more intriguing.

*Enough!*

In three strides, he stood in front of her. She made a high, surprised noise as he tugged her close. Without giving her a chance to protest further, he swooped down and took her lips with his.

She tasted glorious. Like a shot of premium tequila on a sultry night. Like warm sunshine and decadent, sticky desserts. Like jumping off the highest peak of an icy mountain with nothing beneath him but air and infinite possibilities.

Narciso's lids slid shut against the drugging sensation of her lips.

*Madre di Dio!* He was hard. Harder than he'd ever been. And he'd only been kissing her a few seconds.

She made another sound in her throat and her lips parted. Her tongue darted out to meet his and he plunged in, desperate for more, desperate to discover her every secret.

He deepened the kiss and groaned as her hands slid up his biceps to entwine around his shoulders. In a curiously innocent move, she tentatively caressed his nape before boldly spiking her fingers into his hair.

The scrape of her fingers against his scalp made him shudder with escalating arousal. Raising his head, he gazed down into eyes darkened with desire. *'Amante,* you already know what pleases me.'

Shock clouded her expression, as if what she'd achieved had stunned her.

Without giving her a chance to speak, he took her luscious mouth again. The highly potent sound of their kisses echoed in the room as they devoured each other.

Pulling her even closer, he finally touched the pulse that had taunted him all evening. It sang beneath his touch, racing with her excitement.

She inhaled deeply, and her breasts smashed against his

chest. He cupped one, glorying in the weight and perfect fit of it as his thumb brushed across one rigid nub.

She jerked and her teeth sank into her bottom lip. With a rough sound, she pulled away.

Narciso continued to play with her nipple as they stared at each other. Her mouth, wet and slightly swollen, parted as she sucked in panicked breaths.

'You like the way I make you feel?' He brought his other hand up from her waist and cupped her other breast, attending to the equally stiff and aching peak. 'I promise I will make you feel even better. Now take your hair down and show me how gorgeous you really are.'

The words pulled Ruby from the drugged stupor she was drowning in. Reality didn't rush in, it trickled in slowly.

Blinking eyelids heavy with desire, she tried to focus on something other than his arrestingly gorgeous face—the part not covered by his mask.

First, she noticed the stunning chandelier. Then a repeat of that bold dragon motif from downstairs on the wall behind his shoulder. Reality rushed in faster. Stunningly designed black velvet sofas, including an authentic French chaise longue perfect for reclining in...

Then her focus drew in closer. She glanced down at the powerful hands cupping her breasts.

The sight was so erotically intoxicating it nearly knocked her off her feet.

Sensation shot between her thighs, stinging so painfully, she wanted to place her hand there, seek some sort of relief.

'Take your hair down for me,' he insisted again.

She came plunging back down to earth. 'No!'

Telling herself she didn't care about the jaw that tightened in displeasure, she took several steps away from his hot, tempting body.

*Focus, Ruby!*

The last time she'd mixed business with pleasure, she'd almost ended up becoming the one thing she despised above all else—a participant in infidelity. It didn't matter that she hadn't known Simon was married. The very thought of what could've happened made shame lodge in her belly.

She was here to get Narciso Valentino to honour his deal with her, not to get pulled into the same dangerous vortex of emotions that led to nothing but pain and heartache.

Her father's inability to limit his sexual urges to his marital bed and her mother's indecision whether to fight or turn a blind eye had made her childhood a living hell. It'd been the reason why she'd slept most nights with her headphones on and music blaring in her ears. Even then she'd been unable to block out the blistering rows or her mother's heart-wrenching sobs.

And after her experience with Simon, there was no way would she allow herself to jump on that unpredictable roller coaster.

She took another step back, despite the magnetic pull of desire dragging her to Narciso. Despite the soul-deep notion that sex with him would be pulse-poundingly breathtaking. Despite—

*Despite nothing!*

Her treacherous genetic make-up didn't mean she would allow herself to fall into the same trap as her mother just because an unrepentant, unscrupulous playboy like Narciso Valentino crooked his wicked finger.

*But* she couldn't risk alienating him before she got what she'd come here for. Licking tingling lips, she forced her brain to track.

She cast her gaze around the large, luxuriously appointed suite. Seeing the extensive, well-stocked bar on the far side of the room, she made a beeline for it. 'Here, let me get you another drink.'

'You don't need to get me drunk to have your way with me, *amante.*'

She flushed and stopped, whirling to find him directly behind her. The sheer size of him, the arousal stamped so clearly in his eyes, made her breath fracture. 'Stop calling me that.'

A small smile played around his exquisite mouth. 'You know what it means.'

She nodded. 'Yes, I'm Italian.'

'And I'm Sicilian. Big difference, but we will speak your language for now.'

'Whatever language we speak, I don't want you referring to me as a…as your…'

'Lover?'

'Yes. I don't like it.'

'What do you want me to call you?'

'Just call me Ruby.' She didn't mind telling him her name. In order to explain her presence here, she would have to disclose who she was.

So no harm done.

'Ruby.'

Definitely lots and lots of harm done. The way he said her name—wrapped his mouth and tongue around it in a slow caress—made her pulse leap crazily.

'Ruby. It suits you perfectly,' he murmured.

Against her will, his response drew her interest. 'How do you mean?'

'Your name matches the shade of your mouth after I've thoroughly kissed it. I imagine the same would apply to other parts of your body by the time we're done.'

Her flush deepened. *'Seriously?'*

He laughed but the hunger in his eyes didn't abate. 'Too much?'

'*Much* too much.'

He shrugged and nodded to the bar. 'I'll give you the reprieve you seek. But only for a little while.'

She dived behind the bar and gathered the first bottles that came to hand. Almost on automatic she replicated one of her favourite creations and slid it across the shiny surface.

He picked it up and sipped without taking his eyes off her.

He rolled the drink in his mouth before his eyes slowly widened. 'You're very talented.'

Pleasure rushed through her. 'Thank you.'

*'Prego.'* He threw back the rest of the drink and set the glass down with a decisive click. 'But enough with the foreplay, Ruby. Come here.'

Heart pounding, with nowhere to hide, she approached him.

'Give me what I want. Now.'

She debated for a tense few seconds. Then, figuring she had nothing to lose, she complied.

Her hair was thick, long and often times unmanageable. She'd spent almost an hour wrestling it into place tonight and in the end had chosen to wear it up. Her effort to straighten it would've worn out by now, and she couldn't help but fidget when his gaze raked over the golden-brown tresses once, twice and over again.

'You're exquisite,' he breathed after an endless moment during which her stomach churned with alien emotion. 'Your skin is flawless and I want to drown in your eyes, watch them light up with pleasure when I take you.'

Ruby couldn't believe mere words could create such heat inside her. Hell, everything about him made her hot and edgy.

She needed to nip this insanity in the bud before it went any further. 'I'm sorry if I gave you the impression that something more was going to happen between us. You won't be… taking me.'

'Will I not?' he asked silkily, his finger drifting down her cheek to settle beneath her chin. 'And what makes you say that?'

'Because you don't really want me.'

His laugh was rich, deep and incredibly seductive.

'Every nerve in my body disagrees with that statement. But if you need proof…' He bent low, scooped her up and threw her over his shoulder.

His laughter increased at her outraged squeal. 'Put me down!'

The hallway passed in a blur as he took her deeper into the

suite. Her hair entangled with his long legs as he strode with unwavering purpose.

'I don't know what the hell you think you're doing but I demand you put me down right—' Her breath whooshed out of her lungs as she was dumped on a bed. A very large emperor-size bed with slate-coloured sheets and over a dozen pillows.

'You were saying?'

She brushed her hair out of her eyes and saw him tugging off his shoes. When he unhooked his belt, she scrambled off the bed.

He caught her easily and placed her back in the centre. 'Are you going to be a good girl and wait for me?' Silver eyes speared her.

'Wait for... Hell, no!'

He stepped forward and caught her chin in his hand. When his head started to descend, she jerked away. 'What the hell do you think you're doing?'

'Capturing your attention for a moment. You don't need to be frightened, *dolce mia*. Nothing will happen in this room without your consent.'

Oddly, she believed him. 'You don't need to kiss me to capture my attention.'

Slowly he straightened and dropped his hand. 'Shame. Let me remind you of some ground rules before we proceed. We're not supposed to reveal ourselves to each other. However, since you've done me the honour of revealing your name to me, I'll grant you the courtesy of removing my mask. But you'll give me your word that it will stay between us, *sì*?' He started unbuttoning his shirt, revealing mouth-watering inches of golden skin.

Heat slammed into her chest and she sucked in a gulping breath.

Crunch time. Time to get this dangerously bizarre situation over and done with.

'There's no need. I already know who you are. You're Narciso Valentino. You're the reason I'm here in Macau.'

# CHAPTER FOUR

HE FROZE AT her announcement. A second later, he drew the mask over his head, and Ruby got her first full glimpse of Narciso Valentino.

He was breathtakingly gorgeous. With a definite edge of danger that sent her already thundering pulse straight into bungee-jump mode.

She watched his face grow taut. Watchful…condemning.

'You know who I am.' His words were icily precise, the warmth in his tone completely gone.

Licking dry lips, she nodded. His other hand dropped from his belt, leaving her curiously disappointed.

'You're American.'

'Yes, I live in New York, same as you. That's where I came from.'

'And you followed me all the way to Macau. Why?' The clipped demand came with eyes narrowed into cold slits.

A mixture of anger and trepidation rushed through her, propelling her from the bed.

He caught her easily. 'Move again and I'll be forced to restrain you.'

Panic flared through her. Tugging at his hands, she fought to free herself. Before she could fathom his intentions, her wrists were bound to the bedpost with velvet rope he'd pulled from the side of the bed.

She looked from her wrists to his face, unable to believe what was happening. He tossed his mask on the bed, whipped the unbound tie from his neck and flung it across the room, barely suppressed fury in the movement. 'Okay, fine, you've made your point. But you can't keep me prisoner for ever.'

'Watch me.'

'I could scream, you know.'

*Nice, Ruby. Nice.*

'You could. And I can turn you over to the management and let them deal with what can only be regarded as a security breach. Trust me, breaches aren't taken lightly.'

She tugged at her bound wrists. 'I can't believe you tied me up.'

'You left me no choice. Now start talking before I call security.'

Her breath caught as images tumbled through her head of being stuck in a foreign prison. Aside from her roommate, Annie, no one knew her whereabouts. And even if Annie tracked her down to Macau, she wouldn't have the first clue where to find her.

'Tell me what you want to know,' she offered in a rush.

'Is Ruby really your name?' he asked, his gaze dropping to her lips.

Remembering what he'd said about her mouth, she felt heat spike through her belly again.

'Yes.'

'And your earlier assurance that we hadn't met before?'

'Is true. Although we almost did…last week.'

One sleek brow shot upward. 'How?'

'I tried to find you at a nightclub—Riga—but you were leaving when I arrived.'

He prowled closer to the bed, and a fresh load of anxiety coursed through her system. Hands poised on lean hips, he stared down at her.

'I've had women do…unexpected things to get my attention but I don't think I've had the privilege of a full-blown crazy stalker before.' His eyes raked her from head to toe. 'Perhaps I should've made it happen sooner.'

'I'm not a crazy stalker!' She yanked at the restraints and only succeeded in tightening them.

'Of course not. Because those ones readily admit to their charges.'

'Look, I can explain. Just…untie me.'

He ignored her and leaned down, placing his palms flat on the bed so his face was level with hers. 'We could've had so much fun, *amante*. Why did you have to spoil it?' There was genuine regret in his tone, but bitterness had crept in with the iciness.

'I have a genuine reason for being here.'

'For your own sake, I hope so. I don't take lightly to being manipulated.'

Her mind flashed to earlier in the evening. Watching him toy with his opponent had shown her just how dangerous this man was. Despite the outward charm and spellbinding magnetism, he could become lethal on the turn of a dime.

He turned and prowled to the window. With jerky movements, he tore off his expensive shirt, sending cufflinks she was almost certain were made with black diamonds pinging across the room.

Tossing the shirt the way his bow tie had gone, he shoved his hands into his pockets.

The movement contracted his bronzed, strongly muscled back. Among the electrons firing crazily in her brain came the thought that this was the first time she'd come this close to a semi-naked man worth looking at.

He turned and the sight of his naked torso was almost too much to bear. A light smattering of hair grew outward from the middle of his sculpted chest and arrowed down to disappear into his waistband.

Heat intensified as her gaze landed on his flat brown nipples. A decadent shudder coursed through her. She grasped the sturdy, intricately carved bedpost made of highly polished Chinese cedarwood, pulled herself closer to the edge of the bed and peered closer at the intricate knots that bound her.

'Where do you think you're going?' he rasped.

'I can't stay trussed up like a Thanksgiving turkey all night long.'

'Answer my questions and I'll consider freeing you.'

'You'll *consider* it?'

'Have you forgotten already that I hold all the cards here?' He sauntered back and stopped in front of her.

Suddenly, Ruby wished she'd stayed put in the middle of the bed. *This* close the heat emanating from his satin-like skin blanketed her. The urge to move her fingers just that little bit and touch the skin covering his ribcage was immense.

'Go ahead,' he invited softly. Silkily.

Flames leapt through her bloodstream. 'Excuse me?'

'You want to touch me. Go ahead. We can pick up this conversation in a moment once you've satisfied your craving.'

'I… You're wrong. I don't want to touch you. There's no craving. What I want is to be set free—'

Her words froze when he placed large hands on her hips and pulled her into his body.

'Well, despite you ruining my evening, I *still* have a craving for you.'

He smothered her protests by capturing her mouth again. It was as potent as before but this time there was a rough demand in his kiss that spoke of his fury beneath all that outward calm.

But rough didn't mean less pleasurable. Her lips parted, welcoming the jagged thrust of his tongue and the domineering pressure of his kiss.

She moaned before she could stop herself, flexing fingers that wouldn't obey their order to stay put, and touching the velvety smoothness of his neck and collarbone.

By the time he lifted his head, they were both panting. He slowly licked his lips, savouring her taste. The sight of his wet tongue sent liquid fire straight to that raging hunger between her thighs.

Ruby shut her eyes in shuddering despair and opened them to find him sliding off her shoes.

'God, will you please stop doing things like that?' she snapped.

'I'm into kinky when the occasion calls for it, but I don't generally risk puncturing a lung with stiletto heels unless the payback is worth it.' He flung her shoes away. 'Do you need help with your dress?'

'No! Why on earth would I want that?' She edged away from him, the fear that her emotions wouldn't be as easy to control around this man spiking through her.

'It's nearly two a.m. And we're yet to have our little tête-à-tête. But if you want to keep cutting off your circulation in that restricting dress, suit yourself. Tell me why you're here,' he bit out, as if he wanted to be done with the conversation.

'Release me first,' she insisted.

'I released you three minutes ago.'

Shocked, Ruby glanced down at her wrists. Sure enough, the velvet rope was loose enough to free herself. She'd been too spellbound by his kiss to notice.

She met his hard, mocking gaze. Rubbing her right wrist, she encountered his watch. She pulled it off and held it out to him.

He didn't take it. 'I'm waiting for an answer.'

'My name is Ruby Trevelli.'

He continued to stare at her. 'Should that mean anything to me?'

Despite knowing how self-absorbed he was, that flippant question hurt. She flung his watch on the bed. He calmly retrieved it, took hold of her wrist, slipped it back on, and returned to his predator-like position.

'What—?'

'Answer me. Should your name mean anything to me?'

'Yes. I was recently voted Élite Chef.'

His lips twisted. 'My apologies. I don't keep up with pop culture,' he said.

'Well, you should. Your TV company sponsored the show.'

He frowned. 'I have over sixty media companies scattered

all over the world. It would be impossible to keep up with every progamme that's aired through my networks. So you're here to collect some sort of prize—is that it?' The disappointment she'd heard earlier was back, accompanied this time by a flash of weariness that disappeared as quickly as it'd arrived.

'You make it sound like a whimsical endeavour. I assure you, it's not.'

'Enlighten me, then, Miss Contest Winner. Why have you flown thousands of miles to accost me?'

Put like that it *did* sound whimsical. Except this was her life and livelihood they were talking about, the independent life she'd worked hard for so she wouldn't be pulled into her parents' damaging orbit. The life that was being threatened by a loan shark.

'I want your company to honour its agreement and pay me what I'm owed.'

His face hardened into a taut, formidable mask of disdain. 'You came after me because of *money?*' His sneer had thickened.

Ruby couldn't really dwell on that. She needed to state her purpose and leave this room, this suite. He was close, so tantalisingly close, the warmth of his skin and the spicy scent of his aftershave made stringing words together an increasingly difficult task. He smelled like heaven. And she wanted to drown in it.

'Prize money, yes.'

His eyes narrowed. 'But why come after me? Why not go after the man I've put in place to head NMC?'

'You think I haven't tried? No one would take my calls.'

'Really? No one in a company with over a thousand employees?'

'No. Trust me, I have the phone bill to prove it.'

'Well, clearly, I need to hire better staff.'

'I don't like your tone,' Ruby snapped. She sidled towards the edge of the bed.

He caught her and placed her back in front of him, keeping her captive with one large hand on her waist.

'What tone do you mean?' Silver eyes gleamed with cynical amusement.

With every breath she took, the imprint of his hand seared her skin. 'You obviously don't believe me. Why would I travel thousands of miles unless it was because I'd hit a brick wall?'

'Or you'd hoped an extra tight dress and body that won't quit would get you an even better deal?'

The image his words conjured up made blood leach from her face. It was one she'd vowed never to portray. 'I understand you don't know me, Mr Valentino, but I've never used sex or my sexuality to further my career. You can be as offensive and as delusional as you want. The simple fact is Nigel Stone never took my call in the two dozen times I tried to reach him.'

His eyes narrowed at her furious words but he kept silent.

'We can resolve this very quickly. Call him now, get him to talk to me. Then I'll get out of your hair.'

'It's Saturday morning back in the States. I make it a point never to disturb my employees during the weekend.'

Anger stiffened her spine. 'Yeah, right.'

His cynical smile widened. 'You don't believe me?'

'I believe you do exactly what you want when you want. If it suited you, you'd be on the phone right now.'

His shrug outlined sleek muscle beneath his skin. He moved with an innate grace that made Ruby's pulse race shamefully. 'Fine. I admit I ride my employees hard when I have to. But I also recognise their need for down time the same way I recognise the need for mine.'

'You're telling me you need your beauty sleep to function?' she snapped.

'Down time doesn't necessarily mean sleep, *amante*. Tonight, I was counting on wild, unfettered sex,' he delivered smoothly.

She flung herself away from him, from the temptation his words dredged up inside her, before that Trevelli gene she so feared could be fully activated.

Far too often since she'd clapped eyes on him, she'd found herself imagining what sex would be like. Her roommate had referred to the best sex as sheet-clawing, toe-curling. At the time Ruby had silently scoffed at how anything besides the best, decadently prepared dessert would feel that great.

Now she couldn't stop herself from wondering…

Disgust at herself propelled her off the bed. She refused to sink into the quagmire of rampant promiscuity.

Her feet hit the luxurious carpet, bringing a much-needed return to reality. She darted out of the door and hurried along the long hallway towards the main suite doors.

With relief, she grasped the door handle and yanked it down. Nothing happened. She pulled harder.

Glancing around wildly, she spotted the electronic panel and pressed the most obvious-looking button.

Nothing.

'You can't get out unless I allow you out.'

She whirled. He casually leaned one shoulder against the hallway wall. The sight of him standing there, looking sexily tousled and half naked, made panic flare anew inside her.

'Then let me out.'

'I could. But once I do, any hope of a discussion about why you're here ends. My company, if it's liable as you say, owes you nothing the minute you walk out of here.'

'That's preposterous! I signed a contract. *You* signed a contract. You can't just back out on a whim.'

'Think about it, Ruby. You've travelled thousands of miles to get my attention. I intend to give you that attention. Do you think it prudent to walk out now, when you could be so close?'

'I…' She sucked in a breath as overwhelming feelings swamped her. 'Why can't we discuss it now?'

'Because I don't like to discuss business without a clear head. And since you've plied me with exquisite cocktails all evening, I'd be making those decisions under severe influence.' He tilted his head again in that alarmingly endearing way and a lock of hair fell over his eyes.

*Dear God.* This man was truly lethal. He oozed sex and sensuality without so much as lifting a finger.

'You didn't ply me with all those drinks in order to take advantage of me, did you? Because that would be horrifyingly disappointing.'

Outraged, she gasped. 'I most certainly did not.'

Slowly, he extended a hand to her. 'In that case, Ruby Trevelli, there's no earthly reason not to stay. Is there?'

Narciso was doing his best to stop his fury from showing. The same way he was doing his best to keep from kicking himself for ignoring the alarm bells.

Usually he could spot chancers and gold-diggers a mile away, be they tuxedo-clad or dressed in designer gowns that looked too small for them.

For a moment he wished she'd kept her mouth shut until after he'd slept with her to make her avarice known. He would've been a lot more generous than he was feeling now.

*He would also have felt used.*

Fury mounted and his frustrated erection threatened to cut him in half as she stayed out of his reach. Out of his arms.

Recalling her responsiveness, the gut-clenching potency of her kiss, he nearly growled.

She kissed as if she were born for it. Narciso wondered how many men she'd kissed like that in the past and felt a red haze wash over his fury.

*Dio,* what was wrong with him? He should find the nearest phone and report her to management.

Zeus, his host and owner of the club, had so far excelled in keeping people like Ruby away from *Q Virtus* guests. Sure, most *Petit Qs* would accept a generous gift from a guest, but blatant stalking wasn't tolerated.

Except, his stalker seemed eager to get *away* from him, her catlike blue eyes apprehensive as she glanced at his outstretched hand.

'Come here,' he commanded.

She swayed towards him, then abruptly halted her forward momentum. 'If you're too drunk to talk, what other reason is there for me to stay? And don't mention wild sex. Because that's not going to happen.'

Contrary to what he'd said, his mind was as clear and as sharp as a fillet knife. And it sensed a curious dichotomy in her words and actions. The dress, make-up and screw-me stilettos said one thing. Her words indicated another.

He intended to burrow until he found the truth.

*Nice choice of words, Narciso,* he thought as arousal spiked higher in his blood. Lowering his hand, he turned abruptly.

'I'm returning to the bedroom. If you're not there within the next minute, I'll take it that our business is concluded,' he said over his shoulder.

'Wait! You can't do that…'

Narciso smiled with satisfaction at her frustration. Whether she followed him or not, there was no way he was letting her out of his suite tonight. Not until he'd had her checked out thoroughly and satisfied himself what sort of threat she posed.

He recalled the circumstances of their meeting. Of all the tables she could've been hostessing, she'd been at Giacomo's table.

This time he didn't ignore the churning in his gut. Giacomo had played that game before…

He turned and found her two steps behind him but any satisfaction was marred by the new set of questions clamouring for answers.

'Why are you really here, Ruby? Did the old man send you?'

Fresh trepidation flared in her eyes at his harsh tone. 'Who… Oh, that guy you were playing with? No, I have no idea who he is and I'd never met him before tonight.'

He tried to read her. Surely, even seasoned liars couldn't look him straight in the eye as she was without flinching?

'Be warned, if I find that to be untrue, there'll be hell to pay.'

'I'm telling you, I don't know him.' Her fingers meshed together and she began to fidget. But not once did her stare waver from his.

Narciso decided to be satisfied. For now. He entered the bedroom and crossed to the en suite.

'So I'm here. Now what?' she asked.

'I'm going to take a shower. You do whatever you want. As long as you don't leave this room.'

'God, this is nuts,' he heard her mutter as he entered the bathroom. Despite the volatile emotions churning through him, he smiled. From the corner of his eye, he watched her head once more to the stunning view of Macau City.

Silhouetted against the view, her body was so perfectly stunning, his mouth dried. Disappointment welled in his chest but he suppressed it as he undressed.

The cold shower was bracing enough to calm his arousal but not enough to wash away the bitterness as he replayed his evening.

Giacomo was bent on trying to take Narciso down.

Well, that suited Narciso fine. Although Narciso could've destroyed him with that last move, the notion of leaving him dangling a little bit longer had been irresistible.

The opportunity would present itself again soon enough. Giacomo was predictable in his hatred for him, if for nothing else.

And at thirty, exactly ten years after his father's most cutting betrayal, the need for vengeance burned just as brightly in Narciso's veins.

For as long as he'd been old enough to retain his memories, Narciso had known that Giacomo bore him a deep, abiding hatred. As a child he'd been bewildered as to why nothing he did pleased or satisfied the man he once called Papa.

On his eleventh birthday, a whisky-soaked Giacomo had finally revealed to him the reason he detested the sight of his son. At first, even reeling from the shock of the discovery, Narciso had stupidly believed he could turn things around, make his father, if not love him, at least learn to cohabit peacefully with him. He'd made sure his grades were perfect, that he was quiet and obedient and exemplary in all things.

Narciso's mouth twisted. That had lasted all of a year before he'd accepted he was flogging a dead horse. When his thirteenth birthday had come and gone without so much as a single lit candle on a store-bought birthday cake, he'd finally admitted that war was the only way forward.

He'd suppressed whatever heartache had threatened to catch him unawares in the dead of night and used animosity to feed his ambitions to succeed. He'd won scholarships to the best colleges in the world. His head for figures had seen him attain his first million by eighteen. By twenty he'd been a multi-millionaire.

Twenty…also the age he'd met Maria, the unexpected tool his father had used against him. The wound gaped another inch.

With a sharp curse, he shut off the shower. Snapping up a towel, he tied it around his waist.

Maria was dead to him, but, in a way, he was pleased for her transient presence in his life ten years ago. She'd reinforced his belief that lowering his guard, even for a moment, was foolhardy. That even fake love came at a steep price.

Money and sex were the two things he thrived on now. Emotions…connections, hell, *love,* were a complete waste of his time.

He entered the bedroom and found Ruby reclining on the bed, legs crossed, one bare foot tapping in agitation. She shot upright at his entry. After that one quick look, Narciso barely glanced in her direction as he walked to the connecting dressing room.

The whole evening was screwed up. His thwarted efforts to bed her, and now his unexplained trip down memory lane had left him in an edgy mood. Snatching at his fast-dwindling control, he reached for the rarely used silk pajama bottoms and dropped his towel.

The choking sound made him glance over his shoulder through the open door. She sat frozen on the bed, her eyes wide with astonishment.

'Something wrong?' he asked as he stabbed one leg into the garment. At her silence, he started to turn.

She shut her eyes and jerked away from him. He pulled the bottoms on and entered the bedroom. 'Open your eyes. It's safe to look now.'

She opened her eyes but kept her gaze averted.

'Come on, now, the way you're acting you'd think I was the first naked male you'd ever seen.'

That gurgling sound came again and Narciso shook his head. 'I have very little interest in virgins, *amante*. If you hope to snag my attention, I suggest you drop that particular act.'

She inhaled sharply. 'It's not an—' She bit off the rest of her answer as he drew back the sheets.

Four of the six pillows he threw to the floor before he got in. The sight of her sitting so stiffly made his jaw tighten. Reaching across, he pulled her into the middle and pulled the sheet over them.

'You were saying?'

She shook her head. 'Nothing. Are you really going to sleep?'

'Yes. I suggest you get some sleep too even though I fear for your circulation in that dress you're wearing.'

'I'm fine.'

'If you say so.' He relaxed against the pillows. Sleep would be elusive with her so close. For a moment he wondered why he was torturing himself like this.

*Keep your friends close and your stalkers closer?*

He suppressed a grim smile, grabbed the remote and doused the light in the bedroom. But with one sensory factor taken away, her erratic breathing became amplified.

*Good.* If he was to be tortured with images of what sex between them would be like, it was only fair she experienced the same fate.

'What happens tomorrow?' she asked quietly.

'Tomorrow we talk. And by talk I mean you come clean, completely, as to why you're here. Because if you hold anything back from me, I won't hesitate to throw you to the wolves.'

# CHAPTER FIVE

RUBY WOKE WITH the distinct feeling that something had changed. It took a millisecond to realise what that *something* was.

'You took my clothes off?' she screeched, her fingers flying to the hem of the black T-shirt that had miraculously appeared on her body.

The man who lay so languidly beside her, his head propped up on his hand, nodded.

'I feared you'd suffocate in your sleep in that dress. Despite your dubious reasons for being here, even I would find it difficult to explain death by designer gown to the authorities. You were quite co-operative. I think it was the only time you've been co-operative since we reached my suite, which tells me you were as uncomfortable as I suspected.'

She licked her lips and struggled not to squirm under his scrutiny. At least her bra and panties were intact. But the fact was she didn't recall what had happened. And there was only one worrying explanation for that. 'I was tired,' she bluffed.

'Right.' Silver eyes bore into her until she felt like a fly hooked on a pin.

His gaze dropped to her twisting fingers, and she abruptly stilled the movement. 'Tell me what happened. *Exactly.*'

One brow rose at her firm directive but Ruby was desperate to know what had happened during the night. She'd tossed and turned in agitation until sheer exhaustion had finally pulled her under some time before dawn.

'You tried to escape a few times. I brought you back to bed.'
*God. No. It'd happened again…*

Definitely time to leave. She tried to move, and felt a snag on her foot. Shoving aside tangled sheets, she stared in horror at the rope tied around her ankle.

'You tied me up again! Do you have a thing for bondage?'

His eyes gleamed. 'Until last night, I'd never needed to tie a woman to keep her with me.'

'Oh, well, lucky me. Did you tie me before or after you took off my dress?'

'After the second time you tried to take the door off its hinges to make your escape, we came back here and I relieved you of your suicidal gown and put the T-shirt on—' A deep frown slashed his face. 'Are you saying you don't remember any of this?'

She sucked in a slow breath and looked away.

He caught her chin in his hand and forced her to look at him, his steady gaze demanding an answer. '*Dio,* you really don't remember?'

Ruby had no choice but to come clean. 'No. sometimes I… sleepwalk.'

His brows hit his hairline. 'You *sleepwalk?* How often is sometimes?'

'Not for a while, to my knowledge. It only happens when I'm…distressed.'

His frown intensified. 'You found last night distressing?'

'Being tied up and kept prisoner? No, that was a picnic in the park.' She tugged at her ankle restraint. 'And now I'm tied up again.'

'It was for your own good. After I put the restraint on, you stopped making a run for it. I think secretly you liked it.' His fingers caressed along her jaw, his eyes lowering to her lips.

Instantly the mood changed, thickened with sensual promise. 'I'm *not* into bondage.' Or sex with playboys, or anyone for that matter!

'How do you know? Have you ever tried it?'

'No. But I've never jumped off a cliff either, and I'm certain I wouldn't enjoy that experience.'

'Fair point. For the record, I have. With the right equipment, all experiences can be extremely enjoyable. Exhilarating even.'

She watched, terrified and mesmerised, as his head started to lower. 'What are you doing?'

'I'm kissing you *bon giornu, bedda*. Relax.'

That was easier said than done when every nerve in her body was strained in anticipation of the touch of his mouth on hers. She told herself she was sluggish because she was sleep deprived. But it was a lie.

As much as she yearned to deny it, she wanted the pressure of his demanding kiss and the heady racing of her blood through her veins.

His moan as he deepened the kiss echoed the piercing need inside her.

One hand clamped on her hip, drew her sideways into him. At the sensation of his sleep-warmed body against hers, she moaned. The fact that she was clothed from neck to hip and he was clothed from hip to ankle didn't alter the stormy sensation of their bodies meshing together.

Nipples, stung to life at the touch of his mouth on hers, peaked and ached as they brushed his chest.

When his hand moved under the T-shirt and skimmed over her panties, Ruby jerked at the vicious punch of desire that threatened to flatten her.

She was drowning. And she didn't want to be rescued.

'*Dio mio,* you're addictive, *bedda,*' he murmured against her mouth before plunging back in. His tongue shot between her lips to slide against hers. He staked his claim on her until she couldn't think straight. Even when his mouth left hers to nibble along her jaw, she strained closer, her hand sliding up his chest in a bold caress that shocked and thrilled her at the same time.

When her nail grazed his nipple, he hissed. Stunned at the surge of power that action gave her, she flicked her nail again.

'Careful, *amante,* or I might have to repay the kindness.'

Lost in a swirl of desire, she barely heeded the warning. Bringing up her other hand between them, she flicked both flat nipples at once.

*'Maledizione!'* He pushed her back onto the bed and yanked up her T-shirt.

Danger shrieked in her head a second before his mouth closed over her nipple. Tonguing, licking, he pulled the willing flesh deep into his mouth.

Sensation as she'd never felt before tore through her. Between her legs where her need burned fiercest, liquid heat fuelled her raging desire.

Her fingers curled up and spiked into his hair as he transferred his attention to her other nipple. A little rougher than before, he used his teeth this time.

Her tiny scream echoed through the bedroom as her head slammed back against the pillow.

Feeling his thick arousal against her thigh, she moved her leg, eager to rub closer against the potent evidence of his need.

The snap of the ankle rope broke through her haze. The reality of what she was doing hit Ruby with the force of a two-by-four.

'No!' She pushed at his shoulders until he lifted his head. The sight of her nipples, reddened and wet from his ministrations, made dismay slither through her in equal measures. She was nothing like her parents. Nothing—

'What's wrong, *bedda?*' he grated huskily.

'What's wrong? Everything!'

'Everything is a huge undertaking. Narrow it down for me a little. I'll take care of it.'

She pushed harder. 'For a start. Get. Off. Me.'

His nostrils flared with displeasure and his fingers bit into her hip. 'You were moaning your willingness a moment ago.'

'Thankfully, I've come to my senses. Get off me and take off that…shackle you've placed on my ankle.'

He slowly levered himself off her but not before she got

another sensation of his thick arousal. Flames rushed up her cheeks.

Back in his previous position, he dropped his gaze from hers to her breasts. Realising she was still exposed, she yanked her bra cups into place and tugged down the T-shirt. A T-shirt that bore his unique scent, which chose that moment to wash over her again. As if she weren't suffering enough.

'I don't like women who blow hot and cold, *tesoro*.'

'Where I come from a woman still has the right to say no.'

'A stance I fully respect. Except your actions and your words are at direct variance with each other. You crave me almost as much as I crave you. I can only conclude that this is a ploy to string me along until I'm too whipped to put up much protest against your demands.'

Again his description of her behaviour struck painfully close to the bone, pushing all her fears to the fore. Struggling to hide it, she raised an eyebrow.

'Wow, you really have a low opinion of yourself, don't you? Or is that a high opinion on my sexual prowess?'

'Unlike you, I'm not afraid to admit my desire for you. It's almost enough to tempt me to tell you to name your price so we can be done with this…*aperitivo* and get to the main course.' There was a hard bite to his voice that instinctively warned her to do that would be a mistake.

'I only want you to hear me out. You said we'd talk this morning.'

He got up from the bed in a sleek, graceful move that brought to mind a jungle creature.

The unmistakable evidence of his arousal when he faced her made her swallow. He showed no embarrassment in his blatant display of manhood. Even in thwarted desire, Narciso Valentino wore his male confidence with envy-inducing ease. Whereas she remained cowering beneath the sheets, afraid of the sensual waves threatening to drown her.

'And so we will. Come through to the kitchen. Caffeine is a

poor substitute for sex but it'll have to do.' With that pithy pronouncement, he walked out of the bedroom.

She lay there, floundering in a sea of panic and confusion. If anyone had told her she'd be in Narciso Valentino's bed mere hours after meeting him, she'd have laughed herself hoarse. Particularly since she'd vowed never to mix business with pleasure after what had happened with Simon.

But what Narciso had roused in her just now had frightened and excited her. Kissing him had been holding a live, dangerous firework in the palm of her hand. She hadn't been sure whether she would experience the most spectacular show of lights or blow herself to smithereens with it.

And yet she'd been almost desolate when the kiss ended. Which showed how badly things could get out of hand.

Squeezing her eyes shut, she counted to ten. The earlier she finished her business with Narciso and got on the plane back to New York, the better.

Throwing off the sheet, she glanced at the velvet rope around her ankle. Twisting her body into the appropriate position, she tugged on the double knot, surprised when it came loose easily.

Again, the realisation that she could've freed herself at any time made her view of him alter a little. Her fingers lingered on the rope warmed from her body.

Bondage sex. Until now, the scenario had never even crossed her mind. But suddenly, the thought of being tied down while Narciso laid her inhibitions to waste took up centre stage in her mind.

Heat flaming her whole body, she jumped from the bed. Upright, his T-shirt reached well past her knees, and covered her arms to her elbows.

She glanced at her gown, laid carefully over the arm of the chaise longue, and made up her mind. She would dress after they'd had their talk. She couldn't bear being restrained in the too-tight dress just yet. Ditto for her heels.

Stilettos and a T-shirt in the presence of a dangerously sexual man like Narciso Valentino evoked an image she didn't want to tempt into life now, or ever.

For some reason, her body turned him on. She wasn't stupid enough to bait the lion more than he was already baited.

Barefoot, she left the bedroom and went in search of the kitchen.

He stood at a centre island in a kitchen that made the chef in her want to weep with envy. State-of-the-art equipment lined the surfaces and walls and through a short alcove a floor-to-ceiling wine rack displayed exquisite vintages.

'You get all this for a two-day stay?'

He jerked at her question. Before he could cover his emotions, Ruby glimpsed a painfully bleak look in his eyes.

A second later, the look was gone as he shrugged. 'It suits my needs.'

'Your needs… I'd kill for a kitchen like this in my restaurant.'

'You own a restaurant?' he asked.

She concluded her survey of the appliances and faced him. 'Not yet. I would've been on my way to opening Dolce Italia by now if NMC had honoured its commitments.'

'Ah, the sins of imaginary corporate sharks.'

The coffee machine finished going through its wake-up motions. He pressed a button and the beans started to churn.

'Not imaginary.' Ruby stepped forward when she realised what he was doing. 'Wait, you're doing it wrong. We're in a warm climate. The coffee beans expand in warm weather so you need to grind them looser to extract the maximum taste. Here let me do it.' Even though stepping closer would bring her dangerously close to his sleek frame, she seized the opportunity to make herself useful and not just stare at his broad, naked back. A back she could suddenly picture herself clawing in the heat of desire.

Just as she tried not to stare when he leaned his hip against the counter and crossed his arms over his bare chest.

'How are you at multitasking?' he asked.

'It's essential in my line of business.' Content with the set-

ting, she pressed the button to resume the grinding and went
to the fridge. She grabbed the creamer, and forced herself not
to gape at the mouth-watering ingredients in there.

'Good, then you can talk while you prepare the coffee. Tell
me everything I need to know.' His brisk tone was all business.

Quickly, she summarised the events of the past two months.

'So you entered this competition as a chef?' he asked.

'Yes, I have a degree in hospitality management and a di-
ploma in gourmet cuisine and I'm an approved board-certified
mixologist.'

He grinned. 'You have to go to college to mix drinks?'

'You have to go to school to wash dishes right these days or
someone will sue your ass.' She started to grin, then stopped
herself. 'I mean…if you don't want to be sued for accidentally
poisoning someone. Besides, I plan to make my cocktail bar
accessible to allergy-sufferers, too, so I need to know what
I'm doing.'

'Which of your drinks is your favourite?' he fired back.

The question threw her for a second. Then she shrugged.
'They're all my favourite.'

'Describe the taste of your signature drink,' he pressed.

She went in search of coffee cups, opening several cabinets
before she located them. She had to reach up to grab them and
the cool air that passed over the backs of her legs reminded her
how exposed she was.

'Umm, I don't actually like cocktails that much,' she blurted
to distract herself from her state of undress.

'You're a mixologist who doesn't like her own creations?
How do you know you're not poisoning the general population?'

'Because nobody's died yet sampling my drinks. And as to
how I know my drinks rock? I try them out on my roommate.'

'You want me to invest…how much does my company owe
you?'

'Two hundred thousand dollars to help towards construction
and advertising costs for Dolce Italia.'

'Right, two hundred thousand dollars, based on your room-mate's assessment of your talent?'

She poured and passed him a cup, forcing herself not to react to the spark of electricity when their fingers brushed. 'You threw away thirty million last night without blinking but you're grilling me over two hundred thousand?'

He stiffened. 'That was different.' His voice held icy warning.

She heeded it. *'Anyway,'* she hurried on, 'thousands of people voted for me to win *your* show based on three of my best dishes and cocktails.'

His gaze drifted over her, lingered at her breasts then down her legs before he came back to her face. 'Are you sure that's the only reason they voted?'

The sudden tremble in her fingers made her set the cup down. 'You're an ass for making that inference.' Again, much too close to home. Too many times her mother had been ridiculed for using her sexuality to boost ratings, a fact Ruby had burned with humiliation for every single time.

'What inference?' he asked with a sly grin.

'The stupid sexist one you're making. Are you saying they voted for me because I have boobs?' Her rough accusation finally got his attention. The smile slid from his face but not the stark hunger in his eyes.

'Very nice ones.'

Despite her annoyance, heat rushed through her. 'Yeah, well, two of the other contestants had boobs, too.'

'I have no interest in theirs,' he returned blandly.

She picked up her cup and started to blow on her coffee, noticed his intense gaze on her mouth and thought better of it. 'Are you really that shallow?'

'*Sì,* I am.'

'No, you're not.'

'You wound me.'

'You wound yourself. You're clearly intelligent—'

'*Grazie*—'

'Or you wouldn't be worth billions. I fail to see why you feel the need to add this to the equation.'

'Tell me, sweet Ruby, why is it sexist to state that I appreciate an attractive body when I see it?'

Her mouth tightened. 'It's sexist when you imply I got where I am by flaunting it when you couldn't be more wrong.'

'Point taken.' He said nothing further.

'Is that supposed to be an apology?'

'Yes, I apologise unreservedly for making observations about your body.'

'That's almost as bad as saying "I apologise if your feelings are hurt" instead of "I'm sorry for hurting your feelings".'

'Let's not dwell on the pedantic. You have my unreserved apologies.' His gaze was steady and clear.

Ruby chose to believe he meant it. 'Thank you.'

'Good. I tried to reach Stone. I've been informed he's on vacation and can't be reached.'

She took a huge gulp of coffee and nearly groaned at the superb taste. Then his words broke through. 'Right. I wasn't born yesterday, you know.'

The seriously gorgeous grin returned. 'I know, and I'm very grateful for that.'

'Get to the point, *please*.'

'Stone is trekking in the Amazon for the next three weeks.'

Alarm skated through her. 'I can't wait another three weeks. I'll lose everything I've poured into getting the restaurant off the ground so far.'

'Which is what exactly?'

'Simon secured the rent but I put up my own money for the conversion of the space and the catering equipment.'

He froze. 'Who is Simon?' he asked in a silky tone threaded with steel.

'My ex-business partner.'

'Enlighten me why he's your ex,' he said in that abrupt, imperious way she'd come to expect.

The ache from Simon's betrayal flared anew. 'We didn't see eye to eye so we parted ways.'

Narciso's eyes narrowed. 'Was he your lover?'

She hesitated. 'Almost,' she finally admitted. 'We met in college, but lost touch for a while. A year ago we met again in New York. I told him about opening my restaurant and he offered to become my partner. We got close…'

He tensed. 'But?'

'But he neglected to tell me he had a pregnant wife at home and…I almost slept with him. He almost made me an accomplice in his infidelity.' The thought sent cold anger through her.

'How did you find out?'

Her hand tightened around her coffee cup. 'We were on our way to Connecticut for a romantic getaway when his wife called to say she'd gone into labour. I trusted him, and he turned out to be no better than…' She shook her head angrily and jumped when his fingers touched hers. Looking up, her eyes connected with his surprisingly gentle ones.

'I think you'll agree he takes the douche-bag crown, no?'

She swallowed the lump in her throat. 'Yes.'

He remained silent for several minutes, then he drained his cup. 'So my company's contribution is to help finish your restaurant?'

'That and the advertising costs for the first six months.'

'Do you have any paperwork?'

'Not with me, no. I couldn't exactly bring a briefcase to the job last night. But Nigel can prove it…'

'I'm taking over from Nigel,' he said abruptly.

'Excuse me?'

He set his cup down. 'As of now, I've relieved him of his duty to you. You'll now deal with me and me alone.'

That felt a little too…sudden… Ruby assured herself it was the reason why her heartbeat had suddenly escalated. She refused to let hope rise until she'd read the small print in his words. 'So…you'll sign over what NMC promised me?'

His eyes gleamed as he regarded her. 'Eventually,' he said lazily.

'Ah, there it is. The big, fat catch. What does *eventually* mean?' she demanded.

'I need proof that you're as good as you say you are. I don't endorse mediocre ventures.'

'Wow, are you always this insulting in the morning?'

'Sexual frustration doesn't sit well with any man, *amante,* least of all me.'

'And you think bringing your sexual frustration into a business discussion is appropriate?'

Silver eyes impaled her where she stood. 'You followed me thousands of miles and inveigled yourself into my company under false pretenses. You wish to discuss who holds the monopoly on what's appropriate right now?'

'What other choice did I have? I couldn't lose everything I've worked for because your employee is chasing orangutans in the Amazon.'

'I may be way off the mark but I don't think there are any orangutans in the Amazon. Borneo, on the other hand—'

'I didn't mean it literally. I meant…' She sighed. 'Bottom line is, NMC agreed to help me launch my business and it's reneging on the deal.'

'And I'm giving you a chance to get things back on track.'

'By making me jump through even more hoops?'

'I employ the best people. There must be a reason why Stone delayed in honouring the agreement.'

'And you think the fault is mine?' Irritation bristled under her skin. He stood there, arrogant and nonchalant as she flailed against the emotional and professional sands shifting under her feet.

'I'm trying to meet you in the middle.'

'All you have to do is review the show's footage. There were world-renowned food critics who judged my cuisine and cocktails the best. I won fair and square.'

'So you keep saying. And yet I'm wondering if there's something else going on here. If everything was above board, why didn't you use lawyers to hold my company to account? Why the very personal touch?'

'I don't have the kind of money it takes to involve lawyers. Besides, I was hoping you'd be reasonable.'

He moved towards her, his gaze pinned on her face. Danger blazed from his eyes. Along with hunger, passion and a need to win at all costs.

Her heart hammered as she forced herself to return his stare.

'You lied in order to get close to me. And you continued to lie until we were alone together. Having caught a glimpse of who I am, Ruby, how reasonable do you think I am?' His tone was silky soft, but she wasn't fooled. Underneath the lethally thrilling charm and the man who'd shown a surprising gentle side moments ago lay a ruthless mogul who ate amateurs for breakfast.

During her internet trawl she'd come across his moniker—The Warlock of Wall Street.

It took a special kind of genius to reach multibillionaire status by twenty-five and even more to attain the kind of wealth and influence Narciso Valentino wielded by his thirtieth birthday. If she didn't tread carefully, she'd leave Macau the same way she'd arrived—with nothing.

'I'm not unwilling to renegotiate our terms, Mr Valentino...' she ventured.

'I've had my mouth on parts of your body that I believe have earned me the right to hear you say my first name.'

Her blush was fierce and horrifyingly embarrassing. 'Fine! You can have thirty per cent,' she blurted.

His eyebrows shot up. 'Thirty per cent of your body?'

'What are you talking about? God, you think I'm renegotiating with my *body*?' She gasped in shocked horror. 'I'll have you know that I'd rather *die* than do something like that!'

His discomfiture was evident as he slowly straightened and spiked a hand through his hair. 'I'm...sorry,' he murmured.

A touch of warmth dispelled the ice. 'Apology accepted.'

'*Per favore,* enlighten me as to what you meant.'

'Part of the deal for winning was that you'd help with the cash prize and advertising and I'd give you a twenty-five-per-cent share in my business for the first three years. After that I'd have the option to buy it back from you. I'm willing to go up to thirty per cent.'

His shook his head. 'I have a new proposal for you. Agree to it and you can keep your extra five per cent.'

'Do I have a choice?'

'There's always a choice, *cara.*'

'Okay, let's hear it.'

'Convince me of your talent. If you're good enough, I'll hire you to cater my upcoming VIP party. If you're better than good, I'll recommend you to a few people. Now, the only thing you need to decide is if it's a choice you wish for yourself.'

'But I've already proved I deserve this by winning the show.'

'Then this should be a doozy.' He raised an eyebrow. 'Do you agree to my terms?'

The sense of injustice burned within her, the need to stand her ground and demand her due strong.

But from what she'd seen of him so far he could destroy her just as easily as he'd offered to help her. He'd rightly pointed out that she'd sought him out under false pretences. She should be thanking her lucky stars he hadn't turned her over to the security guards.

The small print in her *Petit Q* contract had warned of serious repercussions if she breached confidentiality or behaved inappropriately towards a *Q Virtus* member.

So far she'd breached several of those guidelines. It was therefore in her interest to stay on the right side of Narciso Valentino.

If he could throw away thirty million dollars with the careless flick of those elegant fingers, surely it was worth her while to endure this small sacrifice to prove herself to Narciso. Getting her restaurant opening back on track would also send her parents the message once and for all that she had no intention of bowing to their pressure to join the family business.

She sucked in a breath, which hopelessly stalled when his eyes darkened. 'Yes, I agree to your terms.'

He didn't move. He just stood there staring at her. Ruby had the weird sensation he was weighing her up, judging her…

Unable to stand his stare, she started to turn away. His eyes dropped to her bare legs, heat flaring in his gaze. The power of it was so forceful she took a step back. Then another.

'Stop,' he rasped.

'Why?'

'I need you.'

Her heart hammered. 'What?'

His nostrils flared as he reached and captured her arm. Strong fingers slid down her elbow to her wrist. Ruby's pulse raced harder under the pressure of his fingers as he raised her right arm.

The electronic beep as he activated the smartwatch on her wrist knocked her out of her lust haze. Biting the inside of her cheek to bring her down to reality worked for a few seconds, until he started to speak.

Sicilian wasn't in any way similar to the language she'd learnt growing up, but she managed to pick up a few words that had her frowning.

'You're not returning to New York?'

'Not yet. My plan was to take a long-needed vacation after Macau.'

Her heart sank. 'So I still have to wait until you come to New York to finalise this agreement.'

'Not at all, Ruby. I leave for Belize tonight. And you're coming with me.'

The sight of her open-mouthed was almost amusing. Almost. Had he not been caught up in the maelstrom of severely thwarted desire, Narciso would've laughed at her expression.

As it was, he couldn't see beyond the need to experience again the sensational taste of those lips.

Pure sin. Wrapped in sweet, angelic deliciousness.

He'd never kissed lips like hers. Or tasted nipples like hers. In fact, so far Ruby Trevelli was proving disconcertingly unique in all aspects. Even the confession of her bastard of an ex's betrayal had touched him in a way he most definitely did not desire.

The flash of pain he'd seen had made his insides clench with an alien emotion that had set even more alarm bells clanging.

He hadn't intended to go to Belize till after the party he'd planned for when his Russian deal was completed.

But he was nothing if not adaptable.

'Belize?' Astonishment blazed from her stunning blue eyes.

'Yes. I have a yacht moored there. We'll sail around along the coast, dive in the Blue Hole. And in between, you'll stun me with your culinary delights. But be warned, nothing short of perfection will satisfy me.'

'I've never provided anything short of that. But…' She hesitated, again displaying that reticence he'd sensed in her earlier. If she wanted to play hard to get, she was going about it the right way. He wanted her…hard. But he was no pushover.

'But what?'

'We need to agree on one thing.' Her pulse throbbed under his thumb. He wanted to stop himself from caressing the silky, delicate skin but he couldn't help himself.

'*Si?*'

'From now on things remain strictly business between us. The next time we have a discussion, I'd rather do it without the need for ropes.'

The hard tug of arousal the image brought almost made him groan out loud. 'I guarantee you, *amante,* the next time I tie you up, it'll be because you beg me to.'

She snatched her wrist from his grasp.

'Okay. And Superman rides on a unicorn, right?'

'I have no idea about that. Ropes, on the other hand—'

'Will play no part in our interaction for the duration I'm to prove myself to you. Unless, of course, you're bringing your girlfriend along. In which case, what you get up to with her is your business.'

Irritation fizzed inside him. Having the attraction he knew she reciprocated dismissed so casually stuck like a barb under his skin. 'I'm currently unattached. But I don't think I'll stay that way for much longer,' he said.

Her eyes widened but her lips pursed. Again arousal bit deep.

Suddenly, he wanted to leave Macau. Wanted to be alone with her so he could probe her deeper. The double entendre brought a grim smile.

Veering away from her, he stalked out of the kitchen.

The case he'd asked his personal butler to fetch was standing by the sofa in the living room. She spotted it the same time he did.

'You had my things removed from my room?' The incredulity in her voice amused and irritated him at once.

'I don't believe in wasting time when my mind is made up.'

'And what about *my* mind? You didn't know what choice I would make!'

'That's where you're wrong. I did. I'm very familiar with the concept of supply and demand. You want something only I can provide. You wanted it enough to hop on a plane on the strength of an eavesdropped conversation between complete strangers. I wagered on you being ambitious enough to agree to my demands.'

'You make me sound so mercenary.'

'On the contrary. I like a woman who states what she wants upfront. Subterfuge and false coyness are traits I actively despise.'

'Somehow I don't believe that.'

'You think I like liars?'

Her gaze slid away. 'I didn't say that.'

He forced himself to turn away, resume his path towards his bathroom and another cold shower. *Maledizione!*

'As for your case, I had it brought here to avoid any awkwardness. Or would you rather have answered questions as to why you've been absent from your duties for the last several hours?'

She groaned. 'Oh, God! What will they think?'

'They'll think the obvious. But you're with me, so no one will question you about it.'

'I...I...'

'The words you're looking for are *thank you*. You can use the second bedroom suite to get ready. I have a brunch meeting in the Dragon Room in half an hour.'

'And you want me to come with you?'

'Of course. From here on in, you serve no one but me.' His words echoed in his head and his fists clenched.

For the second time in less than ten minutes another unwanted emotion sideswiped him. *Possessiveness*.

Just as he'd trained himself not to trust, he'd trained himself not to become attached. Possessiveness suggested an attachment to something...*someone*.

Narciso didn't *do* attachment. And yet—

'What happens after your meeting?'

He forced nonchalance into his voice. 'We return here to indulge in...whatever we please. Tomorrow when the lock down is lifted, we leave.'

# CHAPTER SIX

THE REST OF the morning turned out to be a study in how the very rich and influential operated. Having grown up in relative wealth and seen the lengths to which people went to keep what they had, Ruby had imagined she knew how power and influence were wielded.

Watching Narciso Valentino command a room just by walking into it took her education to a whole different level. People's attitude transformed just by him entering their presence, despite his mask now being back firmly in place.

Although dressed more casually than he'd been last night, he exuded the same authority and attention as he moved from room to room, chatting with other well-heeled guests. The brief time he left her to attend his meeting, Ruby was left with a floundering feeling in her stomach that irritated and shocked her at the same time.

She was finishing her buttered brioche and café Americano when she sensed a gaze on her. Anticipating another of the speculative looks she'd been on the receiving end of since she came downstairs with Narciso, she stemmed her apprehension and raised her head.

The man who'd played against Narciso last night and won thirty million dollars was watching her with stormy grey eyes.

He moved forward and pulled out a chair. 'May I join you?' He sat down before she could stop him.

'Sure. It's a free country, I think.'

His smile didn't quite reach his eyes. He steepled his fingers together and stared at her. 'Where's my... Where's your companion?'

'At a meeting...' She paused and stared down at his wrist. 'I thought those smartwatches could tell you where each guest is. Why are you asking me?'

'Perhaps I just wanted a conversation opener.'

'Needing an opener would mean you have something specific to discuss with me. I don't see what that could be.' Her discomfort grew underneath that unwavering, hostile stare. She started to put her flatware down, thought better of it and hung on to the knife.

His gaze went to it and swung back to hers. 'You won't be needing that.'

'I'll be the judge of that. Now, can I help you with something?' As she'd thought last night, there was something vaguely familiar about him. But like every single guest present, his mask was back on and nothing of the rest of his features was enough to pinpoint where she might have seen him before, and she was not going to commit another faux pas by asking him his name.

'I merely came to offer you a warning. Stay away from The Warlock.'

'Considering you won over thirty million dollars from him last night, I'd have thought you'd be in a better frame of mind, perhaps even celebrating your huge windfall, not wasting your time casting aspersions on someone you defeated.'

'He thinks he has bested me but he'll soon learn the error of his ways.'

'Right. Okay...was that all?' she asked, but his eyes had taken on a faraway look, as if he were somewhere else entirely.

'He's been poison ever since...' His mouth tightened and his eyes grew colder. 'For as long as I've had to deal with him, he's been nothing but trouble. He was given his name for a reason.'

'The Warlock?'

His hand fluttered in a dismissive gesture. 'No, I meant his real name. Take my advice and remember that once he tells you who he really is.'

'I'm not supposed to know who he is, so what you're saying means less than nothing to me.'

'Or you could understand perfectly what I mean.' His upper lips twisted. 'Unless spreading your legs for him has robbed you of all common sense.'

The barb struck too close to home. 'How dare you?' She jerked back at the sheer hatred pouring from him. Ice-cold sensation drenched her veins at the same time as warm hands cupped her shoulders.

'Ruby?' Narciso clipped out her name. 'What's going on here?' The question was quite rhetorical because she was sure he'd caught part of the exchange.

Certainly, his flint-hard gaze and tense jaw made her think of her earlier assessment of just how dangerous an opponent he could be.

For whatever reason, the man sitting across from her spewing vitriol had wronged Narciso Valentino on a very deep level. The skin around his mouth was white and the hands curved over her shoulders were a little less than gentle.

Ruby carefully set her knife down and took a deep breath. 'Nothing. He was just leaving. Weren't you?'

The older man smiled and took his time to rise. His eyes locked on Narciso's and for a moment Ruby thought she understood the connection, then dismissed it. What she was imagining couldn't be possible.

Pure visceral hate existed between these two men. It coloured the air and crawled over her skin.

In her darkest days before she'd actively distanced herself from her parents, her father's behaviour had permeated every single corner of her existence and she'd imagined she hated him. She could never accept the way Ricardo Trevelli lived his life, or the careless way he treated her mother. But she'd never encountered hate this strong. It was a potent, living thing.

She shivered. Narciso felt it and glanced down at her before refocusing on her unwanted guest.

'Do I need to teach you another lesson, old man?'

'Keep your money, hotshot. I understand the need to brag in front of your woman. Shame it had to cost you so much last night.'

'It was worth it to see your face. If you need a refresher on how to win, I can accommodate you.'

The old man sneered. 'The time is coming when I'll wipe that smug look off your face once and for all.'

Narciso's smile was arctic. 'Do it quickly, then. I'm growing tired of your empty promises.'

Ruby sucked in a shocked breath at the blatant taunt. With a thick swear word that would singe the ears off a Sicilian donkey, the old man swivelled on his heel and walked away.

Narciso pulled back her chair, caught her up and swung her around to face him. 'What did he say to you?' he demanded, his nostrils pinched hard with the anger he was holding back.

'Oh, he was educating me on the real meaning of your name, albeit very cryptically. Who is he anyway?'

He looked after the departing man and visibly inhaled.

'I told you—he's no one important. But I want you to stay away from him.'

'That would be difficult since I don't even know who he is.'

Tucking her arm through the crook of his elbow, he led her out of the dining area styled with large, exquisitely scrolled Chinese screens. She'd heard one of the guests comment that the stands holding up the scrolls were made of solid gold. *Q Virtus,* its mysterious owner, Zeus…in fact this whole place was insane with its surrealistic extravagance, secrecy and decadence.

'You're an intelligent woman, hopefully equipped with enough of that intuition you women are so proud of. Use it and stay clear of him.'

'Funny, he said the same thing about you. And why does that sound suspiciously like a threat?'

He led her into another express lift and used his thumbprint and her smartwatch to activate the panel before pressing the button for the sub-basement.

'Because it is one.'

'So we've graduated from ropes to threats?' Her attempt at humour fell flat when his face tightened further.

'Don't tempt me. I'm this close to breaking point.' He held two fingers together for emphasis.

She froze when the arm imprisoning hers drew her closer to his warm body. 'Did something go wrong with your meeting? A deal fall through or something?'

'What makes you ask that?'

'Aside from the confrontation just now, you seem to be in a foul mood. Did something happen?'

'No, sweet Ruby. The "network hard" part of my day is ticking along nicely. It's the "play harder" part that has failed miserably.'

So she was partly to blame for his disagreeable mood.

Time for a subject change.

'Where to now?'

'The champagne mixer in the Blue Dungeon. Then we're leaving,' he clipped out.

'I thought we couldn't leave until the lock down was lifted tonight?'

'I've asked for a special dispensation from Zeus,' he said, his gaze on the downward-moving arrow. They were sinking deeper into the bowels of the building. Ruby felt as if she were disappearing into Alice's Wonderland. 'The dispensation should be coming through on your smartwatch any minute now. Let me know when it does.'

'The owner's name really *is* Zeus. Seriously?'

'You don't find my moniker incredulous.'

'That's because...' She paused, unwilling to voice the thought rattling through her head.

'Because?'

She shrugged. 'The Warlock suits you, somehow.'

He faced her fully, his gaze raking her face in that intensely raw way that made her feel vulnerable, exposed.

'In what way does it suit me?' he asked silkily.

*Because you mesmerise me with very little effort.* Ruby cleared her throat.

'You're obviously a genius at what you do.'

'And you think my success stems from sorcery?'

She shrugged. 'Not in the chicken bones and goat sacrificing sense but in other ways.'

One hand rose, trailed down her jaw to rest on the pulse pounding at her throat. 'And will I be able to sway you into my bed with this potent magic of mine?'

'No.'

His smile this time was genuine. And devastating to her senses. 'You sound so very sure.'

'Because I am. I told you, I don't mix business and pleasure.'

His smile dimmed. 'Would this have anything to do with your ex-almost-lover?'

'I believe it's a sound work ethic,' she answered.

Once Narciso had left her on her own, she'd replayed the events of last night and this morning. Shame at her behaviour had charged through her, forcing her to quickly reinforce her crumbling self-control.

Letting her feelings run wild and free was not an option. Heartache and devastation could be the only result if she didn't get herself back under control.

'So you intend to let him win?' Narciso queried softly.

'This is *my* choice.'

'If you say so.'

She had no chance to respond before the doors opened and they entered the most surreal room Ruby had ever seen. Blue lights had been placed strategically on the floors, walls and ceilings of a huge cavern. And bottles of champagne hung on wires, their labels combined with the words *QV Macau*.

'What does *Q Virtus* mean?' she asked.

His smile was mysterious. 'I could tell you but I'd have to—'

'Oh, never mind.' She turned as an excited murmur went through the crowd.

Six acrobats clad in LED-lit costumes swung from tension cables from one end of the room to the other.

She couldn't help her gasp of wonder at their movement. 'Oh, my God.'

'So *that's* what it'll sound like.' The wicked rasp was for her ears alone. His warm breath tickled her ear, sending a tingle right to her toes.

'What *what* will sound like?'

'Your gasp of wonder when I'm deep inside you.' His lips touched her lobe and she jerked at the electric sensation.

'Since that's never going to happen, you'll just have to keep guessing,' she replied.

He merely laughed and plucked two glasses off a sterling-silver tray that dropped down from the ceiling as if by magic. 'Champagne?' He passed her a glass.

She took it simply for something to do besides staring at his gorgeous face, which had transformed dramatically from his earlier formidable demeanour. He clinked glasses with her and raised his in a toast. 'To the thrill of the challenge.'

'I won't participate.'

'Too late. You threw the gauntlet. I accepted. Drink your champagne. That's a five-thousand-dollar glass you're holding.'

She stared down into the golden liquid before answering. 'I don't really drink that much.'

'I guessed as much. Another souvenir from the ex?'

The pain of the memory scythed through her before she could guard herself against it. She shook her head.

'Why don't you drink, Ruby?' His voice was hypnotic, pulling on a cord deep inside that made her want to reveal everything to him.

'I don't like the loss of control it gives me.'

Silver eyes narrowed. 'Something happened to you?'

'You could say that.'

'Something bad?'

'Depends on your definition of bad. Someone upset me. I thought getting drunk would solve the problem. It didn't. It made it worse.'

'Who was it?'

'My father—' She stopped as she realised how much she was revealing to him.

'Ah, *sì*. Fathers. It's such a shame they're necessary for evolution, isn't it?' Although his words were light, his eyes had taken on that haunted look she'd glimpsed this morning in his kitchen.

Out of nowhere came the overwhelming urge to take his pain away. 'I can't believe we're standing in one of the most spectacular rooms I've ever seen, discussing our daddy issues.'

'You're discussing *your* daddy issues. I have none.'

She frowned. 'But you just said—'

His mouth tightened. 'I merely expressed a view on evolution.' He took a large slug of his drink and set the glass aside. 'Come, the show's about to begin.'

He walked her deeper into the room, to an even larger space where a stage was brightly lit in hues of blue and green.

Several more acrobats struck different poses from their ropes but as the oriental-themed music filled the room they started to perform as one. Immediately she recognised the world-renowned group whose exclusivity was reserved to royalty and the crème de la crème of A-listers.

The fluidity of their movement and sheer talent taken to hone such an awe-inspiring performance kept Ruby mesmerised for several minutes, until she noticed Narciso's renewed tension. A glimpse at his profile showed a tense jaw and tightly pursed lips.

She debated for a second, then took a breath.

'It's okay if you don't want to admit to having daddy issues. I lived in denial myself for a long time,' she whispered, aware several guests stood close by.

'Excuse me?' he rasped.

'I could apologise but I thought we were…you know…sharing.'

'I don't *share,* Ruby. At least not in that way.'

'Listen—'

'You're missing the show,' he cut across her.

Forced to curb her reply, she resumed watching the show, aware that he grew tenser with every passing minute.

A particularly daring acrobat surged right over their heads. Narciso's hand tightened around hers. Thinking he was reacting to the spectacular display, she glanced at him, to find his gaze fixed across the stage, on the man who'd confronted her less than an hour ago.

In that instant, the resemblance between them struck her hard. Their similar heights, their silver eyes, the proud, arrogant way they viewed the world. How could she not have seen it until now?

*'Oh, my God, he's your father.'*

He stiffened and glanced down at her with cold, grim eyes. 'He's a man whose DNA I happen to share. Nothing more.'

Applause broke through the crowd as the show finished in a crescendo of dives and leaps choreographed so fabulously, she couldn't help but clap despite her shocking discovery.

*They were father and son.* And they hated each other with a passion that was almost a separate being every time they were within feet of each other.

She wanted to know what had placed such a wide divide between them but she held her tongue. She had no right to pry into anyone's life. Her own baggage was enough to be dealing with. After fighting for so long and so hard to get away from the noxious environment her parents chose to inhabit, the last thing she wanted was for someone like Narciso Valentino to dredge it all up.

The smartwatch on her wrist beeped twice.

Narciso glanced down at it. 'We're leaving.'

Her heart climbed into her throat, and she fought the snap of excitement fizzing through her. What on earth was wrong with her? She couldn't be secretly thrilled with the thought of being alone with this man.

Could she?

Within minutes their cases were being loaded into the trunk of the stretch limo that stood idling in the underground car park, with a smartly dressed driver poised at the door. She slid in and Narciso joined her.

The moment the door shut, she wanted to fling it open and dive out. She'd thought she was venturing into the unknown by coming to Macau.

By agreeing to go to Belize with The Warlock of Wall Street, she was really stepping into an abyss.

'I…don't think I can…' She stopped. What was she doing? She'd forced herself to endure a TV show after Simon had convinced her it was the only way she could fund Dolce Italia.

She'd plunged herself into the very environment she'd grown up in and actively detested just so she could establish her independence. Now she stood on the threshold of seeing it pay off.

'Having second thoughts?' he asked as the car rolled up a ramp and exited into bright mid-afternoon sunshine.

'No. I'm not,' she insisted more to herself than to him.

'Good.'

The smartwatch emitted several discreet beeps. 'What's it doing?'

'It's erasing the evidence of my activities here.'

'Wow, you're not part of the CIA, are you?'

'I could be if spies are your thing.' He gave another of those wicked smiles and her mouth dried.

'I'll pass, thanks. Although I'm curious what you have to do to belong to a club like that.' She took the watch off and examined its multifaceted detail.

'It involves a lot more than chicken bones and goat sacrifices, I can assure you.'

Against her will, a smile tugged at her mouth. Letting go, she laughed. He joined her, his perfectly even teeth flashing in the sunlight. The deep sound echoed in the enclosed space and wrapped itself around her.

*Danger!* Her senses screamed again. But it was a seductive

danger, akin to knowing that extra mouthful of rich, decadent mousse was deadly for you but being unable to resist the taste.

And she'd quickly discovered that if she let herself fall under his spell, he would completely bypass her hips and go straight to her heart.

'Here, take this back.' She held out his watch, stressing to herself that she didn't miss having something of his so close to her skin.

'Keep it. It's yours.'

'Are you serious?' she gasped. 'But what about its value—'

'I wasn't thinking of its monetary value when I offered it. And if you're thinking about pawning it, think twice.'

'I meant its sentimental value to you, of your visit here? And I'd never pawn a gift!'

'I'm happy to hear it. As for sentiments, I prefer mine to be warm-blooded.' He took off his mask and laid it on his knee. 'Luckily, I have you.'

The statement sent equal parts of apprehension and excitement through her. She slowly slid the watch back onto her wrist, and watched as they approached the Pearl River. Luxury super yachts in all shapes and sizes lined the marina.

The limo drew to a stop beside a sleek speedboat and Narciso helped her out. The driver held out a leather case, its velvet inside carved in the exact shape of his mask. Narciso placed the mask inside, shut the case and handed it to the driver.

Seconds after their luggage was loaded, the pilot guided the boat towards the open river.

'I've spent a lot of time asking you where we're going but I need to ask you one more time.'

'Don't you trust me?' he asked with a mockingly raised brow.

'No.'

He laughed again. And again, the sound tugged deep inside.

'We're heading to the airport. My private jet will fly us to Belize.'

Nodding, she watched the disappearing skyline of Macau City. It'd earned its name, Vegas of the East, but there was also soul in this place, and in other circumstances Ruby would've loved to explore a lot more.

She turned to find him watching her. The hunger was back in his eyes, coupled with a dangerous restlessness.

'What?' she demanded when she couldn't stand his intense scrutiny any longer.

'I came here for a purpose. You succeeded in swaying me from that purpose. I intend to find out why.'

'Was that purpose to destroy your father?' she asked before she thought better of it.

He immediately stiffened. The breeze rushing over the water ruffled his hair. He slowly scythed his fingers through it without taking his eyes off her.

'Among other things.'

'But you decided to spare him at the last minute.'

'A very puzzling notion indeed.'

Her heart hammered as his speculative gaze rested on her lips.

'I don't think it's puzzling at all. I think you knew exactly what you were doing.'

His eyes narrowed. 'And what would that be, O Wise One?'

'You were extending the thrill of the chase, delaying the gratification of the kill blow.'

'How very astute of you.'

'So what were the other things?'

'*Perdono?*'

'You said among other things.'

His gaze drifted down the neckline of her black tube dress, again a tighter fit than she would've preferred. 'What do you think?'

'According to online sources you have an IQ of a hundred and forty-eight.'

'It's closer to one-fifty but who's counting?'

Her mouth pursed. 'It also says you're a rampantly rabid playboy who thinks about nothing else but the next woman he intends to sleep with. It's a shame you've chosen to use *all* hundred and fifty to chase skirts.'

He grinned. 'No, I only use one hundred and forty-eight. I need the other two to walk and talk.'

She rolled her eyes even though the corners of her mouth curved. The boat pulled up to a jetty, beyond which she could see several planes parked on tarmac.

Narciso's plane was the same silver shade as his eyes, with a black trim that made it stand out among the other jets.

He lived a life of extreme luxury and decadence, while making people like her jump through hoops to claim what was rightfully theirs.

'What's wrong? You're frowning.'

'You're asking me to spend time and energy claiming something that should be already mine. I'm trying to see the fairness in that.'

'Something about going the extra mile? Doing whatever it takes?' he mocked, but his eyes held a flash of warning. 'Get on the plane, Ruby.'

'Or what?'

'Or you lose everything. Because I won't renegotiate and I despise being thwarted.'

Her feet remained leaden. Her instinct warned her she wouldn't emerge unscathed if she went with him.

'Is this how you do business? You strike a deal, you renegotiate, then you renege?' he demanded.

'Of course not. I'm only here because *your* company reneged on the deal it struck with me!'

'A fact I'm yet to verify. The quicker you get on the plane, the quicker this can be resolved.'

She had no argument against that. And the reality was she'd come too far to turn back. And there was the small problem of Simon's loan shark lurking in the background.

Taking a deep breath, she started to mount the steps. Recalling something he'd said, she twisted and nearly collided with his lean, muscular frame. The steadying hand he threw around her waist burned through to her skin. This close, without the hindrance of his mask, she could see how his envy-inducing cheekbones and long eyelashes framed his impossibly handsome face.

'What did you mean about being thwarted?'

'Sex, Ruby. I meant sex. We're going to have it together. It's going to be spectacular and, yes, I know you're going to protest. But it will happen. So prepare yourself for it.'

She was still reeling from the raw, brazen words hours later as she tried to doze in her fully reclined seat two rows from where he conducted a teleconference call.

She had no idea how long the flight to Belize would take. She had no idea what the temperature would be this time of year.

In fact, her mind was empty of everything but the words Narciso had uttered to her on the steps of his plane.

Punching her pillow, she silently cursed herself for dwelling on it. It was *never* going to happen. She'd have to be ten kinds of fool to repeat what she'd nearly gone through with Simon—

'If you punch that pillow one more time, it'll give up its secrets, I'm sure of it.'

She twisted around and found him standing beside her seat, one hand held out.

'Sleep is eluding you. Let's spend some time together.'

'No, thanks.'

He dropped his hand and shoved it into his pocket. Ruby tried not to stare at the way his shoulders flexed under the snow-white T-shirt he'd changed into. 'Please yourself. But if you end up serving me food that I find abhorrent because you haven't done your homework, you'll only have yourself to blame.'

The challenge had the desired effect. Pushing aside the cashmere throw the stewardess had provided, she went after him.

He smiled mockingly and waved her into the club chair opposite his.

Ruby smoothed her dishevelled hair down, and activated her tablet. 'Okay, shoot. What's your favourite food?'

'Life offers such vast richness. Having favourites is severely restricting.'

She sighed. 'This isn't going to be easy, is it?'

He shrugged. 'I take entertainment where I can get it.'

'Okay, next question. Any food allergies?'

'Peanuts and avocado.'

Her head snapped up. 'Seriously?'

'I don't joke with my health, *amante*.'

She noted it on her tablet. 'How do you feel about Sicilian food?'

'I'm completely indifferent.'

She looked up in surprise. 'Really? Most Sicilians are passionate about everything to do with their homeland.'

'Probably because they have a connection to be passionate about—' He stopped suddenly and his jaw clenched.

She watched him try to rein in his control and her chest tightened. 'And you don't?'

Tension gripped his frame. 'Not for a long time.'

Her tablet dimmed, but she didn't reactivate it. The flash of anguish in his eyes snagged her attention.

'Because of your father?' she pushed.

His eyes narrowed. 'Why does this interest you so much?'

The question took her aback, made her ask herself the same thing. 'I...I thought we were making conversation.'

'This is one subject I prefer to steer clear of. *Capisce?*'

'Because you find it upsetting.'

He cursed under his breath and raked back his hair as that stubborn lock fell over his forehead again. 'Not at all. The subject of my father fires up my blood. I just prefer not to discuss it with near strangers.'

Despite cautioning herself to stick to business, she found herself replying, 'Haven't you heard of the saying make love not war?'

'Why do I need to choose one when I can have both? I'll make love to you and I make war with Giacomo.'

'For how long?'

'How long can I make love to you? Is that another challenge to my manhood?'

'I meant your father, and you know it.'

'I intend to keep going until one of us is in the ground.'

She gasped. 'You don't really mean that, do you?'

Again that flash of pain, gone before it'd even formed. '*Sì*, I do.'

'You know, he called you poison.'

This time the anguish stayed for several seconds, shattered his expression. Her heart fractured at the pain she glimpsed before his face settled into neutral indifference. 'He's right. I am poison.'

His unflinching admission made her heart contract. 'What happened between you two?'

'I was born.'

Narciso watched her try to make sense of his reply. She frowned, then shook her head. 'I don't understand.'

He wanted to laugh but the vice gripping his chest every time he thought of Giacomo made that impossible. He rose and walked to the bar at the mid-section of his plane. Pouring two glasses of mineral water, he brought one to her and gulped down the other. 'That's because you're trying to decipher a hidden meaning. There is none. I was born. And Giacomo has hated that reality ever since.'

'He hates being a father?'

He paused before answering, unwilling to utter the words he hadn't said aloud for a very long time, not since he'd wailed it as a pathetic little boy to the housekeeper who'd been the closest thing he'd known to a mother.

'No. He hates me.'

Shock darkened Ruby's eyes.

He sat back down abruptly, and willed back the control he'd

felt slipping from him since he'd walked into the poker den in Macau last night. He glanced up and saw sympathy blazing from Ruby's face. The rawness abated a little but, no matter how much he tried, he couldn't shake off the unsettling emptiness inside him.

He swallowed his water and set the glass down.

'Enough about me. Tell me about *your* father.'

She stiffened. 'I'd rather not.'

'You were ready to *share* just a little while ago.' He settled deeper into his seat and watched her face. And it was a stunning face. The combination of innocence and defiance in her eyes kept him intrigued. She didn't hide her emotions very well. Right now, she was fighting pain and squirming with a desire to change the subject.

The sudden urge to help her, to offer the same sympathy she'd just exhibited, took him by surprise.

*Dio,* what was wrong with him?

This woman who'd flown thousands of miles after him was an enigma. An enigma with daddy issues. He should be staying well clear.

He leaned forward. 'Since you seem shocked by the depth of my…feelings towards Giacomo, I'm assuming your feelings towards your father are much less…volatile?'

Those full lips he wanted to taste again so badly pressed together for a moment. 'I don't hate my father, no. But I prefer to keep my distance from them.'

'*Them?*'

She fidgeted. 'You're going to find out anyway. My parents are Ricardo and Paloma Trevelli.'

Her stare held a little defiance and a whole load of vulnerability. 'Sorry, you lost me.'

A delicate frown marred her perfect skin. Again his fingers ached to touch. Soon, he promised himself.

'How come you own several media companies and yet have no clue what goes on in the world?'

'My line of work doesn't mean I compromise my privacy. So your parents are famous?'

Her eyelids swept down to cover her expression. 'You could say that. They're famous celebrity TV chefs.'

'And their fame disgusts you?' he deduced.

Blue eyes flicked to his. 'I didn't say that.'

'Your voice. Your eyes. Your body. They all give you away, Ruby Trevelli.' He loved the way her name sounded on his lips. He wanted to keep saying it… 'So you despise them for being famous and cashing in on it. Isn't that what you're doing?'

'No! I'd never whore myself the way—' She stopped and bit her lip.

'Do they know you have this view of them?' he asked.

She shrugged. 'They've chosen a lifestyle I prefer not to be a part of. It's that simple.'

'Ruby…' he waited until her eyes met his '…we both know it's not that simple.'

Shadows chased across her face and her mouth trembled before she firmed it again. Before he could think twice, he reached out and touched her hand.

She swallowed hard, then pulled her tablet towards her. 'How many people will I be catering for at your event?'

He told himself he wasn't disappointed by her withdrawal. 'Are we back to all business again?'

'Yes. I think it's safer, don't you?'

Narciso couldn't deny the veracity of that. Dredging up his past was the last thing he'd intended when he'd boarded his plane. And yet, he resented her switch to all-business mode.

'If you say so,' he replied. 'You think you can handle a VIP dinner?'

'I believe in my talent as much as you believe in your abilities as the Warlock of Wall Street. If I say I'll rock your socks off, I will.'

A reluctant smile tugged at his lips. 'A confident woman is such a turn-on.'

She glared at him. 'If you say so,' she replied sweetly. 'Is there a guest of honour that I should pay particular attention to?'

'Vladimir Rudenko. I'm in the last stages of ironing out a deal with him. He's the VIP guest.'

She started to make another note when her tablet pinged. He heard her sharp intake of breath before she paled.

'What is it?'

'It's nothing.'

The blatant lie set his teeth on edge. 'Don't lie to me.' He reached for the tablet but she snatched it off the table.

'It's a private thing, all right?'

'A private thing that's obviously upset you.' He watched her chest rise and fall in agitation and experienced that disconcerting urge to help again.

'Yes, but it's my problem and I'll deal with it.'

Before he could probe further, she jumped up. 'You said I could use the bedroom if I wanted. I'll go finish making my notes now and get some sleep, if that's okay?'

It wasn't okay with him. Nothing had been okay since he met Ruby Trevelli. But short of physically restraining her, an action sure to bring brimstone upon his head, he let her go.

'We won't be landing for another six hours. I'll wake you before we do.'

She nodded quickly. 'Thanks.'

He watched her walk away, her short, tight black dress framing her body so deliciously, his groin hardened. He couldn't suppress his frustrated growl as the bedroom door shut after her.

The image of her lying in his bed haunted him. But those images were soon replaced by other, more disturbing ones as his thoughts turned to their earlier conversation.

His father.

He shoved a hand through his hair. He'd come so close to revealing the old, bottled-up pain. Hell, he'd even contemplated spilling his guts about Maria.

Maria. The tool his father had used to hammer home how much he detested his son.

His laptop beeped with an incoming message. Casting another glance at the bedroom door, Narciso pursed his lips.

The next six hours would be devoted to clearing his schedule.

Because once they were in Belize, he would devote his time to deciphering the code that was Ruby Trevelli and why she had succeeded in getting under his skin.

# CHAPTER SEVEN

SHE WAS WARM. And comfortable. The steady sound drumming in her ears soothed her, made her feel safe from the erratic dreams that still played in her mind.

But she wanted to get warmer still. Wanted to burrow in the solid strength surrounding her.

The heart beating underneath her cheek—

Ruby jerked awake.

'Easy now, tigress. You'll do yourself an injury.'

'What the hell…? What are you doing here?'

'Sharing the bed. As you can see, once again I managed to restrain myself. And this time we're both fully clothed. That means I win brownie points.'

'You win nothing for letting yourself into my bed uninvited.'

'Technically, this is my bed, Goldilocks. Besides, you were muttering in your sleep and tossing and turning when I looked in on you. I had to make sure you didn't sleepwalk yourself out of an emergency exit in your agitation.'

Ruby tried to pry herself away from the inviting length of his warm body, but the arm clamped around her waist refused to move. 'I wasn't that agitated.'

Silver eyes pinned hers. 'Yes, you were. Tell me what upset you.' His voice was cajoling, hypnotic.

She wanted to tell him about the undeniable threat in the email that had made a shaft of ice pierce her nape and shimmer down her spine. The loan shark had stepped up his threat level, implicating her mother.

Ironic that Narciso, the world-famous playboy and media mogul, had no idea who her mother was but some two-bit loan shark who inhabited the dregs of society knew who Paloma Trevelli was enough to threaten to break her legs if Ruby didn't reply with a timescale of payment.

Her reply had bought her a few more days but there was no way she intended to tell Narciso what was going on.

'I told you. It's my business to handle.'

'Not if it will potentially impede your ability to perform your job.'

'I can cook blindfolded.'

'That I would pay good money to see.' He pulled her closer, wedging his thigh more firmly between hers so she was trapped. Some time during sleep, she'd curled her hand over his chest. Now, firm muscles transmitted heat to her fingers, making them tingle.

Awareness jolted through her when his lips drifted up her cheek to her temple. 'If we weren't landing in less than thirty minutes, I'd take this a step further, use other means to find out what's going on.'

'You're operating under the assumption that I would've permitted it.'

He laughed, then sobered. 'It wasn't your father, was it?'

'No, it wasn't.'

He stared down at her for a long time, then nodded. 'I did some research while you were asleep. I know about your parents.'

'Oh?' She couldn't help the wave of anxiety that washed over her.

His eyes narrowed. 'Has it always been like that with them?'

That mingled thread of pain and humiliation when she thought of them tightened like a vice around her heart. 'You mean the crazy circus?'

He nodded.

'Until I went to college, yes. I didn't return home afterward. And I have minimal contact these days. Any more and it gets… unpleasant.'

'For whom?'

'For everyone. My father is a serial adulterer who doesn't understand why I won't condone his behaviour. My mother doesn't understand why I don't forgive my father every time he strays. They both want me to join the family business. The same business for which they shamelessly exploit their fame, their family, their friends—' She ground to a halt and tried to breathe around the pain in her chest.

His hand stroked down her cheek. 'You hate yourself for the way you feel.'

Feeling exposed, she tried to pull away. He held her firmer. 'Ruby *mio,* I think you'll agree we went way past business when we spent the night together in my bed. Talk to me,' he coaxed.

She drew in a shaky breath and reassured herself that they were talking. Just talking. 'I hate that my family is broken and I can't see a way to fix it without being forced to live my life in a media circus.'

'And yet you chose that avenue to fund your business.'

'Believe me, it wasn't my first choice.'

'Then why did you do it?'

'We'd tried getting loans from the banks with no success. Simon heard about the show and convinced me to enter. Taking three weeks out of my life to be on the show felt like a worthy sacrifice.'

'So you returned to the thing you hate the most in order to achieve your goal.'

'Does that make me a fool?'

'No, it makes you brave.'

The unexpected compliment made her heart stutter. Silver eyes rested on her, assessing her so thoroughly, she squirmed. Of course the movement made her body rub dangerously against his.

He emitted a leonine growl and the arm around her waist

tightened. One hand caught her bent leg and hitched it higher between his legs. The bold imprint of his erection seared her thigh. Heat flared between them, raw and fervent.

'So you don't think it's wrong to do whatever it takes to achieve one's dreams?'

His eyes darkened. 'No. In fact, it's a trait I wholeheartedly admire.'

Her throat clogged at the sincerity in his voice. The barriers she'd tried so hard to shore up threatened to crumble again. A pithy, mocking Narciso was bad enough. A gentle, caring Narciso in whose eyes she saw nothing but admiration and praise was even more dangerous to her already fragile emotions.

Scrambling to regroup, she laughed. 'Dear God, am I dreaming? That's two compliments within—'

'Enough,' he snapped. Then he kissed her.

Ruby's heart soared at the ferocity of his kiss. Desire swept over her, burying the volatile memories under even more turbulent currents of passion as he mercilessly explored her mouth with a skill that left her reeling.

Narciso could kiss. She already had proof of that. But this time the sharper edge of hunger added another dimension that made her heart pump frantically, as she saw no let-up in the erotic torrents buffeting her.

When he sank back against the pillows and pulled her on top of him, she went willingly. Strong, demanding hands slid up her bare thighs to cup her bottom, press her against that solid evidence of his need.

Unfamiliar hunger shot through her belly to arrow between her legs. Desperate to ease it, she rocked her hips deeper into him.

His thick groan echoed between their fused lips. He surged up to meet her, thrusting against her in an undeniable move that made her blood pound harder.

With her damp centre plastered so firmly and fully against him, she moaned as the beginnings of a tingle seized her spine. Hunger tore through her as rough fingers bit into her hips, keeping her firmly in place as they found a superb synchronicity that needed no words.

The first wave of sensation hit her from nowhere. She cried out, her fingers spiking into his hair as she grasped stability in a world gone haywire.

'*Dio!* Let go, baby. Let go.'

The hot words, crooned in her ear from a voice she'd found mesmerising from the very first, were the final catalyst. With a jagged moan, Ruby gave into the bliss smashing through her. She melted on top of him, giving in to the hands petting down her back as her shudders eased.

'I don't know whether to celebrate for making you come while we're both fully dressed or spank you for your appalling timing.'

Slowly, the realisation of what she'd just done pierced her euphoria.

Beneath her cheek, his heart raced. She could feel his erection still raging, strong and vital.

She'd orgasmed on top of Narciso Valentino and he hadn't even needed to undress her.

'*Oh, God.*'

Narciso held himself very still. He had to, or risk tearing her clothes off and taking her with the force of a rutting bull.

'God isn't going to help you now, naughty Ruby. You have to deal with me.'

'I… That shouldn't have happened.'

He nodded grimly. 'I agree.'

Wide blue eyes locked on his. 'You do?'

He swallowed hard. 'It should've happened when I was inside you. Now I feel woefully deprived.' Unable to stop himself, he moved his hands up and down her back. He tensed as her breathing changed. Desire thickened the air once more. Sensing her about to bolt, he flipped her over and trapped her underneath him. 'But I have you now.'

She tried to wriggle away but all she did was exacerbate the flashflood of desire drowning them both.

'No, I can't… We can't do this.'

He stiffened. 'Why not?'

'It won't end well. Simon—'

His eyes narrowed into warning slits. 'Was a cheating low-life who didn't deserve you. You and I together…we're different. We deserve each other.'

Narciso speared his fingers into her soft hair. But instead of kissing her, he grazed his lips along her jaw and down her throat to the pulse racing crazily there. He drew down her sleeves, exposing her breasts to his mouth. His mind screamed at him to stop before it was too late, but he was already sliding his tongue over one nipple.

*Dio!* He'd never known a woman to smash so effortlessly through his defences.

Her nails raked his nape and he groaned in approval. By the time he turned his attention to her other nipple, her whimpers were adding fire to his raging arousal.

She tugged on his shirt and he gave in to her demand. With a ragged laugh, he helped her reef it over his head and divested her of her dress.

Stark hunger consumed him as he took a moment to feast his eyes on her exposed body. 'You're so beautiful.' He drifted a hand down her chest and over her stomach to the top of her panties.

That disconcerting throb of possessiveness rocked through him again. He didn't want to know who else she'd been with but, in that moment, Narciso was glad her ex-business partner had failed to make her his. He settled himself over her, taking her mouth in a scorching kiss that obliterated words and feelings he didn't want to examine too closely.

His hand slid over her panties, hungrily seeking the heart of her. Her breath caught as his fingers breached her dampness and flicked over her sensitive flesh.

She jerked and squeezed her eyes tightly shut.

'Open your eyes, *amante*,' he commanded. He wanted…no, *needed* to see her, to assure himself that she was sliding into insanity just as quickly as he was. When she refused to comply, he applied more pressure. 'Do it or I'll stop.'

Eyes full of arousal slowly opened. His breath fractured at the electrifying connection. His whole body tightened to breaking point and he mentally shook his head.

*What the hell was happening here?*

Her delicate shudder slowed his flailing thoughts. Absorbing her reaction, he inserted one finger inside her, drinking in her hitched cry as she shuddered again.

'*Dio,* you're so tight.' He waited until she'd adjusted, then pressed in another finger.

Narciso was unprepared for her wince.

Instantly alert, he asked, 'What's wrong?'

She shook her head but he could see the trepidation in her eyes.

Those now familiar alarm bells shrieked. 'Answer me, Ruby.'

Nervously, she licked her lips. 'I'm…a virgin.'

Shock doused him in ice. For several seconds he couldn't move. Then the realisation of how close he'd come to taking her, to staking a claim on what he had no right to, hit him like a ton of bricks.

He surged back from her, reefing a hand through his hair as he inhaled sharply.

'You're a virgin,' he repeated numbly.

Raising her chin, she stared back at him. 'Yes.'

Several puzzle pieces finally slotted into place—the touches of innocence he'd spotted, her bolshiness even as she seemed out of her depth.

*Her trepidation.*

What had he said a moment ago—they *deserved* each other? Not any more.

Regret bit deep as he forced himself off the bed. 'Then, *cara mia,* this is over.'

Ruby came out of the bathroom of her cabin and slowed to a stop. Glancing around her room, she tried again to grapple with the sheer opulence around her. The three-decked yacht, complete with helicopter landing pad, had made her jaw drop the first time she'd seen it two days ago.

But the inside of Narciso's yacht was even more luxurious.

Black with a silver trim on the outside, it was an exact reverse on the inside. Silver and platinum vied with Carrara marble mined from the exclusive quarries north of Tuscany.

Her suite, complete with queen-size bed, sunken Jacuzzi bath and expensive toiletries, was the last word in luxury.

But all the opulence couldn't stem the curious emptiness inside her.

Since her arrival in Belize, she'd barely seen Narciso. The only times she saw him was when she served the list of meals he'd approved the day they'd boarded *The Warlock*.

At first the studied consideration with which he'd treated her after she'd blurted her confession had surprised her. Who knew he was the sort of playboy who treated virgins as if they were sacred treasures?

But then she'd seen the look in his eyes. The regret. The banked pain. Her surprise had morphed into confusion.

She was still confused now as she tugged off her towel and headed for the drawer that held her meagre clothes. Only to stop dead at the sight of the monogrammed leather suitcase standing at the bottom of the bed.

She opened it. Silk sarongs, bikinis, sundresses, designer shoes and slippers fell out of the case as she dug through it, her stomach hollowing out with incredulity.

Dressing in the jeans and top she'd travelled to Macau in and taken to wearing since her arrival simply because the three evening gowns were totally out of the question, she went in search of the elusive Sicilian who seemed hell-bent on keeping her permanently off balance.

She found him on the middle deck, after getting lost twice. He wore white linen shorts and a dark blue polo shirt. The early evening sun slanted over jet-black hair, highlighting its vibrancy and making her recall how it had felt to run her hands through the strands.

The sight of his bare legs made her swallow before she reminded herself she wasn't going to be affected by his stunning physique any longer. He'd pointedly avoided her for two whole days. She was damned if she'd let him catch her drinking him in as if he were her last hope for sustenance.

She was here to do a job. Whatever closeness they'd shared on his plane was gone, a temporary aberration never to be repeated. Her focus now needed to be on what she'd come here to do. But before that…

'You bought me clothes?' she asked.

He turned around, casually shoving his hands into his pockets. When his eyes met hers, she couldn't read a single expression in the silver depths. The Narciso who'd alternately laughed, mocked and devoured her with his eyes was gone. In his place was a coolly remote stranger.

'The size of your suitcase suggested you'd packed for a short stay. This is a solution to a potential problem. Unless you plan on wearing those jeans every day for the next week?'

True, in the strong Belizean sun, they felt hot and sticky on her skin. Not to mention they were totally inappropriate for the job she was here to do. When she cooked, she preferred looser, comfortable clothes.

But still. 'I could've sorted my own wardrobe.'

'You're here on my schedule. Making time for you to go shopping doesn't feature on there.'

'I wouldn't have—'

'It was no big deal, Ruby. Let's move on. It's time to step up your game. I want to see how you fare with a three-course meal. Michel will assist you if you need it.' He glanced at his watch. 'I'd like to eat at seven, which gives you two hours.'

The arrogant dismissal made her hackles rise. The distance between them made her feel on edge, bereft.

She assured herself it was better this way. But deep down, an ache took root.

Michel, Narciso's chef, greeted her with an openly friendly smile when she entered the kitchen.

'What do you have in mind for today for *monsieur?*' the Frenchman asked. Deep blue eyes remained contemplative as he stared at her.

'He wants to eat at seven so I was thinking of making a special bruschetta to start and chicken parmigiana main if we have the ingredients?'

'Of course. I bought fresh supplies this morning from town.'

The mention of town made her wonder when Narciso had bought her clothes. Had he shopped for them himself or given instructions?

Shaking her head to dispel the useless wondering, she followed Michel into the pantry. 'Oh…heaven!' She fell on the plump tomatoes and aubergines and squealed when she saw the large heads of truffles carefully packed in a box.

Freshly sliced prosciutto hung from specially lined containers that kept it from drying out and Parma ham stayed cool in a nearby chiller.

Michel took out the deboned chicken breast in the fridge. 'Would you like me to cut it up for you?'

'Normally, I'd say yes, but I think it's best if I do everything myself.' She smiled to take the sting out of the refusal.

He shrugged. 'Shout if you need anything.' After helping himself to a bottle of water, he left her alone.

Ruby selected the best knife and began chopping garlic, onions and the fresh herbs Michel kept in the special potted containers in the pantry.

The sense of calm and pure joy in bringing the ingredients together finally soothed the unsettled feeling she'd experienced for the last forty-eight hours.

Time and anxiety suspended, and her thoughts floated away as she immersed herself in her one salvation—the joy of cooking.

She started on the caviar-topped bruschetta with ricotta and peppers while the parmigiana was in the last stages of cooking.

Setting it out on a sterling-silver tray, she headed upstairs to where the crew had set the table.

Her feet slowed when she saw the extra place setting, then she stopped completely at the intimacy created by the dim lighting and lit candles. Her stomach fluttered wildly as steel butterflies took flight inside her.

'Are you going to stand there all evening?' Narciso quipped from where he sat on a sofa that hugged the U-shape of the room.

'I…thought I was cooking for just you.'

'You thought wrong.' He stood, came over and pulled out her chair. 'Tonight we eat together.' His gaze took in her jeans. 'Right after you change.'

'I don't need to change.'

'One rule of business is to learn to let the little things slide. Standing on principle and antagonising your potential business partner doesn't make for a very good impression.'

'I really appreciate you helping me out but—'

'I would personally prefer not to eat with a dinner companion wearing clothes smeared with food.'

Ruby glanced down and, sure enough, a large oily streak had soiled her vest top.

He'd gone to the trouble of providing new clothes for her comfort. Would it hurt to show some appreciation? In a few days, she'd be back in New York, hopefully with a contract firmly in her pocket. He'd made it clear she was no longer attractive to him in the sexual sense, so she had nothing to fear there.

'I'll go and change,' she murmured around the disquiet spreading through her.

'*Grazie,*' he replied.

Returning to her suite, she quickly undressed and selected a soft peach, knee-length sundress with capped sleeves. Slipping her feet into three-inch wedged sandals, she tied her hair back and returned to the deck.

His gaze slid over her but his face remained neutral as he pulled out her chair.

'Sit, and tell me what you've made for us.'

The intimate *us* made her hand tremble. Taking a deep breath, she described the first course. He picked up a piece of bruschetta, slid it into his mouth and chewed.

The process of watching him eat something she'd made with her two hands was so strangely unsettling and erotic her fingers clenched on her napkin.

'Hmm, good enough.' He picked up another piece and popped it in his mouth.

When she found herself staring at his strong jaw and throat, she averted her gaze, picked up a piece and nibbled on the edge. 'Damned with faint praise.'

'The cracked pepper adds a zing. I like it.'

Heady pleasure flowed through her. 'Really?'

'I always mean what I say, Ruby.' His grave tone told her they weren't talking about just food.

'O...okay,' she answered. 'I have to check on the parmigiana in ten minutes.'

'That's more than enough time for a drink.'

Abandoning her half-eaten bruschetta, Ruby headed for the extensive bar, only to stop dead.

'We're no longer moored?' The bright lights of the marina had disappeared, leaving only the stunning dark orange of the setting sun as their backdrop.

'No, we're sailing along the coast. Tomorrow morning, I intend to dive the Blue Hole. Do you dive?' he asked.

She continued to the bar, her nerves jumpier than they had been a minute ago. 'I did, a long time ago.'

'Good. You'll join me.'

'Is that a request or a demand?'

He'd ignored her for the past two days. The idea that he now wanted to spend time with her jangled her fraying nerves. As she recalled what had happened on the plane heat and confusion spiked anew through her.

'It's a very civilised request.'

And yet...

Regardless of what Narciso was requesting, the last thing she needed to be doing was anticipating spending any time in his company. He made her lose control. She only had to look into his eyes to feel herself skating close to emotional meltdown.

The last thing she'd wanted when she met Narciso was to give in to the attraction she'd felt for him. But perversely, now he'd made it clear he intended to give her a wide berth, her mind kept conjuring up scenarios of how things could be between them.

She'd been wrong to compare Narciso to Simon, or even to her father. Despite the playboy exterior, she'd glimpsed a core of integrity in her potential new business partner that was markedly absent from the men she'd so far encountered.

*Potential new business partner...*

Therein lay her next problem. Whether active or passive, if she passed his test, Narciso would own a share in her business. They'd have a *business* relationship.

*Which meant, nothing could be allowed to develop between them personally.*

She worked almost absent-mindedly and only realised the drink she'd made after she opened the cocktail shaker. Aghast, she stared into the bold red drink.

'Are you going to serve...what is that anyway?'

Flames surged up her cheeks. 'Allow me to present the *Afrodisiaco*.'

One brow cocked; a touch of the irreverence she'd become used to darted over his features. 'Is there a message in there somewhere?'

That she'd produced one of the most suggestive cocktails on her list made her pulse jump as she poured it. 'It's just a name.'

He immediately shook his head. 'I've learned that nothing is ever what its face value suggests.' He sipped the cocktail, swirled it around in his mouth. 'Although now I've tasted this, I'm willing to alter that view.'

'Narciso...' The moment she uttered his name he froze. Another crack forked through the severely compromised foundation of her resistance as she watched his eyes darken.

'No, Ruby *mio,* you don't get to say my name for the first time like that.'

She paused. 'I'm sorry, but you need to explain to me what the last two days have been about.'

*'Basta...'* His voice held stark warning.

*'Non abbastanza!* I didn't ask you to seduce me on your plane. In fact, I made it very clear I wanted to be left alone because I knew— I wasn't... Look, whatever experiences you've had in the past are your own. But you told me you didn't like women who blew hot and cold. Well, guess what, that's exactly what you're doing!'

'Are you quite finished?' he grated out, his face a mask of taut control.

She gripped the counter until her knuckles whitened and she stared down at her dress. 'As a matter of fact, I'm not. Thank you for buying the clothes. If I appeared unappreciative before it was because I've learnt that nothing comes for free.'

'You're welcome,' he replied coolly. 'Now am I allowed to respond to that diatribe?'

'No. I have to check on the chicken parmagiana. The last thing I want to do is jeopardise my chances by serving you burnt food.' She rounded the bar and walked past him.

He grasped her wrist, easily imprisoning her.

Instantly, heat and electricity flooded through her. 'Let me go!'

'I haven't been blowing hot and cold.'

'You've certainly made avoiding me an art form.'

'I was trying to save us both from making a mistake, *tesoro.*'

The realisation that she didn't want that choice made for her sent a bolt of shock through her. Sheer self-preservation made her raise her chin. 'Well, you needn't have bothered. In fact you did me a favour back on your plane.'

His hand tightened. 'Really?'

'Yes. You reminded me that you're not my type.'

His nostrils flared. 'And how would you know what your type is considering your lack of experience?'

'I don't need experience to know playboys turn me off.'

His mouth flattened. 'You didn't seem turned off when you climaxed on top of me, then proceeded to writhe beneath me.'

The reminder made her pulse skitter. The hungry demand that hadn't abated since then made her pull harder. He set her free and she retreated fast. 'Maybe I wanted to see what the fuss was all about. Whatever. You helped me refocus on the reason I'm here on your boat. Now if you'll excuse me, I have to check on the main course.'

Narciso watched her go, furious that he'd allowed himself to be drawn into her orbit again.

The way he'd operated the last two days had been the best course.

So what if he'd climbed metaphoric walls while locked in his study? He'd sealed two deals and added to his billions, and he'd even managed to stop thinking about Ruby Trevelli for longer than five minutes.

But then his investigator had presented him with another opportunity to finish off Giacomo. And once again, Narciso had walked away, unable to halt the chain reaction inside that seemed to be scraping raw emotions he'd long ago suppressed; unable to stop his world hurtling towards a place he didn't recognise.

That his first thought had been to seek out Ruby and share his confusion had propelled him in the opposite direction.

His reaction to her continued to baffle him. In the last two days, he'd expended serious brainpower talking himself out of tracking down the woman who kissed like a seductress but whose innocence his conscience battled with him against tainting.

*Dio,* when the hell had he even *grown* a conscience?

With a growl, he grabbed the last of the canapés and munched on it. Delicate flavours exploded on his tongue.

The past two days had shown him how talented Ruby was in the kitchen and behind the bar. Her skill was faultless and she'd risen to his every challenge. In that time, while he'd locked himself in his study to resist temptation, he'd also reviewed the TV show footage and seen why she'd won the contest.

Her skittishness every time the camera had focused on her had also been made apparent.

She hated being under the spotlight. And yet she'd forced herself to do it, just so she could take control of her life.

His admiration for her had grown as he'd watched the footage even as he'd cursed at the knowledge that she was burrowing deeper under his skin.

He looked up as she entered, a silver-topped casserole dish in her hand. The flourish and expertise with which she set the dish down spoke of her pride in her work. He waited until she served them both before he took the first bite.

His hand tightened around his fork. 'Did you cook this for Simon?'

She visibly deflated. 'You don't like it.'

He didn't just like it. He loved it. So much so he was suddenly jealous of her sharing it with anyone else. 'I didn't say that. Did you cook it for him?'

Slowly, she shook her head.

Relief poured through him. 'Good.'

'So, you like it?' she asked again.

'*Sì,* very much,' he responded, his voice gruff.

The pleasure that lit up her face made his heart squeeze. He wanted to keep staring at her, bathe in her delight.

*Dio,* he was losing it.

He reached for the bottle to pour her a glass of chilled Chablis.

'No, thanks,' she said.

His hand tightened around the bottle. 'You have nothing to fear by drinking around me, Ruby.'

She raised her head and he saw a mixture of anguish and sadness displayed in her eyes. In that moment, Narciso wanted to hunt down the parents who'd done this to her and deliver unforgettable punishment.

'I know, but I'd like to keep a clear head, all the same.'

He set the wine aside and reached for the mineral water. 'Well, getting blind drunk on my own is no fun, so I guess we're teetotalling.'

She rolled her eyes and smiled, and his gut clenched hard.

'We haven't discussed wines yet. When we're done meet me at the upper deck. And wear a swimsuit. The sun may have gone down but you'll still boil out there in that dress.'

The tension in his body eased when she nodded.

After dinner, he made his way up to the deck. They could do this… They could have a conversation despite the spiked awareness of each other. Or the hunger that burned relentlessly through him—

Five minutes later, she mounted the stairs to the deck and his thoughts scattered.

*Madre di Dio!*

The body he could see beneath the sarong was spectacular. But he couldn't see enough of it. And he wanted to, despite the *off limits* signs he'd mentally slapped on her.

*Seeing doesn't mean touching.*

'Drop the sarong. You don't need it here.'

She fidgeted with the knot and his temperature rose higher. It loosened as she walked over to the lounger. She finally dropped it, sat down, and crossed her legs. Minutes ticked by. She recrossed her legs.

'Stop fidgeting.'

She blew out a sigh. 'I can't stand the tension.'

'Well, running away won't make it go away.'

'I wasn't planning to run,' she replied. 'You wanted to talk about wines, remember?'

He nodded, although he'd lost interest in that subject. Forcing himself to look away from the temptation of the small waist that flared into very feminine hips and long, shapely legs, he stared at the moon rising over the water.

'Or I could easily return to my cabin and we can continue to treat each other like strangers.'

He considered the idea for exactly two seconds before he tossed it.

'What the hell, Ruby *mio*, let's give civility a try.'

She exhaled, sat up and poured a glass of mineral water from the jug nearby. 'Okay, first, I have to ask—what the heck is up with your name, anyway?'

He smiled despite the poker-sharp pain in his gut. 'You don't like it?'

'It's…different.'

'It was Giacomo's idea of a joke. But I've grown into it, don't you think?' Despite his joviality, the pain in his chest grew. Her eyes stayed on him and he saw when she noticed it. For some reason, revealing himself in that way didn't disturb him as much as he'd thought it would. In fact, talking to her soothed him.

'You've never wanted to change it?'

'It's just a name. I'm sure a few people will agree I can be narcissistic on occasion. I have no problems in pleasing number one.'

Her eyes gleamed with speculative interest. 'It really doesn't bother you, does it?'

'It may have, once upon a time,' he confessed. 'But not any more.'

Sympathy filled her eyes. 'I'm sorry.'

He tried to speak but words locked in his throat. Two simple words. Powerful words that calmed his roiling emotions. *'Grazie,'* he murmured.

His eyes caught and held hers. Something shifted, settled between them. An acknowledgement that neither of them were whole or without a history of buried hurt.

'The email on the plane. What was that about?' he asked abruptly.

She slowly inhaled. 'Before I tell you, promise me it won't

affect the outcome of this test run.' Her imploring look almost made him reply in the affirmative.

He hardened his resolve when he realised she was doing it again. Getting under his skin. Making a nonsense of his common sense.

'Sorry, *amante,* I don't make blind promises when it comes to business.'

Her lips firmed. 'Simon sold his share of the business to a guy who doesn't see eye to eye with my business plan.' In low tones, she elaborated.

He jerked upright. 'You're being threatened by a loan shark?'

'Yes.'

'And you didn't think to inform me?' he demanded.

'Would you have believed me? Especially in light of how I approached you?'

'Perhaps not right then, but…' The idea that he was prepared to give her the benefit of the doubt gave him a moment's pause. 'What's his name?'

'I don't know—he refused to tell me. All he wants is his money.'

'So I own twenty-five per cent of your business and a loan shark whose name you don't know another twenty-five per cent?'

'Yes.'

He slowly relaxed on his lounger and stared at her. 'You do realise that our agreement is transforming into substantially more than a talent-contest-prize delivery, don't you?'

A flush warmed her skin. 'I'm not sure I know what you mean.'

'What I mean, Ruby *mio,* is that in order to realise my twenty-five-per-cent investment, it seems I have to offer my business expertise. Writing you a cheque after next week and walking away is looking less and less likely.'

Why that thought pleased him so much, Narciso refused to examine.

# CHAPTER EIGHT

'I DON'T REMEMBER the last time I sunbathed.'

'I can tell.'

Blue eyes glared at him and his pulse rocketed. Narciso tried to talk himself calmer. No one else was to blame since *he'd* invited her to go scuba-diving with him. *After* another sleepless night battling unrelenting sexual frustration.

'How can you tell? And don't tell me it's because you're a warlock.'

'I don't need otherworldly powers, *cara*. Your skin is so pale it's almost translucent and there are no visible tan lines.'

She glanced down at herself. 'Oh.'

'Here.' He grabbed the sun protection, started to move towards her, changed his mind at the last minute and tossed it to her.

'Thanks.' She sat on the same lounger as last night. But this time, the smell of her skin and the drying sea water made his blood heat.

'Where did you learn to dive?' he asked to distract himself from following the slim fingers that worked their way up her leg.

She smiled. 'I spent a few summers working at a hotel in Florida when I was in high school. I worked in the kitchens and got to dive in my spare time.'

'Have you always known you wanted to be a chef?'

Her smile immediately dimmed and he cursed himself for broaching a touchy subject.

'I knew I had my parents' talent but I resisted it for a long time.'

'I've seen the footage of the contest. You're not a natural in front of the camera.'

One brow rose. 'Gee, thanks.'

'What I mean is, you can easily prove to your parents that they're wasting their time trying to recruit you.'

'It won't stop them from trying.'

He shrugged. 'Then tell them you have a demanding new business partner.'

She shook her head. 'I'd rather not.'

'You want to keep me your dirty little secret, *tesoro?*'

She smiled but the light in her eyes remained dim. 'Something like that. What about you? Have you always known you wanted to be a warlock?'

He laughed, experiencing a new lightness inside. When her lips curved in response, he forcibly clenched his hands to stop from reaching for her. 'Ever since I made my first million at eighteen.'

'Wow, that must have brought the girls running.'

He shrugged, suddenly reluctant to dwell on past conquests. 'It gave me the ammunition I needed…'

She frowned slightly. 'Ammunition. To fight your father?'

'To fight Giacomo, yes.'

'Why do you call him Giacomo?'

He exhaled. 'Because he was never a *father* to me.'

She paused and that soft look entered her eyes. The realisation that he didn't mind talking to her about his past shocked him. He tried to tell himself it meant nothing, but he knew he was deluding himself.

'What about your mother? Is she alive?'

Sharp pain pierced his chest. 'My poor mama is what started this whole nasty business.'

'What do you mean?'

'She died giving birth to me. I was so determined to make

a quick entrance into the world, I caused her to bleed almost to death by the roadside before an ambulance could arrive.'

Her gasp echoed around the sun-dappled deck. 'Surely, you don't think that's your fault?'

'Giacomo certainly seems to think so.'

It occurred to him that Ruby was the first woman he'd actively conversed with. Normally, any conversation was limited to the bedroom. But with sex off the table it seemed *talking* was the next best thing.

'That's why there's so much animosity between you two. He blames you for your mother's death?'

'It may have started out that way, but our *relationship* has evolved…mutated.'

'Into what?'

He started to answer then stopped. 'Into something that's no longer clear-cut.' Shock rolled through him as he accepted the truth. He'd started out wanting to destroy his father. Along the way, and especially lately, the urge to deliver the kill blow had waned. Even toying with his father now no longer held any interest for him.

'So what are you going to do about it?'

*Sì,* what was he going to do?

Call it a day and cut off all ties with Giacomo? The sudden ache in his gut made him stiffen and jerk upright.

'Enough about me. You have an exceptional talent. I'm officially hiring you to cater my dinner party.'

The compliment brought a smile to her lips. Again, he forced himself not to reach out and caress the satin smoothness of her determined jaw. The urge was stronger because he needed something to blot out his confused thoughts of his father.

'Thank you.' She put the sun protection down and glanced at him. 'Can I get you anything?'

He shook his head. 'No more cocktails.'

Her smile widened. 'Then I have the perfect thing.'

She stood and walked to the chiller behind the bar. To his

surprise she returned with an ice-cold beer. 'Sometimes a beer is the perfect solution to thirst.'

Narciso twisted off the cap with relish and took a long swig, and looked over to find her eyes on his throat. The feel of her eyes on him made his temperature shoot sky-high.

'Aren't you having a drink?'

She indicated the glass of water on the table next to her lounger.

'That must be warm by now.'

Wordlessly, he held out the bottle to her. Her eyes met his and sensation skated over him. Their attraction was skittering out of control but he couldn't seem to apply the brakes.

'You're thirsty. Take it.'

Slowly, she took the bottle from him. Her pink tongue darted out to caress the lip of the bottle before she took a small swig.

She held it back out to him. 'Thanks.'

'So beers are an exception to your don't-drink-much rules?'

'A small drink doesn't hurt.'

'Aren't you afraid you'll lose control with me?' he asked roughly.

'We established that anything between us would be a mistake, remember?'

He stepped deeper into quicksand, felt it close dangerously over him but still he didn't retreat.

Eyes on her, he took another swig of beer. 'Perhaps that no longer holds true.'

Her breath audibly hitched. 'Why? Tell me and I'll remind you when things threaten to get out of hand.'

He couldn't stop the laughter that rumbled from his chest. 'You mean as some form of shock therapy?'

'If it's what works for you.'

His gaze slid down her body. Skin made vibrant by the sun and the exertions of their dive this morning offered temptation so strong it was no wonder he could think straight.

'Don't worry, *tesoro,* I'll try and curb my uncontrollable urges.'

'I'm glad you can. I'm not so sure about myself,' she blurted.

For a moment, he thought his hearing was impaired. 'What did you just say?'

She shut her eyes and cursed as he'd only heard a true New Yorker curse. 'I feel as if I'm skidding close to the edge of my control where you're concerned. After Simon—'

'I am *not* Simon,' he grated out.

She trembled. 'Believe me, I know. But even though I keep telling myself what a bad idea this is, I can't stop myself from… wanting you.'

The blunt delivery made his eyes widen. 'You realise how much power you're giving me by telling me?'

'Yes. But I'm hoping you won't take undue advantage of it.'

Slowly, he set the bottle down. 'Come here.'

'Did I not just mention undue advantage?'

'Come here and we'll see if the advantage is undue or not.'

Ruby stood slowly and stepped towards him, fighting for a clear breath as he loomed large, powerful and excruciatingly addictive before her. Her skin burned where he cradled her hips in his palms.

'What do you want, Ruby?' he rasped.

She looked into his face and every self-preservation instinct fled.

She'd never met a man like Narciso Valentino before. Everything she'd found out about him in the last few days had blown her expectations of him sky-high.

His name might indicate self-absorption but she was learning he was anything but. He could've reported her to Zeus when he'd found out she'd applied to be a *Petit Q* under false pretences. He could've sent her packing after she told him about his company owing her. Stopping himself from seducing her and his generosity with the clothes coupled with his easy companionship this morning as they'd scuba-dived at one of the most beautiful places in the world had shown her that Narciso could be nothing like his name.

Little by little, the traits she'd discovered had whittled at her defences.

And now…

'As crazy and stupid as it is, I want to kiss you more than I want to breathe.'

*Dear God, what was wrong with her?*

'*Dio mio.*' He sounded strained…disarmed, as if she'd knocked his feet from under him.

She ought to pull back, retreat to the safety of her cabin. Instead, she took his face in her hands, leaned forward and kissed him.

His grunt of desire slammed into her before he seized her arms. Leaning back against the lounger, he tugged her on top of him. Strong arms imprisoned her as he moulded her body to his.

The evidence of arousal against her belly was unmistakable, gave her strength she hadn't known existed. She plunged her tongue into his mouth, felt the stab of pleasure when he jerked beneath her and groaned long and deep.

Firm hands angled her head for a deeper penetration that made her pulse thud a hundred times faster.

He made love to her with his mouth, lapping at her lips with long strokes that pulled at the hot, demanding place between her legs.

Her hands hungrily explored his warm, firm muscle and hair-roughened chest. When her fingers encountered his nipple, she grazed her nail against it, the way she knew drove him mad.

He tore his mouth from hers, his eyes molten grey as he gazed up at her.

'*Cara mia,* this will not end well for either of us if you don't stop that.'

Brazenly, she repeated the action. And watched in fascination as it puckered and goose bumps rose around the hard disc. Before she could give in to the urge to taste it, Narciso was moving her higher, stark purpose on his face.

'One bad turn deserves another.' Roughly, he tugged at her

bikini string and caught one plump breast in his mouth as they were freed from the garment.

The sight of him feasting on her in the dimming light was so erotic, Ruby's nails dug into his chest.

Her hips bucked against his hardness, that hunger climbing even higher as she rubbed against his full, heavy thickness. The thought of having that power inside her made her whimper. When his teeth tugged at her in response, her moan turned into a cry.

Foolish or not, dangerous or not, she wanted him. More than she'd ever wanted anything in her life. For the first time, Ruby understood a little bit of the passion that drove her parents. Of the need that forced two people wholly unsuited to stay together. If it was anywhere near this addictive, this mad, she could almost sympathise…

'Narciso…please…'

One hand splayed over her bottom, squeezed before grabbing the stretchy material of her bikini. He pulled, sending a million stars bursting behind her closed eyelids as the pressure on her heated clitoris intensified her pleasure. At her shocked gasp, he pulled tighter. Liquid heat rushed to fill her sensitive flesh. Almost immediately, she needed more, so much more that her body was threatening to burst out of her skin. She sank her hands into his hair and bit down on the rough skin of his jaw.

He cursed and froze, hard fingers gripping her hips. When the sensation slid from pleasure to a hint of pain, she lifted her head to gaze drowsily at him.

'What…?'

'Before this goes any further I need to be sure you want this,' he rasped.

She looked down, saw her state of undress, saw his hard, ready body.

Instinctively she went to adjust her clothes, her face flushing with heat. 'God, what's wrong with me?'

He stopped her agitated movements with steady hands. 'Hey,

there's *nothing* wrong with you. You're a sensual creature, with natural needs just like—'

'My father?' she inserted bleakly.

Surprisingly gentle hands framed her face. 'If you were like him you wouldn't still be a virgin. Do you get that?'

Tears prickled her eyes. 'But…I…'

'No, no more excuses. You stopped being their puppet a long time ago—you just forgot to cut the strings.'

Her breath stalled and her vision blurred. He brushed away her tears and she fought to speak. 'What does that say about me?'

His jaw clenched. 'That we sometimes spend too much time looking in the rear-view mirror to see what's ahead.'

She moved on top of him because, despite everything going south, her hunger hadn't abated one iota. His hands clamped down harder on her hips.

'What's in your rear-view mirror?' she asked him softly.

'Too much. Much too much.'

His answer held a depth of anguish that cut to her soul. Heart aching for him, she started to lean down but he caught and held her still.

'No.'

She looked into his face and saw his slightly ashen pallor. 'You don't want me to kiss you?'

His chest heaved and he glanced away.

The realisation hit her like a bolt of lightning. 'You stopped us making love on the plane and just now because you don't think you're worth it, do you? Why not? Because your father told you you weren't?'

'Ruby, stop,' he warned.

She ignored him, the need to offer comfort bleeding through her. She caressed his taut cheek. A pulse beat so hard in his jaw, her fingers tingled from the contact.

'*Cara,* I'm a man on the edge. A man who wants what he shouldn't have. Get off me before I do something we'll both regret, *per favore.*'

Fresh tears prickled her eyes, stung the back of her throat.

If anyone had told her a week ago she'd be lying on top of the world's most notorious playboy, baring her soul to him and catching a glimpse of his ragged soul in return, she'd have called them insane.

Her hands shook as she slowly removed them from his face. Levering herself away from him was equally hard because her knees rebelled at supporting her in her weakened state.

Snatching at her bikini top, desperately trying to ignore his silent scrutiny, she tied the strings as best she could and secured the sarong over her chest.

Her hair was an unruly mess she didn't bother to tackle. What had just happened had gone beyond outer appearances.

She looked down at him and he returned her look, the torture unveiled now. She floundered, torn between helping him and fleeing to examine her own confused emotions. Eventually, she chose the latter. 'I have a few things to take care of in the kitchen before I go to bed. *Bona notti.*'

Slowly, he rose to tower over her, and in the fading daylight she saw his bunched fists at his sides.

His smile was cut from rough stone. 'I've awakened too many demons for me to have a restful night, *tesoro*. But I wish you a good night all the same.'

*I've awakened too many demons...*

Ruby lay in bed a few hours later, wracked with guilt.

She'd pushed him to relive his past, to rake over old wounds because she'd wanted to know the real man underneath the gloss.

*To reassure herself he wouldn't hurt or betray her?*

Shame coiled through her as she acknowledged that she'd been testing him. But then deep down, ever since he'd turned away from her on the plane, she'd known Narciso was nothing like her father. Or Simon.

And still she'd pushed...

She reared up and gripped the side of her bed. Her head

cautioned her against the need to find out if she'd pushed him too far, if the demons were indeed keeping him awake. But her heart propelled her to her feet.

She went down the hallway and knocked on his door before her courage deserted her.

The evidence that he was indeed up came a second later when the door was wrenched open. He was dressed in his silk pajama bottoms and nothing else.

'What the hell are you doing here, Ruby?' he flung at her.

She struggled to look up from his chest. 'I…wanted to make sure you were okay. And to apologise for what happened earlier. I had no right to push you like that.'

His eyes narrowed for several seconds before he turned and strode back into the bedroom. 'I'm learning that warlocks and demons keep good company.' He picked up a crystal tumbler of Scotch, raised it to her and took a sip.

Ruby found herself moving forward before she'd consciously made the decision to.

Her hand closed over the glass and stopped his second sip.

He stepped back away from her but, hampered by the bed, he abruptly sank down. She took the glass from him and set it on the side table.

'Drinking is not the answer. Trust me, I know.'

Strong hands gripped the sheets as if physically stopping himself from reaching for her and he exhaled harshly.

This close, the beauty of him took her breath away. His chest heaved again, the movement emphasising his stunning physique and golden skin.

Fiery desire slammed into her so hard she reeled under the onslaught.

Before she could stop to question herself, she slid her hands over his biceps. Warm muscles rippled under her touch.

'What the hell are you doing?' His voice was rough and gritty with need.

Her face flamed but a deeper fire of determination burned

within her. 'I have a feeling it's called seduction. I don't know because I've never done this before.'

She leaned in closer. He groaned as her hardened T-shirt-covered nipples grazed his chest. '*Per amore di Dio,* why are you doing it now?'

She placed a finger over his lip and felt a tiny jolt of triumph when it puckered slightly against her touch. 'Because it's driving me as insane. And because I don't want to live in fear of what I might become if I let go. So this is me owning my fear.'

He cursed again and he shook his head. Knowing he was about to deny her, she pushed him onto the bed and sealed her mouth over his.

He groaned and accepted her kiss with a demanding roughness that threatened to blow her away. Encouraged by that almost helpless response, she threw one leg over him and straddled his big body.

Immediately, his already potent arousal thickened, lengthened, found the cradle between her legs. Before she lost her mind completely, Ruby reached out to both sides of the bed and loosened the ties she needed, then she worked quickly before he could stop her.

He wrenched his mouth from hers, and glanced up. Silver eyes darkening in shock, then disbelief. *'Hai perso la tua mente?'*

'No, I haven't lost my mind.'

'Clearly, you have.' He yanked on the binds but they only tightened further. 'Release me, Ruby.'

'Nope. What goes around comes around, *tesoro.*'

Feeling a little bit bolder now she knew he wouldn't easily overpower her or dismiss her, she took a deep breath, drew her T-shirt over her head and flung it away.

'Ruby…' Warning tinged his low growl.

She wavered but the look in his eyes stalled her breath—hunger, anger, a touch of admiration, that little bit of wonder and vulnerability she'd seen earlier on the deck all mingled in his hypnotic eyes.

'I would, but the look in your eyes is scaring me right now. What's to say you won't devour me the minute I set you free?' She trailed a finger down his chest and revelled in his hitched breathing.

'I won't,' he bit out.

She shivered again at the menace in his voice. 'Liar, liar.'

'*Madre di Dio,* do you really want to lose your virginity so badly?'

She shook her head and her hair came free from the loose knot she'd put it into. 'No, it isn't actually that important to me. What I want, what I crave, is to make love with you.'

His eyes darkened. 'Why?'

She tamped down on what she really wanted to say. That he'd shown her another way to view herself. Another way that didn't make her skin crawl for feeling sensual pleasure.

'Do I have to have some noble reason? Isn't crazy chemistry enough? I was absolutely fine before you touched me. You woke this hunger inside me. Now because of some stupid principle, you're trying to deny me what I want. What we both want. I won't let you.'

His chest heaved. 'I won't let you either. Not like this.' The roughness in his tone gave her pause. When she looked into his eyes, that bleakness she'd spotted in the kitchen on their first morning in Macau was back. 'If you want me, release me.'

She wanted to kiss that look away, to utterly and totally eradicate it so it never returned. Leaning down, she did exactly that, luxuriating in the velvety feel of his warm lips. He kissed her back but she could sense the agitation clawing under his skin and she drew back a little. Caressing his chest and shoulders, she touched her lips to his again in a gentle offer of solace from whatever demons were eating him alive.

A rough sigh rumbled from his chest.

'Narciso…'

His lips trembled against hers. 'Release me, Ruby.'

Heart in her throat, she repeated the words he'd said to her in Macau. 'I already have.'

Shocked eyes darted upward. A split second later he was flipping her beneath him, ripping away her panties and flinging them over his shoulder.

Molten eyes speared her as he tugged off his pyjamas, his gaze settling possessively on her damp, exposed sex. 'Sorry, Ruby *mio,* I lied.'

'About what?' Her voice trembled.

'About not devouring you.'

Hot, sensual lips grazed down her cleavage to her navel, the rasp of his growing stubble sending electrifying tingles racing through her body. His tongue circled her navel, then strong teeth bit the skin just below.

Her shudder threatened to lift her off the bed.

One large hand splayed on her stomach and the other parted her legs wider. Watching him watch her was the most erotic experience of her life so far.

She didn't need a crystal ball to know there was more, so much more in store for her.

He bypassed her most sensitive place, lifted one leg to bend it at the knee. Hot kisses trailed down her inside thigh. Again the graze of his stubble added a rough, pleasurable edge that made her breath come out in agitated gasps.

Nibbling his way down, he soothed his bites with open-mouthed kisses that sparked a yearning for that mouth at her core.

But he took his time. Leisurely, he kissed his way down her other thigh, all the while widening her thighs, those molten eyes not leaving her heated sex.

Ruby wondered why she wasn't dying with embarrassment. But seeing the effect the sight of her had on him—nostrils flared as he breathed her in, his fingers trembling slightly as he gripped her knee—she had little room for anything but desire.

*'Lei è sfarzoso,'* he muttered thickly.

She *felt* gorgeous, a million miles from what she'd always feared she would feel when it came to sex. She blinked back tears and cried out as sublime pleasure roared through her.

Lips, tongue, teeth. True to his words Narciso devoured her with a singular, greedy purpose.

From far away, she heard her cries of ecstasy, smelled the heat of his skin coupled with the scent of her arousal as she writhed with bliss beneath him.

Just when she thought she would burst out of her skin, he raised his head.

'I'd had this thought in my head that the first time I took you I'd torture you for hours with pleasure.' Still holding her down, he pulled open the beside drawer and grabbed a condom. Impatiently, he ripped it open with his teeth. 'But I can't wait one more second, *amante*.'

'I don't want you to.'

Hooded eyes regarded her. 'I can't promise it will be gentle. I could hurt you.'

The slight note of apprehension washed away when she recalled what had happened on the deck earlier this evening. Despite the volatile emotions that had raged between them, he'd never hurt her.

She laid her hand over the one he'd flattened on her belly. 'I'm ready.'

He leaned back and she saw him, really saw him for the first time. The erection that sprang from his groin was powerful and proud. Another testament to how well his name suited him. Judging from the size of him, he had a lot to crow about in that department, too.

Holding himself in one fist, he rolled on the condom and settled stormy eyes on her. 'Are you sure about this?' he rasped.

'Right this moment, my confidence is wavering a little,' she confessed, her voice shaky with the knowledge that he would soon be inside her.

He inhaled deeply. 'I promise to go as fast or as slow as you desire,' he said in a deep solemn voice.

Unable to speak, Ruby nodded. In a slow, predatory crawl he surged over her. Dark hair fell over his forehead in that care-

less way she found irresistible. She had a second to weave her
fingers through it before he was kissing her again.

By the time he lifted his head hers was swimming. The flush
that scoured his cheekbones signalled his fast-slipping control.
His erection pulsed against her thigh and the very air crackled
with sensual expectation so thick, all her confidence from minutes ago oozed out of her like air from a balloon.

'What do I do now?'

He glanced down to where her hunger raged, to the glisten-
ing entrance to her body. 'Open wider for me,' he breathed.

Every single atom in her body poised with tingling expectation as she complied with his command and spread her thighs
wider. 'Now what?'

Silver eyes returned to hers. 'Now…you breathe, Ruby *mio*.'
He took her lips in a quick, hard kiss. 'This will be no fun at
all if you pass out.'

Reeling from the sensation coursing through her, she sucked
air through her mouth.

'That's it. Eyes on me and don't move,' he instructed.

The first push inside her threatened to expel the air she'd
fed her starving lungs. From head to toe, Ruby was soaked in
indescribable sensation.

'Oh!' She breathed out again, her hands tightening on his
shoulders as her craving escalated. 'More.'

He shut his eyes for a split second, then he pushed in further,
carefully gauging her reaction as he deepened the penetration.

The need clawing through her sharpened, deepened. Unable
to lie still, she twisted upward to meet him.

'*Dio!* Don't do that.'

'But I like it.' She twisted higher, then gave a cry as pain
ripped through her pelvis.

'*Per amore di*… I told you not to move.' His lips were
tension-white and sweat beaded his forehead.

He started to withdraw but the pain was already fading.
Quickly she clamped her legs around his waist.

'No.' He levered his arms on either side of her in preparation to remove himself from her body. The knowledge that he was holding himself back so forcefully sent a different sensation through her.

Her hand trailed up his throat to clutch his nape, holding him prisoner. 'Yes.'

Tightening her grip, she forced her hips up. He slid deeper to fully embed himself within her and she cried out in pleasure.

'Ruby…'

'Make love to me, Narciso,' she pleaded, because she knew that whatever she was feeling right now, there was so much more to come. 'Please.'

With a groan, he sealed his body fully with hers.

Sizzling pleasure raced up her spine as he set a thrusting rhythm designed to drive her out of her mind. Considering she was already halfway there, it didn't take long before Ruby stopped breathing again, poised on the edge of some unknown precipice that beckoned with seductive sorcery.

Against her lips, Narciso murmured thick, hot words in native Sicilian. Those that she understood would've made her blush if her whole body wasn't already burning from the fierce power of his possession.

His lips grazed along her jaw, down her throat to enslave one nipple in his mouth. His tongue lapped her in rhythm with his thrusts, adding another dimension to the sensations flowing through her.

One hand hooked under her thigh, spreading her even wider. He groaned at the altered angle just as she began to fracture.

He raised his head from her breast and locked his gaze on hers. The connection, deep, hot and direct, was the final straw.

Convulsions tore through her, rocking her from head to toe with indescribable bliss that wrenched a scream from the depths of her soul.

Lost in the maelstrom of ecstasy, she heard him groan deeply before long shudders seized his frame.

His damp forehead touched hers, then his head found the

curve of her shoulder. Hot, agitated breaths bathed her neck as his heartbeat thundered in tandem with hers.

In that moment, she experienced a closeness she'd never experienced with another human being. She told herself it was a false sensation but still she basked in it, unable to stop the giddy, happy feeling washing over her. Her arms tightened around him and she would gladly have stayed there for ever but he moved, turning sideways to lie on the bed.

'I don't want to crush you.' His voice was thick, almost gruff.

'Don't worry, I'm stronger than I look.'

He half growled. 'I guessed as much earlier. Where did you learn to make ties like that?'

'Tying up chickens and turkeys for roasting.'

He grimaced. 'I'm flattered.'

'Don't worry, Narciso. I'll never mistake you for a chicken.'

His laughter caused her heart to soar, the simple pleasure of making him laugh lifting her spirits.

Resting her chin on his chest, she looked into his eyes. *'Grazie.'*

He caught a curl and twisted it around his finger. *'Per quello che?'*

'For making my first so memorable.'

'It was a first for me, too, after a fashion.'

A thousand questions smashed through her brain but she forced herself to push them away. 'Hmm, I guess it was.'

They lay in replete silence for several more minutes. And then the atmosphere began to change.

She started to move but his arm tightened around her. A deep swallow moved his Adam's apple.

'Tomorrow, we'll talk properly, *sì?*'

Heart in her throat, she nodded. *'Sì.'*

'Good. Now I get to show you my favourite knot.'

# CHAPTER NINE

'*Ciao*.'

The deep voice roused her from languor and she opened her eyes to find Narciso standing over her lounger, cell phone in one hand.

The midmorning sun blazed on the private deck outside his bedroom suite and Ruby squirmed under his gaze as it raked her.

'*Ciao*. I can't believe I let you convince me to sunbathe nude.'

'Not completely nude.' He eyed her bikini bottoms.

Heat crawled up her neck and she hurriedly changed the subject. 'Was your call successful?'

'*Sì*, but then all my negotiations are,' he said with a smug smile.

'Your modesty is so refreshing. I guess making a million dollars by age eighteen tends to go to one's head.'

'On the contrary, my head was very clear. I had only one goal in mind.'

Despite the sun's blaze, she shivered. 'So it started that long ago, this feud between you two?'

He tossed his phone onto the table and stretched out on the lounger next to hers. Ruby fought not to ogle the broad, firm expanse of skin she'd taken delight in exploring last night. The grim look on his face helped her resist the temptation.

'Believe it or not, there was a time when I toyed with the idea of abandoning it.'

Surprise scythed through her. 'Really?'

'*Sì,*' he replied, almost inaudibly.

'What happened?'

'I graduated from Harvard a year early and decided to spend my gap year in Sicily. I knew Giacomo would be there. And I knew he couldn't throw me out because the house he lived in belonged to my mother and she'd willed it to me when I turned eighteen. I…hoped that being under the same roof again for the first time in five years would give us a different perspective.'

'It didn't?'

The hand on his thigh slowly curled into a fist. 'No. We clashed harder than ever.'

She couldn't mistake the ragged edge in his voice. 'If he hated you being there so much, why didn't he leave?'

'That would've meant I'd won. Besides, he took pleasure in reminding me I'd killed my mother on the street right outside her home.'

Ice drenched her veins. 'What happened to her?'

'She suffered a placental abruption three weeks before I was due. She'd gone for a walk and was returning home. By the time she dragged herself up the road to the house to alert anyone, she'd lost too much blood. Apparently, the doctor said he could only save one of us. Giacomo asked him to save my mother. She died anyway. I survived.'

Ruby reached out and covered his fist with her hand. He tensed for a second, then his hand wrapped around hers.

'How can anyone in their right mind believe that something so tragic was your fault?'

'Giacomo believed it. That was enough. And he was right to demand that the doctor save my mother.'

She flinched. 'How can you say that?'

'Because he knew what I would become.'

'A wildly successful businessman who donates millions of dollars each year to fund neo-natal research among other charitable organisations?'

He jerked in surprise. 'How do you know that?'

A blush crept up her cheeks. 'When I did a web search on you a few things popped up.'

He shrugged. 'My accountants tell me funding charities is a good way to get tax breaks. Don't read more into the situation than there is, *amante*.'

Lowering her gaze, she watched their meshed fingers. The feel of his skin against hers made her heart skip several beats. 'I think we're past the point where you can convince me you're all bad, Narciso,' she dared.

He remained silent for so long she thought he'd refused to pick up the thread of their conversation. Then his breath shuddered out. 'Giacomo believes that.'

'Because you perpetuate that image?'

His smile was grim but it held speculation. 'Perhaps, but it's an image I'm growing tired of.'

Her breath caught.

His eyes met hers and he reached across and took her hand. 'Does that surprise you? That I'm thinking it's time to end this vendetta?'

'Why the change of heart?' she asked.

His casual shrug looked a little stiff. 'Perhaps it's time to force another mutation of our relationship,' he said obliquely.

'And if it fails?'

His eyes darkened before his lashes swept down to veil his expression. 'I'm very good at adapting, *amante*.' He stood up abruptly and pulled her up. 'Time for a shower.'

She waited until they were both naked in the bedroom before she spoke.

'All that with Giacomo. I'm sorry it happened to you.'

His nostrils flared as bleakness washed over his face. Then slowly, he reasserted control.

Intense silver eyes travelled over her, lingering on her bare breasts with fierce hunger that made her nipples pucker. 'Don't be. Our feud brought me to Macau. Macau brought you to me. I call that a win-win situation, *amante*.'

He lunged up and grabbed her. Swinging her up in his arms, he crossed the suite and entered the adjoining bathroom.

'Wait, we haven't finished talking.'

'*Sì*, we have. I've revealed more of my past to you than to any other living soul. If I'm The Warlock you should be renamed The Sorceress.'

Demanding hands reached for her, propelled her backwards into the warm shower he'd turned on.

'But I don't know you nearly enough.'

He yanked the shower head from its cradle and aimed the nozzle in the curve of her neck. Water set to the perfect temperature soothed her and she allowed her mind to slide free of the questions that raced through her thoughts.

Understanding the boy he'd been, caught in the hell of a father who hated the very sight of him, Ruby found it wasn't a stretch to understand why he'd closed himself off.

But she'd seen beneath the façade, knew the playboy persona was just a defence mechanism. His relationship with Giacomo meant more to him than he was willing to admit.

As if reading her thoughts, he sent her a narrow-eyed glare. 'Don't try and *understand* me, Ruby. You may not like what you discover.'

'What's that supposed to mean?'

His eyes met hers and she glimpsed the dark river of anguish. 'It means there may never be enough underneath the surface to be worth your time.'

'Shouldn't I be the judge of that?'

He stepped forward and aimed the shower right between her thighs. Ruby gasped as sensation weakened her knees. She reached out for something to steady her and got a handful of warm, vibrant flesh. He angled the showerhead and she let out a strangled moan.

'No. This conversation is over, *amante*,' he growled. 'Now, open wider for me.'

Despite his clipped words of warning and the blatantly sexual way he chose to end their conversation, Narciso proceeded to wash her with an almost worshipful gentleness that undid her. When he sank down in front of her and washed between her legs, tears prickled her eyes.

*Hell, she was losing her mind.* Right from the beginning, she'd primed herself to hate this skilled playboy for his shallow feelings and careless attitude towards women and sex.

Instead she'd discovered that beneath the glossy veneer lurked a wounded soul, hurting from a tortured past.

She wanted to touch him the way he'd touched her. She reached out, but he grasped her hand in his, surged upright and set the showerhead back in its cradle. Beside the expensive gels and lotions a stack of condoms rested. Her heart lurched as she saw him reach for one and tear it open.

Grasping her waist, he whirled her around, then meshed his fingers through hers before raising them to rest above her head.

'*This* is the only conversation I want to continue. Are you ready?' he rasped low in her ear.

His thickness pressed against her bottom. Recalling the pleasure she'd experienced before, she could no more stop herself from answering in the affirmative than she could stop herself from breathing.

He slid slowly into her, leaving her ample time to adjust to his size. Pleasure shot through her, imprisoning her in its merciless talons.

Her groan mingled with his as steam rose around and engulfed them in a cocoon of rough kisses and wet bodies.

Narciso let pleasure wash over him, erasing, if only temporarily, the cutting pain of the past rehashed. The raw agony of recollection eased as he surged deeper into her and, even though he refused to acknowledge that her touch, her warmth and soft words eased his pain, he hung on to the feel of being in her arms.

She rewarded him by crying out as her muscles tightened around him.

*Dio mio,* she was unbelievable! And she'd got under his skin with minimum effort. But he'd get his control back.

He had to.

Because this unravelling, as much as it soothed the deep wound in his heart, couldn't continue. For now, though, he intended to lose his mind in the most spectacular way. He slid his hands down her sides, glorying in her supple wet skin. Encircling her tiny waist, he threw his head back and let desire roar through his body.

She woke to a silent room and a half-cold bed.

Ruby didn't need a crystal ball to know regret played a part in Narciso's absence. She felt equally exposed and vulnerable in the light of day at how they'd bared their pasts to each other.

But as much as she wanted to stay hidden beneath the covers, she forced herself to leave Narciso's bed. Shoving her hand through her hair, she picked up the T-shirt she'd brazenly discarded during her seduction routine. Her ripped-beyond-redemption panties she quickly balled up in her fist.

Luckily, she met no one on the way to her own cabin.

Ten minutes later, and freshly showered, she dressed in white shorts and a sea-green sleeveless top, and opened her door to find a steward waiting outside.

'Mr Valentino would like you to join him for breakfast on the first deck.'

Her pulse raced as trepidation filled her.

Yesterday morning hadn't really counted as *the morning after* because after their shower they'd returned to bed and spent the rest of the day making love.

She entered the salon that led to the sun-dappled dining space on the deck.

Fresh croissants, coffee, juices and two domed dishes had been neatly laid out. But her attention riveted on the man flicking his finger across his electronic tablet.

'Morning,' she said, her voice husky.

His gaze rose and caught hers. 'Feeling rested?'

She managed a nod and glanced around. 'Where are we?' The day before they'd moored at the Bay of Placencia after leaving the spectacular Blue Hole.

'We're just coming into Nicholas Caye. Mexico is just north of us.'

'It's beautiful here,' she said, nerves eating her alive at the intense look in his eyes.

'Sit down and relax, Ruby. It will be hard but I can just about stop myself from jumping on you and devouring you for breakfast.'

Heat shot into her cheeks. 'That wasn't what I was thinking,' she blurted, then pursed her lips and pulled out a chair.

Lifting the dome, she found her favourite breakfast laid out in exquisite presentation. Along with her preferred spear of asparagus. 'You made me Eggs Benedict?' Why the hell was her throat clogged by that revelation?

'I didn't make it myself, *tesoro*. I'm quite useless in the kitchen.'

But he'd taken note somewhere along the way that this was her favourite breakfast meal. 'I… Thank you.'

He snapped shut his tablet, shook out his napkin and laid it over his lap. 'Don't read anything into it, Ruby.'

'You keep saying that. And yet you can't seem to help yourself with your actions.'

He picked up his cutlery. 'I must be losing my edge,' he muttered.

'Or maybe you're rediscovering your human side?'

He smiled mockingly. 'Now I sound like a reformed comic villain.'

'No, that would require a lot of spandex,' she quipped before taking a bite of the perfectly cooked eggs.

He laughed, the sound rich and deep. Ruby barely stopped the food from going down the wrong way when she glimpsed the gorgeously carefree transformation of his face. 'You don't think I'd look good in spandex?' he asked drily.

'I think you'd look good in anything. And I also believe you can do anything you put your mind to.'

He tensed and slowly lowered his knife. 'Is there a hidden message in that statement?'

'No…maybe. This is my first morning-after conversation. I may say things that aren't thought through properly.'

Her gaze connected with his. An untold wealth of emotions swirled through his eyes and her stomach flipped her heart into her throat. 'Now you're selling yourself short. You're one of the most talented, intelligent people I know,' he delivered. 'And the waters are treacherous for me, too.'

'Really?' she whispered.

His lids lowered, breaking the connection. '*Sì*. I think we both know we're under each other's skin. It's up to us to decide what we do with that knowledge. What's your most prized ingredient?'

'The white Alba truffle, hands down,' she blurted, reeling at the abrupt question. 'Truffles make everything taste better.'

He slowly nodded. *'Bene.'* He said nothing else and resumed eating.

Ruby felt as if she'd fallen down the rabbit hole again. The conversation felt surreal. 'Why is that important?'

His jaw clenched slightly. 'I need a truffles day to make me feel better.'

'Why?'

'Because I can't wrap my mind around the things I spilled to you yesterday.'

'I didn't force anything out of you, Narciso.'

'Which makes it even more puzzling. So I need a minute and you're going to give it to me,' he stated blatantly.

'How?'

'We're going to spend the day together. And you're going to tell me every single thought that jumps into your head.'

Her brows rose. 'You want to use me to drown out your thoughts? You realise how unhealthy that sounds, right?'

His grimace was pained. 'Yes, I do, but I'll suffer through it this once in the hope I emerge unscathed.'

'And if you don't?'

Silver eyes darkened as they swept over her. The message in

them when they locked on her lips punched heat into her belly. 'Then I'll have to find a different solution.'

Six hours later, Narciso was wondering if he'd truly lost his mind. Although he'd learned everything about Ruby from the moment she'd learned to speak to the present she'd received from her roommate, Annie, on her last birthday, he yearned to know more.

Never had he taken even the remotest interest in a woman besides her favourite restaurant and what pleased her in bed. The fact that he wanted to know Ruby Trevelli's every thought sent a shiver of apprehension down his spine.

He was unravelling faster than he could keep things under control.

Every emotion he'd tried to lock down since that summer in Sicily threatened to swamp him. He gritted his teeth and watched Ruby surge out of the turquoise sea. She walked towards him, clad in the minuscule bikini he'd supplied her with. Her body—supple, curvy and dripping with water—made his mouth dry. When she dropped down next to him on the deserted beach they'd swum to, he burned with the need to reach for her. *Dio,* with the amount of sex they'd had how could he still be this hungry for her?

'So, is the inquisition over?' she asked playfully.

'*Si,*' he growled. 'It's over.'

Her gaze darted to his and he saw her tense at the coolness in his voice.

'Something wrong?'

'Why would anything be wrong?'

'Because you won the swim race from the yacht and you're not crowing about it. And you're not firing questions at me any more.'

'Perhaps I've had my fill for now.'

'Right. Okay,' she said.

He couldn't dismiss the hurt he heard in her voice. Turning, he watched her slim fingers play with the sugary white sand next to her feet. The desire to have those hands on his body grew until it became a physical pain.

Abruptly, he leaned forward and opened the gourmet picnic basket that had been delivered by his crew. He bypassed the food and reached for the chilled champagne. Popping the cork, he poured a glass and handed it to her.

'What are we celebrating?'

'The end of our beautiful down time. We leave for New York in the morning.'

Her eyes widened. Hell, he was more shocked than she was. His plan had been to stay for a full week. But the restlessness that had pounded through him all day wouldn't abate and he needed to find some perspective before it was too late.

At least once they returned to New York, back into the swing of things, everything would make sense again.

'You've asked my every thought for the last six hours. I think it's my turn now.'

He thought of sparing her the chaos running through his head. Then he mentally shrugged. 'I'm thinking why the thought of being free of you gives me no satisfaction.'

'Wow, you really know how to make a woman feel special, don't you?'

'I don't believe in sugar-coating words.'

'Please, spare me the macho stance. You know how to be gentle. What's going on here, Narciso? Why are you suddenly angry with me?'

He met her cloudy gaze and every thought disappeared but one. 'I'm finding how much I despise the thought of you ever taking another lover.'

Shocked blue eyes darted back to his. 'Narciso—'

'Now I've felt you shatter in my arms, the thought of you with another man makes my head want to explode.'

She gasped. 'Did you really just say that?'

He gave a harsh laugh and shook his head, as if testing his own sanity. '*Sì*, I just did.'

Beautifully curved eyebrows rose. 'And I'm guessing that's the first time you've admitted that to a woman?'

'It's the first time I've *felt* that way about any woman.' He shoved a hand through his hair.

*Dio mio,* he was like a leaking tap! Yesterday, he'd bared his past and his soul as if he were under the influence of a truth serum; today he was contemplating the future and the ache of not having Ruby Trevelli in it.

He knocked back the rest of his drink and surged to his feet. The crew member manning the launch a few dozen metres away looked his way and Narciso beckoned him over.

'It's time to go.' Reality and the cut and thrust of Wall Street would bring some much-needed common sense.

Unlike when they'd donned their swimming gear and laughingly dived from the side of the boat half an hour ago, silence reigned on the way back to *The Warlock*.

When he helped her up from the launch onto the floating swim deck at the back of the yacht, he forced himself to let her go, to stop his hands from lingering on her skin. As much as he wanted to touch her, weave his fingers through the damp hair curling over her shoulders, he couldn't give in to the spell threatening to pull him under.

'I have work to do. I'll catch up with you later.' With his insides twisting into seething knots, he walked away.

Ruby watched him walking away, a giant chasm opening up where pleasure had been half an hour ago. Things had been perfect. So much so, she'd pinched herself a couple of times to make sure the combination of sun, sea and drop-dead-gorgeous companion who'd laughed at her jokes and insisted on knowing every thought in her head was real.

She hadn't told him every thought, of course. For instance, she hadn't admitted that every time he'd touched her she'd heard angels sing to her soul. *That* would've been nuts. As would've been the admission that she was dying to make love with him again.

*No chance of that now...*

The hard-assed, enigmatic Narciso Valentino of three days ago hadn't made a comeback—and Ruby hoped against all hope the Narciso who chose to smother away his pain was gone for good—but a new Narciso had taken his place. One who fully recognised his vulnerabilities but then ignored them.

The need to go after him was so strong, she locked her knees and gripped the steel banister. He needed time.

Heck, *she* needed time to grapple with the mass of chaotic emotions coursing through her.

Scrambling for control, she went into her cabin and showered off the seawater. Clad in a long, flowered dress with a long slit down one side, she returned to the bar and lined bottles on the counter. Work would take her mind off her unsettling thoughts about Narciso Valentino.

She was measuring a shot of tequila into a shaker when one of the crew members approached.

'Can I get miss anything to eat?'

She shook her head. He smiled and turned to leave. 'Wait.' He paused. 'Have you seen my phone? I've been looking for it everywhere.'

He smiled. 'Oh, yes. One of my colleagues found it in the kitchen yesterday and handed it to Mr Valentino.'

Narciso had her phone? 'Thank you,' she murmured. She slowly screwed the top back on the bottle she'd opened and put the lemon wedges back in the cooler. Wiping her hands on a napkin, she left the deck.

His study was on the second level, past a large room with a sunken sitting area perfect for a dinner party. Like the rest of the vessel, every nook and cranny screamed bespoke and breathtaking luxury.

He growled admittance after her tense knock.

Seated in a leather armchair behind a large antique desk, he watched her enter with a frown. 'Is something wrong?'

'As long as you can adequately explain why you've commandeered my phone, no.'

'You're expecting a call?' he asked.

'Whether I am or not is beside the point.' She shut the door and approached his desk. 'You've had it since yesterday. Why didn't you hand it over?'

He shrugged. 'It must have slipped my mind.'

Somehow she doubted that. But watching him, seeing his face set in those stern, bleak lines she'd recognised from before made her heart stutter. She'd seen that look before.

She stepped closer, looked down and saw the pictures and papers strewn on his desk. The date stamp on the nearest one—showing that very morning—made ice slide down her spine. 'This is the business you had to take care of?'

He slowly set down the document in his hand. 'No. Believe it or not, I intended to scrap all this.'

'But?'

'But something came up.'

She glanced down at the photos. All depicted Giacomo. In one of them, the one Narciso had just dropped, he was dining with a stunning woman in her late twenties.

'Is that the *something?*' she asked, telling herself the pain lancing her chest wasn't jealousy.

His mouth tightened. 'We're not having this conversation, Ruby.'

'What happened to the man who was going to try to find a better way than this need to destroy and annihilate?'

His head tilted. 'That means the same thing.'

'Excuse me?'

'Destroy and annihilate—same meaning.'

'Really? That's all you have to contribute to this conversation?'

His jaw tightened. 'I told you I was good at adapting, *cara*. So why are you surprised that I'm adapting to the situation I find myself in? And seriously, screwing my brains out does not entitle you to weigh in on this.' He waved to his desk.

'Then why did you share it with me?' she replied.

For a moment he floundered. The clear vulnerability in his eyes made her breath catch. 'A misjudgment on my part.'

'I don't believe you.'

Shock widened his eyes. It occurred to her that she was probably the only person who'd dared challenge him this way.

Slowly, his face transformed into an inscrutable mask. Hell, he was so expert at hiding his feelings, he didn't need a mask at his next ball, she thought vaguely.

'I don't care whether you believe me or not. All I care about, what *you* should care about, is whether you can deliver on our agreement. I can easily find a replacement for you if you wish to terminate it when we get back to New York. Believe that.'

'Oh, I believe you. I also believe you think you can hide behind hatred and revenge to find the closeness you seek.'

'*Madre di Dio.* When I suggested you tell me every thought that came into your head, I had no idea you were a closet pop psychologist or I'd have thought twice. I unequivocally revoke that request, by the way.'

Listening to him denigrate what had been a perfect few hours in her life made anger and pain rock through her. Stepping back from the desk, she glanced at the picture, pain slashing her insides.

'I'll leave you to your machinations.' She rushed out and hurried up the stairs, swiping at the foolish tears clouding her vision.

If Narciso wanted to bury himself in the past, he was welcome to do so.

# CHAPTER TEN

'THERE'S A NEW recipe I want to try. Care to join me?'

Ruby looked up as Michel approached the counter she'd been working at for the last two hours.

Her mood had vacillated between anger and hurt, undecided on which emotion had the upper hand. Certainly, the piece of meat she'd been hammering was plenty tenderised.

She set it to one side, went to the sink to wash her hands, and rested her hip against the granite trim. 'As long as it's nothing Sicilian. I've had my fill of Sicilians for the foreseeable future.'

Michel cast her a curious glance, then gave a sly smile. 'No, what I'm thinking of is unapologetically French.'

She wiped her hand on her apron. 'Then count me in.'

'Excellent! It's a *sauce au chocolat* with a twist. You're making *croquembouche* for monsieur's dinner party in New York, *oui?*'

'Yes.' Although right now the thought of monsieur himself sautéed in a hot sizzling pan sounded equally satisfying.

'*Bien,* I thought instead of the caramel you could try using chillies.'

'Chilli chocolate? I love the idea. I always convince myself the heat burns away half the calories.'

He gave a very Gallic shrug. 'In my opinion, you do not need to worry about calories, *'moiselle.*'

The compliment took her by surprise. 'Umm, thanks, Michel.'

He shrugged again and started grabbing ingredients off the

shelves. They worked in harmony, measuring, chopping, straining until the scent of the rich chocolate sauce bubbling away in the pan filled the kitchen.

On a whim, she asked, 'Do you have any fresh vanilla pods? I want to try something.'

He nodded. Opening his spice cabinet, he grabbed the one long pod and handed it to her. Ruby cut it open and scraped out the innards. Then, slicing a few strips, she dropped them into the sauce. 'Let that infuse for a few minutes, and we'll try it.'

He rubbed his hands together with a childlike glee that made her laugh. After two minutes he grabbed a clean spoon and scooped a drop of the sauce. 'As the last ingredient was your idea, you sample it first.' He blew on it and held it to her lips.

She tasted it, shut her eyes to better feel the flavours exploding on her tongue. The decadent taste made her groan long and deeply.

'Ruby.'

Her name was a crack of thunder that had her spinning round.

Narciso stood in the doorway, the look on his face as dark and stormy as the tension thickening the air. For several seconds, everyone remained frozen.

Then silver eyes flicked to the Frenchman. 'Leave.'

Michel's eyes widened at the stark dismissal. Narciso took a single step forward to allow the chef to sidle past before he slammed the door shut behind him.

The sound of the lock turning made her nerves scream.

Slowly, Narciso walked towards her. With his every step she willed her feet to move in the other direction, away from the imposing body and icy fury bearing down on her. But she remained frozen.

She held her breath as he stopped a whisper from her.

'My intention was to find you and explain things better, perhaps even apologise for what I said in my study.'

Her heart lifted, then plummeted again when she deciphered his meaning. 'Well, I'm waiting.'

'Oh, you won't be getting an apology from me *now, amante.*'

He leaned over and looked into the copper pan bubbling on the stove. Picking up a spoon, he scooped up some sauce and sampled it.

'Not half bad. What is it?'

'Oh, I thought you'd recognise it, Narciso. This sauce I've named The Valentino Slimeball Special. It'll taste divine with the freshly made Playboy's Puffballs I'm planning on serving them with. You'll love it, trust me.'

Slowly, he lowered the spoon and speared her with those icy silver eyes. 'Say that again.'

'I'm pretty certain there's nothing wrong with your hearing.'

He tossed the spoon into the sink and leaned closer, bracing his hands on either side of her so she was locked in. 'Say it again anyway. I like the way that pretty mouth of yours pouts when you say *puffballs*.'

Despite his indolent words, his eyes glinted with fury. Her instinct warned her to retreat, but caged in like this, watching the erratic pulse beating at his throat, she knew any attempt at escape would be futile.

He was hanging on to his control by a thread. The sudden urge to shatter it the way he seemed to shatter hers so very easily made her stand her ground.

'You'll have to beg me if you want that.'

'Ah, Ruby, shall I let you in on personal insight?'

'Can I stop you?'

'I think you delight in pushing my buttons because you know it'll get you kissed. Am I right?'

'You're wrong.'

'Then why are you licking your lips like that? Anticipation has you almost insane with desperation right now.'

'You have a ridiculously high opinion of yourself.'

'Prove me wrong, then.'

'I won't play your stupid games.'

'Scared?'

'No. Uninterested.'

'Believe me, Ruby, this isn't a game.' When his hands went to undo the tie holding her dress together, she batted them away.

'Stop. What's wrong with you?'

His laugh was filled with bitter incredulity. 'I walk in here to find you moaning for another man and you ask *me* what's wrong with me?'

'You're *jealous?*'

Right before her eyes he seemed to deflate. His hold on her dress ties loosened. And the eyes that speared hers held hellish agitation.

'Yes! I'm jealous. Does that make you happy?'

Her senses screamed yes. Jealousy meant that she mattered in some way to him. The way he'd come to matter to her. 'Why did you come in here, Narciso?'

He sucked in a breath. 'I told you, to apologise.'

'Because my feelings are hurt or because *you* hurt me?'

He lifted a hand and trailed his fingers down her cheek. 'Because I hurt you,' he rasped deeply.

The breath shuddered out of her. 'Thank you for that.'

'Don't thank me, Ruby. What I'm feeling...what you make me feel, I don't know what to do with it. It may well come back and bite us both.'

'But at least you're acknowledging it. So what happened in your study?' she asked before she lost her nerve.

His lips firmed. 'That woman in the picture you saw. Her name is Maria.'

She bit her lip to stem the questions flooding her.

'She's Paolina's—my housekeeper's—granddaughter. I met her that summer ten years ago. She came to visit from Palermo. Paolina brought her to the house and we hung out. By the second week I'd convinced her to stay for the whole summer. I believed myself...infatuated with her.' His lips pinched until the skin showed white. 'I was young and naïve and respected her see-but-don't-touch edict. Until I found out she was giving it up to Giacomo.'

Shock rocked through her. 'She was *sleeping* with your father?'

'Not only sleeping with him. He'd convinced her to make a sex tape, which he forced me to watch on the last day of my stay in Sicily.' Something in the way he said it made her tense.

'What do you mean *forced?*'

His teeth bared in a parody of a smile. 'He had two of his bodyguards hold me down in a chair while the video played on a super-wide screen, complete with surround sound. It was quite the cinematic experience.'

Her mouth gaped. '*Oh, my God.* That's vile!'

'That's Giacomo,' he said simply.

'So, what is he doing with her in New York now?'

His jaw clenched. 'I don't know. The reason I opened the file in the first place was to tell my investigator to toss the case.'

'But now you think he's plotting something?'

'She's broke. Which means she's the perfect pawn for Giacomo.'

Ruby wanted to ask him how he knew that, but the forbidding look in his face, coupled with the anguish lurking in his eyes, changed her mind.

With the evidence of the two people who'd betrayed him before him, he'd have to have been a saint to remain unaffected. Hell, the thought of the double blow of betrayal made her heart twist in pain for him.

'I'm sorry I condemned you. I didn't know.'

Mingled fury and anguish battled in his eyes. 'What about this, Ruby *mio?* Do you know *this?*' he muttered roughly.

He parted her dress and his fingers were drifting down the bare skin of her belly, headed straight for her panty line, before she could exhale. Warm, sure fingers slid between her thighs before Ruby knew what had hit her.

Her cry of astonishment quickly morphed into a moan of need as his thumb flicked against her clitoris.

'Narciso!'

'*Dio,* how can I crave you this badly when I didn't know you a week ago?'

Need rammed through her and she clung to him. 'I don't know. You forget that I should hate this, too. I should hate you.'

He leaned in close, until his hot mouth teased her ear lobe. 'But then that would mean you were conforming to some lofty image you have in your head of your ideal man. You'd be denying that our little tiffs make you so wet you can barely stand it. I turn you on. I heat up your blood and make you feel more alive than you've ever felt. I make you crave all the things you've denied yourself. I know this because it's what you make me feel too. Close your eyes, Ruby.'

'No.' But already her eyelashes were fluttering down, heavy with the drugging desire stealing over her.

The next moment, his breath whispered along her jaw. 'Do you want me to stop?'

She groaned. 'Narciso…'

'Say no and I'll end this.'

She whimpered. 'You're not being fair.'

He laughed again. 'No, I'm not, but I never claimed I was a fair man. And when I feel as if my world is unravelling, halos don't sit well on my head.'

His fingers worked faster, firing up sparks of delight in her that quickly flared into flames.

'Oh! Oh, God.'

He kissed her hard and deep, then nibbled the corner of her mouth as she shattered completely. He ran his free hand down her back in a roughly soothing gesture as she floated back down. The mouth at her ear lobe feathered kisses down her jaw to her throat, then back up again.

'I'm sorry that I hurt you, Ruby. But I'm not sorry that I make you feel like this.'

The New York she'd left just days ago to travel to Macau was the same. Ruby knew that, and yet it was as though she were seeing it for the first time.

As they travelled through midtown towards Narciso's pent-house on the Upper East Side, the sights and sounds appeared more vibrant, soulful.

Part of her knew it was because she was seeing it through different eyes. The eyes of a woman who'd been introduced to passion and intense emotion.

She wanted to push that woman far away, deny all knowledge that she existed. But self-delusion had never been her flaw.

She'd slept for most of the four-hour flight from Belize City, a fact for which she was thankful. Awake and in close proximity to Narciso, she didn't think she could've avoided letting him see her confusion.

Their intense encounter in the kitchen on his yacht had been highly illuminating. Very quickly after granting her most delicious release, he'd walked away, leaving her replete and alarmingly teary.

She'd stood in the kitchen long after he'd left, clutching the sink and fighting a need to run after him and offer him comfort.

But how could she have when his words echoed in her ears.

*I hurt you...I'm sorry...I crave you...*

With each word, her heart had cracked open wider, until she'd been as raw as his voice had been.

As raw as she was now...

The need to run from her thoughts was very tempting. Giving in, she activated her returned phone. Several voice and text messages flooded into her inbox.

Three were from the same number. One she didn't recognise but suspected its origin.

She answered Annie's query as to when she would be returning and declined her invitation to a girls' night out when she was back from the West Coast. She wasn't ready to face anyone yet, least of all her perceptive roommate, when her emotions felt as if they'd been through a shredder.

The second message was from her mother, asking her to get in touch. She tensed as she listened to the message again. On the surface, it sounded innocuous, a mother asking after her child.

But she heard the undercurrents in her mother's voice and the hairs on her neck stood up. The other messages forgotten, she played the message a third time.

'What's wrong?' Narciso's deep voice cut across her flailing emotions.

'Nothing.'

'Ruby.'

She glanced at him, and her heart lurched. 'Don't look at me like that.'

'Like what?'

'Like you care.'

'I care,' he stated simply.

She sucked in a breath. 'How can you? You told me there was nothing beneath the surface, remember?'

She knew she was probably overreacting but the thought that her mother was reaching out to her because her father had in all likelihood had another affair made her stomach clench in anger and despair.

But unlike the numerous times before when she'd been angry with her parent, Ruby was realising just how harshly she'd misjudged her mother.

From the cocoon of self-righteousness, it'd been easy to judge, to see things in black and white. But having experienced how easy it was to lose control beneath the charisma and magnetism of a powerful man, how could she judge her mother?

Sure, she was aware that part of the reason her mother had stuck around was because she craved the fame that came with being part of a power couple. But Ruby also knew, deep down, her mother could be a success on her own.

A strong, warm hand curled over hers. Her gaze flew up to collide with silver eyes. 'I know what I said but I want to know what's going on anyway.'

His concern burrowed deep and found root in her heart. 'My mother left me a message to call her.'

He nodded. 'And this is troubling?'

'Yes. Normally she emails. She only calls me when something…bad happens.'

'Define bad.'

'My father…sleeping with a sous chef, or a waitress, or a member of their filming crew. That kind of *bad*.'

He swore. 'And she calls you to unburden?'

'And to put pressure on me to join their show. She seems to think my presence will curb my father's wandering eyes.'

His gaze remained steady on hers. 'You don't seem angry about it any more.'

Because he'd made her see herself in a different light: one that didn't fill her with bitterness.

Warmth from his hand seeped through, offering comfort she knew was only temporary.

'I've come to accept that sometimes we make choices in the hope that things will turn out okay. We take a leap of faith and stand by our choices. My mother's living in hope. I can't hate her for that.'

A flash of discomfort altered his expression. 'How very accommodating of you.'

'Accommodating? Hardly. Maybe I'm just worn out. Or maybe I'm finally putting myself into someone else's shoes and seeing things from their point of view.'

'And your father?'

'I can't forgive any man who toys with my…a woman's feelings. Who exploits her vulnerabilities and uses them against her.'

His sharp glance told her the barb had hit home. 'If you're referring to what happened in the kitchen—'

'I'm not.' A lance speared her heart. 'I think it's best we forget about that, don't you?'

*I think it's best we forget…*

He had no idea why that statement twisted in his gut but it did long after they'd reached his underground car park and entered the lift to his penthouse. Beside him Ruby stood stiffly, her face turned away from him.

He'd expected her to protest when he'd demanded she stay with him until after his VIP dinner party.

Instead, she'd agreed immediately.

The idea that she couldn't be bothered to argue with him made another layer of irrational anxiety spike through him.

Roughly he pushed the feeling away, meshed his fingers with Ruby's and tugged her after him when the lift doors opened.

Paolina exited one of the many hallways of his duplex penthouse to greet him.

Despite being in her late sixties, his housekeeper was as sprightly as she'd been when he was a boy.

'*Ciao, bambino. Come stai?*'

He responded to the affectionate greeting, let himself be kissed on both cheeks; allowed himself to bask in the warmth of her affection. But only for a second.

Catching Ruby to his side, he introduced her, noting her surprise as he mentioned Paolina's name.

She turned to him as Paolina took control of their luggage and headed to the bedrooms. 'Would this be the same Paolina who's related to Maria?'

His smile felt tight. '*Sì.*'

'I…I thought…'

'That I was a complete monster who cut everyone out of my life because of one incident? I'm not a complete bastard, Ruby.'

'No, you're not,' she murmured.

Her smile held none of the vivacity he'd come to expect. To *crave*. He wanted to win that smile back. Wanted to share what plans he'd put in place before they left Belize. But unfamiliar fear held him back.

Would she judge him for doing too little too late?

He watched her turn a full circle in the large living room, her gaze taking in and dismissing the highly sought-after pieces of art and exclusive decorative accessories most guests tended to gush over. The location of his apartment alone—on a thirtieth floor overlooking Central Park—was enough to pull a strong reaction from even the most jaded guest.

Ruby seemed more interested in the doors leading out of the room. 'Do you mind showing me to the kitchen? I'd like to see where I'll be working and if there's any equipment I need to hire. I should also have the final menu for you shortly. If there's anything you need to change I'd appreciate it if you let me know ASAP.'

Again he felt that unsettled notion of unravelling control. But then…when it came to Ruby, had he held control in the first place?

It certainly hadn't felt like it when he'd walked in on Ruby and Michel. Hearing her moan like that had been a stiletto wound to his heart.

In his jealousy and blind fury had he taken things too far? He tried to catch her eye as he walked beside her towards the kitchen but she refused to look at him.

He'd never had a problem with being given the silent treatment. But right now he wanted Ruby to speak, to tell him what was on her mind.

'What I've seen so far of the menu's fine. It's the perfect blend of continental Europe and good old-fashioned Italian. The guests will appreciate it.'

Her only reaction was to nod. They reached the kitchen and she moved away from him.

She inspected the room with a thoroughness that spoke of a love for her profession. Her long, elegant fingers ran over appliances and worktops and he found his disgruntlement escalating.

*Dio,* was he really so pathetic as to be jealous of stainless-steel gadgets now? He shook his head and stepped back. 'I'm leaving for the office. We will speak this evening.'

Four hours later, he was pacing his office just as he had been last week.

Only this time there was no sign of the ennui that had

gripped him. Instead, a different form of restlessness prowled through him, one that was unfamiliar and mildly terrifying.

He laughed mirthlessly and pushed a hand through his hair. Narciso wasn't afraid to admit so far he wasn't loving being thirty. He seemed to be questioning his every action. He was even stalling on the deal with Vladimir Rudenko. Did he really need to start another media empire in Russia?

Going ahead with it would mean he'd have to spend time in Moscow. Away from New York. Away from Ruby. *Dio,* what the hell was she doing in his head?

Gritting his teeth, he strode to his desk and pressed the intercom that summoned his driver.

The journey from Wall Street to his penthouse took less than twenty minutes but it felt like a lifetime. Slamming the front door, he strode straight into the kitchen. He needed to tell her of his plans. Needed her to know he'd chosen a different path…

She was elbow deep in some sort of mixture. She glanced up, eyes wide with surprise. 'You're back.'

'We need to talk.'

'What about?'

'About Giacomo—' he tensed, then continued '—about my father.'

Her eyes grew wider. 'Yes?'

'I've decided to end—'

A phone beeped on the counter. A look of unease slid over her features as she wiped her hands and activated the message. A few seconds later, all trace of colour left her cheeks. 'I have to go.'

He frowned. 'Go where?'

'Midtown. I'll be back in an hour.'

'I'll drive you—'

'No. I'll be fine. Really. I've been cooped up in here all afternoon. I need the fresh air.'

'Fresh air in New York is a misnomer.' He continued to watch her, noting her edginess. 'Is it your parents?'

Her fingers twisted together. 'No, it's not.' Sincerity shone from her eyes.

He nodded. 'Fine. I just wanted you to know, you have my backing one hundred per cent. After the party, I'll have the papers drawn up to provide the funds you need for the restaurant.'

'Th-thank you. That's good news.' The definite lack of pleasure on her face and voice caused his spine to stiffen. She reached him and tried to slide past.

Unable to help himself, he caught her to him and kissed her soft, tempting mouth. She yielded to the kiss for a single moment before she wrenched herself away.

*'Amante—'*

'I have to go.'

Before he could say another word she snatched her bag from the counter and walked out of the door.

Narciso stood frozen, unable to believe what had happened. By the time he forced himself to move, Ruby was gone.

# CHAPTER ELEVEN

RUBY ENTERED THE upscale restaurant at the stroke of six and gave her name.

A waiter ushered her to a window seat. It took seconds to recognise the man at the table. Shock held her rigid as she stared at him.

Without his mask, Giacomo Valentino bore a striking resemblance to his son. Except his eyes were dull with age and his mouth cruel with entrenched bitterness.

'I knew I recognised you from somewhere, Ruby Trevelli,' Giacomo Valentino said the moment she sat down. 'The wonders of modern technology never cease to amaze me. A few clicks and I had everything I needed to know about you and your parents.'

She tensed. 'What do you want?'

'A way to bring my son down. And you will help me.'

She rushed to her feet. 'You're out of your mind.'

'I met with your loan shark today,' he continued conversationally. 'As of three hours ago, I own twenty-five per cent of your yet-to-be-built restaurant. If you walk out of here, I'll call in the debt immediately.'

Heart in her throat, she slowly sank back into her seat. 'Why are you doing this?'

His face hardened. 'You saw how he humiliated me in Macau.'

'Yes, and since then I've also heard what you did to him. And I know you met with Maria yesterday.'

A flash of fear crossed his face but it was quickly smothered. 'So Narciso knows?'

'Yes.'

The old man visibly paled.

'Give it up, Giacomo. You're out of options because there's no way I'll help you further your vendetta against your own flesh and blood.'

The flash came again, and this time she saw what it was. Deep, dark, twisted pain. 'He's a part of me that should never have come into being.'

She shook her head. 'How can you say that?'

'He took away from me the one thing I treasured most in this world. And he struts around like the world owes him a living.'

Ruby heard the black pain behind his words and finally understood. Deep down, Giacomo Valentino was completely and utterly heartbroken over losing his wife.

A part of her felt sympathy for him. But she could tell Giacomo was too set in his thinking to alter his feelings towards his son.

Narciso, on the other hand, wasn't. Ruby had seen gentleness in him. She'd seen compassion, consideration, even affection towards Paolina, the grandmother of the woman who'd betrayed him. He had the capacity to love, if only he'd step back from the brink of the abyss of revenge he was poised on.

*And will you be the one to save him?*

Why not? He'd helped her come to terms with her own relationship with her parents. She'd called her mother this afternoon, and, sure enough, her father had strayed again. But this time, Ruby had offered her mother a shoulder to cry on. They'd spoken for over an hour. Tears had been shed on both sides. An hour later, she'd received a text from her mother to say she'd contacted an attorney and filed for a divorce from her husband.

Ruby knew the strength it'd taken for her mother to break free. Taking a deep breath, she looked Giacomo in the eye. 'You probably don't want my advice but I'll give it anyway. You and Narciso both lost someone dear to you. You were lucky enough to know her. Have you spared a thought for the child who never knew his mother?'

'*Ascolta—!*'

'No, you listen. Punishing a baby for its mother's death went out with the Dark Ages. Do you have any idea how much he's hurting?'

Pale silver eyes narrowed. 'You're in love with my son.'

Her heart lurched, then hammered as if fighting to get away from the truth staring her in the face. Her fingers tightened on her bag. 'I won't be a party to whatever you're cooking up.'

'You disappoint me, Miss Trevelli. Before you go, I should tell you that your loan shark provided me with an extensive file on you, which details, among other things, a building on Third and Lexington.'

Panic flared high. *'My parents' restaurant?'*

Giacomo gave a careless nod.

'I swear, if you dare harm them I'll—'

Giacomo put a hand on her arm. 'My request is simple.'

She wanted to bolt but she remained seated.

His speculative gaze rested on her. 'My son is taken with you. More than he has been with any other woman.'

Her insides clenched hard. 'You're wrong—'

'I'm right.' He leaned forward suddenly. 'I want you to end your relationship with him.'

Her mouth dried. 'There is no relationship.'

'End it. Sever all ties with him and I'll make sure your parents' livelihood remains intact. I'll even become your benefactor with your restaurant.'

Frantically she shook her head. 'I don't want your charity.'

His eyes narrowed. 'Do you really want to risk crossing me? I urge you to remember where my son inherited his thirst for revenge from.'

Feeling numb, she rose. This time he didn't stop her.

Her thin sweater did nothing to hold the April chill at bay

as she blindly struck through the evening crowd. She only re-alised where she was headed when the subway train pulled into the familiar station.

Her apartment was soothingly quiet. Dropping her bag, she went to the small bar she'd installed when she moved in.

Blanking her thoughts, she went to work, mixing liqueurs with juices, spirits with the bottle of champagne she'd been gifted on her birthday. Carefully she lined up the mixtures that worked and discarded the rest. She was on her last set when she heard the pounding on the door.

Breath catching, she went to the door and glanced into the peeper.

Narciso loomed large and imposing outside her door. Jump-ing back, she toyed with not answering.

'Let me in, Ruby. Or so help me, I'll break this door down.'

With shaking hands, she released the latch.

He took a single, lunging step in and slammed the door be-hind him. 'You said you'd be an hour, tops.' Silver eyes bore into her, intense and frighteningly invasive.

She forced a shrug. 'I lost track of time.'

'If you wanted to return here all you needed was to say.' There was concern in his voice, coupled with the vulnerability he'd been unable to hide on the yacht.

Knowing what had put that vulnerability there, knowing what his father's lack of love had done to him, made her chest tighten. She so desperately wanted to reach for him, to soothe his pain away.

But in light of what she faced, there was only one recourse where Narciso was concerned. 'I didn't realise I had to answer to you for my movements.'

He frowned and speared a hand through his hair. The way it fell made her guess he'd been doing it for a while. Swallow-ing hard, she forced her gaze away and walked into the small living room.

He followed. 'You don't,' he answered. 'But you said you'd come back. And you didn't.'

'It's no big deal, Narciso. I wanted to return home for a bit.'

'Are you ready to return now?' he shot back, his gaze probing.

The need to say yes sliced through her. 'No. I think I'll spend the night here.'

He started to speak. Stopped, and looked around. She didn't even bother to look at her apartment through his eyes. Annie had used the term shabby chic when they'd picked up knick-knacks from flea markets and second-hand shops to furnish their apartment. The plump sofas were mismatched, as were the lamps and cushions. The pictures that hung on the walls were from sidewalk artists whose talent had caught Ruby's eye.

'Why are you here, Narciso?'

Narciso walked over to a lampshade and touched the bohemian fringe. 'I tried to tell you earlier. I've called off the vendetta with my father.'

Shock rocked through her, followed swiftly by sharp regret. 'Why?'

He shoved his hand into his pockets and inhaled. 'In a word? *You.* You're the reason.' Again that vulnerability blazed from his eyes. Along with a wariness as she remained frozen.

'I shouldn't be the reason, Narciso. You should do it for yourself.'

He shrugged. 'I'm working my way to that, *amante*. But I need your help. You set me on this road. You can't walk away now.'

*Oh, God!*

She choked back a sob and fled to the bar. He followed and saw the drinks lined up on the counter.

'You were working?'

'I never stop.'

'What have you come up with?' There was a genuine interest in his tone. For whatever reason, he wanted to know more about her passion.

His softening attitude towards her sent her emotions into panicked freefall. Belize had warned her she was at serious risk of developing feelings for Narciso Valentino. Seeing him in her home, touching her things, making monumental confessions, made her want to rush to him and burrow into his chest, hear his heart pounding against her own. But she couldn't. Not now.

She shoved her hands into her jeans pockets and shrugged. 'This and that.'

He flicked a glance at her. Then he picked up the nearest drink and took a sip. 'What's this one called?'

*Push him away!*

She took a deep, frantic breath. '*Sleazy Playboy*. The one next to it is *The Studly Warlock*, the blue one is the *Belize Bender*, and the pink one I've termed *The Virgin Sacrifice*.'

He stiffened.

'There's a black Sambuca one I'm intending to call *Crazy, Stupid Revenge*—'

'Enough, Ruby. I get the message. I've upset you. Again. Tell me how to make it better.' He looked over at her and his eyes held a simple, honest plea.

*Dear God.* Narciso wasn't all gone at all. In fact, right at that moment, he was the single, most appealing thing in her life.

Heat and need and panic and lust surged under her skin as his gaze remained steady on hers. With every fibre in her being she wanted to cross the room and launch herself into his arms.

Giacomo's face flashed across her mind.

'There's nothing to make better because there's nothing between us.'

His eyes widened. *'Scusi?'*

'We had what we had, Narciso. Let's not prolong it any further.'

His eyes slowly hardened. In quick strides, he crossed the room and jerked her into his body. The contact threatened to sizzle her brain. Throwing out her hands against his chest, she tried to break free. He held tight.

'Let me go!'

'Why? Scared I'll prove you wrong?'

'Not at all—'

He swooped down and captured her mouth. His kiss was raw, possessive and needy.

'What the hell's happening, Ruby?' he whispered raggedly against her mouth.

Again her heart skittered.

Briefly, she thought to come clean, tell him where she'd been. Panic won out.

'Dammit, Ruby, kiss me back!' he pleaded raggedly against her lips.

She couldn't deny him any more than she could deny herself what would surely be her last time of experiencing this magic with him.

Desperate hands grazed over his chest to his taut stomach. Grasping the bottom of his T-shirt, she pulled it up. He helped her by tugging it over his head and flinging it away. Eyes blazing with an emotion she was too afraid to name met hers. Stepping forward, she placed an open-mouthed kiss on his collarbone.

His hiss of arousal echoed around the room. Emboldened, she used her teeth, tongue and mouth to drive them both crazy. When he stumbled slightly, she realised she'd pushed him towards the sofa. With a hard push she sent him sprawling backwards. Within seconds he was naked, his perfect body beckoning irresistibly. Driven by guilt and hunger, she stripped off her T-shirt and bra and unsnapped her jeans.

With a shake of his head, he covered her hands with his. 'Let me.'

The slow slide downward was accompanied by hot, worshipful kisses that brought tears to her eyes. Afraid her emotions would give her away, she hurriedly stepped out of the jeans and pushed him back down again and resumed the path she'd charted moments before.

His groan when her lips touched the tip of his shaft was ragged and raw. But encouraging hands speared through her hair, holding her to her task.

Boldly, she took him in her mouth. *'Dio,* Ruby!'

She looked up at him. His eyes were closed, his neck muscles taut from holding on to his control. Taking him deeper, she lost herself in the newfound power and pleasure, her heart singing with an almost frightening joy at being able to do this, one last time.

Tomorrow would bring its own heartache but for now—

'*Basta!*' he rasped. 'As much as I'd love to finish in your mouth, my need to be inside you is even greater.'

He pulled her up and astride him. Reaching for his discarded jeans, he took a condom from his back pocket.

The thought that he'd come prepared dimmed her pleasure for a second. But realising what the alternative would've meant, she took the condom from him, tore it open and slipped it on his thick shaft, experiencing a momentary pang at how big he was.

Silver eyes gleamed at her. 'We fit together perfectly, *tesoro,* remember?' he encouraged gently.

Nodding, she raised her hips and took him inside her.

Delicious, sensational pleasure built inside her, setting off fireworks in her body. His face a taut mask of pleasure, his hands settled on her thighs and he allowed her to set the pace. But this new, deeper penetration was her undoing. Within minutes, her spine tingled with impending climax. She had no resistance when Narciso reared up, sucked one nipple into his mouth and sent her over the edge.

She surfaced from the most blissful release to find their positions reversed. Narciso's fingers were tangled in her hair and his mouth buried in her throat.

When he raised his head, the depth of emotion on his face made her breath catch.

'I need you, Ruby,' he repeated his earlier statement. Only this time, she was sure he didn't mean sexually.

The knowledge that things would never be right between them sent pure, white-hot pain through her heart.

Unable to find the right words to respond, she cradled his face. Locked in that position, his eyes not leaving hers, he surged inside her and resumed the exquisite, soul-searing love-making. Eventually, he groaned his release and took her mouth in a soft, gentle kiss, murmuring words she understood but refused to allow into her heart.

Tears sprang into her eyes and she rapidly blinked them away, glad that he was rising and putting his clothes back on.

'I can stay here, or we can return to my place.' Although his tone wasn't as forceful as before, she knew he wouldn't accept a third choice.

'I'll come back with you.' Despite all that had happened, she still had his dinner party to cater for.

They dressed in silence and she studiously avoided the puzzled glances he sent her way.

When he caught her hand in his in the lift on the way to the ground floor, she let him. When he brought the back of her hand to his lips and kissed it, she sucked in a deep breath to stop the tears clogging her throat from suffocating her.

In his car, he pulled her close, clamped both arms around her and tucked her head beneath his chin. In the long drive back to the Upper East side, neither of them spoke but he took every opportunity to run gentle hands down her arms and over her hair.

Unable to stop herself, she felt tears slide down her cheeks. *Dear God,* what the hell had she done? Of all the foolish decisions she could've made, she'd gone and fallen in love with Narciso Valentino.

*'Qualunque cosa che, oi facevo io sono spiacente,'* he murmured raggedly in her ear. *Whatever I did, I'm sorry.*

The tears fell harder, silent guilty sobs racking her frame.

He led her to the shower the moment they returned to his penthouse. Again, in silence, he washed her, then pulled a clean T-shirt of his over her head. Pulling back the covers to his bed, he tugged her close and turned out the lights.

'We'll talk in the morning, Ruby. Whatever is happening between us, we'll work it out, *sì?*'

She nodded, closed her eyes and drifted off to a troubled sleep.

She jerked awake just after 5:00 a.m., fear and anguish

churning through her body. The need to tell Narciso the truth burned through her.

She needed to tell him about the meeting last night. Needed to let him know that Giacomo's thirst for revenge burned brighter than ever.

Her fear for her parents had blinded her to the fact that she was stronger than Giacomo's blackmail threats. There was no way Ruby would do as Giacomo asked.

She loved Narciso, and, if there was any way he reciprocated those feelings, she didn't intend to walk away.

But she had to warn him that Giacomo might come at him by a different means once he found out Ruby had no intention of walking away.

Turning her head, she watched Narciso's peaceful profile as he slept. Her heart squeezed and she sucked in a breath as tears threatened.

She'd never have believed she could fall in love so quickly and so deeply. But in less than a week she'd fallen for the world's number-one playboy.

But there was far more to Narciso than that. And if there was a chance for them…

Vowing to speak to him after the party, she slid out of bed, dressed without waking him and left the bedroom.

Armed with the black card he'd given her yesterday, she went outside and hailed a taxi. The market in Greenwich was bustling by the time she arrived just before six. For the next hour, she lost herself in picking the freshest vegetables, fruit and staples she needed for the dinner party.

Next, she stopped at the upmarket wine stockist.

Narciso had enough wine and vintage champagne so she only selected the spirits and liqueurs she needed for her cocktails.

She was leaving the shop when her phone buzzed. Heart jumping into her throat because she knew who it would be, she answered.

'You left without waking me,' came the quiet accusation.

'I needed to get to the market before sunrise.'

He sighed. 'I'm sorely tempted to cancel this event but I have several guests flying in specially.'

'Why would you want to cancel it?'

'Because it's coming between me and what I want right now.'

Her heart thundered. 'Wh-what do you want?'

'You. Alone. A proper conversation with no disturbances. To get to the bottom of whatever last night was about.'

'I'm sorry, I should've told you…' She stopped as a phone rang in the background.

'*Scusi,*' he excused himself, only to return a minute later. 'I need to head to the office but I'll be back by five tonight, *si?*'

'Okay, I'll see you then.'

He paused, as if he wanted to say something. Then he ended the call.

Ruby was glad for the distraction of getting everything ready for the dinner party. By the time Michel showed up midafternoon, she'd almost finished her preparations.

They talked through the recipes she'd planned and settled on the timing.

'Monsieur tells me you'll be manning the bar tonight?'

'The idea is to divide my time between the bar and the kitchen. I know I can trust you to hold the fort here?'

'Of course.' He peered closer at her. 'Is everything all right?'

She busied herself placing large chunks of freshly cut salmon in its foil wrappings.

'It will be when the evening's over. I always get the jitters at these events.'

His knowing glance told her he hadn't missed her evasiveness. Thankfully, Paolina entered the kitchen and Ruby sighed with relief.

The planning team arrived at four. After that, deliveries flooded in. Flowers, a DJ and lighting specialists who set up on the terrace.

But the most unexpected delivery came in the form of a couture designer bearing a zipped-up garment bag, which she handed over and promptly departed. The note pinned to the stunning powder-blue floor-length gown was simple—*a beautiful gown for a beautiful woman.*

Joy burst through her heart, made her smile for the first time that day.

For the job she had to do tonight, it was severely impractical, as were the silver shoes almost the exact shade as Narciso's eyes, but as she walked into Narciso's bedroom and hung up the dress she knew she would wear it.

Narciso was late. He arrived barely a half-hour before his guests were due to arrive and walked into the bedroom just as she was putting finishing touches to her upswept hair.

He froze in the doorway, and stared. 'You look gorgeous, *bellissima.*'

She turned from the mirror, a cascade of love, trepidation and anxiety smashing through her. How would he take the news of his father's continued scheming?

*Remember where my son inherited his thirst for revenge...*

Forcing down the shiver of apprehension, she murmured, *'Grazie.'*

His eyes darkened with pleasure. 'You need to speak more Italian. Or better still Sicilian. I'll teach you,' he said as he shrugged off his jacket and tugged at his tie.

Then he strode to where she stood. Snaking a large hand around her nape, he pulled her in for a long, deep kiss. Then with a groan he stepped back.

'Give me fifteen minutes and I'll be with you.'

'Okay.'

*'Dio,* I must be growing a conscience, *bellissima,* since I keep dismissing the idea of calling this party off.'

She forced a laugh. 'You must be.'

Shaking his head, he entered the bathroom. She stood there until the sound of the shower pulled her from her troubled thoughts.

She was behind the bar, pouring the first of the cocktails into glasses, when he emerged.

The sight of him in a superbly cut grey suit and a blue shirt that matched her dress made her heart slam into her throat. He'd taken a single step towards her when the doorbell rang.

He rolled his eyes dramatically, then his gaze drifted over her in heated promise before he nodded for the butler to answer the door.

For the next two hours, Ruby let her skills take over, serving food that drew several compliments from the dinner guests.

She declined when Narciso invited her to join them at the dinner table. Although his eyes narrowed in displeasure, there was very little he could do about it, much to her relief.

She was preparing a round of after-dinner cocktails when she looked up and gasped.

Giacomo was framed in the penthouse doorway.

Her gaze swung to Narciso; frozen, she watched his head turn and his body tense as he saw his father.

For several seconds, they eyed each other across the room.

Giacomo sauntered in as if he belonged. Several guests, sensing the altered atmosphere, glanced between father and son.

'Hey, watch it!'

She jerked and looked down to find she'd overfilled a glass and the lime-green cocktail was spilling over the counter.

Setting the shaker down, she grabbed a napkin.

'*Bona sira,* Ruby,' came the mocking voice. 'How lovely you look.'

Her head snapped up and connected with Giacomo's steely gaze. Surprise that he hadn't headed straight for his son held her immobile. Long enough for him to calmly reach across the counter, take her hand and press a kiss on her knuckles.

She tried to snatch her hand away but he held on tight, a triumphant smile playing about his lips. 'Play along, little one, and all your problems will go away,' he said in a low voice.

'I have no intention of playing along with anything.'

'It doesn't matter one way or the other. Narciso is infatuated with you. He'll see what I want him to see.'

With the clarity of a klaxon, everything fell into place.

She'd been played. Giacomo had always intended *this* to be his revenge. By meeting with him last night, she'd only given him more ammunition.

Heart shattering, she glanced over to where Narciso stood stock still, his eyes icy lakes of shock.

# CHAPTER TWELVE

'Narciso—'

'Don't speak.'

Narciso paced in his office, marvelling at how his voice emerged so calm, so collected, when his insides bled from a million poisonous cuts.

'Listen to him, *bedda*. He's prone to childish tantrums when he's upset. Just look at how he threw out all his guests a few minutes ago—'

'Shut up, old man, or so help me I'll bury my fist in your face.'

Giacomo shook his head and glanced at Ruby in a *what-did-I-say?* manner.

'What the hell are you doing here?'

'Ruby told me you were having a party. I decided to invite myself.'

'I didn't—!'

'*Ruby* told you? When?' Narciso's gaze swung to her, then returned to his father.

'Last night, when she met me for dinner.'

'He's lying, Narciso.' He heard the plea in her voice and tried to think, to rationalise what was unfolding before him. Unfortunately his brain seemed to have stopped working.

From the moment he'd seen Giacomo take her hand and kiss it, time had jerked to a stop, then rewound furiously, throwing up old memories that refused to be banished.

Forcing himself into the present, he stared at Ruby. The gorgeous firecracker who'd got under his skin. The woman who'd made love to him last night in her apartment as if her soul belonged to him.

Waking up this morning to find her gone had rocked him to his soul. The realisation that he wanted her in his bed and in his arms every morning and night for the rest of his life had been shocking but slowly, as the idea had embedded itself into his heart, he'd known it was what he wanted.

He loved her. He, who'd never loved anything or anyone in his life, had fallen in love...

With a woman who would meet with his father and not tell him...allow Giacomo to put his hand on her.

No! He couldn't have made the same mistake twice.

*Ruby was different...*

Wasn't she? Reeling, he watched Giacomo stroll to the large sofa in the room and ease himself into it. His attitude reeked a confidence that shook Narciso to the core.

He forced himself to speak. 'Ruby, is this true?'

She shook her head so emphatically, tendrils fell down her graceful neck. 'No, it's not. I only—'

'You have a spy following me around. I know you do. He reports to you twice a week. Today is one of those days, I believe,' Giacomo said.

Narciso's fists tightened. 'Not any more.'

Surprise lit the old man's eyes. 'Really? You must be going soft. Luckily, I had my own pictures taken.'

Giacomo reached into his pocket and threw down a set of photos on the coffee table.

Narciso felt his body tremble as he moved towards the table. For the first time in his life, he knew genuine fear. He glanced up to see Ruby's eyes on his face.

'Please, Narciso, it's not what you think. I can explain.'

He took another step. And there in Technicolor was the woman he loved, with the man he'd believed until very recently he hated most in his life.

Ironically, it was Ruby who'd made him look deeper into himself and acknowledge the fact that it wasn't hate that drove him but a desperate need to connect with the person who should've loved him.

His legs lost the ability to support him and he sank into his chair. Vicious pain slashed at his heart and he fought against the need to howl in agony.

'Leave,' he rasped.

'I warned you you would never best me,' his father crooned.

Slowly, Narciso raised his head and looked at his father. Despite his triumph, he looked haggard. The years of bitterness had taken their toll. It was what he'd risked becoming…

'She insisted on saving you, do you know that?'

Ice filled his gut. *'Scusi?'*

Giacomo's gaze scoured him. 'Your *mamma*. She had a chance to live. The doctor who arrived could only save one of you. She had a chance and she chose you.' Bitterness coated every word.

'And you've hated me for it ever since, haven't you?'

Giacomo's face hardened. 'I never wanted children. She knew that. If she'd only listened to me, she'd still be alive.' He inhaled and surged to his feet. 'What does it matter? Come, Ruby. You're no longer wanted here.'

Narciso snarled. 'Lay another finger on her and it's the last thing you'll ever do.'

His father jerked in shock, then his face took on a grey hue. Narciso watched, stunned, as Giacomo clutched his chest and began to crumple.

'Narciso, I think he's having a heart attack!'

For several seconds Ruby's words didn't compute. When the meaning spiked, poker hot, into his brain, he reached out and caught Giacomo as he fell.

Behind him he heard Ruby dialling and speaking to emergency personnel as he tore open his father's shirt and began chest compressions.

'*Madre di Dio, non,*' he whispered, the fear clutching his chest beginning to spread as his father lay still.

The next fifteen minutes passed by in a blur. The ER helicopter landed on the penthouse roof and emergency personnel took over.

He sagged against a wall when they informed him Giacomo was still alive but would need intensive care immediately.

'He'll pull through. I'm sure of it.'

He looked up to find Ruby in front of him, holding out a glass of whisky. He took it and knocked it back in one gulp.

It did nothing to thaw the ice freezing his heart.

'Leave.' He repeated the word he'd said what seemed like a lifetime ago.

Shock rushed over her face.

'Narciso—'

He threw the glass across the room and heard it shatter. 'No. You don't get to say my name. Never again.'

He took satisfaction in seeing tears fill her eyes. 'I can explain—'

'It's too late. I told you this thing between Giacomo and I was over. I'd trusted your counsel, taken your advice and abandoned this godforsaken vendetta. But where was your trust, *tesoro mio*? You knew this was coming. And you said nothing!'

'He threatened my parents!'

His expression softened for a split second. Then grew granite hard. 'Of course he did. But his threats meant more to you than your belief that I would help you. That we could fight him together!' He couldn't hide the raw pain that flowed out of his voice.

'I didn't want to fight! And I was going to tell you. Tonight after the party.'

'We'll never know now, will we?' he said scathingly.

'Narciso—'

'Your actions spoke clearly for you. Unfortunately for you, you made the same mistake Maria did. *You chose the wrong side.*'

* * *

Ruby smoothed her hand down the sea-green dress and tried to stem the butterflies.

In less than half an hour, the grand opening of Dolce Italia would be under way.

Two months of sheer, sometimes blessedly mind-numbing, hard work. She'd volunteered for every job that didn't require specialist training in the blind hope of drowning out the acute pain and devastation of having to live without Narciso. Her success rate had been woefully pathetic...

'Are you ready yet, *bella bambina?* The paparazzi will be here in a minute.' Her mother entered, wearing an orange silk gown that pleasantly complemented her slim figure. Despite being in her late forties, Paloma looked ten years younger. With her divorce from her philandering husband firmly underway, she appeared to have acquired a new lease on life. The spring in her step had grown even bolder when Ruby had allowed her to take a financial stake in the restaurant.

She stopped in the middle of the small room they'd converted to a dressing room at the back of the two-storey restaurant and cocktail bar in the prime location in Manhattan.

'Oh, you look stunning,' she said, then her eyes darkened with worry. 'A little on the thin side, though.'

'Don't fuss, Mamma.'

'It's my job to fuss. A job I neglected for years.'

Knowing she was about to lapse into another self-recriminating rant, Ruby rushed forward and hugged her. 'What's done is done, Mamma. Now we look forward.'

Her mother blinked brown eyes bright with unshed tears and nodded. 'Speaking of moving forward, the most exquisite bouquet of flowers arrived for you.'

Ruby's breath caught, then rushed out in a gush of pain. 'I don't want them.'

Her mother frowned. 'What woman doesn't want flowers on the most spectacular night of her life?'

'Me.'

'Are you sure you're all right? Last week you sent back that superb crate of white Alba truffles, the week before you refused the diamond tennis bracelet. I wish you'd tell me who all these gifts are from.'

'It doesn't matter who they're from. I don't want any of them.' She fought the rising emotions back. She'd shed enough tears to last her a lifetime.

*Not tonight.* With her mother as her new business partner, she'd paid off Giacomo's loan and closed that chapter.

Tonight, she would push Narciso and his in-your-face gifts out of her mind and bask in her accomplishment.

'I'm ready.'

They entered the large reception area to find a three-deep row of photographers and film crew awaiting them. In the time she'd decided to open the restaurant with her mother, Paloma had guided her in how to deal with the press. Where her reaction to them had been led by fear and resentment, now she used banter and firmness to achieve her aim.

With the press conferences and TV junkets taken care off, her mother passed her the scissors and she moved to a large white ribbon.

'Ladies and gentlemen, my mother, Paloma, and I are proud to declare Dolce Italia open—'

At first she thought she was hallucinating. Then the face became clearer.

Narciso stood to one side of the group, his silver eyes square on her face.

'Ruby?' she heard her mother's concerned voice from far away as the heavy scissors slipped from her grasp.

'Ruby!'

She turned and fled.

'Ruby.' He breathed her name as if it were a life-giving force, pulling her from the murky depth of pain. 'Open the door, *per favore.*'

She snatched the door she'd slammed shut moments ago

wide open. 'You ruined my opening. Weeks of preparation, of breaking my back to make this perfect, and you swooped in with your stupid face and your stupid body and *ruined* it.' She found herself inspecting his face and body and tore her gaze away.

'*Mi dispiace.* I wanted…I *needed* to see you.'

'Why? What could you possibly have to say to me that you haven't already said?'

His jaw tightened. 'A lot. You returned all my gifts.'

'I didn't want them.'

He took a step into the room. 'And the NMC cheque? You returned it to me ripped into a hundred pieces.'

'I was making a point. Why did you keep sending me stuff?'

'Because I refused to contemplate giving up. I refused to imagine what my life would be like without the thinnest thread of hope keeping me going.'

She wanted to keep her gaze averted, but, like a magnet, it swung towards him.

He looked incredible, the five-o'clock shadow gracing his jaw making him look even more stunning. But a closer look pinpointed a few surprising changes.

'You've lost weight,' she murmured.

He shut the door behind him and she caught the faint snick of the lock. 'So have you. At least I have an excuse.'

'Really?'

'*Sì,* Michel threatened to quit. We agreed on a month-long vacation.'

'You don't deserve him.'

He grimaced. 'That's entirely true. He wasn't happy when he realised his culinary efforts were going to waste.' He threaded his fingers together and stared down at them. When he looked back up, his eyes were bleak, infinitely miserable. Her heart kicked hard. 'I can't eat, Ruby. I've barely slept since you left.'

'And this is my fault? I didn't *leave*. You threw me out, remember?'

He paled and nodded, his nostrils thinning as he sucked in

a long, ragged breath. 'I was wrong. So very wrong to believe even for a second that you were anything like Maria.'

'And you've suddenly arrived at this conclusion?'

'No. All the signs were there. I just refused to see them because I'd programmed myself to believe the worst.'

Her heart kicked again, this time with the smallest surge of hope. 'What signs?'

'Your determination to push me away when I came to your apartment. Your tears in the car on the way back home. Your clear distress when my father touched you. Why would you encourage me to reconcile with my father and turn round and betray me?'

'I wouldn't… I didn't.'

He shook his head. 'I know. I condemned you for something that never happened. Something you tried to tell me you would never do. But I was so bitter and twisted I couldn't see what was in front of me.'

'What was that?'

'The love I have for you and the probability that you could perhaps love me, too.'

Her breath caught. 'W-what?'

'I know I've blown all that now—'

'You mean you don't love me?'

He speared a hand through his hair and jumped up. 'Of course I love you. That's not the point here, I meant—'

'I think you'll find that's the whole point, Narciso,' she murmured, her heart racing.

He stopped. Stared down at her. Slowly his eyes widened. Ruby knew what he was seeing in her face. The love she'd tried for so long and so hard to smother was finally bursting out of her.

*'Dio mio,'* he breathed.

'You can say that again.'

*'Dio mio,'* he repeated as he sank onto his knees in front of her. 'Please tell me I'm not dreaming?'

'I love you, Narciso. Despite you being a horrible pain in the ass. There, does that help?'

With a groan, he rose, took her face in his hands and kissed her long and deep. 'I'll dedicate every single moment of the rest of my life to making you forget that incident.'

'That sounds like a great deal.'

'Can I also convince you to let me back Dolce Italia in any way I can?'

Despite the guilt she saw in his face, she shook her head. 'No. It's now a mother-daughter venture. I want to keep it that way.'

'What about your father?' he asked.

'He consults…from afar. We'll never be close but he's my blood. I can't completely cut him off.'

'*Prezioso,* you humble me with how giving you are.'

'You should've remembered that before you pushed me away.'

'I've relived the hell of it every single second since I lost you.'

'Keep telling me that and I may allow you to earn some brownie points.'

He smiled. 'Can we discuss accumulative points?'

'I may be open to suggestions.'

He kissed her until her heart threatened to give out.

'Wow, okay. That could work.'

'How about this, too?'

He reached behind him and presented her with a large leather, velvet-trimmed box. It was far too large to contain a ring but her heart still thundered as she opened it.

The mask was breathtaking. Bronze-trimmed around blue velvet, it was the exact colour of the waters of Belize. Peacock feathers sprouted from the top in a splash of Technicolor, and two lace ties were folded and held down by diamond pins.

'It's beautiful.'

'It's yours if you choose to accompany me on the next *Q Virtus* event.'

'I want to know more about your super-secret club.'

A sly smile curved his lips. 'I could tell you all the secrets, but then I'd have to make love to you for days to make you forget.'

'Hmm, I suppose I'd just have to suffer through it.'

He laughed, pulled her close and kissed her again. She pulled away before things got heavy.

'Tell me what you've done to my mother.'

'She promised to hold the fort on condition I did everything in my power to exit this room as her future son-in-law.'

Ruby gasped. 'She didn't! God, first you muscle in on my opening, then you strike deals behind my back.'

'What can I say? She drives a hard bargain.' He pulled back and stared down at her, a hint of uncertainty in his eyes. 'So will you give me an answer?'

Her arms rose to curl over his shoulders. 'That depends.'

'On what?'

'On whether white Alba truffles come with the deal.'

He pulled her close and squeezed her tight. 'I'll keep you supplied every day for the rest of your life if that's what it takes, *amante*.'

*Isla de Margarita, Venezuela*

Narciso leaned against the side of the cabana and watched his wife wow the crowd with her latest range of cocktails. Although her mask covered most of her face, he could tell she was smiling.

Music pumped from the speakers strategically placed around the pool area and all around him *Q Virtus* members let their inhibitions fly musically and otherwise.

He raised his specially prepared cocktail to his lips and paused as the lights caught his new wedding ring.

He'd wanted a big wedding for Ruby but she'd insisted on a small, intimate ceremony at the Sicilian villa where he'd been born.

In the end, they'd settled for fifty guests including her

mother, and Nicandro Carvalho and Ryzard Vrbancic, the two men he considered his closest friends.

Although they were working on their relationship, he and Giacomo had a way to go before all the heartache could be set aside.

'So...*last three bachelors standing* becomes two. How the hell are Nicandro and I going to handle all these women by ourselves, huh, my friend?'

Laughing, he turned to Ryzard. 'That's your problem. I'm willingly and utterly taken.' He glanced over and saw Ruby's eyes on him. He raised his glass and winked.

Ryzard shuddered. 'That's almost sickening to watch.'

'If you're going to throw up, do it somewhere else.'

Shaking his head, his friend started to walk away, then Narciso saw him freeze. The woman who had caught his attention was dancing by herself in a corner. Although she had a full mask over her face, her other attributes clearly had an effect on Ryzard.

Smiling, Narciso turned to watch his wife emerge from behind the bar and walk towards him, her stunning body swaying beneath her sarong in a way that made his throat dry.

She reached him and handed him another drink. 'What was that all about?'

'Just me bragging shamelessly on how lucky I am to have found you.'

She laughed. 'Yeah, about that. You might need to pull back on the gushing a bit. You're putting our friends off.'

He caught her around her waist, tugged her mask aside and kissed her thoroughly. 'I have no intention of pulling back. Anyone who dares to approach me will be told how wonderful and gorgeous my wife is.'

His pulse soared when her fingers caressed his collarbone. 'I love you, Narciso.'

'And I love that I've made you happy enough to keep you from sleepwalking lately.'

'That reminder just lost you one brownie point.'

He pulled her closer. 'Tell me how to win it back, *per favore*,' he whispered fervently against her lips.

'Dance with me. And never stop telling me how much you love me.'

'For as long as I live, you'll know it, *amante*. That is my promise to you.'

\* \* \* \* \*

## It was becoming dangerous...this thing with Julian.

It was too fun and too easy. "Is your brother looking this way, Jules?"

"I don't know. I'm looking at you."

It was the tone he used, deep and husky as a country love song, that made Molly almost forget that this was just an act.

"I'm pretty sure he's watching," she whispered, moving closer to Julian's ear. She leaned against his chest and whispered, "I'm thinking we could just stroll off somewhere private and return a little disheveled, you know. Let his imagination run wild with jealousy."

She could feel the coiled tension in the muscles underneath Julian's shirt as he dropped his head to whisper back into her ear, his lips grazing her earlobe.

"As you wish."

**Red Garnier** is a fan of books, chocolate and happily-ever-afters. What better way to spend the day than combining all three? Travelling frequently between the United States and Mexico, Red likes to call Texas home. She'd love to hear from her readers at redgarnier@gmail.com For more on upcoming books and current contests, please visit her website: www.redgarnier.com.

**Recent titles by the same author:**

ONCE PREGNANT, TWICE SHY
PAPER MARRIAGE PROPOSITION
THE SECRETARY'S BOSSMAN BARGAIN

**Did you know these are also available as eBooks?**
**Visit www.millsandboon.co.uk**

# WRONG MAN, RIGHT KISS

BY
RED GARNIER

Published in Great Britain 2014
by Mills & Boon, an imprint of Harlequin (UK) Limited,
Eton House, 18-24 Paradise Road, Richmond, Surrey, TW9 1SR

© 2013 Red Garnier

ISBN: 978 0 263 24669 8

Printed and bound in Spain
by Blackprint CPI, Barcelona

# WRONG MAN, RIGHT KISS

As always, with my deepest thanks to everyone at Harlequin Desire—who make the best team of editors I've ever come across! Thank you for making this book shine.

This book is dedicated to my flesh-and-blood hero and our two little ones, who it turns out are not so little anymore.

# One

Molly Devaney needed a hero.

She could think of no other way to solve her dilemma.

She'd been tossing and turning at night for the past two weeks, obsessing over what she'd done, wishing and praying and hoping she could figure out how to fix things and fix them fast.

It had taken fifteen days and fifteen hellish nights to come to the conclusion that she needed some help—and pronto—and there was only one man who could save the day, just like he'd previously saved her on plenty of other days.

Her hero of all times, ever since she was three and he was six, and Molly and her sister, Kate, recently orphaned, had ended up living with his rich and wonderful family in their San Antonio mansion.

Julian John Gage.

Okay. The guy was definitely no saint. He was a ladies' man down to his very sexy bones. He could have any woman he wanted, in any way he preferred, at any time he felt like, and the stupid meathead *knew* this. Which meant he was determined to sample them *all*.

It really rankled her sometimes.

But while he was an incorrigible rake with the ladies, a handful to the press due to his position as head of PR for the *San Antonio Daily,* a problem to his brothers and a bane to his own mother, to Molly, Julian John Gage was nothing short of the bomb. He was her greatest friend, the reason she'd never really found a man until now and the only person on this earth who would be honest enough to tell her how to seduce his hardheaded, annoying older brother.

The problem now was that Molly could've found a better time to expose her wicked plans to him. Bursting into his apartment on a Sunday morning was not her brightest idea. But then she was losing precious time and urgently needed Garrett, his older brother, to realize he loved her before she all but died from the misery of it all.

Now, if only Julian would stop staring at her as if she'd lost it big-time—which he'd been doing for the past couple of minutes, ever since she'd blurted out her plans.

The guy just stood there, easily the most magnificent work of art in his flawless contemporary apartment, his feet braced apart and his steely jaw hanging slightly ajar.

"I can't have heard right." When at last he spoke, his husky morning voice was laden with incredulousness. "Did you just ask me to help you seduce my own brother?"

Molly stopped pacing around the coffee table and, all of a sudden, she felt very much like a tramp. "Well…I didn't actually say *seduce*. Did I?"

An awkward silence followed as they both thought back to five minutes ago. Julian lifted a lone eyebrow. "You didn't?"

Molly sighed. She couldn't remember, either. She'd been a little tongue-tied when the living sculpture—aka Julian—had opened the door, gloriously bare-chested and wearing only a pair of low-slung drawstring linen pajama pants. The pants were so low-slung and sheer, in fact, that Molly could clearly make out the dark V of hair starting just under Julian's flat, bronzed navel, a tidbit which was playing havoc with her mind since she'd never seen a man partly naked before.

Plus, Julian was not just any man. He looked more like David Beckham's younger brother.

*The hotter one.*

Good thing their friendship made Molly immune.

"Okay, maybe I did say that, I can't remember." Molly shook her head and fought to get back on track. "It's only that I've just realized I need to do something drastic before some bimbo steals him from me for good. I need to get him, Julian. And you're the expert seducer, so I need *you* to tell me what to do."

His eyes—green like the leaves of the oaks outside—flared slightly in concern. "Look, Molls. I don't quite know how to explain this to you, so let me just get it out there." He started pacing. "We all grew up together. My brothers and I saw you in diapers. There's no way Garrett will ever look at you and see anything else but a little sister, the key words here being *little* and *sister.*"

"All right, so it's too late to do anything about the Pampers issue, I get it, but I have solid reasons to believe Garrett's feelings toward me have changed! I mean, has he ever even said he only thinks of me as a little sister, Julian? I'm already twenty-three. He may actually think I've grown up to be quite a sophisticated and sexy lady." *With really nice breasts that he quite happily fondled at the masquerade,* she thought smugly.

But Julian regarded her attire—certainly not one of her best outfits, she'd grant him that—with a look that was the opposite of thrilled.

"Your sister, Kate, is sophisticated and sexy. But you?" He stared pointedly at her boho skirt and paint-splattered tank top, then plunged his hand through his sun-streaked hair as though supremely frustrated. "God, Molls, have you stopped by a mirror recently? You look like you've been smacked, kicked, then put for a spin inside a blender."

"Julian John Gage!" Molly gasped, so genuinely hurt her heart constricted. "My next New York solo exhibit happens to be in four weeks—I don't have time to care about how I look! Plus I can't believe you're giving me crap about my work clothes when you stand there half nak—"

A door slammed shut in the depths of the apartment, and Molly whirled around with a scowl, ready to keep shouting. But she spotted someone approaching out of the corner of her eye and in that instant, she lost all power of speech. That someone was, of course, a woman.

The leggiest, blondest blonde Molly had ever seen was currently stepping out of Julian's bedroom. She was carrying a gold clutch purse and wearing a pair of crimson stilettos and one of Julian's button-down shirts, which seemed to barely contain what was easily a set of enormous breasts that made Molly's girls suddenly shrink before her eyes.

Now *that* woman looked as if she'd been inside a blender. But at a really marvelous speed. Molly wished she could pull off that tumbled look so well.

"I have to go," the mystery woman told Julian sultrily from afar. "I left my number on your pillow, so…" She made the universal call-me sign and puckered her lips. "It was really nice meeting you last night. I hope you don't mind me borrowing a shirt? My dress didn't seem to fare as well as I did." She released a soft giggle, and when Julian remained unmoved by her sexiness and Molly only gaped, she gracefully crossed the room to leave.

The instant the elevator doors shut behind her, Molly's gaze jerked back to Julian. "Seriously?" Annoyance flared through her with such force that she stalked forward and shoved his rigid shoulder. That *womanizer!* "Seriously, Julian? Do you have to sleep with every woman you meet?"

She shoved him again, but his shoulder budged as much as a concrete building would.

With a rumbling chuckle, Julian grabbed her hand and forced her fingers into a fist. "We aren't talking about my love life. We're talking about yours." He frowned down at their fisted hands and briskly released her. "And the fact that you have paint on your nose, in your hair and on your shoes, and this starving-artist look is not going to do anything for my brother."

Molly shot him a harsh glare, then shoved past him and stormed down the hall. "Oh, just let me grab one of your shirts! I'm sure that will do wonders for my pitifully *un*sexy and *un*sophisticated looks."

"Aw, heck. Molly! Come on, Molls. Moo, baby. Get back here and just let me wrap my head around all this, all right? You know you've always been pretty, and I know that's why you don't give a damn."

Julian reached her in three long strides, promptly snatched her arm and dragged her back to the living room. Molly glared at him at first, but when she heard the low, deep sigh that worked its way up his chest, the sigh that said he just didn't know what to do with her anymore, her anger vanished.

It was just too hard to stay angry with Julian John.

Molly knew he'd do anything for her—and maybe that was why she was here. On a Sunday morning. And why she continued to be a pain in his great-looking butt. Because nobody had ever done the things that Julian John had done to make sure she was safe and protected, except maybe her sister, who had practically assumed the role of a mother when they were orphaned.

Kate had put her through school, coddled her, raised her and loved her every second of growing up without a mom and a dad. So the fact that Julian had been there for her almost as much as Kate said a lot about a man who insisted on pretending he was nothing but a playboy.

Which he first and foremost was.

But that was precisely why Molly was happy that he was just her friend and *not* the man she had set her romantic sights on.

"Look," she said as he released her, feeling herself blush as she remembered her and Garrett's stolen kiss. "I know you might not understand this. But I love your brother so much, I—"

"Since freaking when, Molls? He's always annoyed the crap out of both of us."

She stiffened defensively. "True, okay. But that was when he was so rigid, you know. Before."

"Before what?"

"Before…before I realized that he…" *Wants me. Before he said the things he said to me when he kissed me.* Her stomach wrenched at the painful memory. Anxiously, she pushed her red tresses back behind her shoulders and tried again. "I—I really can't explain it, but something has monumentally changed. And I just know he loves me back, I just know it in my soul, Julian—please don't laugh."

She couldn't bring herself to look him in the eyes for some inexplicable reason, so she spun around and slumped down on the leather sofa. The silence ticked by, and within seconds, she became aware of some extremely strange vibes coming from the vicinity of where Julian stood.

The laugh that broke the silence was worst of all. It was anything but mirthful. "I can't freaking believe this."

Molly held her breath and peered up at him, finding that a harsh frown had settled on his strong, tanned face. She had never seen Julian truly mad, but if that black scowl was a good indicator, he was getting there, and fast.

Her stomach clenched when she once again took a peek at his flat, muscled navel, the dark V dipping into those superloose drawstring pants and leading into— Okay, enough of that. She had to focus on getting Garrett. *Now*.

"Julian…" She really had to say something. Sighing, she signaled at that perfectly tanned, perfectly perfect torso. "Look. While we discuss this, can you put on one of your remaining shirts? The chest and the six-pack and all that you've got going on are just… Let's just say it makes me want to go take a peek at Garrett."

Julian scoffed and flexed seriously impressive biceps. "You know damned well my brother doesn't have these guns."

"He does, too."

He flexed his other biceps. "I may be his baby brother, but I can take the guy down in five seconds flat with these."

"Oh, puleeze. The only thing you're probably better at doing than him is screwing around—and you *deserve* that after saying I look like I live in a blender."

"Ahh. So once again, you missed the part where I said you were pretty." Julian fell down on a chair and for a long moment, they sat there, both staring pensively into space.

When he at last spoke, Molly was relieved to hear that his voice had regained its usual playful note. "Yeah. You're right. I am better at screwing around than both my brothers put together. Not that Landon would ever look at another woman now that he's married."

He leaned back and watched her with the beginnings of a smile that carried a hint of danger while he linked his hands behind his head in a deceptively relaxed pose.

"So let's screw around with Garrett. Why not? He's always been ridiculously protective of you and Kate. He'd go Donkey Kong if he ever found out you were dating someone. Especially someone with a bad reputation. You don't even really have to date the guy, just make him agree to play your doting lover for a while, ask him to be convincing enough to yank ole Garrett's chain."

Delighted that Julian was at last addressing her predicament, Molly almost jumped out of her seat and found herself clapping twice. "Yes! Yes! He sounds charming. But the question is, do I actually know such a man?"

Julian's smile was perfectly wolfish. "Baby, you're looking right at him."

His words appeared to strike Molly like an electric shock, and Julian wondered if that was a good thing, a bad thing or totally irrelevant to his newly hatched plan.

"Excuse me?" She jerked upright on his couch and gripped the leather cushions with such force that it looked as if she was on a roller-coaster ride. "I'm sure I heard wrong. Did you just offer to be my boyfriend or something?"

"Or something," Julian agreed, his lips curling upward.

He knew he looked calm. Collected. But inside his head, the wheels were turning with particularly inspiring ideas. Ideas he might later regret. But they were still damned good.

"Wh-what do you mean 'or something'?" she asked him.

Julian could hardly get over how adorable she looked

sitting there, shocked and disbelieving as if she'd just won the Megabucks.

Her eyes were just so wide and so damned blue you'd have to be made of freaking stone not to be willing to move mountains for her. Honestly, he'd never seen such expressive, genuinely innocent eyes in his life. It was a guarantee that Molly would lose every poker game she ever played, her expressions were so real and so clear. Hell, just the way she *looked* at him with those eyes made him feel like some sort of superhero. Not even his own mother gazed at him like Molly did.

With an amused smile, one he sometimes found himself wearing when he was with her, he explained, "'Or something' means I don't have girlfriends, Molly. I have lovers. And I'd be happy to pretend to be yours."

He'd meant to emphasize the word *pretend,* but somehow when he spoke, the only word he seemed to be able to emphasize was *yours.*

Because obviously he would only ever do this kind of stuff for Molly.

"You're kidding me, Jules," she said as she somberly scanned his face. She was not even moving, had practically become a statue on the couch.

He might have laughed at that, except to his own disbelief and amazement, he was dead serious. Dead. As *heck.* Serious. And now he needed to know if *she* was, too. "I may like to kid around, Molls, but I wouldn't kid you with this."

"So you're prepared to pretend to be in love with me?"

He nodded, and his hands itched to wipe away a green smudge of paint from her forehead and a red one from her cheek. "I figure I've probably done worse, Moo. Like that girl who just left…not really prime in the head, if you get me."

He tapped his forehead, but she wasn't even paying attention.

As though in a trance, Molly rose to her feet, all five feet of chaotic red hair and heavy turquoise necklaces and creamy paint-streaked skin, her eyes shining as his proposal finally seemed to dawn on her. "And Garrett will see us together and be madly jealous! Oh, my God, yes, yes, this is brilliant, Julian! How long do you think it will take to get him to realize he loves me? A couple of days? A week?"

Julian stared at her in silence. She really sounded... enamored. Didn't she?

He thought about it for a bit, and with each passing second, he grew more and more baffled. Suddenly all he wanted was for somebody to please tell him what in the *hell* was going on here. Was this some sort of lame-ass *joke?* Molly? Dreaming about his older brother? For real?

If the ten-year age difference wasn't an issue, the fact that the Gages had grown up with strict codes of conduct regarding the Devaney girls should matter. And tons. Especially to Garrett, who never, ever broke a rule. Had his brother done something to give Molly the impression of being interested?

Dammit, this just struck him as so, so wrong, he didn't even know where to begin.

His brother Garrett was ridiculously overprotective of the Devaney girls. The reason they'd become orphans in the first place was because their only living parent, who had been the Gages' bodyguard, had died in the line of duty protecting Julian's father and Garrett from an armed gang hired by the Mexican mafia to murder Julian's father for newspaper coverage disclosing their names and operations. But the Gages' bodyguard had died protecting Garrett, too. Though the gang members had been sentenced to life in prison, as the lone survivor of that bloody night two decades ago, Garrett had been sentenced to a life in hell.

Now he lived with a boatload of guilt and regret. When their widowed mother had taken the girls under their wing, Garrett had been rabid to protect them, even, apparently, from Julian—who had liked to tickle the hell out of Molly and make her giggle… Well, Garrett had always ridden Julian's goddamn back about the rules where the Devaney sisters were concerned. This annoyed not only Julian but also Molly—who loved being tickled by him.

So now, after Molly had complained a thousand times that Garrett never let Julian and her have any fun, it was damned hard to believe that she suddenly had the hots for Garrett.

What in the hell was that about?

Julian and Molly were friends. Honest-to-God, die-for-you, chase-a-killer-for-you and do-all-kinds-of-strange-stuff-for-you friends.

Julian was Molly's one, two and three on her freaking speed dial. The first number was for his office, the second for his cell phone and the third for his home. Molly even frequently admitted that their friendship was better than a romantic relationship, and it sure as hell had lasted longer than any marriage these days.

But after hearing her profess her love for Garrett several times today, Julian had realized that if she was serious— and apparently she was—he would have to help her.

He was going to "help" her realize that she was not in love with Garrett Gage. *Period.*

"I think we can get Garrett where we want him in about a month," he finally assured her, gazing deeply into her eyes in an attempt to gauge how deeply in love she believed herself to be. Knowing what a romantic Molly was, he actually dreaded the answer.

Hell, she was probably already hearing wedding bells; she looked positively love-struck. Which just hit the wrong chord with him. Oh, boy, did it ever.

"Do you really think he'll go for it? He's so difficult to read most of the time," Molly said in a dubious tone.

"Molly, no man in his right mind would stand by and watch his brother put his paws on his girl."

Blushing in excitement, Molly leaped forward and hugged him tight, kissing his stubbled cheek. "You'd really do this just for me? You're the best, Jules. Thank you so much."

As her slim, warm arms tightened around his narrow waist, Julian's entire frame stiffened as if she'd just zapped him. He was naked from the waist up, and he suddenly could feel Molly everywhere he didn't want to. Warm and smelling of sweet things.

Worst of all was that she snuggled in comfortably, turned her face into his neck and whispered, "You're the best part of my life, you know that, Jules? I never know how to thank you properly for everything you do."

Was she for real?

Because the ideas those words put into his head were so, so wrong, Julian could've shot himself.

He tried remembering his past lovers' names, in alphabetical order, but still could not relax a single inch until Molly extracted herself.

Letting go a long, long breath, he avoided her inquisitive gaze and grumbled, "Don't thank me yet, Molls. Let's just see how it goes, all right?"

"It'll go splendidly, Julian, I just know it. Before the month ends, I'll probably be wearing an engagement ring."

He rolled his eyes because he still could not even believe this was happening. "Well, let's not call the wedding planner yet, all right? Just remember that for this month, you're with me, and heads up, baby, the rest of my family isn't going to be too happy about it."

She frowned in puzzlement and planted her hands on her hips. "Why on earth not? Am I not good enough for you?"

"No, Molls. It's me." He turned to gaze sightlessly out the window as a heaviness settled painfully atop his chest. "They think I'm no good for you."

# Two

"You're jerking me around, toad, I just know it!"

Julian leaned back in his swivel chair and suppressed a smile as he watched his brother pace across the state-of-the-art conference room on the top floor of the *San Antonio Daily,* a thriving business the Gage family had run since the 1930s.

"Brother," Julian tsked, "I realize I'm younger than you, but don't forget I *am* stronger and I *will* take you down if you keep pissing me off."

"So you're basically admitting that you're sleeping with our little Molls?"

"I never said that. I said we're dating and she's moving in with me." This last was something Julian hadn't discussed with Molly before, but it had suddenly seemed like a good idea. And when Garrett's complexion turned the color of a ripe cherry tomato, Julian knew he'd struck the jackpot.

Garrett was livid.

Julian and Molly had discussed some basic rules yesterday—like no dating anyone else, a good dose of PDA for show when around family and strangers, and how neither would ever, ever disclose to anyone that their romantic liaison had been fake. This seemed especially important to Molly, who seemed to think it of utmost importance to be convincing in their new "relationship."

Julian was right on board with that.

Hell, he was on board with anything that meant pushing Garrett's buttons.

Not that he had anything against the guy, except the fact that he was maybe too honorable for his own damned good, and ever since Landon, the eldest brother, had embarked on a much deserved sixty-day honeymoon, Garrett seemed to think he carried the weight of the world on his shoulders. Or at least, of the family business.

There was plenty of love among the three, yeah, but Julian had been planning to exact a special brotherly revenge on Garrett for a long. Long. Time.

A revenge made all the sweeter by the fact that Molly suddenly had it in her pretty head to get Garrett's *personal* attention.

Hell, Julian hadn't had a wink of sleep last night just thinking about it.

Now he took a moment to enjoy the fact that his brother's face was taut with displeasure, his knuckles jutting out as he gripped his coffee cup. He stopped his pacing and stood across from Julian at the conference table, where they'd just wrapped up a meeting with their top executives. "Since when are you two interested in each other?" Garrett demanded.

"Since we started sexting," Julian returned, unflinching. Then, before Garrett could ask more, Julian lifted his cell phone and read a message. "Damn, this girl turns me on." He pretended to text Molly back and took his sweet, sweet time about it. Though in reality he was just telling her:

He knows. Guy's going bananas. Tell you about it @ dinner.

Garrett shot him a murderous glare. "Does Kate know about this sexting/moving-in...relationship?"

"Probably, unless she's too busy catering for her next event. She is Molly's sister, after all."

Just then, Molly's response popped up:

No wonder Kate and Garrett get along so well.

Julian quickly typed in:

I suppose Kate no longer worships the ground I tread on?

Molly replied:

Affirmative. Be careful, lover. She has a spatula and she's not afraid to use it as a weapon.

Julian's lips curled in amusement. Ahh, Molly. Light of his life.

"So which part was it?"

Julian gazed blankly up at Garrett, who almost had steam coming out of his ears. "Which part was what?" he asked.

"Which part of what Mother, Landon and I have been telling you for, oh...say, two decades, did you not *get?* The part that Molly Devaney was *hands-off?* The part that you could be *disowned* if you harmed her in any way?"

Julian nodded to placate him. "I heard you all. I heard you the first time, the tenth time, the hundredth time and I hear you now. Now hear this, bro." He leaned forward across the conference table and scowled. "I don't. Freaking. Care. Do *you*...get *that?*"

Garrett clenched his jaw and drew in a breath that inflated his chest. The guy was so rankled, he was probably about a step away from banging his chest like Tarzan. "I'm going to have words with Molly, as I am sure it is in her best interests to reconsider this stupidity. Just know this, Julian...if you hurt her, if you so much as harm a hair on her head..."

He didn't know if it was the threat, or the possessive way Garrett was acting toward Molly or the simple fact that Molly fancied herself in love with the guy. Worse, he feared it might be due to the fact that Garrett wanted Molly for himself. But Julian's cool began to fade, and it took an inhuman effort to keep the mask on his face.

Suddenly transported back to his teenage years, he too easily remembered all those damned times he and Molly tried to get close. The special bond you forged with someone, one that is rare and precious and you'd be lucky to find in your lifetime—Julian had always had that with her. But every time their friendship threatened to develop into something more romantic, his family would panic and they'd swoop down like vultures to emotionally blackmail, harass and coerce him to keep them apart. More than once, he'd even been sent abroad for months, the first time apparently because Julian had been "looking" at Molly in a way that neither Kate, Landon, nor their mother—and especially not Garrett—had liked.

Julian had told himself time and again that he didn't care. And once he was an adult, they'd made him believe he was a playboy until he had no other choice but to play the part. He could have any woman—they always told him—except Kate or Molly. That was the rule.

And every year of his life, that single, simple rule had made him feel tied up, caged like a lion, and as unhappy as a penned-up bull.

Now the command from his brother to stay away from the only woman who truly knew him made a fresh surge of anger rise up from within him. No matter what Molly thought now, or what Garrett planned to do, this was Julian's future on the line—and he had been planning it for years. No one was going to mess with that future. Or with his red-haired, paint-streaked little gypsy girl. Or with him.

Especially when he intended to use this fake relationship with Molly to explore his very real feelings for her.

Quietly and with deliberate slowness, Julian rose to his feet, came around the table and set a hand on his brother's shoulder. Then he whispered, very mildly, but with an edge, "Stay out of this, Garrett. I don't want to hurt you, man, and I definitely don't want to hurt her. So just stay the hell out of this."

Then he grabbed his jacket, reclaimed his cool and stalked out of his office.

"I can't believe it. I really can't. I just know you're pulling my leg, Molly."

Propped up on a stool by the granite island in the Devaneys' kitchen while her sister decorated newly baked cookies, Molly focused on filing her nails, her stomach fluttering with excitement over this being her first night as Julian's fake girlfriend. She could hardly wait to see the expression on Garrett's dark, riveting face when he eventually saw them together. Hopefully, Julian would drape his arm around her shoulders in that aloof, sexy manner he had, in a way that said *she's my girl and aren't I the hottest ticket around?*

"I'm not pulling anything, I swear," Molly assured her. "You can totally call Julian and ask him."

Kate held up her spatula in the air, her auburn-red hair—the same shade as Molly's—haphazardly knotted atop her beautiful face. She exuded such raw sexiness while wearing that frilly white apron that Molly could've hated her if she didn't love her sister so utterly.

If there was one word to describe Kate Devaney, it would be *alive*. Kate thrived doing everything and anything, which explained the rocking success of her catering business; she was a killer cook with killer curves, tall and tanned and confident and fun.

The only thing Molly truly had that might surpass Kate in the looks department was her really nice bust, but then she went through so much effort to hide it, in the end it didn't amount to much of an advantage.

"Julian and *you?* Together? I just can't give credit to this. His girls are always so—"

"Don't say it or I'll hate you," Molly grumbled, smacking her nail file down.

Kate sighed, scooped up cookies from the baking sheet and began packaging them in single decorative cellophane wraps. "Fine. I won't say it. But you know what I mean, don't you?"

Molly stood and went to look at herself in the mirror by the foyer, trying not to remember how Julian's words had hurt her yesterday morning. "You're right, I know they don't look like me," she said as she ambled back with an expression of total displeasure on her face. "They're tall and sexy and sophisticated." *But I don't care because I don't want Julian, I want Garrett,* she reminded herself.

Her lips still burned with the memory of his scorching

kiss, the incredibly sexy rumble of him growling against her mouth, as if Molly's lips were something to suckle on and bite on and feast on…

Everything inside her turned hot, and Molly shook the images aside.

Kate looked at Molly and burst out laughing. "You've really fallen for him, haven't you? I love Julian, Molls, but even I admit that whoever marries him is a fool. And I don't want *you* to be that fool, Moo."

Molly was about to assure her she would never be so stupid as to fall for Julian John. She had never seen a man so determined to sleep with so many women in her life. It was as if he had an itch he needed to get scratched and none of them seemed to cut it for him. She was about to express all of this to Kate, but then she remembered she was *supposed* to be his girlfriend already—or yeah, his *lover,* since Julian was too worldly to have girlfriends—so she clamped her mouth shut and privately thanked her lucky stars that she truly had better sense than to become notch number 1,000,340 on the mysterious and uncatch-able Julian John Gage's bedpost.

Kate paused in her cookie wrapping and lifted two winged eyebrows in question. "So how did it happen? Did he just suddenly—?"

"Did I realize what a fool I've been not to finally admit little Molls is the one for me? Yeah. Exactly like that." The deep baritone that interrupted them startled Molly so much that her arms broke out in goose bumps.

She spun around as Julian shut the front door after him, and her stomach sank in mortification when she realized that once again he would find her in paint-splattered work clothes. Then she remembered she didn't care. This was Julian John and she didn't need to impress him. He already thought she looked like a by-product of a blender. Why ruin it for him?

But it seemed wholly unfair that she would be wearing paint marks up to her hair and he would look so clean and male and good. Black jacket slung over his shoulder, his burgundy Gucci tie almost undone, he looked sexily tousled and delicious. Not that Molly wanted a bite of him or anything, but she supposed another woman would. Hell, they all did.

But Molly had common sense in regards to him.

She mentally patted herself on the back once more while Julian stalked forward as if he owned the place, wearing that playful grin he'd given her ever since they were kids.

"Whatever Kate has said about me, Mopey, don't believe her. It's all due to the fact that she wanted me first." His strong arms coiled like a steel vise around her waist while that Beckham-blond head dipped toward hers.

Molly didn't see it coming. He moved too fast and had incredible strength, and she was only five feet tall and easily handled. Before she could even realize what was happening, Julian had already reeled her in, crushing her breasts against his rock-hard pecs as his mouth settled firmly over hers, expertly, perfectly, oh so hotly.

And ooh. *Oooh.* A tiny working part of her mind frantically screamed at her to push him away. The only one she should be kissing now was Garrett! But the fact was, Julian kissed like his brother. Except Julian tasted clean and minty and not of wine, and he kissed her as if he had all the time in the world.

Those silken playboy's lips pressed with painstaking gentleness against hers and moved so languorously that all her senses began to spin out of control. Molly became magnetized. *Hypnotized.* Almost transported to the night her entire world had flipped upside down, and she'd glanced down to find her heart had been stolen from her chest.

She wasn't even sure she was standing anymore, but trusted that Julian would always catch her fall. The sudden desperate urge to press closer to him flitted through her, burned through her being as he lingered in his kiss for a thrilling, electrifying second, and then he was gone. Leaving her dazed and surprised and scatterbrained as he set her away—thankfully keeping a steady hand on her elbow until she found her ground.

He said something once it was over. She thought it was hello.

Molly pushed her hair back, feeling dazed. "Uh—hi."

He asked her something, his voice huskier than usual, his eyes at half-mast, and she stared at his mouth. His soft yet strong lips became the center of her attention, for she wondered what exactly it was about those lips that had felt so incredibly good when he'd put them on hers.

Even her knees had taken a hit.

She fought to calm down, but remained so shaken she ended up snapping at him for catching her unaware. "What are you doing here, JJ?" she asked, glaring, using his old kiddie nickname just to punish him.

Julian remained aloof and calmly popped a cookie straight from the baking sheet into his mouth. "Nothing, pumpkin buns. Just wanted to check in on my girl." He strode over and squeezed her butt, whispering only for her ears, "JJ? You're going to pay for that, Molls."

She fake giggled so Kate wouldn't notice anything strange and pulled away, her buttocks aflame from his touch. How to get back at him? She said the first thing that came to mind when she caught Kate's confused expression. "JJ loves for me to call him all sorts of pet names when we're…you know," she told her.

"JJ?" Kate turned to Julian, hands on hips, spatula held like a sword. "I thought you absolutely loathed that nickname."

Julian shot Molly a warning look. "I do," he said, jaw square as a cutting board. "But little Molls calls me JJ exclusively when she wants me to spank her."

Molly's satisfaction in getting back at him vanished.

Her cheeks burst into flames. She wanted to die of embarrassment, for now her sister would forever believe her to be into that kind of kinky stuff.

"Baby, its barely afternoon and I still need to make myself sexy and sophisticated for you," she told him as she went around the kitchen and shot him a scowl from behind Kate's shoulders. "Not all of us come by it naturally. Now you'll have to wait for me a bit. I'm sure Kate and her spatula would love to keep you company, though."

He moved fluidly, nonplussed. "I have a better idea, bun-buns. Why don't I help you get dressed, hmm?" Before Molly could deny him, he'd followed her into her bedroom and locked them inside while Kate remained in the kitchen, no doubt still wide-eyed.

"Will you *puleeze* stop provoking me," Molly hissed, pushing him against the door. "Stop calling me bun-buns."

He leaned forward with gritted teeth. "Who's provoking who? You know I freaking hate JJ!"

"And don't you dare kiss me again without warning like you just did!"

"If you ever call me JJ again, I'm going to kiss you—with tongue. So *don't,* otherwise I'll think you *want* my tongue inside your mouth!"

He glared at her and she glared back, wishing that a stream of butterflies hadn't just migrated to her stomach. She couldn't help but wonder what Julian did with his loathed tongue that drove all women crazy, crazy, *crazy*....

"Are we clear about this, Molls?" he demanded, using his thumb and forefinger to tip her head back and force her to meet his gaze. She was appalled to realize she had apparently been staring dumbly at his mouth.

She nodded so that he would release her and swallowed, some rebel inside her wanting to test him and say: *Yes, JJ.*

Then she groaned and thrust him away. "Why, oh, why did you have to tell her you spanked me?" She shook her head and rubbed her temples in complete mortification.

"Because sometimes I swear to God you want me to." He swatted her butt and strolled to the closet, leaving her to grapple with incredibly strange and powerful emotions and an uncomfortably stinging butt.

"So." He yanked out a huge suitcase, turned back and cocked a devilish eyebrow at her. "I told the love of your life that you were moving in with me. What do you say about that, my little Picasso?"

"Was he jealous?"

That smile again. "About as close to banging his head on a wall as I've seen him."

Molly yanked her panty drawer open. "Then I'd be delighted."

# Three

"So what else did the love of my life say?" Molly asked as they made a pit stop for food on their way back to Julian's place. He was always hungry. It seemed that his muscles needed a lot of glucose, all the time. The man had a friends group for every sport he participated in: soccer, basketball, kayaks, zip-lining, even the more extreme hang-gliding gigs.

Those hard, taut muscles on his arms and legs and abs and the magnificent golden hue of his skin obviously didn't come from being in an office all day.

He was so lean, he could probably tackle a decathlon as easily as he tackled women in bed.... Hmm, she wondered if Garrett would soon tackle *her* in bed.

"Wait here," he said as he slid his silver Aston Martin into the only vacant parking slot in front of a frozen yogurt chain.

"Hey will you get me an Oreo milk shake with—"

"Three cherries on top—one for chewing, one for sucking and one to leave at the bottom?"

Molly grinned and nodded, and she could still hear his rumbling chuckle even after he'd closed the door.

Minutes later, he returned, and she found herself scowling down at her milk shake. "Why is there a phone number written on my milk shake cup?"

With an easy flick of his wrist, he turned the key and his car engine roared back to life.

"Julian!"

He flung his hands up in exasperation. "I didn't ask for it, Molls."

She shook her head in distaste. But then, could she blame the cashier or whoever had scrambled to write her hopes on Molly's milk shake? Julian was graced with both a face and body that made women gape, stammer and stutter—then behave like twits. That was a fact. And there was nothing Molly—or even Julian—could do about it.

Still, it rankled, and Molly kept shaking her head. "Honestly. I have no idea who in their right mind would hook up with you."

He shifted sideways and put the car in Reverse, then reached out and chucked her chin. "Apparently *you*."

Molly laughed and started chewing her first cherry. "You haven't told me what the love of my life has to say about me—his one true love—hanging out with the likes of you."

Julian turned the wheel, shifted gears and sped onto the highway. "He mentioned guns. At dawn."

Molly sucked on her second cherry. "Just please don't make me a widow before I even marry him."

"*Marry.* Whoa. Now there's a big word."

"There's nothing wrong with the word *marriage.*"

"I said it was a big word."

She stopped sucking on her cherry and stared at him in suspicion, pushing the cherry to one side of her mouth as she talked. "And please don't tell me when you said guns you were talking about your biceps again?"

He just smiled that sexy smile. As if he knew a secret Molly didn't. Or as if he'd seen her naked without her knowledge. *Oops, where did that thought come from?*

Her stomach jittered all of a sudden, and she figured she might be cold. It had started raining when they loaded up her suitcases, and now her clothes were soaked and clinging to her skin. Which was unfortunate, because she'd changed into something Julian might even consider sexy and sophisticated. Not because she cared what he thought, but just to prove to him that Molly Devaney had money of her own, had success on her own and only dressed comfortably because she believed inner beauty was more important than material stuff.

Now as she contemplated her soggy outfit, she didn't know if her goose bumps were due to her wet tank or the cold milk shake or excitement.

Julian became pensive as he drove, but that was fine with her. Molly chattered on in her excitement about how she was going to get Garrett, how she could use one of Julian's spare bedrooms if she felt suddenly inspired and had to paint... She *did* have an exhibition soon and needed to finish two more pieces within the next month.

When they arrived at his apartment building, he asked her if he could show her something and Molly nodded eagerly. Eduardo, one of the doormen, took charge of delivering her bags to the twelfth floor while Julian guided her to another elevator and pressed P. They were carried up to the penthouse.

What greeted them when the elevator doors opened was an enormous white space, with floor-to-ceiling windows in every corner and the smell of fresh paint lingering in the air.

"Wow. What is this?"

He met her gaze, and she was mesmerized by the proud gleam in his eyes, could even hear the pride in his gruff voice. "These just so happen to be my future offices."

Molly's eyes rounded in surprise. "You—what do you mean? Is the *Daily* moving from downtown?"

The Gage family owned the most thriving and successful newspaper conglomerate in all of Texas, which included several print publications, internet news sites and some cable-TV channels, all working under the umbrella of their first paper, the *San Antonio Daily*. It was a business of three generations and one that gave the family immense wealth and untold power. Their offices occupied an entire block downtown, so Molly couldn't quite believe the move would be so easy.

A second passed before Julian answered, and it was as though he was selecting his words carefully. "No. I'm the only one moving out, Molls."

Molly stared at his somber expression, loud warning bells chiming in her head. She immediately sensed this development was not a positive thing for the family. "Do your brothers know about this, Jules?" she asked, treading cautiously.

"They will."

Molly took a couple of minutes to digest this shocking news. Her stomach did weird things at the thought of drama within the family, which had always seemed to revolve around Julian and his rebel ways. She still remembered each one of the times he'd been sent abroad for who knew what kinds of wrongdoing. Molly had missed her friend terribly, like she'd miss a thumb or an arm or a crucial and important part of her. All she remembered about those wretched months was that she'd cried. A lot.

Now she watched him move lithely across his new office area, easily stepping over plastic tarps while he surveyed the electrical wires that stuck out from the scattered pillars, and she wondered why he'd want to bail out on the family's extremely successful newspaper and publishing business.

As the head of PR and chief of advertising for the company, Julian had the best part of the pie, in her humble opinion. He had the same whopping salary, just as many shares in the company as his brothers but the fewest responsibilities, which allowed him to have the most fun, the most women and the most time for hobbies like flying that Cessna plane he so loved and doing all the sports he enjoyed. Why would he leave the *San Antonio Daily*?

"I had no idea you were unhappy where you were," she said as she caught up with him, searching his face.

He stared out the wide windows and the sunlight caught a dozen golden flecks in his green eyes. "I'm dissatisfied with my life, though not necessarily unhappy. A change was in order."

Her heart clenched with a strange emotion; she supposed it might be disappointment, for she'd believed they were close enough for him to share this important information with her sooner. As in, before he signed the lease for the penthouse. But then Julian was very reserved with his emotions, which was why people thought he had none. "So…" She walked through the space with him, taking in each new desk waiting for its worker. "How long have you been planning this?"

She wanted to know more but also knew Julian disliked being pushed too far, and she sensed that this was all she would get for now.

"A couple of years. Maybe my whole life."

He smiled down at her, a truly honest and content smile, and captivated by it, she returned it in kind, was helpless not to. But while a part of her wanted to clap and say *good for you!* there was another part, the one that was also loyal to the entire Gage family, that wished he'd reconsider. For Molly's entire life, she'd sided with Julian about everything, anytime and anywhere, yet now she felt torn. Because she'd given her heart to Garrett two weeks ago and knew for certain that she'd never get it back. And she knew Garrett would fight tooth and claw to keep Julian in the business.

He was one of their greatest assets and the only Gage brother cocky enough to neither worry nor care about appearances. His suave manner and mysterious ways seemed to both annoy and charm the competition, and made him the best PR person in the state. Molly doubted the *Daily* would have even half the amount of advertisers it did when Julian no longer had a hand in reeling them in. Maybe he would reconsider in due time?

Continuing their stroll with a sigh, she nearly bumped into a blank wall. "All this white space could use something, you know," she suddenly said aloud.

From a few feet away, Julian chuckled, and the husky sound created a compelling echo in the wide-open room. "Now, why did I know you were going to say that?" he asked as he came over.

She grinned and wrinkled her nose at him. "Maybe because I don't like blank walls and you've known this for twenty years or more."

Stopping just an arm's length away, he smoothed the wrinkle in her nose with one lone fingertip. "Then make a mural for me. This entire wall—make it yours."

Molly held his penetrating stare, her nose itching where

he'd touched it. As the wheels in her head started spinning, she turned to the wall and found that her muse had already jumped with an idea. "Are you high? My individual paintings already command five-figure prices. A mural would run at least 150,000 and it would take me months. I need to talk to my gallerist."

Her gallerist had once represented Warhol and he was the savviest art dealer around, selling the craziest, most daring and contemporary art in the world. He was also Julian's friend.

"Leave Blackstone out of it. A hundred and fifty it is."

She gasped. "Jules, I can't charge you that, it feels like I'm robbing my best friend."

"Then it should be fun. A hundred-fifty K, Molls, but make it real pretty for me. As pretty as you." His smile flashed charmingly, and a bucket of excitement settled in Molly's stomach until she could hardly stand it. She didn't know if it was due to the fabulous deal she'd just closed or to being called pretty for once without it being accompanied by an insult to her clothes attached. Perhaps it was both.

"Of course, Jules!" Pulling herself up by grabbing onto the collar of his shirt, she quickly kissed his hard jaw, then wished she hadn't, because he totally stiffened. "Thanks. When can I start?"

He spun for the elevator and cranked his neck as though it had cramped on him. "Tomorrow if you'd like," he said.

Molly floated in a cloud of bliss as she followed him. Had she really just landed an enormous work space just upstairs for the time being?

Had she just been commissioned for her first *mural?*

She could hardly believe her good fortune, although she'd always enjoyed a certain share of luck when it came to her art. The sudden interest from a top New York gallery a couple of years before had placed her works in several important collectors' homes, and before she knew it her name was being piled up next to contemporary artists like David Salle and Sean Scully; big, big, *big* names in the art world. Now for the first time in her twenty-three years, maybe some of that creative luck would rub off on her sadly lacking love life. Maybe she was close to getting what she wanted with Garrett.

Thanks to Julian, for sure.

Because she'd suddenly realized that, just as her canvases did not miraculously paint themselves, her love life wouldn't happen without some encouragement. And that was where Julian's help making Garrett jealous fit in.

Once back in Julian's spacious apartment, Molly chose the guest bedroom to the left of his room, a space done in a pastel blue-and-green palette that she'd always found soothing. She retrieved her night creams, day creams, moisturizing creams, shampoos and toothbrush and aligned them all on the sink, then peeled out of her still-damp clothes, showered and slipped into her sleep shirt, which was actually an old T-shirt Julian had used in high school and his mother had sent to the Donation Station. Nobody knew Molly had fished this shirt out of the garbage bag for being the softest and most worn, and Julian would hardly remember he'd ever owned it.

Once ready for bed, she went out in the hall to look for him and hoped to propose they watch a movie, but his bedroom door was closed. Disappointment crept in, so then she went to bed and lay there, gazing at the walls, the curtains and the ceiling fan for hours.

Sleep eluded her, and her thoughts kept drifting toward Garrett. His black hair, those onyx eyes with the sooty lashes, and *oh, God,* the way he'd kissed her two weeks ago. She remembered that kiss so perfectly that she'd been reliving it nightly, in bed, as she futilely tried to fall asleep.

"I think I'd like to be a spinster," Molly had told Kate that evening as they stood out on the terrace of the Gage mansion, gazing into the brightly lit masquerade party transpiring inside the sprawling 10,000-square-foot home.

Kate had obviously laughed. "Molls. Why on earth would you say that?" She'd lovingly tousled her hair, which Molly had worn loose for the evening. "You're beautiful and sweet and any man would be lucky to have you."

"It's just that no man seems to live up to my expectations."

With a dreary sigh, Molly showed Kate the picture of the three Gage brothers she carried in her iPhone. It featured the gray-eyed, responsible Landon, the dark-haired, honorable Garrett and of course the sex god playboy, Julian. As her favorite Gage brother, Julian was everything that a good husband was *not*.

"I know what you mean," Kate said softly, staring longingly at the picture.

It couldn't have been easy for her to play both mother and father to Molly while she herself had been barely a teen. Although Eleanor Gage had been a stand-in mother for both of them, she was a stern woman, and as one did when running on survival instincts, both girls had tried to put on their best behavior and their whitest smiles with the person who'd given them food and shelter. But when alone, Molly would seek out Kate's warmth and support like she'd seek out a pillow and blanket. Especially during those lonely times when Julian had been sent away. Sometimes Molly even wondered if she wasn't to blame for Kate's lack of a love life, a husband and a family of her own. The thought made her stomach feel heavy.

"You deserve someone, too," Molly whispered.

Kate smiled brightly and winked at her. "Then let's go find one," she teased and rushed for the double doors that led inside, but Molly groaned and stayed back, loathing her stupid costume.

She had been dared by Julian to dress as a tavern wench tonight. And of course he knew Molly could never ignore a dare that he delivered. Alas, now here she was. In an outfit so tight she was barely able to breathe, which showcased her breasts in a way that made her feel as if she'd just stepped out of a porn magazine.

She had never felt so exposed in her life, and as soon as she saw Julian, probably dressed like some evil creature, for sure, Molly was going to tell him off for being such a cad. "I'll catch up in a sec," she lied to Kate before her sister disappeared inside.

Instead of following, she edged farther out on the terrace, where it was dark and the air was fresh from the gardens and nobody would see her in her corseted wench costume.

A silhouette by the banister caught her attention.

Someone was coming toward her. Zorro? she wondered. Or was it the Phantom of the Opera? Or maybe it was Westley, the dangerously sexy man from Molly's favorite movie, *The Princess Bride*.

Whoever he was, he was hot. Clad all in black: black cape, a cloth mask covering both his hair and the upper part of his face. Black boots. And that smile. It just had to be Julian. Nobody smiled like Julian. He smiled like a wolf and made you want to be the lamb he was going to eat; it was very, very bizarre how he pulled that off.

She suddenly caught his glimmering eyes straying to her prominent cleavage and she felt something hot coil inside her belly.

"Well, well, well…" he murmured as he continued to approach.

His voice was thick and slurred, and she wondered how much he'd drunk tonight. He didn't sound like himself at all.

He smiled again and her stomach tightened under his appreciation.

He had a drink in his hand, and when he raised it to his lips, watching her with those eerily sparkling eyes, she noticed that his glass was empty. He cursed under his breath, shook his head and swung around to leave, murmuring something about being crazy.

She frowned when she realized she would not be getting to tell him off just yet. "You're going to leave me all alone out here?" she playfully called after him.

He paused for a moment, then turned, set the cup aside, and started for her with sudden purpose. With each long, determined stride, he dived deeper into the shadows Molly had been trying to hide herself in.

He was not smiling now. Something in his approach, in the tension in his shoulders, made her heart begin to pound. And pound faster. Faster. The way he moved, the way he frightened her…

It couldn't possibly, possibly, be Julian.

She began, "What—?"

He pulled her up against him, so fast that her lips flew open and she sucked in a shocked mouthful of air. In one fluid move, he pinned her hands at her sides, then bent his face to hers, mask to mask. Molly had stopped breathing.

It was too dark to make out this stranger's eye color, but she could still sense that gaze like a laser beam boring into her being. Her heart faltered when he made a sound, low and completely unrecognizable—a rumbling groan that was so hot and so male her toes curled.

His lips touched hers. The lightest of touches. Just a graze. Like the tiny spark that sets loose a wildfire. And Molly exploded with a rush of wanting so powerful it scorched every inch of her insides, infusing every particle of her being with heat.

Her lips opened as though on their own, and her body melted under his as a strange, embarrassing little moan escaped her. He seemed to like it, for his answering growl vibrated in her mouth as his lips latched firmly over hers.

He kissed her so possessively, a tornado of pleasure shot through her veins and her heartbeat skyrocketed to the ozone layer. His fingers bit into her buttocks as he dragged her up against him. Closer. Closest. Thrusting his tongue into her mouth with a groan of pleasure.

She tasted wine and immediately felt drunk on him. High on him. Wild for him. She was lost to a staggering rush of sensations as their mouths devoured each other with wet, greedy licks and suckles, her skin screaming with delicious agony as his hand stroked up her arms, caressing her. She had never felt so alive, so connected to another human being, as though her body were an extension of his larger, stronger one.

It was like being caught in a deluge of rain, and now she could feel his desire pour over her. Swimming in sensations, she felt the warm metal of a ring sliding upward as he stroked her shoulders, and her eyes jerked open when she realized this man kissing her, this man was...

Garrett?

How could it be?

He rarely put so much as a finger on her, he was so protective. Julian was always pawing her and she loved the little ways his touch made her feel. But while Garrett rarely reached out for her, when he did, Molly always felt this thick, smooth ring anywhere he put his hand. When he grasped her hand in his—ring. When he petted the top of her head—ring. When he secured her elbow to keep her from falling—aha. Ring.

Now Garrett was kissing her as if he was eating her alive, his ring almost like a brand across her skin as his hand greedily stroked her shoulders, then suddenly her throat, down her collarbone, to the top swell of her breast, tracing the shape of her.

He mumbled something, but she could hardly hear him through the roaring of her own heartbeat, his voice sounding alien and lust-roughened as he fiercely bent down to lick the exposed skin.

Rocked with the realization that this man, untouchable to her like all the Gages had been for her entire life, had thrown all caution to the wind and was kissing her as if his life depended on it left her knees in such a weakened state that she clung to him even while she tried to edge back to steal a quick peek at his ring.

The platinum band glinted in the shadows as he fondled her breasts, and yes, it was the same one-of-a-kind ring Garrett always wore, with a blue diamond at its center.

It *was* Garrett fondling her shamelessly.

And it felt so good, his touch so arousing, a rush of liquid heat flooded her between her thighs.

He groaned in misery when she went still with shock, yet he pulled her tighter against him anyway, as though her lips were powerful magnets for his. "Shh," she heard him say, cooing to her, calming her as if she were both precious and wild. "Shh…"

When he edged his knee between her legs to part them, the skirt of her dress rose, and he expertly eased his hand through the layers of fabric to cup her between her legs, right where she'd grown wet for him. The heat of his palm burned through her panties, and her bones seemed to disintegrate into nothing. Nothing but heat and pleasure and sensation.

"Oh," she gasped, body tensing as his fingers began stroking in slow, lazy circles, her head exploding in disbelief and excitement as a rush of hot lightning coursed through her.

His touch consumed her.

He touched her as if he owned her. As if he *knew* and *cherished* everything about her.

She'd never known she could respond like this to another human being.

She'd tried never to feel anything romantic for any of these Gage men—because they were her protectors and Kate said they were like their brothers and were therefore unavailable. But this one…this one wanted her and clearly didn't give one whit about what Kate said. What anyone said. And Molly hadn't realized she wanted him back so much until this very moment, when she was melting in his arms in a way she had never, ever imagined.

Needy sounds bubbled up in her throat as she rocked her hips against him, helpless to stop herself, her body a puppet to masterful hands that continued expertly stroking her. The sensations were so powerful she whimpered in mingled fear and longing, her insides coiling tightly like springs.

He groaned and bent his head to her ear, biting the lobe hungrily, desperately, those gut-wrenchingly sexy noises from his throat shooting arrows of heat to her nerve endings. His hungry mouth traveled all over her neck, leaving a wet path that sizzled as he pressed the heel of his palm seductively between her legs, rubbing and stroking exactly the parts that most ached and hurt and burned.

And then the worst part was that, with one more expert touch, one firm press with the heel of his hand, she'd exploded.

Molly still remembered the way she had trembled with that touch alone, and then she had wanted to cry, because she'd never had an orgasm before. Embarrassed to her core, she'd pushed him away as soon as she was able and gritted, "Don't touch me. Don't even talk to me! This never happened—never!"

And she'd yanked off her stupid mask, flung it aside and left.

The next day, Garrett had pretended that nothing happened, just as she'd told him to. And when she'd gone to talk to Julian about it, he'd been too hung over to focus and in a pissy mood. So she'd kept it to herself for over a dozen nights, her sexual siren having been awakened, now hungry for more and determined to do something about it. Once again, Molly wanted to weep in her bed in silence.

She wished she hadn't kissed him.

She wished she hadn't stopped.

She wished she hadn't pushed him away.

She wished she'd had the courage to face the music, so that he would have done the same.

But more than anything, she wished to feel again like she'd felt that night.

Garrett had broken down and revealed his feelings for her in an unmistakable way, and though Molly had gloried in his intimate touch and his incredible kiss, she'd gotten scared in the end.

She wished she hadn't given out the message that she wasn't receptive to more of his delicious kisses and touches. Because the more she thought of and relived that kiss, the more she was convinced that unique connection wasn't typical and that she'd just found her *soul mate*.

Without words, she'd been able to feel his love so powerfully that her own heart had sung inside her chest, and she ached desperately to be with him again.

Swallowing back a lump in her throat, she pounded the pillow and shifted to lie facedown on the bed. *Go to sleep, Molly, and tomorrow you can show Garrett what he's missing.*

But rather than give her comfort, the thought only made her realize that the one person who had been missing out on the best things in life was Molly.

Julian knew exactly why he couldn't sleep, why he was feeling so cranky and why everything felt like crap lately.

It was all Molly Devaney's fault.

She was driving him crazy in every possible way he could imagine.

First with the Garrett thing. And now just thinking about her sleeping next door made him toss restlessly in bed, frustrated beyond measure.

Tonight, it had been raining outside when they loaded up her suitcases. By the time Molly had stepped into his apartment, she'd looked so...wet. God, he'd really tried not to look at the way she needed to peel her shirt back from her breasts, but he lacked the willpower.

Lying back in his bed, he tried to cool down his roiling blood, his head swimming with the sight of her breasts, perfectly round, with those pointy nipples straining against the fabric of her top.

And when she'd kissed him upstairs, so happy to be painting the mural for him, it had taken all his willpower not to turn his face and capture that kiss with his lips, kiss her long and hard as if he'd wanted to back in her apartment—where she'd been flushed and gasping for breath after the silly little peck he'd given her. And those cherries. Goddamn the sounds she made as she ate those miserable cherries!

It had been a miracle Julian hadn't lunged across the seat of his car, taken her face between his hands and suckled each and every cherry from her cool and sassy mouth.

*Hell, this is the worst idea I've ever had in my life.*

For years, Julian had grown up with rules that he'd tried to follow, knowing the only girl he'd ever respected and admired was out of his reach. Molly was the one woman Julian would want to be locked in a closet with. Stranded on a deserted island with. She was the only good and pure thing in his life, and despite some failed efforts, he'd tried to keep it that way. Unsullied and unsoiled, happy and protected.

Growing up, he'd always imagined they would have each other. Molly had never liked to date, and she'd always needed Julian. Julian had kept his hands off her and *on* just about anyone else in his efforts to keep busy, stay focused and more importantly, stay away from Molly.

But now—she wanted Garrett.

A Gage.

Julian's stomach roiled with nausea at the reminder. God. He'd never imagined this could ever happen.

At first, he'd thought she was pulling his leg, or trying to make *him* jealous. In the back of his mind, he'd always imagined that if Molly ever fell in love with one of the Gage brothers, it would be…him. Dammit, him and *only* him. Because she sure as hell never seemed to look at anyone else.

Even his family had thought Molly wanted him, which was why every time he got close to Molly, all hell would break loose. His mother, Landon, Garrett, even Kate would pounce. Julian had suffered endless lectures from them all about being good to Molly, staying away from Molly, respecting Molly or finding another home. For the most part, he had been good. Really good.

But now, years and what felt like aeons later, the fact that Molly wanted his brother was a game changer. Julian had been living in this hell long enough, and he could no longer kid himself that the magic, the pull, the impossible chemistry between Molly and him was only due to friendship. He knew full well that when she made his groin throb with her smiles, they were not friendly feelings. Much less brotherly ones.

He'd been dreaming about her for *years*. Powerful dreams. Sexual dreams. Dreams that left him drenched in sweat and groaning in pain and reaching for the first pair of female legs that passed him.

Yeah, he'd thought if he'd had sex more often, his powerful reactions to her would diminish. But all it did was make him want her more—because none of those women were Molly.

No. *No one* could ever even compare to that effervescent little bombshell—no one.

Now he just needed to play his game right. Julian might have a long comfortable fuse where his temper was concerned, but when it came to Molly, his fuse had run damn short. If she kept this up he was going to do something reckless and stupid.

And he didn't want to be reckless and stupid.

He'd been moving his pieces all in the direction of one goal so he could stake his claim on her once and for all.

Now he'd prove to his family that he did not need them, and that he would never hurt a single hair on Molly's beautiful head. He needed them to see that he was worthy of her, that he wanted her for real and not just for sex—though of course when that happened, it was going to be damned amazing, too. But more importantly, he needed to show them that he would do whatever it took to have her. Even cut his ties with them *all*.

If Molly was ever going to settle down with a guy, she was settling down with Julian. Whether they liked it or not.

And as for Molly…

He had to make her see that *he* was the man for her and always had been—and once and for all, he had to finish what he'd started the night he'd kissed her heart out at the masquerade party.

# Four

Something about sleeping in Julian's apartment made Molly restless.

Well past midnight, still tortured by the memory of Garrett's kiss, she found herself tiptoeing down the hall toward the kitchen in the hopes of finding some sort of sleep aid in his cupboards. She had her heart set on Sleepytime Tea, but valerian root or chamomile would do, too. Hey, at this point, she'd take anything as long as it meant quieting her troubled brain and getting some rest.

But what she found on her way to the cupboards was a beautifully sculpted, seminaked man instead—and the sight of him was sure to give her permanent insomnia.

Wearing only a pair of white cotton briefs that hugged his buttocks perfectly, he leaned against the open refrigerator door, his head stuck inside as he surveyed the food.

Molly stopped in her tracks, her heart flying to her throat.

The warm fridge light silhouetted Julian's magnificent form, shamelessly caressing every dent, every shadow and every sharp rise of lean, ripped muscle. Her breasts pricked unexpectedly. And suddenly he was not just Julian.

He was every inch…Julian John Gage.

Sexy playboy, dangerous male.

Not a hero, not harmless and definitely not just a friend.

A tremor rushed down her legs as her eyes helplessly drank up what was so blatantly on display, aided by the moonlight that filtered through the windows; she took in the sinewy arm folded above his head as he leaned forward, the broad muscled back, the lean hips and…the rest. His long, muscled calves and hamstrings, his hard buttocks under that snug white cotton.

Her temperature skyrocketed. Not because he was utterly sexy in a way that made her want to swim in ice right now, but because she was here. With him. At midnight. And he was about 90 percent *naked*. When it should be Garrett here, Garrett almost naked, Garrett in her head.

Her hormones clearly knew nothing of reason. They burst into action until she could feel the hot little pinpricks all over her body, to her utter confusion and despair.

Even her fingers tingled at her sides with a painful itch to trace the muscles on his back, determine the texture, the hardness, paint the thick ropes straining in his forearms. For a wild moment she kidded herself that it was the artist in her; it had to be. For she felt the same fever she did when she was gripped with the need to paint.

Except now she was gripped with the need to trace the length of Julian John.

With finger paint. All of him. She thought wildly that if he were a canvas, she would not leave an inch of him unpainted except his lips. He was just too masculine to wear them any way but bare.

But she could still trace them with her fingertips and find out what sort of power they held when they kissed her. She could explore the thick bottom one and then the top one and she might even kiss them again just to be sure her memory wasn't failing her…

*Molly, you love Garrett, you tramp!*

Shocked by the untoward thoughts, she snapped back to the present and swallowed a lump in her throat. An awful guilt surfaced inside her. Had she actually been thinking of accosting Julian in his own kitchen? What was wrong with her?

Ever since that evening at the masquerade, it felt as if her entire life had been flipped over as easily as a pancake.

Now she could not stop thinking about kissing, touching, tasting, wanting. Garrett had awakened the desperate needs of a woman inside her, and Molly felt so hyperaware of her body now, even her reactions to Julian were uncommonly, embarrassingly…unsettling.

*See what you've done to me, Garrett? Apparently I'm a nymphomaniac now.*

"Um. Did you forget you have a guest here?" she blurted out from her spot a few feet away.

Julian's shoulders stiffened almost imperceptibly. His head dropped an inch or so, that gorgeous mane with sun-streaked strands that were lighter than the others. "Damn—you're supposed to be asleep, Molls." He pulled his head out of the fridge, his chin dropping an inch or so as he faced her, his hair catching the light just right.

"People with insomnia don't sleep, Jules."

Molly should go back to her bedroom, she supposed, but being squeamish about a man's near-nakedness did not go with her artistic persona. She had to treat it as a natural state of being, or at least that was what she told herself as she woodenly walked over and opened and shut cabinet doors in search of her tea.

"Here, have some milk, always works for me." He shoved the carton he'd just drunk from in her direction.

Molly took it and set her lips over the place his mouth had been, trying not to get too hooked on that discomforting detail as she downed a big gulp. Swallowing, she said, "Ah, it's cold," and handed it back, all her efforts focused solely on not noticing how velvety smooth and hairless his massive chest was.

She had never felt five feet tall when she was with Julian until today. When he seemed to hulk over her, appearing for the first time in her life almost…threatening. Extremely male.

"I'm going back to bed," he said, shoving the milk back into the fridge and shutting the door.

"Can I come sleep with you?" Molly blurted out to his retreating back.

Suddenly she just knew if she went back to sleep alone in her room, she would be haunted. By her masked man. And by Julian in sexy white cotton briefs. She desperately wanted to watch a movie with him and snuggle and sleep and get her best friend back. She ached for him to make her feel…safe. Like when they were kids.

"No," he answered without a single backward glance.

"Don't be a jackass, Jules."

"I don't sleep with women I can't take to bed," he yelled back.

"I'm not women. I'm just *me*."

"Precisely."

She scowled and said, "Just put some pants on and I'll bring my pillow. Come on, don't be mean."

She heard silence, then receding footsteps down the hall.

"Julian?" she called back tentatively.

His laugh made her hope for a moment, but then he spoke. "Good night, Molls!"

And so Molly cursed him all the way to her room, climbed alone into her bed and didn't sleep a wink.

She didn't fare so well on the second night, or on the third, either. Even though she tried every night to get him to invite her for a sleepover, the man's will was iron. She was surprised she couldn't bend him to her plea at all, but she was more surprised by the amount of effort Garrett had been putting into stopping her from getting into a "relationship" with Julian. Which amounted to zero so far.

That was not the approach of a man in love!

Then again, Garrett had always been the most hard-headed of the three, so he'd probably need extra incentives in order to react to her provocations.

Molly fantasized about the sexy clothing she could wear to catch his attention. She was growing so desperate, she even imagined pulling out that stupid wench costume again—but what sane person wore that? Nobody, that was who. Only Molly Devaney on a *dare* from *Julian*.

By the sixth night and seventh morning at Julian's, Molly decided she was being tortured. Cranky from lack of sleep and out of sorts from painting all night, she began to wonder if she might have taken too deep of a plunge into this whole "relationship." She'd barely even seen Garrett, much less talked to him, yet oh, boy, she'd been seeing plenty of Julian John.

Of course seeing him seminaked in the kitchen that first night took the gold.

But the close silver went to the times when he had breakfast in those linen drawstring pants that drove her crazy. He had several in different colors, and when the

sunlight hit them at just the right angle, she could almost see through them. It was torture trying *not* to.

Like having an open chocolate bar stare back at you for hours and trying not to eat it. It was *crazy*.

And then watching all those bare shoulders and biceps and triceps and lats and traps and pecs and all that hairless tanned skin moving and flexing as he had breakfast nearly catapulted her to internal combustion. He was just too…defined. His virility too overwhelming to endure when she'd had no sleep.

But on the other hand, the bantering between them was wonderful.

Julian usually read the paper while Molly eyed all the junk mail, and this morning he'd accused her of being the only person he knew who actually enjoyed reading it. They'd laughed about that, among other stuff. And yet there were also moments that felt…serious. Too serious.

Every time Molly rose for more coffee, she caught Julian staring at her bare legs that peeked from under her long T-shirt. She had never in her life been more self-conscious of her walk until she came back to the table with his smooth green eyes admiring her every step. To cover up her awkwardness, she'd blurt out a silly question and Julian would jerk his gaze back to her face, asking a distracted, "What?" as if he had not even heard her.

It was not like him at all; he was usually as sharp as a tack.

Today, his teasing had continued as he drove her to her old place. Once again he mentioned her clothes. But this time his remarks had felt strangely…intimate.

He didn't exactly say her flowered sundress came from her "blender" collection, he merely said, eyes glinting in mirth, "You almost look naked without a single paint mark on you."

*Naked.*

Molly still wondered why her stomach had twisted like a pretzel at the word, but just the prospect of him seeing her naked made her head spin wildly. Now she waved goodbye to Julian from her front door as his Aston Martin rolled around the curve, a dazed smile lingering on her lips.

She'd promised to catch a ride home with Kate later today, once she managed to pack more of her paint supplies and found herself a dress to wear to tonight's event, a small housewarming for Landon and his wife, Beth. Although the couple had been married for two years, they'd never really taken the time to honeymoon until now. At first, they'd married because it suited Landon's business purposes and would help Beth could regain custody of her son, David. But soon they'd fallen madly in love. Now their turbulent waters had calmed and they had one of the most loving marriages Molly had ever seen.

This was the first time Julian and Molly would face all the Gages at once.

The first time they would face Garrett and make him realize he was an *idiot* for letting Molly go.

And suddenly, sexy and sophisticated wouldn't do.

Suddenly it was *crucial* that Molly look *stunning.*

Using the key neatly hidden in the potted fern outside her door, she quickly entered the apartment to the aroma of baking: cinnamon, cardamom and every scent she associated with home.

Her heart swelled at the sight of their nice, tidy place looking cozy as usual. It was prime-time girly, scattered with lacy pillows and throws on the couches and colorful accessories. Even Molly's old teddy bear sat contentedly under a Tiffany lamp.

After sequestering herself for days in an ultramasculine bachelor pad, the feminine vibe in their small one-story home appealed to her. Right then, she decided to take some of her pink pillows to Julian's place. She needed to make herself more at home if she was going to be there for a while, plus she definitely planned to stock up his cupboards with her beloved Sleepytime Tea.

"Okay, what is going on with you?"

Molly spun around to find Kate standing in the kitchen archway, her red hair tied in a ponytail, a frilly apron around her waist and a what-in-the-world expression on her face.

People used to say Kate had so much energy the sun would burn out before she did. They were right; she was always doing something.

"I just came for some more clothes. Julian's car is so impractical a kid can fit more stuff in a bike basket, I swear," Molly said.

When Kate's expression didn't soften, Molly went to the kitchen to give her a hug, which might have been easier if Kate wasn't holding a bowl.

"I can smell something's cooking, Molly. I'm like your mother and sister and father all in one."

"And *I* smell cinnamon."

Molly peeked at all the yummy offerings on the kitchen island and selected several muffins to take to Julian. She shoved them into a brown paper bag and rolled it closed with a lot of noise.

"Aww, you always do this to me," Kate said, exasperated, setting down her bowl with a plunk. "Those muffins happen to be for Landon and Beth's welcome-back party, Moo. I'll bake some for you tomorrow, okay?"

"Fine," Molly grumbled. Already halfway to her room, she retraced her path to where her sister stood and handed her the paper bag. Instead of leaving, though, she stared into eyes that were clear and blue and almost identical to hers.

Her chest felt so heavy today, she just ached to be truthful with her sister.

They'd always been close with each other. As tight as two people who were left alone in the world could possibly be. But both of them were creatively inclined and tended to disappear into their own private bubbles of imagination half the time. Molly had been known to spend months locked away, painting away her restlessness. Kate cooked her heart out as well so that by the end of the day they were both too tired to even remember that they had lives outside their jobs, jobs which also happened to be their hobbies.

Kate had always been there for Molly, a shoulder to lean on, always supportive but not suffocating. But rarely in all these years had they actually discussed men. Or the strange feelings a woman might have toward them.

It was as though they both tried to pretend men did not exist in their lives. Or maybe just pretend that, other than their wonderful relationship with the Gages, they didn't need any man *at all*.

Molly had been perfectly content with that pretense because she had Julian John's friendship. And he counted for a hundred men. So she'd never felt she lacked any male attention at all.

Until that one night, when *his brother* had made her feel *wanted*.

Until that one night when she'd been kissed and fondled until she'd burst. Literally.

Now Molly couldn't seem to stop craving that extra spark in her life. That wonderful feeling she'd felt as those hot lips, those expert hands, had reminded her she was a living, breathing woman who deserved a man's love. Because why the hell not?

But how to inform Kate of her masquerade escapade with one brother when she was now supposed to be the other's lover?

Molly just couldn't talk about Garrett yet. It was still impossible to mention that kiss that had flipped her whole life upside down. But at least she could mention something else that was gnawing at her.

"Julian hates my wardrobe," she blurted at last. She hated how her stomach cramped at the admission. And she loathed remembering how cockily Julian had assured her that this "starving artist look" would not do anything for Garrett. Damn him anyway for making her feel insecure.

Kate's eyes widened, then she cocked an I-told-you-so brow. "Now, why am I not surprised to hear that?"

"Because you've said the same. There. Does it please you, Kay? That he thinks I dress bad? Because the last thing it gives me is pleasure."

Suddenly, just remembering the sexiness of that woman she'd seen in Julian's apartment made Molly flush in anger all over again. She had to look better than *her*. She had *so* many other looks in her wardrobe, not just the "blender" ones. Jules would see.

Eyebrows joining over a nose that was dotted with freckles, Kate took a step to scrutinize Molly more closely. "Molly, I don't get you. You haven't called in days and when I text you, you tell me you're flying in Julian's airplane over to South Padre Island to get an hour of suntanning with him? Your last two unfinished paintings for the exhibit sit all alone down the hall in your studio with your deadline looming…and after years of listening to me beg you to let me give you a makeover, you finally decide to do it because of what *he* said? What is going on with you two? I couldn't sleep last night—I had to call Garrett. I'm worried sick!"

"*Garrett?* Well, what did he say?"

Looking genuinely mortified, Kate shook her ponytail and rubbed her temples. "He said to relax, that he'll talk to you. I just don't understand how this could come on so suddenly without me noticing what you two were up to. I thought this would happen later, when you were more experienced and mature."

"Forget that! Tell me what tone Garrett used. Was he angry? Concerned? Kind of possessive?"

Maybe the idiot was so arrogantly certain of Molly and her feelings for him, he thought he still had her in his grasp. Well! She'd just have to set the man straight, wouldn't she? And play harder to get with him than ever. In fact, Julian would know just how to take care of that tonight.

"I don't remember exactly what else he said, but I'm truly mortified over this. Moo, I thought you were a virgin until now?"

Kate seized her shoulders, and as her wide blue eyes searched deep into her own, Molly dropped her gaze to the floor, feeling suddenly transparent. "I *am* a virgin," she whispered, then she realized what she'd admitted to, and that the truth, right now, wouldn't do. "I mean I *was* before Jules…"

"Were you hurt your first time, Molly? Did he hurt you?"

That soft question, full of caring and concern, sent Molly for a loop. Suddenly she felt like the very red center spot of the Target sign. That was what liars felt like when they were put on the spot. So now she was going to have to draw on her imagination.

"He didn't mean to hurt me, but you know…" She trailed off and hoped to leave Kate to her own conclusion.

Which, judging by her struck expression, wasn't all that good. "I could kill him!"

"No! No! It was amazing, he was…" Helplessly hooked into an image of Julian John making love to her, Molly trailed off. Or was it Garrett she was fantasizing about? Her mouth felt so moist all of a sudden, she had to swallow. "It was actually perfect," she finished in a whisper.

"But anyway, my pride is smarting like crazy after he insulted my dress choice," she continued after a moment. "I'm truly torn, Kate. I want to show him that I can look fantastic but don't care what he thinks, either. I know you're catering for our event tonight, but do you think you can take an hour off to help make me look good?"

"Good enough to make Jules eat his words?"

"Yes!" Molly laughed, grabbing a frilly pink pillow and playfully smacking Kate with it.

She pictured Julian's face when he saw her walk through those elevator doors. Oooooh, it would be priceless. He'd look stunned and shocked and he would definitely no longer think Molly needed a new mirror.

And Garrett? He would regret every hour of these days they had been spending apart when they could have spent them together. Necking.

Kate slapped the pillow back at Molly, laughing. "Yes, I'll give you a makeover. But Molls?"

"Hmm?" Molly was already storming into her bedroom, rummaging through her closet in search of options that would make a man's mouth water. She didn't have a lot. But she still found a very nice dress in Kate's closet. She extended it to her sister, loving how the sapphire silk fabric shimmered in the light. "It has the tag on," Molly said aloud.

"Take it off," Kate said excitedly, and pulled on the plastic.

Molly shook her head. "But it's new. I can't wear this."

"Yes, you can. I was saving it for a rainy day. You'd look so lovely, Moo."

"I wish you'd stop calling me Moo. I feel like a cow." Molly hung the dress back up with a sigh, and her heart clenched for her sister. "I'll borrow this one day, but only after *you* wear it. When it rains."

They shared a smile, and minutes later, Molly found another dress in her sister's closet. It was black, fitted, and had an open back that was to die for. Molly tried it on backward and loved it so much, she decided she was doing things her own special way and cut off the label. She'd wear it this way and show plenty of cleavage tonight.

By that evening, after spending a wonderful day with Kate, getting her makeover and even helping her sister finish loading some of tonight's munchies into the catering van, Molly arrived at Julian's posh apartment building, her heart pounding in anticipation.

Her hair was held loosely by a shimmering crystal butterfly clasp, with a few soft tendrils escaping along her temples. She wasn't used to pulling her hair back, but it seemed to emphasize her features this way. Her round cheekbones, her plump lips.

Her insecurities flickered to the forefront as she asked the bellhop to hold her canvases and paints below until she rang for them. He kept staring at her as if he'd never seen her before, and she wanted to run back home and put on a boho skirt, let her hair down and grab a huge pair of earrings.

But no. This was not the time to feel insecure.

She would show Julian sexy and confident if it killed her.

She crossed the marble lobby with purpose, aware of her hips swaying, the material clinging to her skin. Garrett was going to like what she was wearing; if he'd liked the wench costume, then he would love this one for sure. And if Julian didn't like it? Her stomach did a twist inside her, and she wondered what that meant. Hopefully it meant *screw him*.

She wasn't wearing this for him. *At all*.

Taking in a deep breath, she waved at the receptionist and pushed the elevator's up button.

*All right. Here goes nothing....*

The elevator chimed, and Julian glanced up from the bar and almost dropped the bottle of wine he'd been examining. It was a Penfolds Grange Hermitage 1951—so rare and prized, only twenty bottles were left in the entire world, with the last having sold at auction for almost fifty thousand dollars.

But who cared about that now?

Because an exotic-looking creature resembling Molly had just stepped off the elevator, and something that felt like a paddle struck him in the chest, the gut and right between his straining eyeballs.

*Holy mama.*

He'd though this morning had been tough, watching that redheaded little package prance around in an old T-shirt of his with those curvy bare legs begging to be stroked.

And now...

He was certain that never in his life, after dating models, actresses and even a pampered princess, had he been as fired up by the sight of a woman as he was this instant, watching Molly Devaney and her pinup body walk toward him in that minuscule black dress.

She looked like a sexpot. A sex goddess. A sex *bomb*. Awakening every Neanderthal instinct inside of him.

Julian could hardly take her all in with one long sweep of his eyes, he was so dumbstruck.

Her titian hair was drawn back into some sort of careless knot, but several soft wisps escaped to frame her lovely face, the overall look enhancing the delicacy of her doll-like features. Her lovely, heart-shaped lips shone with a peach-colored gloss, and whatever silver-gray shade of eye shadow she'd worn made her eyes look even rounder and bluer than usual. Her earrings were small pearly dots, unlike her usual flashy chandelier style, and they made her look so elegant he wanted to fly her to Monaco on his jet right now and seat her next to him at a baccarat table.

Then the dress. Ahh, the dress. The satiny black fabric fell from her nape to drape over a pair of beautiful round breasts he'd kill to taste while the plunging neckline revealed inches and inches of smooth porcelain skin in the cleavage between. The skirt was barely a couple of inches long, and it hugged her rounded hips like Lycra. Suddenly he wanted to be that skirt. That dress. That cloth that molded to her and felt her and hugged her and practically rode those curves all over the place.

Molly had always been the funniest baby, the happiest baby he'd ever seen in his life. She cackled all the time. Especially with him. Now she was entirely, 100 percent, take-me-serious woman. And Julian was primed to stop mucking around with her and ready to do some serious, serious things with her. Aww, *crap!*

This was going to be a long night.

Schooling his expression, he set the wine bottle down and noticed his hand wasn't so steady. Not while his heart was doing vaults and backflips. "Is something wrong with your usual clothes, Molls?" He was amazed his voice made it past his dry throat.

"As a matter of fact, yes." She planted her hands on her

hips, thrusting her chin up in a silent dare. "They're not sophisticated and sexy, according to you."

He cocked a brow and remained silent, mentally deliberating what in the world to do now. A part of him wanted to escort this impostor out the door and demand to know where his red-haired, paint-streaked imp was. And another part was just thinking of how good this woman would look in his bedroom. Splayed open on his bed…where he would give her a goddamned hickey that would sting like hell tomorrow…

Okay, no.

No.

He was not doing any of that.

Not so soon and not like this.

But hell, had she actually picked this dress for *Garrett?*

His jaw locked in wordless jealousy, his eyes so starved they felt like Ping-Pong balls as they went from her prominent cleavage to her narrow waist to her sexy stilettos and back to the enticing swell of her breasts and to her slim, sleek arms. A torch blazed inside his chest and the heat quickly spread to every corner of his tense body. "You call that sophisticated and sexy?" he asked gruffly.

Yeah. It was definitely sophisticated and it was so damned sexy his eyes were about to burst. But it was also practically nonexistent. And he told her so.

She stuck her little pink tongue out at him. "Eat your heart out, Jules. I look good."

He was not even going to think of all the places he wanted to feel that little tongue. Really. "*Good* is not the word I'd use."

"All right. I look amazing," Molly countered.

"Says who? You?"

"Come on, I can see you struggling, Jules. Be the better man and admit it," Molly teased, clearly enjoying this.

"I'm the only man here, Molls, and I'd gladly admit it if I wasn't so busy looking for the rest of the dress. So? Where's the rest of the goddamned dress?"

Her smile wavered. "You don't like it? Fine. I'm not wearing this to impress you." With a stiff shrug, she breezed past him to her bedroom, where she began shoving her things into a small clutch purse.

Julian followed her to the threshold of her room and watched her buttocks wiggle as she bent over. His mouth watered. She looked so sweet and so delicious he was salivating like a dog.

He'd had mile-long legs wrapped around his body, centerfold lips around his privates and breasts the size of melons in his hands. And he had never, ever, been so turned on.

He wanted Molly so bad he'd die for it.

He wanted to cup her breasts and suckle her until his jaw ached. He wanted to unpin her hair and watch as every fiery-red strand fell to caress the lovely curve of her nape and shoulders. He wanted to take a plunge into her cleavage and lick his way downward until he found the very center of her being—and he wanted to stay there, all night, drinking and feasting and adoring every prized and special inch of her.

He knew this girl like he knew himself. And he still wanted to know her *more*.

He knew he only had Lucky Charms for breakfast when she did, so he could eat her marshmallows. He knew she had her cereal with almond milk. He knew when she got painting fever she would disappear into her studio for months and not care whether the world kept spinning or fell apart, except for taking a moment each day to see him and Kate. He knew she'd secretly donated the first million she'd made to an orphanage and that when she was younger she'd watched *The Princess Bride* about twenty times, rewinding and replaying the part when the hero tells the princess, "As you wish," rather than, "I love you."

He knew that she wanted his praise tonight.

He had seen the uncertainty underneath the confidence in those striking blue eyes of hers, could see the eager rise and fall of her pretty breasts.

More than anything, he wanted to shower her with the praise she wanted. He wanted to take off that slinky black dress with his teeth so she knew how badly he craved her. Then he wanted to take his teeth from her tiny toes and drag them up her shapely ankles, her firm calves, her slim beautiful thighs, and roam his hands up her tiny waist and her beautiful breasts while he buried his lips between her legs and drowned in the intoxicating taste of her. He wanted to take her to heaven, because that was the place where angels live, and he wanted her to ask something of him—anything—so that he could look into her eyes and tell her, "As you wish."

But he did none of that.

Could not do it. Not yet.

Because she'd worn this dress tonight for another man. And the thought of that alone made him feel like kicking a kitten.

"I can feel your eyes on my back, Jules." Molly broke into his thoughts, probably sensing his overwhelming testosterone encircling her.

He leaned on the door frame with his wide shoulders, still struggling to process this new feeling of complete and utter jealousy. "You're showing off so much skin I'm concerned you're contracting pneumonia as you stand there," he said.

She swung around in surprise. Her mouth hung open, and then she tossed her head back and laughed. "Really?

You're concerned about my health? Or about your ego and the fact that you can't even admit to me for one night in my life that I don't look like I came out of a fistfight and a blender?"

His fingers curled into his palms and his lips clamped shut. So…she thought he'd insulted her?

"If you don't want to be mauled the entire evening, I suggest you at least find a sweater," he instructed. He was trying to sound friendly. Like a good friend. A best friend would make such a suggestion, wouldn't he?

"It's a hundred degrees outside. Why would I need a sweater?"

He stared down pointedly at her breasts—yes, so that she noticed—then back up at her until she squirmed under his stare. "Need I remind you you're my lover for the time being? You're like a property of mine and I won't have any of those bastards…staring at your…your *assets*."

"I'm like five feet tall and almost invisible, Jules. Nobody's going to stare except, hopefully, Garrett. And then he'll propose and we'll have babies together."

*Over my dead, rotting body, you will!*

He was a hair from hyperventilating by now. "I didn't sign up to play the part of the freaking fool, Molls. What am I supposed to do while you hold court at the family gathering? You're supposed to be *my* girl!"

Her eyes sparkled in mirth, because she'd probably never seen him worked up to a lather before. "Well, at least you can give your big 'guns' a good workout as you fend off my unwanted suitors, huh."

He stalked over and grabbed her shoulders, not amused and very freaking jealous about all this. "Damned right I will, and you know why?"

"Enlighten me."

"All the guys in attendance, from Landon's friends to

business associates, are going to swarm you like a pack of starving beasts. They always have, and you don't even notice. You're so damned different, Molly..." She had no idea, no idea what she did to him or anyone else. She was not only blind to him, she was blind to all men. The looks she received while she was staring off into space, thinking of a painting, were never even noticed.

Had she forgotten all the invitations she'd had to prom? She hadn't even attended, but she goddamned well had been asked.

"You really think I'm different, Jules? You know, maybe that's because of my special relationship with my Oster!"

He laughed and wondered when the hell he would hear the last of that. *Never,* he thought, then growled in frustration and clenched her shoulders. "You don't need to change one whit about you to catch a man. If you need to change your identity to make him see something great about you, then Garrett doesn't deserve you. None of those bastards do."

Something he said struck a chord. Molly stopped fiddling with the bag and clutched it firmly to her abdomen. She surveyed him in curious speculation and tilted her head a notch, those sky-blue eyes wide with innocent expectation.

"So basically," she said, her lips lifting at the corners, those same lips he wanted to kiss more than anything until they were red and swollen and only his. "So what you're saying is—I *do* look good?"

Julian stood ramrod stiff as he struggled to reply, not wanting her to be seen like this by anyone. Anyone. But he owed her the truth and he had to shove his jealousy aside if it killed him.

And it was. Killing him.

Looking at her like this. Killing him.

Wanting her and having to wait. *Killing him*.

He twirled his finger in the air and thickly commanded, "Give a little spin for me."

She spun, slowly. Yep, killing him. Her butt was so perky and round he could already feel it in his hands. Needing to do something—touch her, anywhere—he reached out to tuck a loose tendril of red hair behind her ear, then his lips curled ever so slightly on one side as he inclined his head just a fraction, and said in a gruff voice, "Yeah, baby. You look good." And he gave that rump a little playful pat because he'd been aching to. "Too damned good."

# Five

"*So do you think Garrett will like my dress, too?*"

Molly's question irritated Julian like a painful snakebite as they drove to Landon and Beth's gated home. He hesitated before at last answering her with a tender squeeze of her hands, which she'd been nervously wringing on her lap. "No doubt about it, Mopey. Just relax, you look stunning."

But now it was he, Julian John Gage, who needed to relax.

He felt like drinking hard, but he wasn't stupid enough to get drunk like the night of the masquerade party, when he'd lost control and acted like some sixteen-year-old dweeb with his first girlfriend.

Oh, no. Tonight he needed all five senses and then some.

Tonight Molly needed him to put on a show and damned if he wasn't aching to give it to her.

To *all* of his family.

But he felt like he had a bomb strapped to his rib cage

and he wondered if he'd be able to keep his usual cool. His success might depend on it. Keeping cool, biding his time, being patient. Logically, that was what he must do. But Molly was in love with his brother, dammit, and both his head and his cool had left him a week ago when he'd learned of it.

Things he had planned to do his whole life were happening, and precipitously. Regrettably, not in the manner he had intended them to.

Never had he imagined he would experience this much jealousy over the girl he'd always planned to have for himself falling in love with his brother.

God, he still couldn't believe this was true.

Still, he was trying very hard to screw his head back on and focus on enjoying the parts of the evening he knew would bring him pleasure.

Like showing off his new "girlfriend" to his family. "Mother, have you met Molly?" he could ask while the unspoken words that floated between them would be, *The woman you warned me never to touch? I'm tumbling her all night now, and she loves it. We both do. Hey, will you excuse us for a moment? We're going to go ahead and have sex out by the bushes....*

But sadly, not even that thought brought him comfort as he handed his keys over to the valet and strode over to help Molly out of the car.

Her scent dizzied him as she stood up from the low seat.

Creamy legs…silken red hair…the sexy-as-hell curve of her neck just begging to be bitten…

He wasn't going to think about that now. In silence, he focused on how warm and calm the night breeze was as he led her up the staircase, her hand unsteady in his.

"Molls?"

"Mmm?"

He wanted to tell her she had never looked more beautiful to him. Instead, he lifted her hand and placed a soft kiss on the back of it, tipping her chin encouragingly with his other hand. "We've got this," he murmured, and her instant smile wrapped around his heart.

Hand in hand, they entered the gleaming foyer of the two-story mansion, where a harpist welcomed them with a slow, haunting tune. The gathering consisted of a small group of friends and family and of course Landon's enormous mastiffs, who were plopped on the rug at the far end of the living room.

Molly had told Julian earlier that Kate and Beth's business, Catering, Canapés and Curry, was handling tonight's party.

So at least the food would be good.

As soon as Julian and Molly were spotted, they were split apart. Kate and Beth sequestered Molly for interrogation while his mother, in an evening dress and a pair of bed slippers, flew over to Julian before he could even find a server with a wine selection. "My dear son! My dear, dear son!" she called from afar, crossing the room toward him. "What's this I hear about you and Molly, JJ?"

"Mother, why did you give me two names if you did not plan to use them?" he said, exasperated.

"All right then, Julian John—answer me now and don't test me. My nerves are frazzled as it is without any help from you these days!"

A fond smile played on his lips as his mother stopped an arm's length away, regal and elegant even in slippers and panting for her breath—something only a matron like Eleanor Gage could pull off.

Julian could already taste the satisfaction of watching the "news" affect and disgruntle his overprotective mother. She, who had sent him to Spain, France, Russia and Africa to separate him from his best friend. She, who had warned him if he ever touched the only girl he'd ever truly cared for, he might as well not consider himself a part of the Gage family anymore.

Yeah, it gave him pleasure, perverse pleasure, to see if she would make good on her threats. A part of him savored the fight with her even though he loved her. It had hurt him, incredibly, to be judged and condemned by his entire family for a sin he hadn't yet committed.

He'd been punished since he was just an adolescent, and he'd been suffering ever since.

Yes. It felt good to rebel against them. To give them the exact thing they were afraid of. Because soon they would see how wrong they'd been about him. Dead. *Wrong.*

So now that she was narrow-eyed and thrusting her chin out in warning, Julian ducked his head to her height and kissed her cheek smoothly, unperturbed by her bravado. "If you heard that Molly is with me, then you heard the truth, Mother. Now you can finally make good on your threat and disown me."

Eleanor drew back with a shocked little breath, genuinely traumatized by his suggestion.

Julian wanted to assure her he didn't need the trust his father had left anymore. He could live lavishly with his savings alone, plus he already had a promising business ready to launch, with several billion-dollar companies lined up as clients for his PR services. Instead, he smiled at her to defuse the tension and tucked a wisp of ebony hair behind her ear.

"You knew this would happen, Mother," he said softly. "Just as I knew someday I'd have to prove to you how much I want her and how far I'm willing to go."

Her eyes, the only ones in the family that were green like his own, flared wide with accusation. Julian waited for her comeback, but words seemed to be failing her at the moment.

He really wished that if his mother was staring at him as if he were a monster, it was because sweet, lovely Molly was crazy about him, couldn't keep her hands off him and was letting him have his way with her in bed, in the shower, in the car, in the kitchen and in every place he could think of. And not because of this idiotic little lie.

He needed her to be his.

He didn't know how much longer he could wait, or what it would take for her to realize she and Garrett weren't compatible in any single way that she and Julian were.

"If you think I'm going to let you use that girl like all those Janes you go out with, you're sorely mistaken, Julian John. I'm like that girl's *mother*."

He nodded in agreement. He had definitely understood the position his mother had been placed in two decades ago when the Devaneys had been brought to the house. She had been a recent widow with three young sons, feeling responsible for the death of an employee who left two young daughters orphaned. His mother, always stern but nonetheless a loving woman, had taken them in, but hardened her position with her sons in the process.

It was too much on her nerves to ever think the boys would harm the girls in any way; after all, they owed them their father. And yet nobody had ever understood that Julian did not want to hurt Molly. Just as he did not want to hurt his mother now. It just was what it was.

He wanted Molly. And no one was going to stop him from having her anymore.

In feigned aloofness, he grasped one of her jeweled hands and indolently patted it between both of his. "Why don't you have a little more faith in me as well, Mother? And let us be happy together, for once." Before he left to greet Landon and his wife, he grumbled, "I'd never hurt Molly. *Ever.* And it hurts me that you even think I would."

Molly stood at the other end of the living room with Kate and Beth, who was being brought up to speed on all the excitement.

"I can't believe this. Landon and I leave for two months, we come back and you and Julian are *dating?*"

Molly waved a hand excitedly. "We're actually way past that, Beth. I've moved in already." She nodded proudly, then added, "But you know, that's exactly how shocked I felt when I emerged from a long creative streak in my studio to find out Landon had remarried. I didn't even have a clue he'd met someone. Julian should've kept me up-to-date all those nights he brought Chinese food!"

Looking past Beth, Molly spotted Landon, another gorgeous Gage specimen. He kept glancing in their direction as he addressed Julian, and although Landon was not a man easily perturbed, even *he* appeared slightly confused as he spoke to his youngest brother this evening. Garrett joined them within seconds, and Molly could just sigh at the sight of his broad back. She could imagine their next kiss and already knew it would be as hot as the first....

With a wistful smile, she watched the three men, all of whom she adored. The chandelier lights caught on Julian's streaked golden hair, which sharply contrasted with both of his older brothers' dark coloring, and she melted with tenderness for him. Just to think Julian might be taking crap from his brothers because he was supposedly dating her only endeared him to her more. Would Garrett do something like this for her?

While Julian lounged around effortlessly, seemingly careless to everything they said, Garrett stood sterner, more tense and, hopefully, already jealous. Landon, however, had never looked so utterly relaxed. Like a man completely satisfied with the state of his life and thoroughly in love, as was evident from the frequent looks he stole in Beth's direction.

"Landon said he always knew this would happen," Bethany offered in a private whisper, oblivious to her husband's attention across the room as she leaned closer to Molly. "When our plane landed, he called his office and heard about you two from Garrett. He wasn't even surprised about it. He said it was inevitable."

"He did?"

It was a shock to Molly.

Because who on earth would ever think Julian and Molly could be more than friends?

It was ridiculous. Molly didn't even like to date. And Julian was a playboy.

Plus, the Gage family still viewed her as a child, except for Garrett, who seemed to be the only one who'd realized she was now a full-grown woman. A *kissable* grown woman.

Still reeling at the idea, she looked back at the group of men, intending to admire Garrett from afar and remind herself why she was so in love with him, but her gaze snagged on Julian as he calmly explained something to his brothers.

Already having disposed of both his black jacket and his silver tie, Jules exuded powerful masculinity and self-assurance as he stood there, the cuffs of his shirt rolled up to his elbows to expose his tanned, thick forearms. His stance was so wide and confident, it seemed to say, *Yeah, baby, I own me, I own this and I own you.*

Before Molly could force her gaze back to the man she loved, Julian seemed to sense her scrutiny, for suddenly, his head turned. The smile he wore gradually vanished.

With the glittering lights overhead, his eyes, those eyes that changed from gray-green to gold-green in a moment, right now looked as green as Colombian emeralds. And they blazed at her from across the room—almost proprietarily, as if he *also* thought he owned the little black dress she wore and the pair of black panties underneath.

*Molly! You did not just think of your panties!*

Mortified, she jerked her gaze away, her stomach clenching, and then she had to look back at Julian. Because…surely she had hallucinated that he was giving her the Wolf vs. Red Riding Hood stare?

He said something to Garrett and started in her direction, and before Molly could understand why her insides spun in turmoil, she realized he must be putting on a show. A show so that Garrett could see that she was desirable to him. And he would get terribly jealous and feel forced to tear them apart and stake his claim on Molly once and for all.

Yes, of course. It was all part of the plan. And it was brilliant.

But as Julian walked toward her with that slow tiger prowl-walk and his stare held her captive, her legs liquefied. She hadn't felt this desirable since the night Garrett had kissed her. The way he stared at her made her feel… wanted. Womanly. So, so, womanly.

Wow, this guy was so good at this.

And he was hot.

And tonight, everyone in this room thought he was *hers*.

"Get over here and dance with me," he prodded as he reached for her with a strong, long-fingered hand.

Molly grinned. "There's no dance floor, you dope."

"Come on, Mo-Mo. There's music and that's all we need."

She smiled and took his hand, and a surprising bolt of

electricity shot through her as he clasped her fingers. He spun her into his arms and yanked her effortlessly against him, almost dizzying her with his strength.

She swallowed a small curse, unprepared to feel his powerful body aligning so perfectly with hers. And suddenly Julian had erased all the distance between them. And Molly had seen him in his *briefs*. And he was so close.

His body warmth enveloped her, causing her muscles to relax while at the same time an odd hyperawareness built inside her midsection. It…disconcerted her.

"You're so good at this, it's almost annoying," she told him with a smile.

And she hardly believed *how* good he was as she wrapped her arms around his strong nape, trying not to think of how utterly helpless she would feel if Julian was to turn on the charm with her like he did with all of his flings. Not that it would ever happen, or even that it would work. Because there could only be one man for her, and he'd *better* be watching them.

"Is Garrett looking?" she whispered, desperate to get this fake-lover charade over with. It was becoming dangerous…playing house with Julian. It was too fun and too easy. "Is he looking this way, Jules?"

"I don't know, Molls, I'm looking at you."

It was the tone he used, deep and husky as a country love song, that made her insides move in a way that made her supremely uncomfortable. Or maybe the sensation was due to the fact that Garrett must be watching them dance. It had to be. For it felt as if the Earth had stopped and not only Garrett, but the entire world, was watching them dance—or at least sway to the harp tune in the middle of Landon's living room.

"I'm pretty sure he's watching," she whispered, moving closer to Julian's ear. There, she leaned against his chest and whispered, "I'm thinking we could just stroll off somewhere and return a little disheveled, you know. Or go lock ourselves in a closet for fifteen minutes and let his imagination run wild."

She could feel the coiled tension in the muscles underneath his shirt as he dropped his head to whisper back into her ear, his lips grazing the lobe. "As you wish."

Fireflies exploded in her stomach, the words were so unexpected, as unexpected as the caressing bump of his lips against her earlobe. Molly drew back with a start, trying to calm her racing heart, telling herself he couldn't possibly know what those words did to her. Or how deeply they spoke to her. "Really?" she whispered, shaking her reaction aside. "It's a good idea?"

He arrested her gaze with tender, heavy-lidded eyes that threatened her equilibrium. All she knew was that in her favorite movie of all time, Westley looked at Buttercup in *just* this manner.

And this was just the way Garrett had to look at her by the end of the evening.

"Yeah." Julian lightly chucked her chin, then with painstakingly slowness, smoothed his calloused thumb across her lower lip in a way that made her shiver. "I've always enjoyed a little closet fun. Let's get lost."

Molly didn't remember moving so fast in her entire life—even though she had to stop several times because she was laughing so hard—than when Julian dragged her down the long hallway. She felt intoxicated with an incredible sense of freedom and mischief and fun—and when she caught a glimpse of Julian's sexy, curvy smile, she wanted to fling herself into his arms and kiss him from the excitement alone.

Within seconds he came to an abrupt stop and efficiently shoved her inside a small downstairs office.

The instant the door closed after him, Molly's heart stopped.

Darkness enveloped them. Silence and seclusion spread between them, around them, like a cloak of velvet. But in this closed space, nearly entirely occupied by a big mahogany desk, Julian's scent suddenly stormed around her like a tornado, and it made her lungs burn. He smelled clean and of spices and within seconds Molly couldn't seem to stand still. Her mouth watered, and she swallowed.

"Do you have lipstick in your purse?" he asked in a voice roughened with exertion.

Her eyes adjusted to the shadows, and she realized with a start that Julian was undoing the top buttons of his white shirt. Molly could barely organize her thoughts at the sight of his tanned throat being exposed, then the hollow between his collarbones, then a part of his pectorals.

She licked her lips and, without even thinking, she lunged at him.

Going straight for the dirty business, she coiled her arms firmly around his neck and kissed his square jaw, pressing her body against his marble-hard one. Next she trailed her lips down the length of his throat. She'd surprised him, she supposed. For he stood utterly still, maybe not even alive.

Oh, no, but he was definitely alive, very much so. His warmth seeped through his clothes and spread heat all the way to her bone marrow. Intoxicated by the incredible feel of his taut, warm skin under her roaming lips, Molly trailed a path of kisses down to his collarbone, where she crazily wondered if she should just go ahead and trace it with her tongue.

"Molly?"

Julian's voice was a thick rasp.

"Mmm," she answered, placing a gentle kiss in that hollow at the base of his throat.

"You could've used your lipstick straight on me, baby. You didn't have to kiss me."

It took a moment for that guttural whisper to register. She had been happily—maybe too happily—dragging her lips along the thick tendons of his throat so that they ended up smeared peach and no one doubted, not even Julian and especially not Garrett, that Molly had kissed him.

She stopped abruptly and backed off in sudden confusion, all of her body heat concentrating on her cheeks. "What do you mean…? I don't even remember where I left my purse, I think Beth has it."

He must have heard the utter embarrassment in her voice, for he gathered her back against him, his voice even thicker and rougher than before. "Shh. Go on then. This works, too."

But she hesitated, her cheeks now scalding. As though encouraging her, Julian undid another button of his shirt, so leisurely that as she watched she began to focus on details she had never thought of before. How gracefully his fingers moved. How both their breaths ricocheted off the walls of the small space.

How she could feel his eyes burn like lasers through the top of her head as she watched him undo another button.

How a hot little tingle spread across every inch of her skin.

And how this would all be so easy to dismiss if she hadn't seen him almost *naked*…

"Now try kissing me a little lower."

He spread his shirt open, fully open, and Molly's windpipe clamped shut. Her knees wobbled in place. Jules could be a sculpture, he was so defined and so lean. At such a short distance, he looked even *more* ripped, like a top athlete. Molly could see every square indentation of his wash-board abs, every sharp rise and fall of muscle.

A tremor rushed through her, and when she didn't move, he slipped his hands onto the back of her head and gently urged her toward him. His fingers were long and felt gentle on her scalp, and as she set her palms on his rib cage and bent her head to his collarbone, she felt his fingertips work on her butterfly clasp and undo her hair.

A hot little shiver rushed from the top of her scalp to the tips of her toes as her hair tumbled to her shoulders. Trembling, she lowered her head and set a dry kiss on the V of his neck. Gingerly at first, holding her breath, trying to suppress another tremor building inside her body. Julian stood utterly still, and she wondered if he held his breath, too. Then she heard him softly say, "Go lower."

Her eyes drifted shut and she set down another kiss, pressing her lips lightly against the tautly stretched skin above his six-pack. She felt the muscles contract under her fingerprints, and her tummy clenched in response. Why did she feel so shaky? Why was her mind spinning inside her cranium? She felt like a teenager stealing a first kiss, like a bad girl misbehaving, which she'd never been before. Of course it was all due to the excitement of making Garrett jealous. She had to remind herself all these emotions were due to the fact that her and Julian's plan was so good, it was going to *work*.

"Lower, baby," he murmured in a thick, raspy voice.

She was so trusting of Julian that she almost automatically obeyed, following his instructions without hesitation, while in the back of her mind she started to wonder how he would get Garrett to see that Molly had kissed his washboard abs, too. Daydreaming of Garrett's jealous face while a strange liquid fire simmered through her veins, she let her lips wander lower, Julian's skin hot and silky under her lips…her heart thundering in her ears as she heard him once again rasp, "Lower." Feeling like she was dreaming, she went lower, her eyes feeling heavy as a strange tremor tingled along her nerve endings, until she heard him unzip his pants.

Startled, she lifted her head in confusion. He was laughing down at her, his eyes sparkling in the shadows, those sensual lips curled at the corners as he zipped back up.

"You're so innocent, Molls. I was wondering when you'd catch on," he said.

She smacked his elbow and straightened, already feeling a rush of color climb up her cheekbones. "You jerk!"

She tried pushing him aside but he seized her wrists and yanked her back to him, his laughter lingering in his voice. "No, no, no, not yet, baby. We need to work on you now."

He rumpled her hair with those long-fingered hands and Molly felt herself clam up, her throat closing with an unnameable emotion. She felt…unsteady. Vulnerable and open to him. Even those feathery touches on her scalp felt special. Electric. Rushing from the roots of her hair to her brain, charging her with inexplicable adrenaline.

As he worked on her hair, the mist of his breath fanned, warm and minty, across her forehead, and she had to use all her effort to fight the impossible flames flicking through her body. His smell was killing her. Dizzying her.

What was happening to her?

This was Julian, not Garrett. *Julian.*

She sucked in an unsteady breath, and his hands went still on the crown of her head. Their eyes locked in the dark as his hands slid down to her nape as he slowly ducked toward her. Closer. Closer.

She was frozen in place, her voice a breathless whisper. "Julian…what are you doing…?"

"Shh. I just want some of your lipstick on my mouth.

Just a little." His breathing changed as he secured her cheeks between his big hands, and she became aware of the bite of something incredibly large and rigid against her stomach.

"Julian…" she said, turning her head to the side. Their noses brushed accidentally, but rather than pull back, Julian dipped his head even farther and scraped his mouth purposely across hers.

The contact singed.

Her mouth parted on a gasp.

Julian pulled back, his eyes gleaming in the darkness. Then he lowered his head and repeated the motion, scraping his mouth across hers. Her legs went rubbery, her core melting like lava.

A little quiver rippled through her, followed by a surge of desire so sharp and powerful, her world tilted on its axis. Not even Garrett's kiss had done this to her. Nothing on this earth had *ever* done this to her. She shouldn't feel such blazing need swimming through her veins, shouldn't want to feel more, feel everything.

But she did, goodness, she did.

His nearness intoxicated her, the brush of his sensual lips fascinated her beyond measure, and she felt weak with wanting, had never wanted anything so much as she ·wanted to be kissed by him. Right now, in this tiny lightless room, this very instant. Kissed thoroughly and deeply by this sex god everyone wanted but no one could ever have. Least of all Molly.

But Julian did not kiss her. Only teased her with the possibility of it. The delicious scent of his body enveloped and dizzied her. It was incredible; this feeling of flying. He was so familiar and at the same time totally new. As if discovering your body could do something you never expected it to. This was how it felt to awaken to Julian John. And that was the only word she could think of. *Awaken.*

*To Julian John.*

He just had to kiss her.

*Please kiss me.*

Her breathing escalated and her lips parted as he scraped his mouth across hers for the third time. She heard a sound come out of herself and almost collapsed in a puddle on the floor when he released her.

"There. I'm probably wearing more lipstick than you are now. Come on, Mo-Mo. Let's get out of here."

He went to open the office door, and light from the corridor spilled in, silhouetting his magnificent form. Their eyes met across the gloom while he waited for her to get her bearings. But her knees felt like soup.

Her legs like noodles.

She blinked but couldn't focus.

She couldn't even breathe.

She didn't know what was wrong with her, but her mind was screaming for him to come back, for him to kiss her, for her to kiss him, for her to do anything to be kissed by Julian John. And suddenly when he swung around to leave, she blurted out, "JJ, wait!"

Her heart stopped when he froze, and for a wild instant, all that was audible in the dark room was both their uneven breathing. Their eyes met again—and something electrifying pulsed between them.

He closed the door so slowly her heart almost disintegrated, and then she heard a click as it hit the doorjamb. Darkness swallowed them again, darkness and something wild and untamable. An unbearable intensity charged the air as he took a step forward.

Molly was not thinking right, felt drunk with sensations. With expectation. *Anticipation.*

"What did you just say?" Julian asked. His voice was very, very soft. Dangerously soft.

Molly held her breath, her lungs near bursting. "I said *JJ*."

His eyes shimmered like lanterns in the night, and her heart rattled in her chest and the blood roared in her ears as he took that last step closer.

With slow, deliberate precision, he placed his hands on either side of her head against the back wall and caged her between his arms as he leaned forward. A gravelly sound stole into his voice as he slid his fingers through her loose hair and encircled the back of her head. "Say it to my face, Molly. Say it one more time to my face. I dare you."

Longing burst open inside her. Hunger. Want. *Everything.*

She knew this was crazy and wrong and yet she couldn't help herself, couldn't stop. Her body was trembling, head-to-toe, trembling. He had been playing a game with her and perhaps she wanted to play back, but this was more than a game.

Maybe?

Was it?

She didn't know anything anymore, except that maybe she should apologize for calling him by his most loathed nickname and just leave.

Maybe she didn't really want to be kissed by Julian John, because she wanted Garrett. Or maybe she'd truly lost her head tonight, because as she met his gaze in the shadows, she heard herself speak between panting breaths.

"I said *JJ,* JJ."

The silence was deafening.

Julian's eyes widened, for he was sure that he hadn't

heard right the first time. But this second time, he just couldn't believe it.

Molly had called him JJ, and he was going to have to make her pay for that. Stat.

In a whiplash move, he yanked her up against him and hoarsely demanded, in a voice as jagged as torn paper, "Do you remember what I told you I would do if you ever, ever called me JJ again?"

Smiling a smile that was all mischief, Molly tilted her back, her breasts rising and falling fast. She nodded slowly, provocatively—tauntingly.

The little she-cat wanted this!

Almost drugged with the thought of exacting his punishment, Julian caressed his hands up her slender arms, savoring the feel of her smooth skin against his calloused palms. "Well, then, I'm going to have to kiss you now," he purred, the words acting like foreplay as he leaned closer. He could almost taste the gloss on her lips already.

"O-okay, Jules," she said, almost a squeak as she gripped the rolled-up sleeves at his elbows as though hanging on to him for dear life.

Swamped with every single emotion in the world and close to exploding with wanting her, he cupped her face between his large hands and lowered his head, his heart going a powerful *baboom baboom baboom*. "'Okay, Jules'? Is that all you have to say? All right, then, you asked for it, Moo…now you're getting it good…"

He started easy, her face framed in his grasp as he lightly set his lips on hers, but with that whisper touch alone, lightning streaked across his veins and seared their mouths like fire. Suddenly, that single, wholly erotic fusion of their bodies lit his entire being on fire. He grabbed her closer, and she slid her hands up his bulging arms, their mouths parting hungrily in unison.

Groaning as her plush lips opened for him, he plowed his tongue into her mouth in a thirsty search for hers. Her soft moan tumbled down his throat as she shyly licked him back.

She tasted like peaches. And he *loved* peaches.

Deepening their kiss, he trailed his open palms down to the small of her back and conformed her curvy body to his. Her breasts softly pressed against his diaphragm, and it drove him crazy when she rubbed the tips of her nipples up against the wall of his chest.

Her nails bit into his shoulders while her mouth eagerly explored his, and when her hips began rocking against his, too, his senses swam with both pain and euphoria. The pain came from his pulsing length pressing against his pants zipper, aching to grind against those luscious hips she taunted him with.

His fingertips dug into her waist as he crushed her tighter to him, and plunged deeper into her mouth, stealing dozens of incredibly sweet and wet tastes of her. Ten. Eleven. Twelve. She tasted pure. And he desperately wanted to make love to her.

Undone by her wildness, he grappled with her hands and lifted them above her head, pinning her against the back wall. This surprised her, and she gasped. He caught the sound and kissed her harder. Wetter. Longer.

His body exploded in chaos as she responded in kind, pulling her arms free and rubbing her hands up his biceps, through his hair, making soft purring sounds against his mouth.

She felt incredible. *Incredible.*

He had never wanted anything or anyone more in his life. Molly. His tiny, sweet little gypsy. He wanted to hear her come undone for him, to lose control like she made him lose his.

But did she really want this? Did she have any idea how serious he was about this, about *her?*

"Molly," he murmured tenderly, then he dived down her neck and twirled a wet path to her delicate collarbone.

"Don't stop yet," she mewed in a little helpless plea, her fingertips sliding back into his hair. "Please let me pretend for a little bit."

His insides twisted with foreboding. "Don't you *dare*—" he came back up and shoved his tongue into her mouth, taking all of her taste, taking all that she could give "—pretend that I'm my brother."

But that tormenting thought now held him back like an iron chain, and he had to rest his forehead against hers with a groan, his breaths jerking in and out as he fought to get a grip. Suddenly, the reminder that Molly was making out with him to make his brother jealous gnawed a hole the size of Texas into his gut.

But her slim arms still clung to him. Her face was still tilted up to his in offering. And he could hardly think straight while she looked up at him as if she adored him.

"You look thoroughly kissed, Molly," he rasped. He cradled her beautiful face with his big hands, drinking up the dewy desire that softened her features.

She licked her lips, her pupils dilating as her gaze darted from his eyes to his mouth, up and down, up and down. He could barely speak, his voice roughened with painful, dizzying arousal.

"Should we just go out there so my brother gets to see what I've been doing to you? He'll probably think I've had my hands all over you this evening."

She made a little choking sound and dropped her face. "Jules, stop. Please don't tease."

Julian's thighs trembled as he fought for control, fought

to keep from doing more, doing everything to her. With her. "I'd just like to know if this kiss was just for Garrett— or because you want me, Molly?"

She kept her head bent, intoxicating him with the smell of raspberry shampoo that wafted to his nostrils. "Everybody wants you, Julian. Everybody. I just can't believe this. What did we do? This was so insane, so stupid!"

"Shh." He pinned her against him when she squirmed, his hands firmly curled around her shoulders as he kissed the top of her head and tried to ease her. "If you can't do this sort of stupid thing with your best friend, then I don't know who the hell you can do it with."

She shook her head but nonetheless buried her nose in the crook of his neck. "I didn't mean for this to happen. All this is your fault! For being such an expert seducer— please don't let go yet. I just want you to hold me. Jules, you smell so good...."

One two three four five six seven eight nine ten eleven twelve...

Not enough. He could count to a million and it was not. Enough. Not enough of her. Not enough time. To hold her. Be with her. Drown in her.

A groan of pent-up desire rumbled up from deep within his throat as his fingers clenched around her waist. "I wasn't seducing you, Molly—but you shouldn't have tempted me to kiss you." Unable to stop himself, he recklessly slid his hands upward to engulf her breasts as he heatedly nibbled on her earlobe. "Now I want to kiss you until you're weak and pliant in my arms. Until you tell me what it is that you really want, because I don't think you even know what you're asking for—"

"*So!* Are you two finished in here—or do we have to call the fire department?"

* * *

The baritone voice that cut through Julian's delicious, seductive words yanked Molly to full wakefulness. She jerked in Julian's arms as if she'd just been dumped into the frigid waters off Alaska and straightened to see Garrett— the man she wanted to marry—standing just outside the open door. Landon stood next to him, and while Landon's expression verged on amusement, Garrett did not look pleased.

*And now he'll think I'm a whore.*

The sudden thought popped into her mind and she almost wanted to groan in self-pity.

Her cheeks glowed hot as Julian pushed her behind him in a stance that reeked of protectiveness, and she was grateful for that. Taking advantage, she hid against his back and frantically struggled to rearrange her dress and hair.

"We'll be done as soon as you two dopes leave us alone."

How Julian could sound so calm and collected, she didn't know, because panic had gripped Molly by the throat and she could hardly even breathe now.

She'd wanted Garrett to imagine she and Julian had shared a little romp this evening. But she had never, ever expected to be caught while doing it.

What had she been thinking? She had clearly been undone by the strange, tantalizing complexity of Julian's male scent, the desperate desires his mouth evoked, his kisses always somehow bringing the heartbreaking reminder of her night with Garrett at the masquerade. Every time she kissed Julian, her chest began to *ache,* and not in a good way.

"We apologize, but Mother sent us," she heard Landon explain to Jules almost apologetically. "Not a task I was looking forward to."

"I'm surprised she didn't summon the whole party to

come stop us," Julian grumbled, and with one of his powerful arms, he slammed the door back shut.

Cursing low in his throat once they were alone, he extended an arm to keep the door closed and glanced past his shoulder.

"You okay?"

"Yes," she said as she arranged herself frantically, wanting the small room to develop an appetite and suddenly swallow her whole. She couldn't believe Julian had touched her *breasts* just now.

"The point was to look disheveled, Molls. And you do."

He sounded calm, almost too calm. When he reached into his pants pocket and handed over her butterfly clasp, Molly reached for it and clipped her hair back as best she could, her hands still trembling when she finished.

She sighed dejectedly.

What Julian had said made sense, of course. But she felt incredibly guilty and maybe still a little aroused. The things he had been saying to her before they were interrupted? The things he had been saying while he was cupping her breasts?

That was major, major stuff he'd been whispering in her ear!

"You're right," she said, avoiding his gaze, his all-knowing gaze that would intuitively pick up on just how far past her comfort zone they had gone. "This is perfect, couldn't be more perfect. You're a master, Jules. Master of disaster." She gave him a quick peck on the cheek and tried to sound businesslike. "Thank you."

Ducking under his arm, she yanked the door open and swept outside. Determinedly, she walked past both the Gage men, who stood like sentinels down the hall, with their black suits and matching impassive expressions on their faces.

She shot each of them a smile, smiling with her in-flamed mouth that had just been kissed like a hussy's.

She even pretended she was proud of it.

But she could feel Julian's eyes on her back, sensed he hadn't moved from the office doorway yet, and as she rounded the corner to the busy and crowded living room, all she wanted was to find a nice spot where she could collapse safely and sort out her out-of-whack emotions.

She heard footsteps and suddenly Garrett loomed at her side, his fingers curling around her elbow. "I'd like to talk to you in private, Molly," he said. "Do you have time tomorrow?"

Surprised, she looked into her beloved's eyes while an avalanche of emotions buffeted her from the inside.

He seemed concerned, intense, his obsidian eyes peer-ing into hers so fiercely, she feared he'd be able to see how aroused and guilty she was.

"Of course," she said with a shaky nod, her voice husky for all the wrong reasons. "I'll stop by your office at noon, Garrett."

"Thank you," he said softly, and placed a kiss on her forehead, his hands lingering on her cheeks for a second.

She was so numb that she couldn't even enjoy his ca-ress that she'd fantasized about feeling again for days and nights.

She could hardly believe that she'd finally caught his attention.

In a daze, she crossed the living room toward Kate and Beth, her thoughts scattered and unfocused. She should be celebrating, she knew. Garrett wanted to talk to her in private tomorrow, and he was, at the very least, concerned. Maybe he was even hiding his jealousy with grave effort. By all appearances, her plan was succeeding. Wasn't that what she'd been dreaming of accomplishing?

But no. She couldn't enjoy her victory because she was too rattled by what she'd done.

What on earth had gotten into her, to tempt Julian the way she had? Were those the actions of a woman in love with another man?

And what if things became awkward with Julian now? What if this stupid charade affected the one relationship in her life she cherished above anything?

"What on earth happened to you?" Kate cried with one startled look at her.

Molly decided she was going to own up to it.

Whatever her sins, whatever her mistake, she was going to *own up to it* if it killed her.

"Julian and I made out in the dark. You should try it sometime, Kate. It was actually fun before those two idiots interrupted."

She glared in the direction of Garrett and Landon, then saw Julian stroll from around the corner of the hall, his hands in his pockets, his blond hair mussed. *Sexy* didn't begin to describe the man. He looked tousled. Delish. Thoroughly kissed, as he'd put it—and there was no question about it. Streaks of what looked like Molly's peach lipstick slashed all over his tan skin. Marking his thick throat, up along his jaw, across the side of his plush lips. He looked so rumpled he could've just battled a Siberian tiger in a cage, and for some reason, knowing the tiger had been *her* caused a pool of liquid heat to rush between her thighs.

"Julian, what happened to you?" Beth asked as he approached.

Julian's green gaze tracked and zeroed in on Molly, and her swollen mouth began to burn under the intimacy of his stare. Between her legs, she burned. Her breasts, the very breasts he had cradled in his enormous hands, pricked hotly in remembrance. Quite simply, and too damn easily, he set her ablaze with his gaze, reminding her of his blatantly sexual words, almost causing her to combust.

"Molls and I had a little fun in the downstairs office. You okay, baby?"

His voice, still husky enough to resemble the timbre he'd used in the dark, did wild things to her overstimulated senses. Awareness had quickly skyrocketed to hyperawareness in that empty office, and now she was frantic to power these sensations off.

While the other women processed his words in stunned silence, Julian made a thorough assessment of Molly's face with a measured expression on his own.

Was he worried they'd gone too far, too?

Trying to offer some reassurance, Molly let her lips curl upward, loathing this awkwardness between them. But thankfully, a playful light kindled to life in his eyes. When he gave her his wolfish smile, Molly almost sagged in relief.

Visibly relaxing, too, Julian put his arms around her and dragged her to his side, and Molly knew as she snuggled against him that whatever happened, it was all going to be all right.

As long as she had Julian.

"You know I love you, don't you?" she whispered up at him once again, kissing his hard cheek. It was not the first time she'd said it, not at all. But this time, he drew back and met her gaze, his smile fading. Then he planted a long, hard kiss on her temple, his voice gruff as he told her, in her ear, so nobody else could hear, "So do I."

# Six

*So here we are now,* Molly thought as she rode the elevator up to the top floor of the *San Antonio Daily* building the next day.

At last Garrett seemed to be ready to do something about her situation with Julian. The question was: What was he going to do?

And how was Molly going to react to it?

She honestly didn't know. Whatever happened today, though, she wore her largest earrings and her thickest bangles and her sassiest attitude to the meeting. It was a trick she used when she needed the extra security boost. There was just something about big jewelry that made her feel better no matter how dreary things looked or how anxious she felt. So now it was one minute until noon, and she was every bit the confident lady as she marched down the long hall that led to the executive offices.

"Molly!" Julian's assistant exclaimed with obvious

warmth, glancing up at her through her spectacles from behind an enormous desk. "I didn't know you were paying a visit! He went out to lunch...."

Smiling, Molly greeted the older woman with an affectionate hug. Ms. Watts had been with Jules forever and sometimes conspired with Molly to pull Julian out of important meetings. Just for fun.

"I'm actually here for Garrett today, Ms. Watts." But her stomach felt queasy, and suddenly she very much wished she was having lunch with Julian instead.

She was led directly into his office by Garrett's assistant, a younger woman who sat at an identically enormous desk not too far away. Molly couldn't help but straighten her spine when she was announced. "Miss Devaney to see you, Mr. Gage," the assistant intoned, and then quickly shut the doors behind her.

Over six feet tall, with dark hair and broad shoulders, Garrett stood by the window with his hands in his jacket pockets, radiating intimidation. Her knees felt knobby as she walked forward, somehow expecting to catch a glimpse of something telling in his expression. But his face revealed nothing at all when he turned around and gave her a brief, almost businesslike smile.

"Molly, I don't think I need to tell you why you're here? Or why Kate—" he signaled to her sister, whom Molly just now noticed sitting behind Garrett's desk, pretty as you please "—and I want to talk to you today."

Molly sat down across the desk from Kate, still absorbing the fact that he had not meant to have a "private" conversation with her at all. Private had merely meant without Julian present.

The realization made her scowl at him, her blackest, angriest scowl.

She couldn't help noticing Garrett seemed so detached

today, unlike the passionate lover of that magical evening. Of course, the man had excellent control, so you never knew with him. That night, he'd sure as hell surprised her, too. Now Molly looked into his eyes but try as she might, she detected no special heat as he looked at her.

Had she completely misread him? Had he been so drunk that just…any "wench" would have done? How could he stand there, so lamplike, after he'd caught her in a dark room with Julian? Even Julian, who was known to be the cool and aloof brother, looked at her with much more… Actually, Julian's looks set her on fire. But enough of that.

They were just different, the two men—and she had to stop comparing them.

She had to get it through her thick skull, once and for all, that those kisses with Julian last night had been pure error. She'd gotten carried away and she wasn't even certain why she'd done something so reckless as to tempt a lion like Julian. Except maybe she knew that he would never take things too far with her.

Or *would he?*

Because last night in bed, she'd been so tormented and confused. The things he'd whispered, the things he'd made her feel as he'd kissed her had been the most intense she'd ever felt in her life, even more than on the night—

No. It couldn't be.

How could anything top what she'd felt that night at the masquerade? Was it right to feel all this excitement and passion when just *any* guy kissed her? No. She knew it was impossible, it was too overpowering, too special.

So then what was the matter with her?

"Can you please explain to us what's going on between you and Julian?" Garrett queried, breaking into her reflections.

Completely disbelieving his tone, Molly leaned back

in her chair and crossed her arms, her bangles making a clanking noise.

Wow.

She'd really made up that whole masquerade soul-mate kiss, hadn't she?

Garrett didn't seem jealous *at all,* and now her silly thoughts of marrying him were quickly being dashed. She'd thought she was luring him in with her plan and now she wondered if he was even hungry for the hook she'd tossed him. Apparently, Garrett only had a weakness for Molly in a *wench* costume and while he was inebriated out of his ever-loving mind.

*Wow.* Really. She was such a dope.

"Are you two seriously going to pretend you don't know? Or do I need to spell it out to you?" Molly asked him, getting supremely irritated by all this. Where was the man who'd kissed her at the masquerade? Where was the hunger that awakened hers? The passion that had ignited hers? Had it all been a joke? A dream? A ruse?

When neither Kate nor Garrett answered and her masquerade man refused to make an appearance, her irritation increased tenfold. So they were going to drill her and intimidate her. Did they interrogate Julian like this, too?

"We're together, Garrett," Molly suddenly said, thrusting her chin out defiantly and sounding damned proud. "I moved in with him. I'm his gi—lover. And I've never been so happy." The last was true. She'd always had the most fun with Jules, had loved him beyond loving anyone else, protected him beyond anyone else. They covered for each other, laughed with each other, fought with each other....

This morning they'd had breakfast together, and they'd laughed. Even after the debacle of last night. They'd laughed.

"Did you know," Garrett said softly, his eyes kind, "this

is exactly what we feared would happen all these years. My mother, Kate, Landon and I. We feared Julian and you would dive headfirst into each other and one of you, especially you, Molly, might not make it out."

With a painful frown, Molly wondered why Garrett didn't just drop the mask already and step into his sexy black masquerade boots. He'd had *guts* that night, taking what he wanted, which had clearly been *her*. Today? He merely seemed concerned, like a brother would be, and that had definitely not been Molly's plan from the start. "Why would you think that about me and Julian?" she challenged, wanting to scoff at the accusation.

His dark eyes widened in surprise, as though Molly were lacking in brainpower to have overlooked something so obvious. Kate stepped in to explain, "Because when you were teens you were infatuated with each other, Molls. You cried when I told you he was like your brother. You cried for days and when I demanded to know why, you told me it was because of what I'd said. Because you wouldn't be able to marry him now."

Molly groaned and rolled her eyes. "I must have been ten, Kate."

"You never cry, Molly. Never. The only times I've seen you cry in your life have been all about Jules."

"Because they sent him away and it sucked!"

"There you go," Garrett said.

She scowled. "I just don't see how our relationship concerns any of you. We've had a bond since the beginning."

In fact, Molly knew the story by heart, for it had been related to her not only by Eleanor Gage, his mother, but later by Landon, Kate, Garrett, even Julian himself.

On the day the Devaney sisters had come to live at the Gage mansion, Molly had been a mere three years old.

She'd been introduced, along with Kate, to all the family members and staff, but she'd hardly paid any attention because she had a lollipop stuck in her mouth and she was gladly sucking it. Embarrassed by this, Kate had tried to convince her to hand over the lollipop, since she'd been the one who'd given it to her in the first place, but it was all to no avail. And yet while they proceeded to do the introductions, Molly's attention had fixated on the blond, green-eyed boy who looked at her in amusement. She toddled over to him, took her lollipop out of her mouth, and graciously offered it to him with a cheeky grin.

Julian had been six at the time, and even when his mother had beamed a silent command at him to refuse the germ-filled offering, Julian had shoved it into his mouth and smiled down at Molly. Just like that, they'd been instant friends.

Now Molly looked pointedly at Garrett and cocked a brow, wondering if he even remembered that story. They'd only told it about twenty times or so, if she recalled correctly. The family laughed about it, joking that what the other brothers accomplished with force, the younger brother accomplished with a grin.

"Molly." Kate clasped her hands before her in a silent plea. "I just need you to assure me that you know what you're doing. Julian's relationships don't last. In fact, he's never even had one, only one-night stands and weekend flings. You're in way over your head here, Moo!"

"I'm not his weekend fling, Kate," she defended, suddenly fierce, determined to show them she was at no risk and meant more to Julian than that, even though what she was defending was a fake liaison intended to make Garrett jealous. "What makes you think Jules would ever hurt me? He's the only guy I know that would give me a kidney if I needed one! In fact, he's so good to me I'll bet he'd even give me two!"

The worry creases on Kate's forehead only seemed to double. "You've really fallen for him, haven't you?"

It killed Molly not to be able to tell her sister the truth, so she could at least wipe that worry off her pretty face, but then how could she assure her what a lie her relationship with Julian was, when she herself couldn't understand why she'd even kissed him yesterday?

Since she'd moved in with him, she'd been bombarded with strange feelings and emotions, hardly getting any sleep as she lay in her bed, wondering about all the *what-ifs* and *could be*s in her life.

Saying good morning to him in his sexy pajamas with his six-pack abs showing was torture. Bantering with him, wanting to be close to him…

She didn't even know what she felt anymore.

She'd wanted to find love in her life, because she'd already found success in her profession. Wasn't it normal to always want something? But this time she sensed that what she wanted was nearby, but she couldn't put a name to it, and that frustrated her out of her mind.

She'd been counting on Garrett to reignite the spark in her today, not leave her feeling cold and empty. She'd been counting on this meeting where he could help her straighten out her head, and more importantly, her emotions.

Instead, she and Julian were being attacked, and it made her want to stick her claws out for him. For them. For what they had, which nobody had ever really understood in the first place.

"Julian would never hurt me," she said as she rose, fighting to keep from shouting. "I promise you if you ever see me cry because of him, I give you permission to shoot me."

"I'd actually prefer to shoot *him*," Garrett said drily.

Whipping around to face him, Molly stared at this large,

handsome man, thinking he'd always been a great influence in her life. He'd always felt responsible for her father's death. Even though the Devaney sisters had never blamed him for what had happened, it seemed as if Garrett would never forgive himself.

Which sometimes made his smiles seem sad. And made him try too hard to make things right for Kate and Molly, protect them. But...protect Molly from Julian? *Oh, puleeze!* Julian had been as crucial as sunshine to her since she was a toddler. He'd been her hero before she even heard of the word or understood its meaning.

Garrett was a good man, a great man, in fact, and Molly knew he would be a faithful and giving husband if he could only give himself a chance. But did he need to be drunk to let go the way he had at the masquerade?

Whatever the reason, she feared that the man who'd kissed her that night was an illusion. And if she'd ever, ever doubted whether she would have to choose between Garrett and Julian, it was an easy choice now that she was faced with it.

Her hero won outright.

"What is your problem with Julian anyway?" Molly asked, aghast and affronted. "Both of you—you're always riding him about something. If I were him, I'd...never talk to you again."

She pivoted for the door, but Garrett's voice stopped her.

"That little toad is my brother. Of course I love him. We merely feel responsible to protect you."

She grabbed the knob and turned. "If I need protecting from anything, I will tell you, but the last person on this earth I need protecting from is Julian." She yanked the door open and then added, "And if you love your brother so much, then I suggest you try to make things work around here before he leaves the *Daily* for good—Lord knows *I* would! Who the hell can even work in peace with this sort of constant criticism? I'm glad he's ready to move on!"

"Excuse me?"

"You heard me!" she shot back.

She gave Kate a look that said *don't do this to me again,* and with that, she stormed outside.

"Molly!" Garrett followed her, stopping her a couple of feet from where his secretary was busily tapping her computer keypad. "Where's my brother going? Is he leaving the *Daily?*"

"I want to go now, Garrett," she grumbled, trying to pull her arm free.

He drew her closer. "He's leaving the *Daily,* isn't he?"

Hating herself for having spoken so rashly, Molly dropped her face. "I think you misunderstood," she hedged.

"No, I didn't. I know he's not happy here, Molly. I've been suspecting for a time now. But if you aren't telling me when he's leaving or where, then at least answer me this. Do you love him?" he asked.

Molly stared up at the man she'd once thought she loved and wondered why her throat closed up in a tight little ball. Why she wanted to wail her heart out to him over that question alone.

Because of course the answer was yes, a thousand times *yes.*

She loved Julian in so many ways, she hadn't even begun to discover them all. And she feared that loving him as a friend was only one of them.

Halting just a few feet from his own office door, Julian saw them. Molly and the "love of her life," together at last.

He saw them say goodbye. Saw his brother pat her back. Saw her take a little sob and drop her face into his jacket. Saw him put his arm around her.

His blood simmered. His heart caved in on itself. And suddenly red-hot anger coursed through his veins and his eyes blurred with the force of his fury. Maybe this was what Molly had wanted all along. She had practiced with Julian last night so she could get out here and make Garrett jealous, make him see her as the lovely, sexy, grown woman that she was.

Perhaps Julian should've stepped back and let his best friend be coddled by the man she wanted to be coddled by.

He should laugh it off, not care. But it mattered very much. *Too* much.

Body shaking, he was amazed he could speak so calmly, so softly, as he walked up to them. "I hate to break up your tête-à-tête, but if you don't take your hands off Molly, I'm going to beat your face until our own mother won't recognize you."

Garrett stiffened, but his arms instantly dropped as his head whipped toward his. "What the hell is wrong with you, Jules?"

Julian gritted his teeth as Molly swung around in surprise. Ignoring Garrett, he stretched out his hand to her, palm up, and gazed intently into her red-rimmed eyes. She'd been crying, or about to cry. Dammit, why? He pursed his lips in anger. At her, at himself, at this entire mess he'd gotten himself into.

He'd wanted time to let things unfold naturally.

He didn't want to pull all the stops he used with other women and seduce the hell out of her. Because this was the only girl who knew him, respected him, admired him— he was *real* with her. He wanted it to be perfectly natural with her. No bull. And it just wasn't happening that way, dammit. "What day is today, Molly?"

She sniffled, then wiped the corner of her eye with one fingertip. "Um?"

"What day is it?"

She told him the date, and he nodded gravely and bent to whisper in her ear so that nobody would hear his words but *Molly.* "Exactly. You're still my girl. Aren't you? We said a month. Didn't we?"

She blinked as he drew back to survey her reaction, and when her gaze strayed to Garrett, Julian's chest tightened with rage.

Garrett, his brother.

Whom he suddenly, profoundly abhorred.

Her tear-streaked blue eyes came back to him, and she nodded and mumbled, "Of course. Take me home, all right?" And to Garrett, she said almost placatingly, "Thanks for the chat. Think about what I told you before I…stepped out, okay?"

Garrett nodded before Julian led Molly by the elbow toward his assistant's desk. He barked a dozen orders, then led Molly with him to the elevators.

Neither spoke on the drive home.

"So tell me," Julian finally said as they entered his apartment, his emotions having fermented during the drive. He was close to exploding now. "Tell me what he did to make you cry like this."

Molly stared at him with wide, shining eyes that made him want to wrap her up in his arms and keep the world from so much as looking at her, she looked so damn lost and so damn vulnerable. Her voice was a soft, puzzled whisper. "What's wrong with you today?"

He drew a deep breath, then let it all out. "He doesn't deserve you, Molly! I know a guy who's so crazy about you, he would do anything to be with you—*anything.* He'd lie for you, cheat for you, steal for you—"

She scoffed, everything sounding more ludicrous to her

by the second. "Are you getting high on my paint supply? Who are you talking about? Who would do such a thing?"

"Take a wild guess, Molls."

"I have no clue what you're talking about!"

"I could kill him for making you cry like this." Julian sat down on the living room sofa and threw his shoes off with a bang. "This obsession with my brother just pisses me the hell off, Molly. Like nothing in my life has ever pissed me off before."

She crossed her arms, suddenly glaring. He might have been pissed off, but he had no idea what was wrong with her. That she cried because she realized the entire masquerade night had been a stupid illusion in the first place. That the man she'd thought she loved…just wasn't the Garrett she knew. And like all the other men she'd ever met in her life, he would end up paling to Julian in every possible way she could imagine.

But how could she admit to this man, whose respect she craved and wanted above all others, that she just might have screwed it all up and was not really in love with Garrett? That the man she wanted was…unattainable. And that his brother and her sister had been warning her away from him because he would hurt her?

Oh, how she'd wanted to tear their eyes out when she heard them! Even if they might be right.

She gnawed on her lower lip and said nothing, focusing instead on getting ready to vent her frustrations on the only person she could vent with.

Julian.

"Just tell me what you see in him all of a sudden that you find so irresistible. Tell me why you'd go cry on his shoulder and not with *me*."

Oh, God, what was happening to her?

Her legs went flaccid with a mere look into those stormy

green eyes. He was so handsome, his jaw square and rigid, his eyebrows two sharp, bleak slashes. He was more enraged than she'd ever seen him before. She could even think he was *jealous,* and the thought summoned a deep, dark stirring in her that she'd been feeling more and more frequently lately—at the most inconvenient times. A powerful little ache in her body that craved for him to wrap his arms around her and… She didn't know what she wanted him to do.

She ached for closeness with him, almost trembled with the need. She wanted to smell his scent all around her and to feel his hands everywhere and enjoy the hardness of those big, big biceps bulge as he held her imprisoned against his body. She wanted him so close, closer, closest. As if mere friendship was no longer enough with him. As if revealing every intimate detail of her life to him, her fears, her desires…

Was. Not. Enough.

Anymore.

"Are you planning to answer me, Molly?"

Molly's throat seemed to be working extra hard to get the words out. She didn't know why her nipples were beaded under her cotton turquoise sundress, why the way Jules was shooting fire at her with his eyes made her breathless and shaky and strange. She fought against the sensations, struggling to focus on his question.

She threw her hands up in the air in frustration. "I don't know, Jules! All right? Maybe I hated when he was overly protective of us, the way he took it upon himself to chaperone you and me. He never let us have fun together, like we were doing something wrong, and we *weren't.* You may be hot for anything that walks but he never realized that we were always just friends. But I truly don't think he was being deliberately mean. Maybe he was just trying to do the noble thing out of caring and respect for me and out of respect for my father, who protected him." She softened her voice as she tried to save the last remains of her hope.

Julian's glare could have melted all the ice in Alaska. "Garrett pulled you away from me because he knew that— He knew I—" His face darkened, and Molly's nipples pricked with wanting as she watched his fingers curl into fists at his sides. An image of those fingers clutching her breasts when he'd whispered sexy confessions into her ear returned to her, and she swallowed. This was *so* not the time to get worked up about that.

Jumping to his feet, he plunged a frustrated hand through his hair and thoroughly ruffled it. "And what about him and Kate? Hell, Molls, have you not seen the way your sister looks at him? You're both pining away for the same man."

Molly blinked in stupefaction, her eyebrows pulling low when she registered what he'd said. "You're lying. You—you can't mean that— Kate doesn't feel that way about him."

"Kate is like a sister to me. I know lust when I see it, Molls."

Horrified, Molly gaped at the thought of her sister loving Garrett. So quietly? And for how long? It couldn't be.

Fiddling with one enormous hoop earring, she shook her head several times. "Jules—you don't understand. Garrett and I have *done* things. We kissed one night and it was… magical, like it was meant to be."

Freezing in place as though she'd said something monumental, Julian openly gawked at her until his expression emptied into such a blank look that it might have been comical if she didn't find it thoroughly alarming. "He *kissed* you?"

Molly offered him an embarrassed little nod, then

groaned in self-pity and buried her face in her hands. "I've never felt such a connection in my life except with you. What I felt that night seemed so real, it was like we recognized each other, like we knew we were soul mates…"

*But it was all an illusion, and I can't understand it and I'm so confused.*

Julian stalked a short distance away as though he didn't know what do with himself, and then he returned, his jaw muscles working restlessly. "You're kidding me, Molly. Say it now, Molls. Right. Now. Tell me you're kidding me, Moo."

She could only imagine how it looked to him, the guy she had been devouring with her lips yesterday, that she'd let his brother do that, too. What was wrong with her? Why had she felt nothing when she'd looked at Garrett today?

But it *had* happened.

Hadn't it?

"I'm not even sure it was real anymore," she admitted as she fell on the couch and covered her face with her hands. "It all happened at that loathsome masquerade, when I was wearing that stupid wench costume you dared me to wear! He…he was wearing all black. I was outside and thought it was you, and then he kissed me, and we did some intimate things, and I noticed the ring he was wearing as he held me, and I knew that it must be him."

The deafening, tomblike silence that followed stretched so long and taut, she sat up in confusion and studied Julian in growing alarm.

Suddenly, he stormed down the hallway like a man possessed, and Molly sighed and rubbed her temples to ward off a headache. She just hoped he hadn't gone to fetch a gun or something, for what was she going to do now? She was usually the impulsive one and always counted on *Jules* being the one with a cool head.

She considered following him, talking some reason into him, explaining that it was just a kiss and all that, but then he returned less than a minute later and produced something shiny from his pants pocket.

He sounded livid now. Livid.

"You mean this ring, Molly?"

# Seven

As Molly stared at the ring he was holding between his two fingers, a horrific sensation crawled up her stomach like a tarantula.

She blinked several times, and her jaw fell open. "Wh-what are you doing with that?"

Garrett used to wear it all day, every day. The platinum was scratched and dented with age, for it had been in the family for generations, boasting at its center a rare blue diamond that was supposed to be worth millions.

"It's my ring. *Mine.* I won it from him. Over a month ago. He bet me that it was worth more than my autographed Mark McGwire seventieth-home-run baseball when he was *really* freaking drunk. He was off by several hundred thousand and lost the bet." Julian smiled at her, a sharp, angry smile that cut through her skin like the clean, expert slice of a dagger. "I just wear the ring to piss him off sometimes when I know I'll be seeing him."

All the color drained from her face, as though all the blood in her body was going straight to her heart, which was racing in her breast like a mad thing. If her ears were hearing correctly and her dazed brain processing correctly, it seemed that he was basically admitting to owning that ring on the night of the masquerade. The night that a stranger had kissed her ever-loving heart out.

*Oh. My. God.*

The conclusion she'd come up with terrified her. Julian…had been the one wearing that ring? Julian had whispered…those sexy words in his raspy voice while his big, long-fingered hands had touched her so provocatively…?

Julian. Her hero. Her protector. Her best friend. Her young crush. Her lifetime love.

It had been Julian who'd kissed her and made her have an orgasm while he'd fondled her? How he must have laughed! Laughed at her naïveté, at her stupidity, at her…

"I can't believe," he breathed softly, his eyes glowing like golden moons, "that you wouldn't know that I was the one who kissed you that night."

Grief and unexpected humiliation cut through her like a thousand knives. Julian had known all this time.

Her chest constricted so tightly she thought she would break apart, but she still stubbornly shook her head from side to side. "I don't understand."

His kisses. Oh, dear, his kisses. Three total. Each one so different. One, passionate and drunk. The next, cocky and trying to show off in front of Kate. And the last one, in a dark room, where it was just him and her, supposedly playing a game….

*Please no, I can't be that stupid.*

"I don't understand," she repeated, more frantic now.

In three steps, he closed the distance between them, and

when his fingers curled around her arm, Molly could feel the leashed power in his hold, see how he visibly fought for control. "I think I do. You thought I was Garrett that night—when I kissed you hard enough to make your mouth swell under mine. You let me put my hands between your legs, touch your breasts, maul you like a—"

"Stop it, Julian. *Stop it!*"

She leaped away and backed off, hardly able to look into those fiercely jealous green eyes, which were only reminding her that he—he who was her *everything*—had done all that. Every bit of what he'd said, and more.

Julian had kissed her, had turned her life upside down with his touch. He'd made her shatter in his arms, and then he'd acted as if it had meant nothing. *Nothing.*

He was her best friend, and yet he'd kept her in the dark all this time. He'd been intimate with her, had made her feel as if he wanted her, cherished her, but instead he'd been happily helping her seduce his own *brother!*

"How *dare* you!" she exploded at that. "How dare you do that to me and then say nothing!"

His eyes flashed, and he threw his arms up in the air. "What did you want me to say? That it was a mistake? That I got carried away by your pretty blue eyes and the way you looked in that scrap of a dress?" he shot back. "You *told me* not to mention it, and since I was drunk and clearly screwed up, I thought it was a damned good idea. You pretended nothing happened the next day, and I *went* with it. At least it gave me time to get it right."

"Get *what* right, you idiot? You just shot our friendship to hell!" She pushed him aside and stormed away to her bedroom, adding as she went, "Now excuse me if I go pack, you...you jerk! How could you even agree to help me seduce Garrett after you touched me like you did, you... Oh! *I can't even think of a word for you!*"

She slammed the door with a bang.

Her lungs burning for air, she fell back weakly against the door and stared at the bed with blurry eyes. She glanced at the walk-in closet, tempted to leave this very second. She would leave. Of course she would. But she needed him to drive her, or Kate to come get her, and she'd die before she made that request of either of them right now.

A desolate sensation weighed heavy on her chest as she thought of the mural waiting upstairs, a safe haven for her to get lost in a sea of color. She had never left a work unfinished and she was not going to start now because of that…that douche!

She would finish it tonight, or at least try to, and then she'd leave tomorrow.

She still couldn't believe it. He had known…all along, all this time. The bastard had already kissed her, fondled her, known how easy it was to make her explode.

What mockery.

That beautiful masquerade kiss now mocked her. Her best friendship in the world—her entire life—mocked her.

One after another, memories flashed before her eyes, and there wasn't a single happy memory that she could remember not featuring Julian. She saw him smiling down at her like a lone wolf, tweaking her nose, rumpling her hair, driving her back home. She saw him snarling at her and teasing her and tickling her, and calling her Mo-Po, Mopey, Moo, Molls, Mo-Mo, Moo-Moo….

Nausea rose up her throat, and she shakily sat down on the edge of the bed, held a pillow to her chest and drew in deep breaths. But she didn't seem capable of filling her lungs. She'd just never felt so empty. So stupid. So used. Nothing in her life had ever hurt this much, not even when Jules had left her all those times.

*But he won't make me cry anymore,* she thought angrily, remembering Kate's recent words.

Teeth gritted, she curled up into a rigid little ball with the pillow firmly grasped to her core, and something very deep inside her clenched tight as the images of that night bombarded her once more.

His mouth, firm and urgent, the roughened sound he made as he kissed the tops of her breasts, as if he'd just entered heaven and they had been made just for him.

The way he'd groaned and bent his head to her ear, biting the lobe hungrily, desperately, and then how he'd soothingly murmured to her, "Shh…shh…"

Her eyes stung with unshed tears. How could she not have known?

She'd been so sure it was him at first, that wolfish smile so familiar to her, but then the way he'd fiercely kissed her had been so completely unlike her cocky best friend. Why did it have to be him? The man couldn't keep his hands to himself and just had to have a piece of her, too?

She'd promised herself when she was a thirteen-year-old girl that she would not shed any more tears for Julian John. He meant too much to her, was too special to her, made her feel like a princess being rescued by a hero. She'd promised herself she would get rid of the infatuation she had with him, her silly crush, because everyone told her he would hurt her and they couldn't all be wrong.

But it was no use because now the truth stared her in the face, and yes, yes, yes, it mocked her, too.

The man she'd felt she'd die if she didn't kiss again…

The man she knew in her gut was her soul mate…

That man was the only man in the world who could really, truly break her heart into such tiny particles she would never be able to piece herself back together.

And now even their friendship, the one golden and steady thing in her life, was gone.

Julian wanted to punch something.

He paced his room for hours, restless, his emotions gone berserk. Jealousy coursed through his veins like some sort of acrid poison as he remembered Molly's moans, the way she'd responded to him the night of their first kiss, like her body was a harp only his fingers knew how to pluck and tune and play...

And all while she'd thought he was Garrett.

His brother.

The guy who'd been holding her when she was in tears today.

The guy who'd owned every one of her desires for weeks.

The guy whom he very much wanted to kill right now.

He replayed the scenes over and over in his mind, recalling the hurt in Molly's eyes when he'd set her little head straight this evening. When he'd told her that he was the man who had kissed her that night, touched her so intimately and made her go off like a hot, beautiful firework in his arms. Goddammit, she'd almost seemed disappointed he hadn't been Garrett!

He gritted his teeth at the thought, deeply regretting not confronting her about it the day after the masquerade. All this time she'd been hunting for his brother thinking of *Julian's kiss*. To hell with whether she wanted to talk about it or not! If he'd done things right, he might have been holding her in his arms all this time—and not under false pretenses—and kept her from noticing Garrett. All these sleepless nights. Nights she'd wanted to have a friendly sleepover with him—yeah, right. As if he could stand being in the same bed with her without turning into some ravenous, sex-starved maniac.

Did she not *see* he'd been crazy about her for twenty years?

He had thought he could screw Molly out of his head, but clearly that had not worked. Okay, so he'd kissed her when he was drunk and hadn't talked to her afterward. Not suave. She'd expected better of him? Yeah, well, that made two of them. He wasn't too pleased to find out that she'd thought all along that it was his brother who'd kissed her.

Now they both felt like fools.

Groaning in despair, he plopped down on the bed, full of rage and agony and disgust. He couldn't stand the impotence he felt. Restless, he changed into his pajama pants and yanked back his bedcovers, but all he did was toss and turn restlessly on the bed.

So maybe he should've talked to her about that evening. Except he'd thought it best to forget about one drunken night's kiss and continue with his plans until he could do things the right way.

Well, he sure as hell was mucking it up right now, wasn't he?

No way was he going to stand for it. Suave Julian, they used to call him. How he was so cool, aloof. Yeah, right. Clearly not where Molly was concerned. His Achilles' heel. But also his greatest strength. If he had become someone and done something with himself, it was all because of that incredible redhead in his life and his desperation to show his family that he was worthy of her.

Shoving the covers aside, he stalked across his bedroom and out to the hall, where moonlight streamed through the living room windows and across his apartment.

He found the door to her bedroom ajar. He rapped his

knuckles on the wood, waited a second, then pushed the door open wider.

Her bed sat empty. It hadn't been slept in.

Scowling, he stalked the entire apartment, every square foot, and found it empty.

Heart pounding seriously hard now, hard enough to crack one of his ribs, he jammed the elevator buttons and rode up to the penthouse, his mind racing with a thousand thoughts per minute, shouting out its conclusion: *she left, she left, she left, you idiot!*

But when the elevator doors opened, he saw her.

She lay on the marble floor of his new offices, dressed in nothing but a giant button-down shirt, her hair a pool of red fanning behind her as she slept with her hands tucked under her left cheek. He drank up her image as he approached her, drinking up her image, the perfect image of this woman he'd loved since they'd first met.

She should not be sleeping on the floor. God, never on the floor.

She deserved a bed, pillows, satin sheets and a man to love her with all the passion that she unfailingly conveyed in each of her artworks.

His eyes glued to her moonlit face, he knelt at her side— she was just so damned beautiful his eyes hurt. A streak of green paint crossed her forearm to her elbow, and he ached to trace it with his fingers, then with his lips. He noticed the empty paint tubes scattered around her sleeping form and glanced up at the colorful wall before him. His heart wrenched with regret when he realized she'd been trying to finish the mural.

So she could leave.

Leave him for good.

Now, when JJG Enterprises was almost ready for his final walk-through and just days away from opening to its employees. Now, when he had grown accustomed to her being here as he met with contractors, architects, painting her heart away on a wall that had been empty before she'd made it come to life with little playful flicks of her dainty hands.

She wanted to leave now, when Julian was days away from fulfilling one of his dreams and ready to focus on the next one—the possibility of sharing the rest of his life with her.

Throat dense with emotion, he stroked the curve of her cheek with the back of one fingertip.

She sighed contentedly at that, relaxed in her sleep. Shoving aside his hesitation, he reached out, gently scooped her up and carried her back to the elevator. She was as light as a feather and as warm as a little chicken, and his chest swelled when she sought out his heat and snuggled closer. But when the audible chime signaled their arrival on his apartment floor, Molly grew heavy in his arms, and he saw her spiky titian lashes flutter open.

Their eyes clashed. Her gaze was dewy, sleepy, and Julian's muscles tensed as he waited for her to speak up, praying her first words weren't "Put me down!"

He tightened his grip as he waited for the inevitable, but instead of kicking or screaming and demanding he release her, Molly hugged him even tighter and buried her face into his neck, where she quietly started sobbing.

The words tumbled out of his throat in an anxious rush. "Molly. Molly, I'm sorry. Don't cry. I'm sorry for what I said."

"No, Jules, I'm s-sorry, too. I—I overreacted, I—I'm s-so stupid. I should've known you anywhere. I should've known it was *you*."

Julian might have been considered a daredevil among

his sports friends, but seeing Molly cry just now tore up his insides.

He didn't think about what he was doing, only followed his instincts and carried her to his bedroom. He sat on the edge of his bed and clutched her quaking body to the exact place where his heart spasmed like an open wound inside his chest.

"I'm sorry, Molly. I should've brought it up and at least apologized," he said, smoothing his hands down her shivering back.

Her chest heaved as she sighed and stayed buried against his throat. "No, no, it was me. How could I not have known...not have *realized?*" She sniffled and glanced up, her eyes wide and blue and glazed with emotion. "At first I thought it was you, but then I felt his ring pressing against my arm. Why were you wearing it? Why didn't you tell me?"

"Baby, I thought you knew it was me that night. I thought you responded because it was *me.* I was going to leave you alone, Molly, but you called me back onto the terrace and I couldn't stop myself."

He had a similar sensation now as he marveled at the incredible feel of her in his arms, warm and shivering and vulnerable, like she'd been that night, ravenous for his mouth and his touches. He wanted to protect her, possess her, claim her, love her, make her never ever think again of anyone but him.

Cradling her face, he wiped her tears with the pads of his thumbs. "Why would you think it was Garrett, Molly? Don't you see the way I look at you? The way I want you? Everyone around us has noticed but you. Do you believe I'd help another man, *any* man, get even a little piece of you, when I've been waiting all my life to claim you as mine?"

She looked into his face, and her eyes widened at his

words, as though she'd only just realized that he *wanted* her. Her hands trembled as she cupped the back of his head, and then she kissed him. Softly. Whispering against his lips, "I love you. I'd die if I lost you, Jules. I'd rather lose my arms and never paint again than lose you."

Her lips pressed lightly against his, the words, the touch sending a shock of awareness bolting through his system. He stiffened under her, his heart kicking full speed, pumping hard and loud as a jolt of arousal coursed through his bloodstream.

When she drew back, her eyes shone like beacons, and the blatant desire he saw in those blue, blue eyes could've toppled him to his knees.

He was having trouble getting a word out, his arms shaking as he palmed her face between his open hands. "Do you want me?" he finally rasped.

His lips tingled from her sweet kiss, and now his mouth burned with the hunger to plunder her lips. Ripe with innocence, wet and pink and waiting to unleash all her passion on him. He needed to make her his. Only his. He couldn't bear another night, another second, another moment of his life without this.

He splayed his fingers across her scalp and gazed into her eyes in the shadows, so intoxicated with her nearness, he could only murmur in a thick whisper, "Do you want me, Molly? Do you want to be with me?" He slid his fingers down her back to palm the round curves of her buttocks, gently pulling her closer.

She nodded, struggling for air.

He gripped her hair within his fists and pinned her in place as he swept down. "I need to kiss you, touch you, make love to you." He fitted his lips perfectly to hers. His tongue plowed, swift and fast, into the warmth of her open mouth, and the pleasure of connection was so intense, a riptide of sensations racked his entire body.

She felt familiar and at the same time exotic and intoxicating to him. She was marshmallows in fire, lollipops under the covers, the best memories of his youth…she was museums, Monaco, fine wine….

She was Molly.

His lovely, effervescent Molly.

And he'd loved her almost as long as he'd been alive.

His arms snaked out to guide her legs around his hips, and suddenly she was straddling him, almost weightless, but burning hot and moving in restless excitement against him, her hands gliding up the bare muscles of his torso, her mouth ravenous on his. "Jules," she murmured. "Jules, I'm sorry for what I said."

"Shh, I'm sorry, too. Let's just forgive each other. You're mine, Molly, and I can't wait to be inside you." He twirled his tongue around hers, her body eagerly rocking over his hardness. Agonizing pleasure ripped through him as her weight bounced seductively over his straining erection.

Things went from slow to urgent in a heartbeat.

He anxiously unbuttoned her shirt, and when she started doing it herself, his hands slid up to caress her face. Panting fast and hard, he stroked her reddened bottom lip with alternating thumbs, her lovely jaw cradled within his cupped palms. He'd never seen so much desire in a woman's eyes. So much emotion. Her lips were so luscious, plump and damp and so unbelievably swollen from his kiss.

Desire pumped, hot and heady, through his bloodstream as he laid her down on the bed and pushed off his drawstring pants, licking her calves, her knees, touching her, looking at her—he couldn't get enough, do it quick enough, couldn't see her naked fast enough.

He wanted to part her slim, white thighs and taste her

honey. He wanted to make her gasp and moan and thrash against him as he introduced her to the greatest pleasures in the world. He was cooking inside of his body and he hadn't even started to do everything he wanted to. He had never thought he could want a woman like this.

He wanted to revere her. Adore her.

Molly was just as desperate, her fingers somehow cramping on the last buttons of her shirt. "I can't get this thing off. Please get it off, get it off, Jules!"

He cursed under his breath and lunged forward. He was being ripped in two from so much desire, so much rapture. He could barely speak from the euphoria, his fingers working as fast as they could through the tremors already shaking him.

"Is this mine? Is this an old shirt of mine?"

She nodded, and he swiftly grabbed it in both fists and tore it open, buttons flying everywhere. His blood roared like a monster in his ears when he parted the material, revealing flawless creamy skin he wanted to devour until tomorrow.

"Is this what you want, Molly?" He ducked to put his mouth on a beaded nipple that thrust up in the air. He laved it thoroughly as he rolled her to her side and sprawled his body right next to her as his hands engulfed the round curves of her buttocks and he drew her tighter against him, enabling him to feast on her breast like a man possessed.

She arched up against him as he twirled his tongue around the protruding tip, her whispers tickling his hair, "Yes, oh, please!"

He groaned, because he could never deny her. *Never.* He wanted her to be certain she wanted him and only him, as a man and as a lover, but she felt so right, was hot and lusty in his arms, in his bed, where he'd spent many sleepless nights as he imagined her lying in her own bed just next door.

No. He couldn't stop if he'd wanted to. For the first time in his life, he would be truly making love with someone.

Heart pounding at what was about to happen, something irrevocable, monumental, something he'd thought about his whole life, Julian turned her onto her back, his hands roaming down her curvy body, squeezing her lovely thighs as he kissed her long and languorously. "I want you. I need you. You feel so perfect. It's like coming home."

Her red hair splayed over his white down pillows. Her chest rose and fell heavily with each breath, her eyes so trusting he could drown in them. "I'm still a virgin, Jules." She reached out to stroke his dampened lips with one fingertip.

He placed a kiss on the tip of that fingertip. "Sweet, sweet baby, you have no idea what knowing that does to me." He was so honored, so turned on that he would be her first, her only. His hands shook as he eased the shirt off her shoulders and helped her pull it off her arms. "I'll be extra careful, but you have to tell me if I ever go too fa— Oh, Molly, *look at you*."

His eyes blurred at the sight of her completely naked. Her slim legs, her tiny hips, the little thatch of red curls at the apex of her thighs, and the two perfect globes of her breasts staring back at him, large and round, with those perky pink nipples that begged to be laved and licked and loved until morning.

She drew his hand up to one large globe, her eyes holding his with such innocent seduction he could've wept. His body trembled with anticipation, excitement.

"Do you want me to kiss you here again?" he gruffly said, and cupped both her breasts in his big hands, gently squeezing. She shivered in pleasure when he began teasing the pink areolae with his thumbs.

He bent his head and took one firm bud between his lips. He flicked it with his tongue first, then drew it deeply into his mouth as his hand trailed down her stomach. She gasped under him. Her hips rolled enticingly as his fingers teased through her moistness.

"You're so damp," he rasped, watching her expression melt as he eased one finger gently inside her. "And so damned tight you're going to make me come before I even get started."

Her honey pooled in his hand as her entry snugly enclosed his penetrating finger. Restless and mewing softly, she arched up on the bed and pressed her breast to his mouth. He suckled her with a growl of pleasure and plunged a second finger inside her.

Her soft moan tumbled into the air, and her hips rocked against his hand in silent plea. He drew back, panting, and met her blue gaze, an ocean of arousal, her lashes heavy, her mouth red, her nipples red…

Undone, he slid down her body and buried his head between her legs, giving her a hungry kiss that penetrated her to her sweet, warm depths. She cried out and pulled helplessly on his hair. "Stop, oh, please stop or you'll make me…"

He lifted his head. Urgency thrummed through his body like a living, breathing thing. He was panting, drowning in ecstasy, in his need to make it special and memorable for her while at the same time trying to withhold his body's natural reactions to tonight. To being with her after wanting her for so long.

"I'll make you what?" he prodded softly, coming up and brushing his nose against hers. "Do you already want to come?"

She nodded, her breath fast and hot against his face.

He wanted to take those breaths and suck them into his body, to take this woman and mark her with his touch, every inch of her, for eternity. Catching her bottom lip between his and gently suckling, he caressed her between the legs again. "But that's a good thing…"

She plunged her hands into his hair and set a kiss on his lips, the tip of his nose, his square jaw. "Not alone—Jules, please. When it happens, I want to feel you inside me. I've always wondered what it… I've been dying to feel this…"

Her fingers delved between their bodies, and he almost yelped at the incredible feel, the amazing feel, of her hand curling around his hard length as if she owned him. "I want you," she breathed, her eyes wide in surprise at what she touched. "I…I want *this*…" She stroked his full length exploratively, and a barrage of pleasure raced through his system. He bit back an oath as his body instantly tensed for release.

He grabbed her wrists and playfully pinned her arms up over her head, then he dived to give her a hot, ravenous kiss on the lips. "If you do that again we won't get to the part of me actually entering you."

She writhed underneath him, her breasts beckoning another kiss. "Please, please."

He was unraveled by her desire, enchanted by her openness to him, his undeniable connection to her. His hands shook with male-hormone overload as he reached out to the nightstand.

He briskly rolled on a condom as fast as he could. Realizing she'd been watching in fascination, he pushed her back down with his weight and reached for both her creamy ankles. He couldn't wait to be inside her. Feel her heat.

*Make her mine, mine, mine.*

"Do you want me inside you…?" he urged as he hooked her legs around his hips, his pulse fluttering like crazy.

"Please, yes. Oh…" She gasped as he penetrated her, firm and slow, pushing in inch by inch, her tender body fighting him. The effort it took to hold back made his every muscle quiver in restraint.

"Ahh, I'm sorry, this is going to hurt you…"

She'd gone motionless beneath him, those trusting, wide eyes clawing at his heart as she clasped his shoulders in a death grip. "Don't tense against me, don't fight me," he cooed, easing back to let her breathe, then carefully guiding himself back in, caressing her nipple tips to incite her relaxation as he gently rocked his hips. "Give yourself to me, Molly. Be mine."

He thumbed the little pearl above the entry of her sex, and he felt her give him another inch, and another, until he was almost buried to the hilt. Suddenly, with fierce determination, Molly thrust her pelvis up against him and they both cried out in surprise—he barked in pleasure, and she moaned in sudden pain, and they both went utterly still, completely joined, his length pulsing inside her, her body snugly wrapped around him.

He took her breathless little mouth and kissed her fiercely as the compact heat of her body adjusted to his length. Struggling to hold back, his heart thundering in his chest, he threw his head back in ecstasy and finally started to withdraw, enjoying every sliding inch. "So good. You feel so. *Good.*" He bent down and kissed her, a hot, wild kiss. "Please stay still, baby, I don't want to hurt you."

He went back in, and she moaned in pleasure, her fingers clenching his buttocks, urging him on. "It's okay now. It's okay. Don't hold back, Julian."

"Oh, Molly…you have no idea what you've been doing to me.…" He rocked his hips gently against hers, the motion slow but deep and incredibly erotic. Excruciating pleasure shot through his system as he continued his rhythmic thrusting, waiting to feel her shudder, waiting for her to come apart in his arms.

Suddenly, their eyes locked, and Molly released an out-of-control moan, her nails biting into his skin as she arched up in pleasure.

She watched him watch her.

She felt like crying, dying, flying.

She thought she'd break when he first entered her, and now the pleasure had overridden anything else.

Julian's eyes were an inferno of passion, eating her up alive. His hands slid like satin on her skin, over her hips, her rib cage, caressing her breasts. Then he ducked his head once more and his velvet tongue branded every inch of her body until every cell and atom felt alive and fevered.

A sheen of perspiration clung to his forehead, and she ached to lick it up and get drunk on him. High on him. She thrashed under his eyes when their gazes met, glorying in the ravaged way he looked at her, the tender words that tumbled off his lips as he took her, words like *adore* and *want you* and *killing me*.

Inside her being, she overflowed with love for him. Him. She wanted all of him, all of Julian John Gage, as she watched his muscles flexing hard with each move of his powerful body against hers.

And when his rhythm turned erratic, her eyes drifted shut and the passion overtook her. She clutched his bulging shoulders with a soft cry of pure, unrefined bliss, hearing him let loose a growl of his own, and they snapped and twisted together, clutching each other, tense and shaking, and then…seconds later…slumping, relaxed and entwined, they felt as if they were one, at last.

* * *

They couldn't get enough of each other.

After less than two hours of sleep, Molly awakened to find Julian's tousled blond head trailing suspiciously down her tummy and heading south, his fingertips sensuously playing between her splayed thighs. Drawing out her wetness, he made her mew in her throat and toss her head back helplessly against the pillow.

When he buried his face in the damp, warm place where his fingers had been, she gripped the sheets at her sides as each hot flick of his knowing tongue set a rampage of sensations loose in her body. She arched and twisted. "Jules, please…" she gasped in the dark. He pushed her to a climax with his tongue, and then he wrapped her legs around his hips and rode her until she was crying out to him in ecstasy.

Less than an hour later, she stirred in bed and searched for his warmth, having somehow been separated from him during sleep. She hooked one leg around his narrow hips and draped her arm around his waist, and as she wiggled to get comfortable, she became aware of the large, prominent erection biting into her hip bone. She stilled, but Julian had already awakened. He groaned and dropped his head in search of her lips in the shadows, and she gave her mouth up to his. Lying on their sides on the bed, he entered her slowly, whispering sweet little nothings in her ears that drove her to a climax that left her gasping for breath and blushing over all the things he said.

They showered together and laughed over "bun-buns" and "JJ," then returned to bed. Then, at 5:00 a.m., while a tiny stream of light filtered through the closed drapes, Molly once again woke up to find herself entangled in Julian's muscled limbs and his Egyptian cotton bedsheets. She couldn't seem go back to sleep. She throbbed all over in such a delicious way. Adrenaline and excitement continued coursing through her system, and she couldn't stop touching him. Kissing him. Smelling his skin, which smelled clean and of his sandalwood soap.

"Jules," she whispered, going breathless at the excitement of waking up with him. "Are you asleep?"

"Not anymore." With an arm draped over his eyes as he lay sprawled on the bed, Julian's chest rose and fell with each breath, his voice groggy and sexy.

Molly sat up and edged closer, waiting for him to stir to action. "I'm still naked," she said, dropping her voice to a seductive purr.

Dropping his arm and cracking his eyes open, Julian stroked his thumb down the length of her arm, his expression deadly serious. "I know what you're begging for, Molls."

Before she could even blink, he'd rolled her over with a lionlike "rawr" that made her squeal and laugh her heart out as he gave her the tickle torture of her life. "Oh, I hate it when you do this, stop it, *stop!*" she squealed in between hysterical laughs, but he didn't pause for a whole half a minute—because it wasn't called torture for nothing. They ended up breathless and grinning from ear to ear when it was finally over.

He turned somber as he gazed down at her flushed features, then he reached out to cup her naked breast and manipulate it as though it were his property to play with. When her nipple responded eagerly, his smile turned wolfish, and a devilish glint appeared in his gaze.

"You sure you can take me?" he said, and bent his head to give her a leisurely good-morning kiss, his seductive lips stirring her senses. "I don't want you hurting all day."

She was still breathless from his torture. "Well, I do."

He laughed. "What an insatiable little devil my little

Molls is turning out to be." He smiled that wolf's smile again, his eyes spelling mischief, then he ducked his blond head and playfully nipped the beaded points of her nipples, and the stimulus was almost too much to bear.

"Thank you for the gift you've given me," he whispered against her flesh, switching from one nipple to the other. "My entire life I worried someone else would take what I wanted."

That husky, unexpected confession turned her on like flicking on a light switch, and together with the nibbles he was giving her? It was a winning combo. Her muscles stiffened as the blissful sensations rippled through her. She clung to his shoulders, squirming as red-hot desire took her over and his warm, wet tongue tortured her beyond measure.

"Oh, Jules," she sighed. "Don't do that unless you... you know."

"Yeah, I know," he said, coming up to her ear, murmuring, "I got you, baby, you know I do."

Molly turned her head, opened her mouth and kissed him, lazily at first, then vigorously. "No. Now it's my turn to torture you," she said sheepishly.

She pushed him under her and he obediently lay on his back as she greedily took in his magnificent body with her eyes. From head to toe, Julian was a masterpiece she wanted to memorize.

Eyes narrowed, he crossed his hands behind his head and let her touch him, like a pasha being pampered and tended to. She bit her bottom lip while her breasts throbbed for his touch and the place between her legs pricked with wanting. Her hands stroked his abs and pectorals and round, hard biceps, and then trailed downward to cup his mesmerizing hardness....

He sucked in a harsh breath through his teeth. Molly's

eyes blurred as she seized his hard length—so big she could not grip him with only one hand. He was so aroused and powerful that she could feel him pulsing underneath her palms and fingers. She wanted to lick him there, lick him everywhere, like a lollipop. "I want to kiss you here, Jules." She patted him gently, her insides clenching with pure, unadulterated lust.

His nostrils flared, his eyes almost black. "Then stop teasing and kiss me."

Molly watched his face as she bent her head, and she would never forget the flaming, pulse-pounding lust in his eyes, as if he could eat her up and not want anything else for the rest of his life. "Like this?" she asked tentatively as she dipped her puckered lips and placed a kiss right on the tip.

His hips bucked wildly, his biceps bulging as he fought to keep his arms back.

"Do you like it, Jules, or—?"

"Baby, I've dreamed of this," he murmured in a coarse, thick voice, his torso rising and falling with each soughing breath. "Morning, noon and night, I've dreamed of this…."

Molly bent her head and watched him, melting in heat at the harsh look of ecstasy on his face. His eyes burned into the top of her head as she snaked out her tongue to lick him in a slow circle around the tip, savoring his taste and the incredible feel of his hardness sliding into her mouth. She opened wider and took the first couple of inches inside of her. His hands rounded over the back of her head and his fingertips delved gently into her hair as he eased her head back so their gazes locked. Her eyes felt heavy with arousal, and his gaze was thick-lashed and stormy.

"Did you think of me, too, baby?" he said in a guttural whisper, and Molly released him, then climbed on top of him and straddled his hips, bending to press her lips hungrily to his.

"So much I've never even looked at another man, Jules," she whispered into his mouth.

She felt the powerful tremor that rushed through his body at her words. Then he took charge and twirled his tongue around hers while his hands slid down her back to grip her buttocks. He squeezed the plump flesh, moving her so their hips aligned and his rigid erection pressed right into the part where she was soaked.

"I've thought of this every day for so damned long. I won't even begin to tell you how many times during the night."

"I want you in me, Jules." She rocked her hips enticingly against his length. She was wonderfully sore and yet needed to feel him again, only to be sure this was real. This was happening. She was his, and he was hers.

Hard and strong, he easily rolled her over and loomed above her now, and the sight of him poised at her entry drove her to the edge. His golden skin glowed with a thin sheen of perspiration, and his shoulders and arms bulged with straining muscles, corded with pumping veins. She couldn't believe that this wonderful creature would want her like he did. Would look at her in the way he was looking down at her now. That her hero and friend and favorite person in the world could also be her lover.

Clutching him closer, she whispered, "I want you, but slowly so it won't hurt."

"I'll be careful with you. Come here, Moo." He gathered her closer, holding her firmly against him as he slowly eased inside her.

"Yes!" she cried out, squeezing her eyes shut against the onslaught of sensation—a deluge of love and passion and everything she'd always wanted. Right here in her arms, after years of being so close to it.

A sound tore from his straining body as he began a hard, thorough pace, his lips dragging wildly over her face, her lips, her cheeks, her temple as his hips rammed against hers and she held on to him for dear life. He drove her to the precipice and made her gasp out his name, and then he followed her with one last thrust, her body clutching his in a long, tight orgasm.

For an hour afterward they lay entangled in bed and remembered their little adventures as teenagers. As Molly drifted off to sleep, she felt so content, so genuinely happy, she thought at last her life was as it should be.

Nothing would come between her and her soul mate any longer.

# Eight

Full sunlight streamed through the windows of Julian's bedroom as Molly cracked open one eye, and then the other. Noticing it was past 10:00 a.m., she moaned languorously and rolled and stretched on the bed, anxious to feel the warm contours of the body she'd snuggled against all night long. But Julian wasn't in bed with her.

Disappointment swept through her as she sat up. Then she spotted the note over his pillow, and she instantly relaxed.

> Good morning, Picasso. Meet me upstairs? Business is ready to open Monday and I'm giving it a thorough check. Hope you don't mind I left another message for you somewhere.
> Yours,
> Julian

The other message, it turned out, was right on her left buttock. Molly gasped when she caught sight of it as she passed by the mirror. It consisted of three red letters, perfectly curved, perfectly marking her fanny like a cattle brand, except he'd used her paint: *JJG*.

She laughed so hard that tears popped into her eyes. She'd never imagined she could wake up feeling so content, so full, so complete, so happy. How could she have spent all these years next to this man she would give her life for, and miss out on all of *this?*

It was as though last night Jules had opened the little box where she'd hidden away entire decades of special, secret feelings for him, and now that those feelings were out, Molly feared she'd burst from the love in her chest.

Scrambling to catch up with him, she showered and found herself drifting off to last night as she shampooed. They'd lain awake remembering stuff about their childhood, then they'd laughed, then their laughter had faded into heat once more, and they'd kissed and made out and made love until they'd exploded.

Hot and bothered by the memory alone, she jumped out of the shower, wrapped herself in a towel and rushed to the walk-in closet to survey her clothes. She settled on a short white jean skirt and a lacy white blouse. Then she fixed coffee and folded two warm croissants she'd heated in the oven into a pair of napkins. She carried the croissants and the two coffee mugs up in the elevator, watching them steam with a smile.

She could too easily picture doing this every day, too easily imagine having her husband's offices in the same building as her apartment. He could come and go as he pleased—take a few moments in his busy day to steal away between meetings and come home and kiss her. Kiss her heart out like at that masquerade, like last night, like, hopefully, later this morning. Her cheeks flamed at the prospect.

The elevator chimed and she stepped out, impressed by the sight that greeted her.

*Wow.*

The place had undergone a huge transformation. She hadn't noticed all this last night when she'd been painting like a fiend. But now full sunlight streamed through the windows, and every inch of the marble floor sparkled clean. Chrome chandeliers hung from the rafters, brand-new computers sat proudly atop their shiny new desks. A main reception desk stood before her, and behind it, the wall of her partly finished mural said a cheery good morning.

Just looking at that explosion of colors made her anxious to work on it some more. But the truth was, she was feverish to see Julian. Her breasts pricked at the thought of kissing his silken lips and wrapping herself around his big, hard body again....

She heard voices then. Angry voices.

Frowning, she went around the wall through a set of glass doors. And that was when she spotted Julian. Beautiful in khaki slacks and a white polo short, his casual weekend clothes. But there was nothing casual in his wide stance, in his massively tense shoulders, the arms that strained at his sides.

And then she saw the second man, his stance as menacing as Julian's.

Garrett.

Molly's heart stopped.

Her eyes wildly searched Julian's profile for clues. He looked more than furious. His nostrils were flaring, and though the movements were almost imperceptible, he kept flexing his fingers as though they were cramping. Or as though he was just aching to throttle someone.

O-oookay. This might just not be the morning she had envisioned while she was taking a shower. What were they arguing about anyway? And why was Garrett here if he didn't know about Julian's new—

Oh, no.

*No, no, no.*

All of a sudden it hit her. And she feared that she knew exactly what the two men were arguing about.

Her own words came back to haunt her like a curse.

*"Who the hell can even work in peace with this sort of constant criticism? I'm glad he's ready to move on!"*

*Oh, no, please no.*

Garrett had sounded less than thrilled when he'd demanded to know if Julian was leaving. She swayed nervously on her feet and a wash of hot coffee spilled across her left wrist. Pain shot up her arm, and when she gasped, both men turned.

She locked gazes with Garrett first, somehow avoiding Julian's gaze out of dread. She didn't want to know if he was angry. Not after the incredible, mesmerizing night they had spent together. But really, how angry could he be? He was naturally an easygoing man and would probably take it well and laugh about it later. It wasn't as if she had revealed super top secret information, had she? *Had she?*

She breathed out slowly and smiled at the window behind their shoulders. "I didn't know we had company, Jules."

"I find that hard to believe, somehow, since you issued the invitation."

Her heart skipped a beat when she heard his voice; it was low and silky as a ribbon, but it was the winter coolness of the tone that made the hairs on the back of her neck stand up in alarm. Her eyes jerked to lock with his, and for a moment she needed to recover from the utter slamming force of his accusing gaze.

"Jules," she said, slowly tossing her hair from side to side. "I didn't invite him here. I did not mean for him to... Uh, here, you can take my coffee, Garrett, if you'd like."

She extended a mug, trying once again to turn this crazy morning around to the morning she wanted. The one she'd dreamed of. If Garrett took the hospitable offering, Julian would have to take the second one and maybe after the croissants they'd all—

"Already bringing coffee to the love of your life, Molly? Too bad he was just leaving. Aren't you, brother?"

Once again, Molly's eyebrows furrowed in confusion over Julian's frigid tone. For a dazed moment, she almost expected Julian to chuckle and admit he was teasing her. Like he did when he dared her to wear that wench costume or asked her to kiss his six-pack and go as low as she would go in the darkened office at Landon's house.

But no laughter followed his words.

"What the hell are you talking about?" Garrett burst out.

Molly realized in dawning horror that Julian had referred to Garrett as the love of her life. She glanced down at the mugs both men had refused and the sticky residue of coffee on her wrist, growing numb in disbelief. Had he been making fun of her having stupidly thought she loved Garrett once upon a time, or did he actually believe it to be *true*?

Drawing in a steadying breath, she walked around and shakily set the mugs and croissants on a nearby desk. A little part of her already wanted to get hysterical, but she tried reminding herself that, although she'd spoken out impulsively, the last thing she'd intended was to harm Julian.

She would have time to explain all of this in a couple of minutes, just a few minutes more....

"Please tell me you're having someone check your god-damned head because you're not making any sense," Garrett thundered, then he turned to her. "Thanks for your visit yesterday, Molly," he said. "And for keeping us in the loop of this development."

Molly froze. She could not even believe he would say that to her in front of Julian. Seriously, she'd never expected things to go south so fast. Suddenly, she trembled with the fantastical urge to fling the coffee mugs at Garrett's face for ruining what should've been a perfect morning, for now there was no doubt whatsoever that Julian would believe she had been a little snitch who had betrayed his confidence and trust.

God. It sounded so bad now that she reflected on it, and yet she wouldn't have even said it at all if they hadn't infuriated her so on Julian's behalf!

Instead of giving Garrett any sort of answer, she pursed her lips and pretended to be super busy sucking the spilled coffee from her left wrist. Garrett had spoken the words in true gratitude, maybe even with a bit of tenderness, but she still loathed the fact that Julian had found out that her mouth had apparently gotten ahead of her brain yesterday.

Garrett sighed and turned to Julian, his timbre hardening. "Think about it, before you do something even stupider," he said, and walked toward the reception area and out to the elevators.

Molly finished sucking up the coffee and suddenly felt too energetic, as if she needed to do something. Parachute, river raft, hike Mount Everest? Artists were solitary people by nature, too emotional, too vulnerable, too incapable of handling awfulness like this. Fighting to stand still, she frantically counted the seconds after Garrett left that Julian remained silent. Just watching her. So very, very silent.

Fifty.

Fifty hellish seconds.

While Molly wanted to hide under the chair, blend with her mural or just scream.

Because she was just coming to realize how big a mistake she'd made. She'd done something very wrong to him. Very, very wrong.

Jules didn't trust anyone. Anyone but *her*. Oh, God, now his family would be riding him hard about coming back. Maybe they couldn't send him away like they used to when they were displeased with him, but did she dare wonder how they could pressure him to bend to their united wills?

What had she just *done* to him?

With a pounding heart, she waited for him to speak, every second eternal, miserable. The top two buttons of his polo shirt were unbuttoned. He wore the masquerade ring on his hand. His fingers were curling and uncurling into fists at his sides.

She wanted to die.

"You ratted me out to my brother."

He spoke softly. Too softly. Way too softly.

She sucked in a breath, surprised by the pain cutting through her rib cage. If he'd said, *You suck. You're a liar. Last night was a mistake,* it might have hurt less. Shame spread through her like wildfire. Because how had she not seen this coming? "It's not how it looks, Jules," she told him, but his expression was so harsh and scary her gaze dipped once more to the floor.

His shoes were so polished and shiny. Were they advancing toward her?

He turned her face up to his with his thumb and forefinger, forcing her to look into his piercing eyes. "You ratted me out to my brother, Molly. How the hell could you do this to me?"

Just to stand there under the searing heat of his reproachful green stare made her empty stomach churn. "I didn't mean to! It slipped. *It slipped.* What? Are you going to hate me now, is that it?"

"Hate? Molly, I freaking *love* you! I can't believe you'd line up with them against me." He raked his hands through his hair and then backed away, as though she had a rash he needed to distance himself from. "You want to know why I would leave a thriving, billion-dollar business, Molly? Fine, let me tell you why. Because as long as I'm under my family's thumb, I'll never be able to be with you."

His expression was grim as he watched her, his eyebrows drawn sharp and sullen over his eyes; eyes that killed her with emotion as he looked at her.

"That day you came to me begging me to help you get another man…I thought to *hell* with my family. I wasn't going to let them ruin my life anymore and let them keep me away from you, Moo."

Molly incongruously wondered why Julian could say *Moo* and make it sound revered and womanly, sexy and beautiful, but she was so distraught over the rest of what he said that she didn't wonder for long. Julian's face had hardened with pain and his voice felt like icicles on her skin. Molly's eyes had blurred with tears because each and every one of the words he'd said was eating her up inside.

"They've sent me away dozens of times, they've threatened to disown me, they've tried every twisted plot to keep me in line. And I'm sick and tired of dancing to their tune. I just want to be with *you*." His green eyes clawed her like talons as he spread his arms out, his jaw clenched so tight she feared it would crack like her heart was cracking. "So this was the plan. This was my plan. With my

full financial independence, I'll need no one—no one—
to tell me what to do, or tell me if I can or can't love you,
Molly. Dammit, I can't freaking believe you'd crucify me
for them—*for him*."

He pulled at the collar of his polo shirt as if he wanted to
rip it off him and then stalked to the floor-to-ceiling window. Molly mourned his affection already. No more sparkling green eyes. There were only tornadoes and storms
now.

And she'd put them there.

A tear slipped down her cheek as her brain replayed his
words over and over in her head, then a second tear followed, and a third, and they wouldn't stop. Julian *loved*
her. Oh, God. To know that he'd cared for her all this time,
had wanted her like she'd secretly wanted him and had
been actually doing something so he could be with her…

To know the truest kind of love could have been hers
all along…

This should have been the happiest day of her life. But
instead it had morphed into the worst.

Because to learn that you had something on the same
day you lost it *sucked.*

Molly wanted to tear her skin off with her nails, her
heart out with her hands so she could show him all she
wanted was to give it to him. "I'm sorry, Jules," she said,
clutching her stomach. "I didn't know it was so important.
I swear I would have watched my mouth better—"

"I trusted you, Molly," he interrupted, shaking his head
over and over again. "You know me better than my family, better than anyone. I've trusted you with everything.
Everything I think and want, and… Jesus, I just can't do
this right now."

He put even more distance between them and jammed his
fingers into his hair as each step carried him farther away.

"You can still trust me, Jules! I was careless, that's all. I mean…you're not going to let Garrett push you into anything you don't want to do. Are you?"

He halted. And she trembled at the expression on his face, so…vacant, as if not only would he never, ever trust her again, but neither would he care to try.

This steely detachment on his part was so new and alarming, when he turned to face the window and gave her a view of his broad, impenetrable back, she actually wanted to flee to her studio and lock herself up the rest of her life in a sanctuary of paint, brushes and blank canvases.

But her life would never be the same without him, would never be the same if she didn't stay here and work things out. Julian was, quite simply, the most valuable and treasured thing in the world to her.

He *had* to forgive her.

So she remained. She remained glued to the floor, to this present, this horrible alternate reality where Julian looked at her as a…fraud.

"Jules?" she prodded when he remained staring silently out the window for too long.

He ran a hand all the way through his hair and gripped the back of his neck, then stared down at the floor. "Was I your consolation prize, Molly? Do you still have…an idea of you and Garrett in your head?"

She opened her mouth to deny it, but only heard a shocked gasp, the question so terribly painful to hear. Did he not realize she *adored* him? Did he think she would spend a night like last night just for the *fun* of it?

"If it had been Garrett kissing you that night at the masquerade, for real, would you even be here with me, Molly? Or would you have left here with him?" he asked, and when he dropped his arm and turned slightly, his empty stare slashed her to bits.

How could he think that?

She wanted to hit him for even thinking it, but she felt shattered inside.

The magic she'd felt in that kiss could never have been there with Garrett or anyone else. It was him, Julian, it always had been, no matter how much she'd tried to fight it. He was The One.

Him and only him.

But she couldn't speak. To her frustration, she was crying now, and with her throat so tight, it was really hard to get a word out.

She'd never imagined she could ever hurt anyone. She loved to laugh, to enjoy life, to paint. She was young at heart and had never seen herself as a threat to anyone— not even to a bug, because she had a habit of escorting them out to the yard and never squashing a single one. She would cut out her eyes for Julian if he needed them, her hands so she could never paint again. She'd give him two kidneys, her liver, and her pancreas and lungs, too! She wouldn't even mention her heart because she'd never really had it to herself in the first place.

She'd given it along with her lollipop to a six-year-old boy a long, long time ago.

"Julian, don't be ridiculous, please. I love you," she said as she wiped her tears, rushing after him when he'd got tired of waiting for her to reply. But he was already boarding the elevator, as proud and stubborn as all the Gage men she'd ever known.

"Get your stuff, Molly. I'm taking you back home. Consider the mural done."

# Nine

For exactly twelve days, eleven hours, forty-seven minutes and thirty-two seconds, Julian buried himself in work, sweat and sports. He hadn't set foot at the *San Antonio Daily* in almost two weeks. Not even to present his damned brothers with his resignation letter.

No. Since then, JJG Enterprises had officially opened for business, so instead he'd buried himself in work from 6:00 a.m. to 6:00 p.m. each day, and after that he had been rowing, paddling, kayaking, running, climbing and sky-diving his freaking heart out.

He would come home at midnight, soaked in sweat, to feed his body, bathe himself and drop down dead on the bed. But it was no use. His head continued swimming with memories of making love to Molly, kissing her sweet lips. Memories of her betrayal.

He'd never thought that a casual, collected guy like

him, with everything under control, would ever get to feel that way.

And every day when he saw her mural upstairs, he wanted to tear that wall down. It was so bright and vivid, so sassy, so Molly. He could bulldoze it to the ground if he didn't have millions invested up there. Millions. Hell, his whole damned heart, since he'd imagined sharing that future with Molly.

Now he didn't even want to wake up.

Even his home, once his sanctuary, seemed to assault him with memories at every turn.

Her scent lingered in the pillows. He kept finding her stuff around the house. Fashion magazines. A random paintbrush. In the kitchen pantry he'd find the artificial sweetener she claimed was the best sitting right next to the honey he liked to gobble. And those damned Sleepytime Teas.

He hadn't realized until the glaring emptiness of life without Molly stared him in the face every day how deeply she had infiltrated his life. She had been involved, in little and big ways, in every part of his day. From the cookies he'd snack on at the office or at home, provided by Molly from Kate's delicious kitchen, to the text messages reminding him of a family gathering to her calls—*Forget to say hi yesterday, moron? Call me. Or else!*

He wanted to forget he'd ever met this woman, forget he'd ever wanted her, forget he'd been prepared to change his whole life around for her....

But he couldn't.

He couldn't forgive her. If only he could just forget her. Forget the way she laughed with him, at him, and poked and prodded him and made his body feel alive in a way nobody else did. He'd had strings of lovers but had never enjoyed sex so much, cherished the moment so fiercely as that night he'd spent with her.

He'd replayed it in his head dozens of times, groaning and suffering like a masochist, but the reality had been so sweet he didn't want to forget that time with her. Ever. To have finally seen her, sprawled and wanting him in his bed, that red hair fanning across his sheets, could still give a grown man wet dreams.

She'd said she loved him a thousand times in her life. He knew she did. As a friend. As a "brother." But did she *love* him? Julian had been inside her, knew every secret of her body, knew where to press her, how to make her moan, what she ate, what she feared, where to tickle her. Would she rather have spent that night with Garrett?

Garrett.

His blood boiled at the thought of his brother. Even though he knew Molly's feelings for Garrett had been based on a kiss that Julian himself had given her, he continued to feel so jealous he couldn't even see straight. He couldn't believe that she would betray him to his brother like she had. So *why* had she?

Had two decades of pure, raw friendship meant nothing to her?

He desperately tried fishing his memories for clues of her and his brother together. Looks he could've missed. Touches that had more weight to them than they should have. But he came up with nothing. Every memory of Molly was tied to one man, and that man was *him*. Maybe he had not always been a man. But when he had been a boy, he had been *her* boy.

*Jules, Jules, gimme a piggyback ride.*

And when Kate had tried to patch her up after a good scrape and would coo down at Molly in a maternal way, "I'm going to kiss your boo-boo better," little Molly would point at Julian across the room and grin. "No, I want him to do it."

And later, as teens: *Teach me to surf, Jules. Will you drive me over to art class, Jules?*

And as an adult: *Coffee? Tea? Call me! I'm still alive, you know, just been painting!*

But now he was alone.

So damned alone.

Yeah, that was him.

The careless playboy with a broken heart.

The sun shone overhead so bright, Molly was surprised she didn't disintegrate like a vampire under its glare. After being locked in her studio for weeks, it was almost a miracle her skin did not instantly peel off from sunlight exposure. She might even deserve such a fate.

At least if you asked Julian, who, she assumed, wanted her dead.

Eyes narrowed to shield herself from some of the sun's brightness, she gazed down at the envelope she gripped in her clammy hands, recognizing the handwriting as that of Julian's assistant, Ms. Watts.

So. This is what their friendship and one-night stand—because truly, that was all they'd managed to have together—had come to.

Communicating through the post office.

She closed her mailbox and had to sit down on the grass next to the sidewalk and just stare down at that white envelope.

Her texts had not been answered.

Her calls went straight to voice mail.

She wanted to kill the jerk for being so silly and dramatic, and at the same time she wanted to slap herself for opening her big mouth to Garrett without thinking.

Julian was, and had always been, an extremely private man. He showed his cool and aloof side to everyone but only showed his true self to a select few. Molly knew, deep down, that no one knew Julian better than she did.

He couldn't stand to talk about politics but oh, he sure loved to steal her Lucky Charms marshmallows. He was a sports and sports-memorabilia fanatic, and if he was not a businessman, he'd probably spend all day doing water sports at the lake surfer, with his suntan and lazy charm and a wakeboard under him. He'd never felt as if he belonged in his family—never really felt as if he belonged anywhere.

And that was why she couldn't stand to remember what she'd unwittingly done to him.

He'd longed for freedom in his life, and instead she'd blown the whistle on him to his family so they could tie him back up and keep him from flying. She had done that. To the man she had constantly, throughout her life, loved in every way a woman could love a man.

The worst part of it was that Julian never let anyone in.

But Molly had always come in through the back door.

And he'd let her. Enjoyed it, even. Cared for her, protected her, coddled her.

And she'd accidentally betrayed him to a man whom he'd believed she wanted over him.

How could she ever make things right if he didn't even want to talk to her?

It had been fifteen days since she'd seen him now, and each day she'd tried to make amends. Her last attempt had been returning every penny of the money he'd wired to her for her unfinished mural. With a note that read, *I've never left a work unfinished until now. Please give me a chance—I'd like to finish this.*

She'd written a thousand notes before settling on that

one. Some had said, *I love you* and *please* and *forgive me.* But she'd been too much of a chicken to send any of those, and so she'd settled on the most businesslike one, thinking it was probably her best chance of getting an entry with him.

She drew a deep breath and peeled the envelope open with shaky fingers. The check she had written to him for the $150,000 fell into her open palm, shredded to pieces. There was no note. Except her own note. Shredded to pieces, as well.

She thought she heard her heart crack.

Her eyes welled with tears and she ducked her face when a car approached. Tires screeched, a motor shut down and doors opened.

Kate and Beth stepped out of the Catering, Canapés and Curry van. "Molly?" Kate said, alarmed.

Molly used her hair to shield her profile from view and jammed the pieces of the check and note back into the envelope, rising to her feet and quickly wiping at her cheeks. "Hey. I'll help you." She didn't look at them as she went to the back of the van and began unloading their empty trays, but she could feel their eyes on her as she headed inside the house.

Beth caught up with her in the kitchen. "Molly?"

Molly prayed to God her eyes weren't red, and even smiled as she set the trays down on the kitchen counter. "Hey, Beth."

She could see the concern in Beth's expression, and she feared that there was even a little pity there, too. "You know, Julian came by the house the other day. To speak to Landon. He resigned from the *Daily.*"

Molly nodded as her airway constricted. "Good for him."

Beth studied her. Molly knew she was a good woman.

She had known heartache and a horrid divorce before she had found true love in her life, and suddenly Molly wanted to wail her heart out to her. Because surely this woman would understand how it felt when you were ripped apart, shredded like your notes and broken. But then Kate's heart would break for Molly if she saw her like this, and Molly didn't want to break her sister's heart.

It was her own fault that all this had happened. Kate had warned her so many times, so, so many times, about Julian. Maybe Molly had even had it coming.

"You know—" Beth grasped her hand and gave her an encouraging squeeze "—if it makes you feel any better, he's not doing too good, either."

Molly looked down at her bare toes, her chest heavy as if it were carrying the weight of a whole country. "It doesn't," she admitted, feeling like a bug as she remembered Julian's anger, his disappointment. The last thing she'd wanted was to make him suffer. "But thanks anyway, Beth."

That afternoon she went back to finishing the two canvases she had left for her exhibit at the Blackstone Gallery in New York. They ended up awful, tenebrous and depressing, reflecting her mood. But she still owed the gallery these two works, and because she had no time to start anew, they would have to do.

At night she lay in bed, her eyes dry as she heard Kate on the phone: "Not doing well... What are we going to do?"

Molly wanted to make a humble suggestion and tell her, and whomever she was talking to, to stay the hell away from her life, but then she just put her pillow over her face and groaned.

"Molly," Kate said from the door, a shaft of light entering with her.

"I heard you, Kate. I have ears, you know, and we don't

live in a mansion," she grumbled angrily, flinging the pillow aside.

The mattress squeaked as her sister sat by her side and took her hand. "I'm sorry, Moo. I think we've made a terrible mistake. With you and Julian, I mean."

"No. You were right all along." Molly rolled to her side and pulled her hand free to stick it under her cheek, suddenly rejecting any physical contact that didn't come from where she most craved it.

"Molly, we're planning something. Garrett, Landon, Beth and I. If I tell you what it is, will you go with it?"

"If it involves me lying again to anyone or pretending to be something I'm not, count me out."

"No, Moo, this is actually a good plan," Kate said, a smile in her voice. "All you'd really need to do is follow some instructions in a note that I'm going to give you this weekend. The note will lead you to Julian."

"I hate him."

"You do?"

"I've never met such a frustrating bastard in my life!"

"All right, then." The bed squeaked again as Kate got up to leave.

Molly sprang back up on the bed, her heart picking up speed as she switched on the lamp, and frantically blurted, "I was never really with him, Kate. It was all a lie. I was confused and thought that Garrett was the one who kissed me that night at the masquerade. I foolishly thought Julian could help me make Garrett jealous so he'd come around, but then I realized all along…"

Kate cocked her head from the doorway, her eyes brimming with understanding. "I know," she said. Coming back, she sat down and ran her hand down the length of Molly's hair. "Do you really think I believed that little act?

You two were so obviously not lovers I could've laughed if I hadn't been so very worried."

"But it was actually Julian who kissed me at the masquerade and I...I got mixed up. It was like my soul recognized him, but my brain *couldn't* or maybe didn't want to. All I know is that I needed to find this man and I needed to be with Julian while I did... It's his fault I can never look at other men, never want to be with anyone else. I even think I was pretending to want to make Garrett jealous but really wanted to make Julian jealous instead."

"I know, I know. Relax. That man is your rock, Molly. And you're his soil. You have to *be* with him. We made a grave mistake keeping you two apart for so long. Garrett is worried sick about him. He's been running himself to death. Not eating. Not opening up to anyone. His family feels responsible for this, even his mother is trying to apologize for all her earlier threats, and he won't hear anything from anyone. He's really hurting, Molly. You want him, don't you?"

"You have no idea," she gasped brokenly, nodding so fast she was almost dizzy. The mere idea of being able to see him again was electrifying. Of talking to him. Touching him, even if only with the merest tip of her littlest finger. Oh, God, it hurt so much to love him from afar, reminding her of all the misery of growing up without him.

She had always dreamed of having a family, because hers had been broken before she'd even gotten to know her own parents. She'd just never tried for one of her own because she'd believed Julian would never be a part of it. Now a little kernel of hope sprang in her center, and she opened her eyes.

But she feared to hope too much and end up wretched. "Why?" she asked Kate. "Why is everyone going to help us, after all this time?"

"Because I love you, Molly. And you love him. And *he* loves you. And we all love you both."

Molly coiled her arms around Kate's waist and squeezed her sister as tight as possible, sighing when Kate squeezed her back just as hard. "I miss him so much, Kate."

"I know, Moo. I know you do."

# Ten

It was a good day to be at the lake house. Sunny and breezy days on the cusp of summer were hard to come by in Texas. But that was just what the Gage family got when they visited their Canyon Lake home on the last Saturday of the month.

Julian had not planned to set foot here, but Landon had insisted, and he'd grudgingly agreed merely because he would be able to water-ski, swim and do the WaveRunner thing. After a day of that, the only thing that would be aching would be his goddamned muscles rather than his heart.

Now the wind slapped him as he roared across the lake on the WaveRunner, racing Garrett on his right and Landon on his left. He squinted in the direction of the mansion, which stood white and regal by the lake, with a small dock and bright pink bougainvillea hanging from the terrace columns. He could see his mother already seated at the long terrace table, calmly pouring glasses of lemonade for the two figures seated with her—Landon's wife, Beth, and his stepson, David.

Julian swerved and spewed water behind him as he jolted the machine to a stop right beside the dock. He tied up the WaveRunner and jumped out, wet suit soaked, dripping a path up the wood planks as he ambled toward the terrace. When he arrived, he plopped down on a chair and took a glass of lemonade from his mother.

"Landon tells me you're not coming back to the *Daily*," his mother said without preamble. "Are you certain about that?"

Julian nodded, not up to explaining the deal he'd made with Landon and his reasons for it. The point was, he would continue to support the *Daily* with JJG Enterprises' services, personally making sure the *Daily*'s client base thrived. But he was riding solo now.

Eleanor patted her bun absently with one hand, making a puppy-dog plea with her eyes until he groaned. "I've got 1,210 businesses already signed up for the services of JJG Enterprises. *No,* Mother. The *Daily* is my past. I'm a free agent from now on."

She relented quickly, and Julian knew it was due to the guilt that gnawed at her over the way she'd attempted to separate him from Molly over the years, and the pain it had ended up causing him now. In fact, she'd even relented about her threat of cutting off his trust fund because he'd quit the family business, though she was still trying to convince him to come back.

Now his brothers strolled over, wet suits soaked, and plopped down just as a redhead emerged from within the house, carrying a salad bowl.

Julian stiffened at the same time Garrett did.

It must have been the red hair, shining in the sun, flowing behind her in the wind. For a blind second, Julian thought it was Molly. He didn't even know how he felt about that, but his heart kicked in his chest like a wild thing. He was relieved when he realized that it was Kate.

He calmed back down while Garrett went over to take the bowl from her hands and whisper something in her ear.

"Hi, Julian," Kate said, spotting him. "You've been so busy all morning I haven't been able to say hi."

"You just did, so now you can sleep soundly," he said.

Then he realized how grumpy he sounded. Well, hell, he could still tackle some kayaks and hike this afternoon to let out some of his frustration. His every muscle ached, but there was still some juice in them, and he didn't want to have a drop left by the time he was finished. It wasn't enough; he needed to push harder. Push every single muscle to failure.

Servants brought out trays of canapés and wine. While the family chatted, Julian sat in silence, brooding when no second redhead came out of the house. Kate had been invited. So where the hell was Molly?

He wanted to ask, his tongue itching in his mouth. He wanted to ask where she was and how she'd been doing and why in the world she had betrayed him. He'd never gone twenty-three days, four hours, thirty-two minutes and about thirty seconds without talking to her. The time had dragged on so hellishly that it felt like years as far as he was concerned. However he measured it, this was proving to be the crappiest period of his life so far.

Kate kept her attention on him, and he could feel her gaze on his profile as she asked, "You're not going to eat anything?"

Julian stared at the salad bowl. Molly used to get all of his croutons and he'd eat all of her raisins.

He shook his head, not even hungry anymore.

Beth and Landon kept squeezing each other's hands tenderly as they nibbled salad and drank their lemonades, and the grenade inside Julian's stomach seemed to be ready to detonate. His oldest brother had a truly doting wife and a great kid, and he doted on them both in return. The family had been thrilled that Landon had been able to find love again after his first wife and their son had died. They thought he'd closed himself off for good, yet Beth had opened him up like a Christmas present and found gold.

Usually, the sight of them brought Julian immense cheer, but today he found it was…difficult. To see that connection.

Because the only person he'd ever had it with was not with him here.

"So how is dear Molly, Kate?" his mother asked, very politically bringing her up, damn her. "I'm so disappointed she couldn't come."

Lips compressed into a thin line, Julian stared at his empty glass of lemonade, wishing he'd gone for vodka.

"She was disappointed, too," Kate said, "but she had that exhibit in New York and had to fly over for the opening."

Julian refused to think about Molly flying all alone to her solo exhibit. Getting chatted up by someone next to her in first class. By her fans and collectors at the gallery. It was an important time in her career. And Molly had celebrated…alone.

He refused to think about how he should've been there, always had been there.

He restlessly shifted in his seat, trying to console himself with the thought that at least Josh Blackstone, her gallerist, would be there with her. Julian's old acquaintance was as ruthless as a hellhound, but fair with his artists and especially with Molly, whom he'd taken under his wing a long time ago when Julian urged her to submit her works for his consideration.

Blackstone had flipped, called it feisty and fresh, and the rest had been history.

"I've always loved her canvases, my dear. So bright and sunny. Like her. No wonder they do so well in the art market," his mother casually told Kate, and the topic only incensed Julian to a whole new level.

"Remember how she used to save all those wrappers," Garrett added in lingering disbelief. "And twine them around the tree trunks to make some weird…"

"Oh, yeah, the candy tree," Landon said, lifting up his glass. "I think she has one in this exhibition. It's considered to be her 'early work.'"

"Remember that one review?" Beth said, turning to Landon. "You know the one, Lan… Where the reviewer said Molly was the kind of artist who could draw a simple sketch on a paper napkin and sign it and with that, not only pay for her dinner tab, but for the entire restaurant's? Like it was rumored Picasso once did."

The chair legs screeched like angry banshees as Julian pushed back his seat and rose, his face black with rage. With a shove-it-where-it-hurts look, he grabbed his drink to leave.

"Oh, Julian, dear," Eleanor said, "Could you tell one of the servants to bring out the pies?"

He realized his drink was empty and slammed it back down. "Tell them yourself."

Ready to call it quits on family time, he marched toward the dry clothes he'd left on a wood bench by the dock, angrily unzipping and yanking the top part of his wet suit down to his hips. His family kept talking of Molly's artworks, how special they were, and yes, they were incredible pieces, amazing. But it was Molly whom he'd always considered the masterpiece. Living and breathing, coloring his world with passion and liveliness, making his every moment…worthwhile. God, he hated to remember how she used to make him feel.

Stopping in his tracks, he scowled at the wood bench. His clothes were nowhere to be found.

He stormed back to the group. "Where the hell is my stuff?"

Kate covered her cheeks with both hands, eyes wide. "Oh, I'm sorry! I hung everything in the closet at the cottage so it wouldn't get wet or wrinkled."

He rolled his eyes and stomped down the path to the spare cottage a good distance from the main house. Once he got there, he slammed the door shut behind him to keep the AC inside and went to the closet.

That was when he caught a shadow moving out of the corner of his eye.

He did a forty-five-degree turn and saw Molly. She stood by the window, like a virgin fire princess ready for the sacrifice of her life, her hair molten lava running down her rounded shoulders, wearing a sexy little strapless dress and glittery sandals, big earrings, big bangles and a big smile.

His body, traitorous, jumped to life at the sight of her as though *twenty-three* miserable, endless days of continual physical exertion were not enough to keep it numb. Oh, no, not around her. Her mere presence had flicked on his power switch. Now his blood rushed through his veins and his mind sparked to awareness, taking in every detail of her porcelain skin, her pale blue eyes, her shiny hair, her sweet, white, tiny little teeth she'd used to bite him lovingly. He took in every detail now only to torture himself with them later.

His palms itched, his breath hitched, and he said, "You."

He heard shuffling outside the door, and then the sound of a bolt sliding into place.

*Plunk.*

And he realized too late, that his family had just locked him in with her.

"Me," Molly agreed calmly.

And suddenly it didn't matter that Julian obviously didn't want to be here, that he didn't want to see her. It didn't matter that his eyes flashed reproachfully at her, that his stance was wide and defensive, that his lips were hard and pressed together in anger. The sight of him after all these painful days made her lungs throb and her head spin with the sheer joy of being able to look at him.

And he looked extremely good.

His torso was damp with lake water and tanned by the sun. His chest looked wider, his athletic form so incredibly sexy in the way the wet suit hung halfway down his body, emphasizing his narrow hips and waist. The shiny black fabric clung seductively to his thighs and to the prominent part of him that had once joined him with her. His hair was damp and slicked back from his face, revealing every inch of his formidable features. The features of a playboy, a Greek god, the man she loved—and the man who wanted nothing to do with her.

Molly trembled with nervousness, desire, regret.

She noticed his hair, still streaked enticingly by the sun, was growing a bit longer, to his nape, and she could smell the woods on him, the oaks and the cedars on the property.

"I thought you had a show," he said, his tone indicating that he didn't really care about her answer.

She still wanted to tell him—because he used to be the only one who truly listened—that it had gone well, that the reviews were excellent and everyone thought she was the luckiest person on earth to have succeeded so young. They thought she had it all.

But she didn't.

She didn't have what she wanted most. Had always wanted.

"I got back from the opening yesterday," she said slowly, her hands restless at her sides, fiddling with the skirt of her dress. "Everyone seemed to like my paintings, except for my two most depressing ones." *The ones that suck because of you.*

"You have no depressing works," he said, pointing at her.

He pursed his lips as he once again scanned his surroundings. Then he shook his head in disgust, marched back to the closet, yanked open the doors and began to pull out his clothes briskly from the hangers.

She felt an unwelcome rush of desire when he began to change right before her eyes. He pulled off his wet suit with a snap, and when he peeled it from his thighs and kicked it off, she saw his nude backside. Glorious muscles rippled and clenched as he put on his Boss underwear and khaki pants. He slipped on a polo shirt and buttoned the two top buttons, then crossed the room toward the cottage door and tried to force the knob. He cursed under his breath when it didn't open and angrily swung around to her.

"So you're into kidnapping now, Molls? Is that your new kick?"

"Yes, as a matter of fact, I'm into spanking, kidnapping and robbing unsuspecting clients of their money while I fail to complete their murals."

Jaw clamped, he stormed to one of the windows and attempted to open it so forcibly the glass rattled in its frame. He acted as if he was in prison and eager to be set free, which just made Molly sigh in despair.

"Look, this wasn't my idea, but I think the plan is brilliant," she said.

"Except for one flaw," he said wickedly, unlocking a second window with a surprising click. He cocked a devil-may-care brow at her and grinned as he pushed upward, only to realize there was another lock on the outside and the glass stayed right in place, no matter how hard he tried to get it open. *"Damn."*

"You don't want to talk to me, Julian, that's fine," Molly said softly. "But I need to talk to you. So now you're going to have to hear me out. Even if you *break* one of those windows, Jules, what are you planning to do? Let in some fresh air?"

He scowled as she pointed at the forged-iron bars on the outside.

"Your mother had that design made specially to keep the drunk teenagers from getting in like they've been doing at other lake houses, and if they can't come in through those bars, I doubt even *you* can go out through them."

The glare he shot her could've been Lucifer's. "I can't believe this idiocy. First they don't want me near you, now they lock me up with you?"

Shaking his head, he paced like a caged lion.

His tumultuous energy spun through the room like a whirlwind, making her want to go over there, wrap her arms around him and calm him down like she had many times before when he was irritated about other things.

But now he saw her as untrustworthy, and he wouldn't want to open up. Now his irritation was caused by the fact that he was locked in the same room as Molly.

"Your family has realized we're miserable and they're trying to make amends. Well, *I* have been miserable," she added, watching him pace. "Jules, will you please look at me so I can talk to you? Or do I need to call you JJ to make you react?"

He stopped in his tracks, his hands curling at his sides, fingers clenching. Although his face was a mask of cold indifference, his eyes blazed with intensity. "Don't even think about provoking me."

"Or you'll what? Kiss me?"

His glare was as bleak as a cemetery. "I'll spank the hell out of you, how about that? I'm *through* with kissing you, Molls."

The decisiveness in his words summoned a fresh wave of outrage from her. "Really? And who says I even *want* you to?"

"A closed door with a lock on it, that's who!" His teeth were clenched so tight, she could see a muscle twitch in the back of his jaw.

She glowered at him, but feared in the innermost part of her, where a candle of hope flickered its last lights, that this battle was already lost. Apparently, not only was her presence not wanted, her kiss was worth nothing to him, either. But she, on the other hand, remembered perfectly all the things she had done as a result of *his* masquerade kiss. "So are you going to listen to me, *JJ?* God, I'm try-ing to fix things here!" she cried.

He looked up at the ceiling and pinched his eyes shut as though supremely tested. She thought she heard him counting under his breath, stopping at thirty-eight, his hands still clenching and unclenching.

Gradually, he turned around to plant his hands on the wall, then stared out the window with his forehead almost touching the glass pane. His voice was a coarsened whis-per. "I'm damned well listening. So talk."

Molly dragged in a breath as she watched his hands splay wider on the wall. She longed to feel those fingers again, feel him touch her, caress her, hold her. "Garrett wanted to talk to me that day I went to his office. He wanted to discuss our relationship."

His hands fisted against the window frame. "Whose?" he asked, his knuckles white. "His and yours?"

"Yours and mine, Jules." She flung her hands up in exasperation. "Obviously! So I told him—"

He spun around like a cyclone. "You told him that I was leaving the *Daily,* and my family could have ruined everything I've planned for years. What *else* did you tell him? You were fishing for his approval by ratting me out, weren't you?"

The hurt that exploded in Molly's chest was so massive that she almost staggered. "Do you really believe that? *Do you?*" Her voice sounded panicked, but she didn't care.

The look he shot back at her was so raw and stark it all but extinguished her candle of hope.

Her voice broke, and she opened her hands out in silent plea. "Look, I'm sorry, Jules. It wasn't on purpose. I was angry about the way they tried to warn me off you and wasn't even thinking clearly. Please, please help me out here. I'm so in love with you I just can't bear this anymore."

"That information wasn't yours to share and *especially* not with them, Moo!" He shook his head and plunged a hand into his damp hair. "Look, I just can't talk to you now. I can't. I'm too goddamned pissed that you would…" A halting hand shot up in the air when she started forward, and she abruptly stopped, her heart in her throat.

He sighed and backed away from her, and every step he took felt like a mile she would never be able to recover. He took a seat on the window bench, and Molly eased back and ended up alone on a floral couch, silent and hurt.

*He didn't say he loves me back* was all she could think. *God, please, doesn't he care for me just a little bit anymore?*

She thought of how easily he had jumped between lovers and beds his entire life and she wondered if there had been women warming his bed all this time, comforting him while she'd been pining for him alone, producing the worst artworks of her life because of him.

*Seduce him,* a little voice whispered. *Make him forgive you.*

But the thought made her feel cheap and as fake as he thought her to be. How could she go through with a seduction? First of all, he wasn't even giving any indication that he still *wanted* her. And it had never been just about sex between them. It had been about friendship and fun and sharing and trust….

Trust.

Once long ago, Molly had been careless and had broken Eleanor Gage's prized crystal figurine, one up on display over the chimney mantel. No matter how Julian tried to help her fix it, the thing could never be properly glued back together without looking pitifully disfigured. Now the thought that she could have shattered Julian's trust just like that dolphin figurine, a figurine they'd ended up *throwing away,* terrified her.

Despair made her sink deeper into her own personal bubble. She'd always felt strong in her life, plunging into adventures without thinking too much about their consequences. But now the source of her strength was gone, and she felt totally lost without him.

The sun began to set outside, the lights of dusk bathing the room in a golden glow. She wondered if some woman had been stroking Julian's Beckham-blond hair a day before. If a woman with model legs and bigger breasts had been feeling his beautiful hands on her skin and sighing under his searing kisses. His beautiful kisses.

"Have you been sleeping around again?" she blurted

out, unable to stand the torment of wondering about it any longer. The jealousy was ripping her insides into shreds.

"I don't feel like sex ever since you and I—" He glared, as though furious he'd revealed as much. Eyebrows pulled downward, he then growled, *"No."*

The relief she felt made her sag back against the couch.

"Have *you?*" he shot back.

"Of course not!" she cried.

His narrowed gaze held hers with magnetic force, and they both fell so quiet that Molly could've heard a pin drop across the room. Unable to bear the strength of his stare, she broke eye contact and surveyed her sandaled feet, her stomach roiling. God, how she missed his oak leaf–green eyes.

"So do they plan to leave us here all night?" Sounding just as thrilled as he had minutes ago—which was not thrilled *at all*—Julian looked around the cozy cottage as though he still hoped to find an escape route.

It made Molly feel about as wanted as an abandoned rug. She nodded dejectedly. "I think they left some food in the kitchenette and water and…champagne."

How foolish to even mention that last item.

As if they would both have something to celebrate. *Uh-huh. Right.*

She had totally underestimated the size of Julian's pride, and the size of her own, and now she just wanted to stop begging and curl up on a pillow and never wake up until the Earth spun the way it was supposed to. The way it used to.

Her eyes blurred as she glanced up at him, but he was looking out the window, still unapproachable, and though she trembled with the urge to feel his arms around her, she curled up on the sofa and grabbed a pillow embroidered with *Home Is Where the Heart Is*. Shutting her eyes tiredly, she cuddled on one corner and strove to pretend Julian wasn't here with her. It was easy. Because she'd never before felt so broken, so somber and so lonely when she was with him.

But then his voice flicked through her, soft and husky enough that she could almost pretend it was a caress.

"Do you remember when you flunked your second driving test, Molly?"

She nodded, throat tightening. He had to bring that up.

"Do you remember taking out Landon's car for a little practice drive and crashing the hell out of it?"

She nodded faster, her throat tightening even more.

"You pulled me out of a damn Spurs game in the final period. And I fixed things. Fixed them so that you'd never be caught, gladly taking the super-fun lecture from my brother and mother for you. I never ratted you out. Never."

Throat burning thick now, she kept her eyes closed and prayed he didn't notice the dampness in her lashes, the tears stealing from between her eyelids to slide down her cheeks and to the pillow. "I'm sorry," she gritted out helplessly, opening her eyes to see the blurry vision of him. "You've always been my hero. I'm *sorry* I turned out to be the villain in *your* plot!"

He laughed, a sarcastic sound that said he didn't even care, and then he said no more and leaned a shoulder on the window and stared outside, probably wishing he was anywhere but here. With her.

"If we hadn't slept together," she asked his profile, "would you still be my best friend and talk to me?"

He rubbed one of his arms absently over his chest as he continued staring out the window. "Ask Garrett to be your bud," he said quietly.

Her eyebrows furrowed, and the anger and injustice that had been building up in her for days overtook her in an explosion. She jumped to her feet, shaking in fury. "You know what, Jules? Go to hell! If you want to hang on to the one thing I've done wrong to you in my life, that's your call. But you know I've been there for you every single second of your life like your own private cheerleader. If you had a fan club you know damned well I'd be the *president*. I happen to think that there's no one in the world as perfectly wonderful and special and incredible as you. But if you think that I would willingly hurt you in any way, for *anyone* else, even your brothers, then you're an idiot. And you don't deserve me *or* my friendship, much less my *love!*"

She was just too hurt and too tired to beg anymore. She'd thought what Julian and she had would survive anything. That they were invincible and powerful.

And now here they were, strangers and almost enemies, as if they hadn't once meant everything to each other.

He didn't reply to her words, but kept staring stiffly out the window, his profile taut.

Molly sighed and dropped back to the sofa, tired from her trip, from twenty-three days without sleep, weeks of wishing to find love and losing everything precious in her life in the process. Tired and frustrated, she tossed and turned on the couch, and she did that until finally sleep took over.

During the night her eyes fluttered open to see him still sitting by the window. Every time she looked, she found those green eyes watching her in the darkness.

The last time she woke up shivering and confused, and when she saw him still sitting there, alone and watching her with eyes that were almost as shadowed as the room, she curled herself into a ball and groggily said, "You should get some sleep, Jules. You can keep on hating me tomorrow."

He started coming over with something in his hands. "People with insomnia don't sleep, Molls," he murmured, and covered her with a blanket.

And that was as close as he got to her.

# Eleven

It was past 7:00 a.m. when Julian heard someone fiddling with the outside bolt, and he stalked across the room like a man chasing a diabolical fiend. He'd slept exactly zero hours, had been torn between taking Molly in his arms and breaking a freaking window with his fist, but he would be damned if he gave his family the satisfaction of doing either.

No. He was through doing whatever they wanted him to do.

They thought he and Molly would have something to celebrate? The only thing Julian was going to celebrate today was ramming his fist into his brothers' jaws.

And that was exactly what he did as soon as the bolt was removed and he pushed the cottage door open to find Garrett outside, turning to leave.

"Good morning," Julian said to make his brother turn back around. He did.

And the force Julian put into his punch was so heavy it floored him instantly. Garrett smacked the ground with a loud thump.

Inside the cottage, Molly jumped to her feet with a start, her eyes wide and startled as she came over and saw the middle Gage brother sprawled at Julian's feet. She whipped her face up to him and fiercely scowled. "Oh, you were just itching to do that, weren't you? You've been talking about your guns for months!"

Frowning, Julian stretched out his fingers in confusion, because damn, that had hurt. Apparently, Garrett was too hardheaded to punch without getting a bit of a jolt in his knuckles, too.

"Yeah," Julian admitted to her. Then he glowered down at his brother and nudged him with his foot. "That felt real good, you son of a bitch!"

Coming up to a sitting position, Garrett wiped the blood off his mouth with the sleeve of his polo shirt and spat out the rest. "We have the same mother, you *moron*."

"I'm going home," he heard Molly mutter under her breath as she stormed toward the terrace, where Julian watched her grab some keys from Kate's purse. A minute later the catering van was pulling out of the driveway.

He wanted to chase her, yell and fight with her, the adrenaline was so off the charts in his body. But his instinct to spare her his rage was still too strong, and he was more bloodthirsty to make his brother his outlet for his rage.

Garrett was pushing to his feet, but Julian didn't let him. He shoved him back down by bracing one knee on his shoulder. "Stop meddling in our lives! We're not your responsibility, or Mother's or anyone else's. And if we wanted to be together, we sure as hell have never needed your idiotic help!"

Garrett pushed him aside and shuffled to his feet, rubbing his sore jaw. "She loves you, Jules. You're being an ass."

"Make that a headline in the paper tomorrow, brother. See if I buy a copy." Julian stalked away and flipped Garrett his two middle fingers without even glancing backward.

"Argh, you hardheaded bastard." Garrett pounced, scowling as he blocked his path. "You're going to make me fight you, aren't you?" Gritting his teeth in obvious frustration, his older brother began rolling up his sleeves.

"Get out of my way," Julian warned.

"Molly didn't betray you, you imbecile! She was furious because we were warning her away from you. She didn't *know* we've been riding you about her for years and she was trying to defend you. Why can you not *see* that?"

Julian wasn't listening. He was still restless, reckless, seething.

All night. All night, watching inches and inches of goose-bump-covered, creamy white skin, lustrous red hair and parted pink lips. All night, torturing himself with wanting her so damned much. He'd had a hard-on for hours. Hours.

"You know that girl loves you more than anyone or anything in this world. Don't you? *Don't you, Julian?*" Garrett demanded.

He glared at his brother. Goddammit, he wished he was sure of her. That she did not want anyone else. That she would never put any other man before him, ever again, before *Julian*.

"And you love her so bad you were ready to dump your whole family just to be with her," Garrett insisted.

Julian was suddenly incensed. "Because she's mine. Mine. Always has been. Always will be. She gave me her

damned lollipop, and I took it, and right then and there—
she was mine, Garrett. *Mine*."

"Well, then. Why are you here arguing with me while
she's on her way home?"

Julian dropped his face with a grimace of pain, remembering her words as he rubbed his throbbing temples.
*Please, please help me out here. I'm so in love with you I
can't bear this anymore.*

If only he could be absolutely sure that she truly loved
him. *Him*.

Not…*his brother*.

"Well? Are you going to let her get away now that you
have her?" Garrett pressed as he signaled at the empty
driveway. "Do you think a good girl like Molly would be
with you if she wasn't all for you, man?"

Julian stared off to where she'd disappeared. "She was
never with me."

"Come again?"

"Molly. It was a lie. Our relationship. She was never
really with me. She wanted…you."

Just saying that to Garrett made him feel sick to his
empty stomach. He didn't even know how he could have
gone along with her foolish plan in the first place.

"Sooooo…*that's* what this is about." Garrett threw his
head back and released one of his few real laughs, the
sound booming across the landscape. "Molly doesn't want
me, Jules. Hell, I sure as hell would know when a woman
does." His gaze strayed over to Kate. She was speaking to
their mother by the docks, and Garrett watched her for a
long, long moment, his eyes on fire with emotion.

He jerked back when he realized he was being watched
and growled, "Molly's loved you her whole life, jerk. She
wanted to marry you when she was younger. She thought
when it was time for her prom, she would be taking *you*.

Kate had to tell her once and for all that she should see you as a brother and start thinking of another boy to invite to prom. She cried for days because she'd never be able to marry you. She even packed her bags and that feisty little girl actually tried to *leave*—said she didn't want to grow up with us and have you as a brother. Our mother forced her to stay, but can you please understand how Mother would remain concerned about this development?"

It took a moment for him to absorb this. He imagined Molly in all her stages. Never once had any man featured in any of them—except for Julian. While he'd known he could never have her and had sought to fill in the void with a thousand different women, she had done the opposite and had wanted no man.

Until one kiss from Julian had awakened her.

God, if he had known that all this time... All. This. Time. She'd wanted to go to *prom* with him? Had wanted to *marry* him?

She'd been his friend, and he'd been hers, and neither had realized that they had truly ever only loved and wanted each other.

His heart soared at the realization, and for the first time in days, he felt as if he could take a normal breath again. But he still glared at his brother for having made his life a living hell where Molly was concerned. "Clearly what you all failed to see is that I *loved* her. I always have, you morons."

Brow rising in interest, Garrett stopped pretending to roll up his sleeves and now began to roll them down. "Oh, well, then. So what are you doing here?"

Julian stared out at the placid lake, and then once again noticed how Garrett kept glancing at Kate on the docks. "You plan to give me advice, old man," Julian dared, pointing at her. "And yet I don't see you following your own. I know you want her, Garrett, I'm not blind. Why don't you freaking do something?"

Garrett stiffened, his face harsh and pained. "The difference between you and me is that you've always known you deserve Molly. And I'll never deserve Kate."

Every muscle tense with longing, Julian thought of Molly as she'd been last night, how vulnerable she'd looked as she slept, how she'd shivered and how he'd watched her, covered her with a blanket while he'd wanted to cover her with his body instead. All night. All night he'd spent memorizing her face, wanting to pretend this little beauty had not hurt him like she had.

*If you had a fan club you know damned well I'd be the* president!

How adorable she'd looked, ranting at him. And he'd been an ass. Unreasonable and closed off to her, not even listening, letting his anger and that damned feeling of jealousy overcome him.

His heart began to race at the thought of losing her, really losing her, for life. No. Never. Because Molly was smarter than he was, and she would not cling to the one thing he'd done wrong in his life. She was better than that.

And he was getting her back. He had to, and this time it would be for life. His heart swelled as he thought of her. His little Moo, his Mo-Po, his Mopey, his Molls, his Picasso, his *Molly.* The one he'd always wanted, with all her paint-streaked skin, frilly skirt and sassy attitude that got her into trouble.

No, Molly had not betrayed him to Garrett intentionally, or out of preference for the other man. She'd been too innocent for her own damn good, which was why she'd always needed Julian in the first place. He'd be damned if his pride and anger and jealousy would keep her away from him now.

"You're right," he said, resolute. "I do deserve Molly, or at least I did."

He started across the gravel path, suddenly wanting to get his favorite pair of Nikes and run like the wind to her home. But then, his Aston Martin was probably faster.

"I'll just go and put some ice on this," Garrett called after him sarcastically, rubbing his jaw.

"I have a better idea. Why don't you let Kate do it," Julian yelled in return, and began sprinting to his car, his heart galloping. He would tear her clothes off when he saw her. He would nibble, lick and kiss her until she couldn't stand it and begged for him to stop. And then he'd stop, only to do it all over again.

His heart pounded as he drove, his mind homing in on one thing, just one thing.

He could barely feel the pain in his muscles now, the synapses in his brain all firing on one word, one thought, one girl.

Outside her place, he grabbed the key they hid in the planter, opened the front door and slammed it shut. He could hear his own footsteps echo as he charged down the hallway to her room.

Her door was open a crack, and he stopped. All of a sudden his system was ready to go haywire, and he wanted to do everything at once.

When he entered her room, he saw her lying facedown on her bed, as if she'd been crying or just tired or—God, he hoped she hadn't been crying.

As he quietly backed out of the room, she sat upright with a start.

Then she saw him and leaped to her feet, her gaze throwing daggers at him. Gone were her earrings, her bangles and her smile. Despite her obvious anger, he was about to detonate with hunger and love for this passionate little redhead. He reversed course and advanced on her with slow purpose, like that night at the masquerade, with the single-minded determination of a man truly possessed. By love, by desire, by a woman. By *his* woman.

She continued to look fiercely at him. "Go back to fight with your brother, Julian," she snapped.

Julian paused in the middle of the hall and spread out his arms in a gesture of pure innocence. "I'd much rather fight with you, Moo."

"Well, I *wouldn't*. I don't plan to fight with you anymore."

He smiled the smile he knew to be irresistible to her, his hands up in the air as if she'd trained a loaded gun on him. "All right, then. Let's make up. What do you say?"

She opened her mouth to answer, then shut it.

At the first sign of her hesitation, Julian dropped his arms and started forward. "I'm so sorry, baby."

She shook her head. "You don't say you're sorry, Julian John. You bring flowers and say, 'Here are your flowers and look outside, there's another truckful for you.'"

"Damn, you're greedy, Moo. I'll get you a whole flower shop as soon as I get my hands off you."

Lines of confusion settled across her features, and suddenly her lips quirked at the ends. "You can't get them off me if you don't have them *on* me, Jules."

"Count to three." He could literally *see* her lovely baby blues start to glow for him once more.

"One," she suddenly whispered.

His heart turned over in his chest, and he almost fell to his knees from his gratitude to her. Struggling to find words, his voice came out rough and uneven. "I'm sorry I was so damned jealous and unreasonable, but please understand there's not a woman in the world who drives me

as crazy as you do. I couldn't stand the thought of you
siding with them, of you putting my brother before me in
any way. The thought of you responding to him like you
respond to me—"

"Jules, no one has ever come before you. It wasn't *him*
I responded to that first night you kissed me, it was *you*.
I realized right away that I was kissing my soul mate."

He charged toward her. "I want to spend the rest of my
life with you, Molly, and I want to know that I will always be your first and foremost, because you're sure as
hell mine."

She lunged forward. "Two, three!"

He laughed in pure male thrill when he opened his arms
at the same time Molly leaped and curled herself around
him. *"I love you,"* she murmured, open-lipped against him.

He slanted his head and fitted his mouth to hers, a sound
of desperation and hunger rumbling up from his throat.
Molly met this sound with her own breathless gasp, her
fingers delving into his hair until he could feel the delicious bite of her nails on his scalp.

*Oh, baby, yeah.*

He could feel her kiss in his every living cell, she kissed
him so thoroughly, so completely. He hungrily squeezed
her buttocks as he suckled her tongue and almost drowned
in the taste of mint and apples and Mopey.

"I missed you so bad I haven't even been myself," he
growled. Ducking his head to her breasts, he pulled down
her strapless dress to find them bare and waiting for him.
He suctioned a nipple between his teeth and closed his
eyes as bliss pummeled him from the inside.

"Jules, I could've killed you for being such a hardheaded, moronic—"

"Shh." His head came up and he silenced her with a fingertip. "Be nice to me or I won't do this, hmm." He stuck

his finger into her mouth and she suckled it greedily while he watched, his eyes feeling heavy.

She mewed in protest when he retrieved his finger, so then he used his lips to part hers wider and thrust his hot, wet tongue inside her. "Please tell me I didn't make you cry, baby," he desperately whispered as he broke their kiss for a moment to slant his head and get a better angle.

She nodded, speaking into his mouth as she gloried in the taste of him. "Like eleven times."

"Now I'll have to make it up to my girl with an hour of this for every time I made her cry." He cupped her breasts lovingly and kissed each one with care.

Molly panted, quivering with arousal as his skillful hands gripped the fabric of her dress at her hips and pulled it over her head, leaving her in her lacy black panties.

"It was really more like thirty-five times. I just didn't want to sound desperate," she confessed, her voice full of yearning as she fondled his dampened lips with her fingertips.

"Poor baby." He drew back to take a good look at her, his eyelids heavy as he caressed her lovely curves with his fingers. "Let me get my math straight…how many times?"

"A hundred times," she concluded, her breasts jerking up and down with her laboring breaths as she tightened her legs around his hips.

"A hundred times that I made my baby cry… I have a lot of making up to do."

Molly shuddered at the words, at the way he muttered them against her swollen breast, the way he laved her nipples and then breathed on them until she thought she would burst.

She'd been waiting for him, praying and plotting and planning to get him back. The one and only man for her.

A little hardheaded, true. But to her, Julian John Gage was still the bomb. The *bomb*.

Now he was here, in her arms, and she never wanted him to leave.

She held her breath as she frantically pulled his shirt over his head, and when he sent it flying across the room, his magnificent muscles bulged.

"I was about to call Garrett and ask him to pretend to love me." She rubbed his hard, square shoulders and delighted over the satin feel of his skin. "Just to see if you came back around."

"Oh, yeah?"

His smile was all cocky as he set her on her feet, then he hooked a finger in her panties and pulled them down, off one leg, then the other. "The difference is," he said as he undid his belt buckle and sent it clattering to the floor, "that he would be pretending. While I never was."

Once he was naked, he kicked the door shut and boosted her up against the wall, guiding her legs around his hips. Molly locked her ankles at the small of his back, clenching him tight between her arms and thighs and never planning to let go. His eyes glowed so bright and tender on her face, the light warmed her to the very depths of her being.

"Make love with me?" he murmured.

She jerked her head breathlessly as he held her hips between his big hands, and then, as sunlight streamed in through her bedroom window and their eyes locked, he thrust inside of her. She cried out with the joy of being physically his again. She'd been so ready to settle for friendship, if that was all she'd get. But in the deepest, most secret parts of her, she had ached for so much more.

"Jules, love me. Say you love me."

"I love you like crazy." He framed her face and looked

into her eyes. "Never doubt it. I love you, I worship you, I adore you, Molly. You and you alone."

His passionate words drove her to the precipice. They came together with tempestuous force, and once their endless shudders subsided, Molly gasped and turned her face into his neck, struggling to catch her breath. She'd felt his warmth spill into her, had felt the powerful contractions that seized his body, and now her heart soared in the sheer joy of being entwined with Julian again.

Panting and sweaty, she lifted her head just as he was ducking to kiss her. Their lips met in a languorous, loving, lazy kiss that left her weak and buzzing. "Every time you kiss me," she said softly, stroking his face as he carried her to the bed, "it feels like the first time." A dreamy sigh escaped her as she remembered that masquerade. "I should've *known* I was being kissed by a playboy."

"Get used to it, Mopey." He set her down on the mattress with a kiss on her forehead, then stretched out beside her and rumpled her hair. "Because I promise you'll never see a playboy more into his wife than I."

Her heart stuttered at the word *wife,* then it just completely stopped beating.

"What do you mean?"

At the sight of her wide eyes, his wolfish smile appeared, and he took her left hand within his. She watched in disbelief as he slid the matte platinum ring, large and masculine, onto her ring finger.

The ring from the masquerade.

"I'll get you a real one tomorrow. One with a white diamond—a big one. This is just so you know my intentions are pure."

"Oh, I have no doubt your intentions are squeaky clean," she laughed as she pointedly glanced down at their nakedness, and then she fell somber as the magnitude of what was happening struck her. Settling her hands on his shoulders, she gazed at the ring, then into those oak leaf-green eyes. She could see his pulse fluttering rapidly at the base of his throat, could see the love and need in his eyes.

"You were meant to be my wife, Molly," he rasped, brushing her hair back, his hands, his tenderness undoing her. "Will you marry me?"

She held his caressing green gaze and nodded, her eyes mirroring the loving way that Julian looked down at her now. Stroking his strong jaw affectionately, she simply said, "As you wish."

\* \* \* \* \*

*Look for Kate's story, coming soon!*
*Only from Red Garnier and Harlequin Desire!*

A *sneaky peek* at next month…

# MODERN™

### POWER, PASSION AND IRRESISTIBLE TEMPTATION

## *My wish list for next month's titles…*

**In stores from 18th July 2014:**

❏ Zarif's Convenient Queen — Lynne Graham

❏ His Forbidden Diamond — Susan Stephens

❏ The Argentinian's Demand — Cathy Williams

❏ The Ultimate Seduction — Dani Collins

**In stores from 1st August 2014:**

❏ Uncovering Her Nine Month Secret — Jennie Lucas

❏ Undone by the Sultan's Touch — Caitlin Crews

❏ Taming the Notorious Sicilian — Michelle Smart

❏ His by Design — Dani Wade

**Available at WHSmith, Tesco, Asda, Eason, Amazon and Apple**

## *Just can't wait?*

# Make it a summer to remember with the fantastic new book from Sarah Morgan

Fiery French chef Elise Philippe has just heard that the delectable Sean O'Neil is back in town. After their electrifying night together last summer, can she stick to her one-night rule?

**Coming soon at millsandboon.co.uk**

Anouska Knight's first book, *Since You've Been Gone*, was a smash hit and crowned the winner of Lorraine's Racy Reads. Anouska returns with *A Part of Me*, which is one not to be missed!

**Get your copy today at:**
**www.millsandboon.co.uk**

Discover more romance at

# www.millsandboon.co.uk

- ❤ WIN great prizes in our exclusive competitions
- ❤ BUY new titles before they hit the shops
- ❤ BROWSE new books and REVIEW your favourites
- ❤ SAVE on new books with the Mills & Boon® Bookclub™
- ❤ DISCOVER new authors

PLUS, to chat about your favourite reads, get the latest news and find special offers:

- Find us on facebook.com/millsandboon
- Follow us on twitter.com/millsandboonuk
- ❤ Sign up to our newsletter at millsandboon.co.uk